Praise for Earl Emerson's firefighting novels

"Emerson, himself a veteran firefighter, deserves a medal . . . for taking us inside the subculture of the men and women who do this dangerous work for a living."
—*The New York Times Book Review*

"A terrific read with rousing scenes of firefighters in action . . . When writer Earl Emerson takes you into a burning building, you believe it."
—Baltimore *Sun*

"The best suspense fiction . . . such chilling, utterly convincing detail that readers may wind up struggling to breathe."
—*Los Angeles Times*

"Reads like James Patterson decked out in fire gear."
—*Booklist*

"Thrilling . . . Emerson depicts [the] dangerous but alluring world of firefighting [with] skill and verve."
—*The Seattle Times*

"Earl Emerson gives the reader enormous insight into the grueling and dangerous lives of firefighters."
—JOHN SAUL

"Scarily authentic and utterly captivating . . . easily one of the most compelling books you'll encounter this year."
—*Mystery Scene*

"Emerson keeps the heat on from start to finish."
—*The Sunday Oregonian*

Praise for Earl Emerson's Thomas Black mystery series

"Emerson is carving his own special niche among a new generation of private-eye writers. . . . He writes lean, muscular prose to carry his fast-moving action."

—*The Washington Post Book World*

"Earl Emerson is one of the best new private eye writers."

—*Chicago Sun-Times*

"Earl Emerson writes with the richness and grace of a poet. This guy is *good.*"

—Robert Crais

"An intrepid private investigator."

—*The New York Times*

"Private eye fans who haven't yet discovered Earl Emerson have the perfect opportunity to do so. . . . Look for strong writing, a likeable hero, and some great characters in this one and you won't be disappointed."

—*Alfred Hitchcock Mystery Magazine*

"Emerson's plotting is original, suspenseful, so well done that the richness of his writing seems almost a bonus. . . . [He] has taken his place in the rarefied air of the best of the best."

—Ann Rule

"Delivers the goods, dishing out humor, suspense, and heart-pounding action in heaping portions."

—*Booklist*

"Witty and fast-moving, with rich, well-drawn characters and a twisting, lively plot . . . Emerson's hard-boiled riff is still state-of-the-art."

—Cleveland *Plain-Dealer*

"Earl Emerson is a master of witty dialogue; clever, complex plotting; and lucid, meaty prose . . . in the best tradition of American crime fiction."

—Aaron Elkins

"Top-notch . . . Emerson infuses a unique sense of humor mixed with the stuff heroes are made of as well as brothers and best friends."

—*Mystery News*

"Emerson justifiably has developed a following for his taut, layered story lines, his sharp dialogue, and his accomplished evocation of place."

—Tacoma *News Tribune*

"The action is always fast in Emerson's books, the clues intriguing, and the danger leavened with humor—black humor, naturally."

—Eugene *Register-Guard*

"First rate. . . . [A] special niche in a new generation of potent private eye writers. . . . and its language muscular in the best sense of the term."

—Milwaukee *Journal Sentinel*

By Earl Emerson

VERTICAL BURN
INTO THE INFERNO
PYRO
THE SMOKE ROOM
FIRETRAP

THE THOMAS BLACK NOVELS
THE RAINY CITY
POVERTY BAY
NERVOUS LAUGHTER
FAT TUESDAY
DEVIANT BEHAVIOR
YELLOW DOG PARTY
THE PORTLAND LAUGHER
THE VANISHING SMILE
THE MILLION-DOLLAR TATTOO
DECEPTION PASS
CATFISH CAFÉ

A Novel of Suspense

EARL EMERSON

BALLANTINE BOOKS • NEW YORK

2007 Ballantine Books Mass Market Edition

Published in the United States by Ballantine Books, an imprint of The Random House Publishing Group, a division of Random House, Inc., New York.

BALLANTINE and colophon are registered trademarks of Random House, Inc.

Originally published in hardcover in the United States by Ballantine Books, an imprint of The Random House Publishing Group, a division of Random House, Inc., in 2006.

This book contains an excerpt from the forthcoming book *Primal Threat* by Earl Emerson. This excerpt has been set for this edition only and may not reflect the final content of the forthcoming edition.

ISBN 978-0-345-46293-0

Cover design: Carl D. Galian

Printed in the United States of America

www.ballantinebooks.com

OPM 9 8 7 6 5 4 3 2 1

For

JOE BLADES,

who's been a splendid editor

and a great friend for over twenty years

ACKNOWLEDGMENTS

Many thanks to Lieutenant Jay Mahnke of Engine 33 and to Erik Lawyer of Ladder 3 for their technical and editorial assistance. Thanks also to Matt Hougan, also on Ladder 3, for the fire scene schematic. Thanks, as always, to my wife, Sandy, for seeing the flaws in the original manuscript and coming up with a whole new plot.

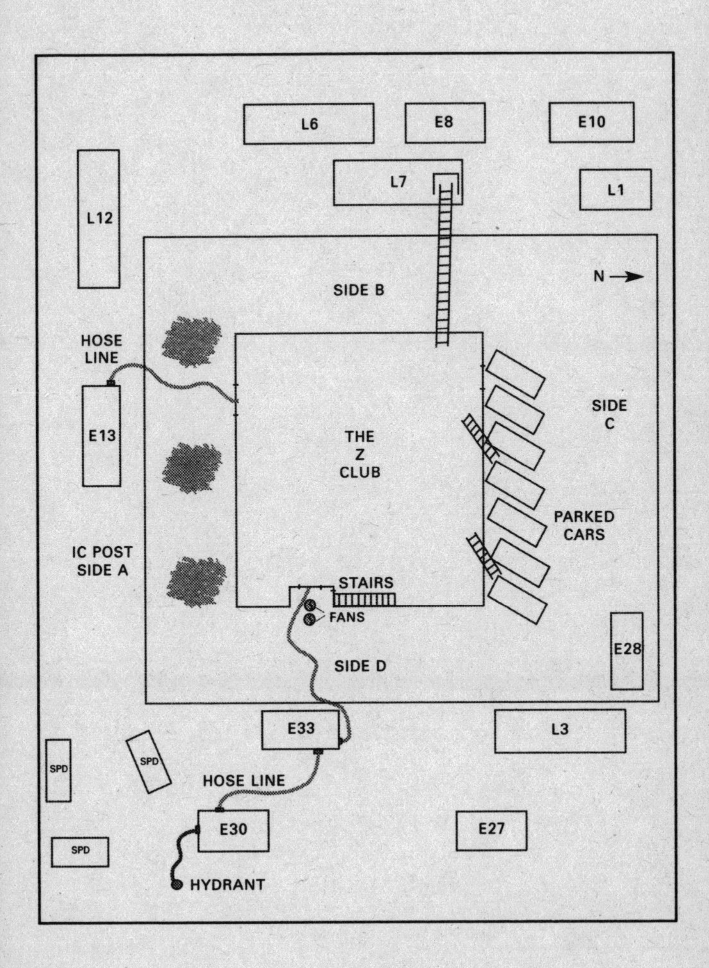
L6
E8
E10
L7
L1
L12
N
SIDE B
HOSE
LINE
E13
THE
Z
CLUB
SIDE
C
PARKED
CARS
IC POST
SIDE A
STAIRS
FANS
E28
SIDE D
E33
L3
SPD
SPD
HOSE LINE
E30
E27
SPD
HYDRANT

1. THE Z CLUB

CAPTAIN TREY BROWN, ENGINE 28, C SHIFT

I was seventeen the first time I stole India from my brother.

They say you never forget your first love, and I guess it's true, because even though I haven't laid eyes on her in almost two decades, I find my thoughts straying in India's direction often. But then, my life changed forever that summer, so why shouldn't my thoughts stray to that time? There were a lot of changes during the course of those months: our oldest brother dying in a car wreck, India's sister the victim of an assault that changed her life and mine forever, the dark evening I got myself blackballed out of the Carmichael family on what was essentially a hand vote.

Perhaps it is because memories of youth are so often marbled with yearning that I believed parts of our summer might one day be recovered. Memories of desire heated to the melting point dim slowly. The summer India and I cheated on my brother, I was seventeen and she had just turned eighteen. At the time I believed we were more in love than any other two people on earth. Had events turned out differently, that feeling might have eased out of my soul of its own accord instead of being jerked out like a gaffed flounder. Oddly, her last name is Carmichael now, a detail that lends more angst to my recollections than anything else.

Being excommunicated from the family was only the beginning of my troubles. At seventeen I came as close as I ever would to a jail cell, and then had the stuffing beaten out of me by two ex-pro boxers while Barry Renfrow stood by and watched. Renfrow's back now, too, which shows how circular life can be.

Though I hadn't laid eyes on India during the intervening years, I'd seen pictures of her in the newspaper: at a Mariners game sitting with the president of the ball club and his wife; a wedding photo the week after she married Stone Carmichael; and more recently, functioning as the hostess at a charity ball attended by Puget Sound's hoity-toity, the odd software billionaire sprinkled in among the five-thousand-dollar gowns and designer tuxedos. For me the photos were freeze-frame glimpses of a life I'd been banished from.

Even now I remember our last night together, the silky feel of her breasts under my touch, the ultimate tension in my loins as her thighs tightened. Oddly enough, she married into the only family on this planet who held me in lower regard than her own family did. But that's a long story. Only weeks ago Seattle suffered its most devastating fire in recent history, and the irony that disaster can reunite us just as disaster once split us apart does not elude me. Today I am a lonely man of common tastes, who wonders occasionally not whether his lost love thinks of him as frequently as he thinks of her, but whether she thinks of him at all.

This morning I debated whether or not to take the Harley to work, but in the end decided the riots would probably be over by six forty-five when I left the house. The radio reported rock throwing in the Rainier Valley, random gunshots on Beacon Hill, bricks thrown at a fire station several blocks from my home. In the nine days I'd been out of town, the public outcry over the fire had snowballed from bitch sessions to rioting. If things continued in this vein, it was only a matter of time before more deaths were added to the fourteen at the Z Club—fifteen if you counted the witness who was murdered two blocks from the fire.

It was four weeks after the tragedy, a Friday morning, early October, and Seattle was sleepwalking through a typical fall of fog-shrouded mornings and hazy afternoons. The news said rain was moving in.

At the intersection of Martin Luther King and Jackson, a gaggle of black teenagers stood idly in the fog. I could tell from their body language that they'd been out all night, hunting up hassles and emboldening one another with tough talk and macho posturing. A small grocery store on the northwest corner revealed broken windows and graffiti streaming across the front door like cartoon captions. As I waited at the red light, one of the boys realized I was the only motorist at the intersection and threw a half-full beer bottle onto Jackson, where it burst twenty feet from my front tire. Several of them laughed, the others waiting for my reaction. I wanted to tell them that if this was a black-white revolution, perhaps they should go after a white guy instead of yours truly, but all I did was blip my throttle a couple of times and roar away when the light changed.

I'd been in a cocoon of my own making for the past nine days, having flown to Las Vegas on my annual trek with my mom and brother, my real family. I hadn't had time to catch up on all the news, but I knew the official fire department report had come out two days ago and yesterday the papers had unloaded a bombshell that made the report look like a pack of lies. Since then, all hell had broken loose. While my minor burns from the Z Club fire had healed, the community rebellion had grown worse.

This would be my first shift on Engine 28 in almost a month, and as much as I detested Las Vegas, making the trip each year specifically for my mother and brother, who couldn't get enough of it, the journey had been a respite from the angry speeches, department arm-twisting, and political diatribes prompted by the Z Club fire.

As did other papers in the country, the *Las Vegas Review-Journal* had carried daily updates on the unrest in Seattle. *USA Today* sported a photo of bodies under a large tarpaulin on the sidewalk outside the Z Club, and it was because of those bodies that last Friday and Saturday night African-American youth rioted in Seattle in a manner that hadn't been seen here since the late sixties. Monday morning, almost sixteen hundred marchers, black and white, forced the mayor to stand in the rain outside the municipal building and give a conciliatory speech about knitting the community back together. So far nobody had been killed in the riots, although one police officer received a broken shoulder when some moron dropped a cinder block from a roof. Each day there had been organized marches, and later, under cover of darkness, a different set of protesters staged mini-riots, break-ins, and looting.

According to reports I heard on the radio, the vice president's visit this morning had forced the SPD to maintain an expansive presence on the streets. I was afraid my little brother Johnny, who had a penchant for lunacy and a compulsion to be part of any crowd, would get sucked into the maelstrom, so I had hoped the ruckus would have died down by the time we returned from Nevada. In fact, we had taken the Vegas trip a month early trusting in just such an eventuality. But instead of dying down, the turmoil had mushroomed.

Thirteen black civilians and one white firefighter had died at the Z Club fire. One version of the story had a mostly white fire department pouring water into the building in a cowardly style from the sidewalk while frantic young blacks tried to escape the premises without any help. Another version painted a picture of firefighters so intent on saving one of their own that they ignored relatively easy civilian rescues, leaving more than a dozen African Americans to die. If I bought into either of those scenarios, I might have been tempted to march in the streets, too.

Yesterday afternoon the mayor's office issued its official reaction to the fire department's report on the Z Club fire and to the news stories yesterday morning which supposedly debunked that report. The TV news had been filled with cautiously worded affirmations from city administrators and fire department brass juxtaposed with statements from the outraged local NAACP chapter president, from angry black ministers, from family and friends of the victims, and from more fortunate partygoers who'd escaped the Z Club that night. Melinda Burns, the lieutenant I would be relieving on Engine 28 this morning, was interviewed during one newscast, announcing rather lamely that it was "always a shame when people had to die at a fire." From the department's perspective, the interview probably wasn't a great idea, since

Melinda was white, the victims were black, and that distinction had been the number one topic of contention from the get-go.

Situated on Rainier Avenue, Station 28, my home away from home, was a stereotypical firehouse with three tall roll-up apparatus bay doors and hard tile floors throughout. Because of the institutional nature of our structure and furnishings, I often thought the building could serve as the living quarters for the staff in a state facility, most likely a nuthouse.

I shut off the Harley and rolled into the station without getting off, walking the bike quietly between the rigs to the rear of the station under the basketball hoop. It was seven A.M., and most of the firefighters from yesterday's shift were just climbing out of their bunks. In half an hour, today's crews would take over and hold the fort until seven-thirty tomorrow morning: four firefighters on Ladder 12, three of us on Engine 28, and two paramedics on Medic 28.

Lieutenant Burns, who met me outside the engine officer's room, was thick through the middle—like someone who'd been drinking beer for too many years—but had been a star athlete in college: rugby and lacrosse. She was anxious about living up to department standards, even though as far as I could tell, she generally surpassed them.

"All heck's been breaking loose," she said.

"Oh, yeah?" I left the door open a few inches while I went into the small engine officer's room, tugged off my motorcycle boots, and stepped into a freshly laundered fire department uniform I'd carried to work in my saddlebags.

"We bunked four times last night," she said from the hallway. "Had two Dumpster fires down near Alaska. Got called to the South Precinct after they pepper-sprayed a couple of guys outside one of the holding cells. They must have had eighteen or twenty people under arrest for rioting. People are really bent out of shape over that report. Tonight might be more of the same."

"Yeah, it's Friday."

It was unexpected and a little sad to see the black community so angry at the fire department. Historically it was the police department that attracted our wrath, as it had not been too long ago when police officers killed a mentally unstable black man who'd held two women hostage for ten hours. Although the guy had been armed only with a kitchen knife, the police shot him seven times, which did a grand job of stirring up righteous indignation. Four months later when the Z Club fire came along, the black community was still simmering.

"By the way, Melinda. I saw you on the news. You looked good."

"The chief called and chewed me out. They want either a chief or the PIO to be talking to the media. Nobody else."

"There was a memo to that effect before I left. You didn't see it?"

"I did, but they stuck a microphone in my face and asked me to say something, and I just went ahead and shot my mouth off. I don't know why."

"So what's going on around here?" I'd changed and was in the corridor, the two of us walking toward the beanery, which had begun to fill up with yawning firefighters from yesterday's shift. Somebody was grinding coffee beans in the kitchen alcove.

The kitchen, or the beanery in department parlance, was a big room suffused with the odors of aftershave, yesterday's cooking, and the residue of smoke from last night's fires. A television sat in the far corner, and a long wooden table dominated the room. One corner had two refrigerators, a range, and a sink. Rank-and-file firefighters slept in the large bunk room on the other side of the apparatus bay, while the engine and truck officers slept in the offices behind us. The medic room was sandwiched between the officers' rooms.

Except for Melinda and one incoming medic, everybody in the room was male. Two firefighters in the corner were discussing a bow-hunting trip. Other than that, all talk centered around the civil unrest. When the phone rang, I snapped it up. "Captain Brown. Station Twenty-eight."

"Cap? This is Garrison. I'm going to be late. I-Five's a parking lot. I heard on the radio there's another protest south of the old Rainier Brewery. If it's like last week, it'll gum things up for hours."

"I'll tell Hannity," I said, picking up the remote off the table and switching the TV to the local news. A chopper was displaying a sky view of about a hundred fifty sign-waving marchers on Interstate 5. They had taken over all four of the northbound lanes, and the southbound lanes were stalled with gapers. "If Hannity can't stay over for you, I'm sure somebody else will."

"All they're doing is making people mad. There's going to be like six thousand people late for work."

"We'll cover for you."

Winston, one of the incoming medics, had been studying the TV images and said, "Gee, I wonder how they work that? Do they call their boss and say, 'I need to take a few hours of comp time so I can be on the freeway fucking up the morning for everybody else?' Or do they call in sick and scam a day off the company? Or maybe they all work the night shift? Maybe they're independent entrepreneurs and are planning to make up the lost time by working this evening. Jesus."

The ridicule in his voice was rich with the implication that none of the black marchers had jobs, thus were able to mess up the day for hardworking white people, who did. The secondary implication was an old one I was familiar with, that the marchers didn't have jobs because they didn't want to work for a living.

"The squeaky wheel gets the grease," said Lieutenant Black cheerfully.

"If you ask me, the squeaky wheel should get greased," growled Winston, making a gesture toward the TV with thumb and forefinger as if shooting someone.

"If I remember correctly, this is still America," I said. "A guy decides to march with a sign, you don't shoot him. That's banana-republic SOP. Besides, their goal isn't to foul up commuters. It's to stall the vice president, who's landing at Boeing Field at eight o'clock. They want to disrupt *his* schedule so they can make the national news. I'm not saying it's right. I'm just saying they're not out to make regular people late."

"Whatever it is, it's a load of crap!" Winston said.

Somebody else said, "You're right, Captain. If they can tie up the vice president on his way to see the mayor, it'll make national."

"The city blew it," Melinda said, "letting that report out without having all the facts. Then that nine-one-one call on the news. That recording: 'Help me. Help me. Please don't leave me here. The firemen keep walking past me.' They've been playing it every half hour. It doesn't sound good."

"It had to be a fake," said Smollen. "No firefighter would leave a victim."

"They got headlines, all right," said Lieutenant Black, who'd picked up the remote and switched to the *Today* show on NBC. The same chopper pictures we'd been viewing locally were being broadcast nationally.

"Anybody read the SFD report?" I asked.

"It's not in the stations yet," said Melinda, "but on the news yesterday they said it absolved the fire department of all wrongdoing."

"As well it should have," said Winston. "I was at that fire. We worked our butts off. Somebody wants to torch a place, there's not a lot you can do to stop them. This is just another . . ." He looked up at me and stopped.

"Go ahead. Say it."

"This is just another case of the black community not being able to face the fact that their problems are of their own making. I'm sorry, but that's the way I feel."

"What about that nine-one-one tape?"

"I don't know about that. I'd like to see them identify those firefighters who supposedly passed that guy up. If they exist."

Most people in the fire department kept their thoughts on race, whatever those thoughts were, to themselves. Winston was one of the outspoken ones, and in some ways I appreciated his candor, if not his attitude. The room grew quiet. As a captain I was the ranking officer as well as the only black man in the room. "Opinions are like assholes," I said. "Everyone has one."

"Yeah, I know," Winston said. "But you don't agree?"

"You mean, do I agree the marchers should be shot?"

"I shouldn't have said that. I mean do you think that tape is legit?"

"It sounded real to me."

Somebody said, "Where'd that nine-one-one tape come from, anyway? Why didn't we have it the first day after the fire?"

"Maybe the dispatcher held it back from the city investigators so the fire department wouldn't look bad," I said.

"So who was bypassing victims?"

"God only knows," I said, although in the back of my mind I had an idea.

The most recent and inflammatory news report had been a clip from a dispatch tape reportedly made on the night of the Z Club fire, in which a man who claimed he was trapped in the fire called the 911 dispatchers on his cell phone to tell them that firemen were passing him by. Sounds of fire and even an MSA mask operating could be heard in the background. They were playing snippets of the tape on every newscast. The pleas had been heartrending, given the fact that the man had apparently died shortly thereafter. No survivors had admitted to making the call, and the phone had been found beside one of the victims on the second floor.

"Okay, they're saying we didn't try hard enough to get those people out because they were black," said Winston. "A lot of firefighters at the Z Club were black. They're trying to make it into this huge racial thing when it wasn't."

The worst part about the controversy for black firefighters was that when we defended the black community, we were looked on with suspicion by white firefighters, and when we stuck up for the fire department, the black community called us Uncle Toms. There was no way to win. But then, there never is.

"They just don't get it," Winston continued. "Not everything is racial."

I said, "That's just it. Everything *is* racial."

"How can you say that?"

"How can you deny it?"

"Because it isn't. Take you, for instance. You're a captain in the fire department. You got that position *because* you were black. Not in spite of it. How do you figure you've been hurt by racism?"

"You got about a year to listen?"

"Don't give me that. The type of racism these people are talking about doesn't exist in Seattle. I doubt it exists anywhere in the country anymore."

"You paint yourself black for a year and then I might give some thought to what you're saying."

"Walk in the other man's shoes? Is that what you're telling me? Why don't you paint yourself white?"

"I've already *been* white." The room grew quiet. One by one we focused on the TV and the vice president's motorcade heading onto the freeway. It was a little like watching the O.J. chase, excruciating in its slowness and in the inevitable knowledge that when the motorcade collided with the protesters, the outcome would be dismaying.

Twenty-five minutes later Clyde Garrison had just signed into the daybook when the bell hit, and Garrison, Kitty Acton, and I rushed out to the apparatus bay and climbed onto Engine 28. It was good to be back.

2. THE VICE PRESIDENT'S LIMO RUNS OVER A FOOT

TREY

Over eighty-five percent of our emergency calls in Seattle are aid calls. This one was in a neighborhood west of the station near the freeway, a few blocks off Graham Street. The house was a pink-and-white rambler on a slight embankment in a pleasant enough neighborhood. I was the first one through the door, followed in rapid succession by Garrison and Acton, lugging the aid kits. The first thing I noticed were two angry black men standing in the kitchen in Raiders jackets, looking as if they'd arrived just moments in front of us.

Our patient was in her sixties, wearing warm clothing but no jacket, the toes of her shoes wet, as if she'd traipsed across the same grass wetted by the overnight fog we'd just crossed. She was weeping so copiously she could barely see us, her raspberry-colored blouse and huge bosom streaked with tiny comets of tears.

"What's going on this morning?" I asked.

"The police sprayed me. I'm sixty-one years old, and they went and sprayed me."

"Were you at the march?" I asked. When she didn't reply, I glanced into the kitchen, where the two brothers had been joined by two more brothers, one wearing a white bandanna on his head. He had watery eyes, too, though he wasn't as bad off as our patient.

"Motherfuckin' president's ride ran over some woman's foot," he said. "We're going to sue that motherfucker."

"How you going to do that? He's going to be outa town in twenty-four hours," said one of the other men.

"Somebody's going to pay."

"It was the *vice* president's motorcade," said Clyde Garrison under his breath. "Not the president's." He took a reading of our patient's blood pressure while I got a quick medical history, and Kitty began irrigating the woman's eyes with lactated ringers from our aid kit.

"Fuckin' tear gas," said one of the men, stepping into the kitchen doorway. "My mother never even got to the demonstration."

"The best treatment is to irrigate with water," I said. "It usually takes about twenty minutes."

"What do you mean, 'irrigate'? I don't want nobody irrigating *my* mother."

"We wash her eyes," said Kitty.

It took just over twenty minutes before she felt better. As we left, the brother with the pepper-sprayed eyes stood in the middle of the living room blocking our exit just enough so that we had to detour around him. He stared at me as if we were about to step into the ring together and said, "If you're done, I want your funky Uncle Tom ass out of here."

One of the older men from the kitchen said, "Hey, thanks for coming," then turned to the man in the bandanna and said, "Shut up, DeShawn."

"You're welcome," I said, staring at the man in the white bandanna as if he'd been the one to thank us.

Outside, Kitty was furious. "They call us for help and then act like we're intruders. There's just no gratitude." During the drive back to the station, Garrison and I kept our thoughts to ourselves while Kitty, a tall, slender woman with a penchant for letting little things eat at her for an entire shift, continued to rant. To make it worse, she found a broken eggshell and a yellow smear of raw egg on top of the crew cab.

When we got back to the station everybody was gathered in the beanery along with our battalion chief and a civilian woman who appeared to be half black and half Filipina. You could tell everybody in the room was being super polite because of her. It suddenly hit me where I knew her from. Her name was—

"Jamie Estevez," said Chief Horst, looking at me, "let me introduce Captain Brown."

She stood and reached for my hand. "I've heard good things about you, Captain."

"You're on the news. Channel Four?"

"I *was* on four. I've signed a contract with KIRO, but I won't be there for a few months."

Although she had never been one of my favorites, I had to admit Jamie Estevez was arguably the best-looking news reporter in the area, and whenever she showed up on TV, somebody in the station remarked on it. She had black shoulder-length hair, mocha skin, dark eyes, and a figure that several of the guys in the room were trying hard not to ogle, currently displayed to good effect in high heels, a hot pink blouse, and a navy skirt and blazer.

When Kitty Acton entered the room, she began plying Estevez with questions about the news business. Chief Horst stared at me through the general chatter that was beginning to fill the room and said, "I've brought a man to replace you for a couple of hours while we go to a meeting. Can Acton act?"

"What's going on?"

"All I know is, I have orders to skip the conference call this morning and drive you and Ms. Estevez to a meeting. They're in a hurry."

"This isn't about the award, is it?"

"I have no idea."

"Do you know what this is about?" I said, interrupting Kitty's interrogation of our guest. I might have waited for her to finish, but Kitty didn't finish anything verbal in less than half an hour; we called her Chatty Kathy.

Estevez turned to me. "Can we talk about it in the chief's car?"

3. WHATEVER YOU DO, DON'T TELL HIM HOW HE FIGURES INTO THIS

JAMIE ESTEVEZ

As we sat around the kitchen table at Station 28, engaging in the kind of chitchat strangers use to whittle down the time they must spend together, I tried to decide whether I'd made a mistake taking on a project that was going to bite a good chunk out of my life, both in terms of time and emotional involvement. Having arrived at Station 28 just as Engine 28 careened out onto Rainier Avenue and sped away, we'd been forced to wait almost thirty-five minutes. I'd caught a fleeting glimpse of Captain Brown as they sped off, a man with a small mustache and a chiseled profile. I hadn't been expecting him to be black, although given the circumstances, it certainly made sense. I had, in the way that I irrationally expect it of all firemen, expected him to be handsome, however, and was not disappointed.

Finally somebody said Engine 28 was returning, and a minute later Captain Brown came shambling through the door as if he owned this half of the world. Even in a room filled with confident firefighters, Captain Brown stood out as the big dog.

Except for Chief Horst, all of the men in the room were big, with thick arms and shoulders, but none were sculpted like a professional athlete until Captain Brown showed up—the kind of macho bastard I'd been falling for my whole life. His skin tone was a couple of shades lighter than mine, and his eyes were gray and bore evidence of more than one Caucasian ancestor. When he spoke, his voice was deep and rumbling, a voice that should have had a tranquilizing effect, yet I found myself nervous and unexpectedly hoping he was either gay or taken.

After we piled into the chief's Suburban, the two men sitting up front, Captain Brown turned around and said, "So what's up?"

I cleared my throat. "I've been retained by a group calling themselves the Z Club Citizens for Truth. They've asked for and received permission to set up an independent inquiry into the Z Club fire, with city funding. They've hired me to investigate the fire and write a report."

"Because of the nine-one-one call?"

"That and other things. Nobody was happy with the official report before that call became public, but now there's even more reason for a second inquiry."

"We've already got a number of investigations, don't we?" Captain Brown asked. "There's the fire department report. Labor and Industries is doing one. And ATF."

"This one will be accountable only to the families of the victims."

"Are you working for KIRO TV or for this group?"

"For the Z Club Citizens for Truth."

"So where are we headed?"

"We're on our way to meet with the committee."

Captain Brown turned to Chief Horst. "I don't understand why I'm here, Chief."

"All I can say is, I got a phone call this morning from Chief Douglas. Said Ms. Estevez was showing up and we were to take you along. Arrange the manpower and be there by nine o'clock. That's all I know. We're already late. Mount Zion Baptist Church."

"Where we'll be talking to community leaders and your big chief," I added. "I assume they're going to give me whatever parameters they feel are necessary, and we'll proceed from there."

"I still don't see why they need me at this meeting."

"I've asked for an assistant from the fire department," I said. "Somebody who knows all the players." Horst, who had warned me not to let on that Captain Brown would be the appointed liaison, tossed me a look over his shoulder.

"You don't think they're going to try to saddle me with it, do you?" Brown asked.

"I'm sure I would look forward to working with you, too."

"That's not what I meant. I meant—"

"I know what you meant," I said, "and I'm sure you don't have anything to worry about."

"Well, I'm glad I'm not going to be part of it. Good luck. This whole thing is going to be explosive. I wouldn't touch it with a ten-foot pole."

It was quiet for a while, our silence punctuated by the sounds of the fire department radio mounted on the dash. Chief Horst and I both knew Captain Brown had already been selected. After a bit, Horst said, "Ms. Estevez started out in radio and TV in Spokane. Isn't that right?" He peered at me in the rearview mirror.

"Something like that. How long have you been in the fire department, Captain Brown?"

"Going on fifteen years."

"You don't look old enough."

"You look like you just got out of high school yourself."

He turned around and faced me, and as he looked me over, I could feel my face heating up.

Probably my biggest flaw—and the reason I wasn't with somebody now—was that I gravitated toward rebels and mavericks (my high school sweetheart got kicked off the football team *and* the basketball team), iconoclasts, people my grandmother would have called dadgummed chicken thieves. It was probably the reason I was mulling over what Chief Horst had told me on the drive to Station 28. He said Brown had pissed off a lot of people downtown by not showing up to accept an award they wanted to give him for his actions at the Z Club fire. To make matters worse, there were people in the black community who interpreted his refusal of the award as support for their contention that the fire had been run badly.

The three of us remained silent for most of the drive. We were headed for the Mount Zion Baptist Church, probably the largest African-American church in the region and certainly in the city, where the pastor and deacons had been instrumental in trying to quell unrest during the past few weeks. Ironically, they'd also been instrumental in stirring up that same unrest with repeated public pronouncements that they suspected a cover-up.

Under the stoplight at 23rd and Jackson, the intersection was mobbed with people waving signs, marching, chanting, and shouting at cars. On the far corner a cluster of black males shouted angrily at passing vehicles. "You can't kill us anymore! You can't kill us anymore!" Several of the signs that people carried had large photographs of victims from the Z Club fire, mostly enlarged high school yearbook photos, grainy and sad in their blurriness. A hundred feet from the intersection a solitary police car was parked on the sidewalk outside a Starbucks coffee shop, two burly officers looking on with what I could only term feigned disinterest.

When we caught the red light and stopped, our fire department vehicle quickly became the focus of a splinter group of sign carriers, all women, stepping into the street to get a gander at the fools in the SFD Suburban. If half an hour earlier

I'd been asked whether five middle-aged women in ski parkas carrying signs on sticks could have frightened the living hell out of me, I would have scoffed at the suggestion. But that's exactly what they were doing: approaching so that their signs rattled against the roof and the spittle from their shouting peppered my window, which they beckoned angrily for me to lower. They shouted at Captain Brown to lower his, too, and for a few moments I was afraid he was going to because he began fumbling with the controls, inexplicably failing at each attempt. Only after we vacated the intersection did he lower the window and then raise it, causing me to laugh nervously at the realization that he'd been toying with them. I wondered if he'd done it out of some warped sense of fun or as a defense mechanism to stall the women.

The chief and captain were both in uniform, but God only knew what the protesters thought I was doing in my pink blouse and navy blazer besides sweating.

I read as many signs as I could. "First the cops/now the firemen." "JUSTice for the Z Club." "What Really Happened?" And my two favorites, probably because of the misspellings: "Stop the Z Club liers." "Give us the truth. Don't let our children die in vane."

As we passed Fire Station 6 three blocks later, we could see where the building had been pelted by stones, vegetables, and eggs, with two windows in the garage doors broken. Somebody had spray painted something on one of the building's cream-colored outer walls, but it had been hastily painted over.

Frankly, if I'd known what a powder keg the situation was, I might not have agreed, but two weeks earlier I'd pledged my support to Miriam Beckmann, the founder of the Z Club Citizens for Truth. She convinced me that my training and my standing in the community made me uniquely qualified to head up a secondary probe, should the results of the first probe turn out to be unsatisfactory.

"Can't investigate yourself," Miriam had said to me on the phone the night before. "And this new tape from the nine-one-one dispatchers proves it."

4. WHITEWASH BY THE WHITE GUYS

TREY

Funny how many times sin brings you closer to the Lord. Years ago I'd been with a woman who belonged to Mount Zion Baptist and tried to coerce me into attending services there. While attractive and well educated, Charlise had been emotionally needy, if not a little nuts, a woman my pal Rumble called high maintenance. She told me repeatedly that if she could turn me into a churchgoer she might think about marrying me, although I'd never seriously contemplated marriage. In fact, the longer I knew her, the less tantalizing the notion became. We broke up after she threw a screaming fit in the lobby of the ACT theater, falsely accusing me of sleeping with not one but two of her girlfriends.

Inside the foyer of the church, Estevez, Horst, and I were directed to a good-size meeting room, where we found eight or ten brothers shaking hands with a group of white guys who'd arrived in front of us. There were thirty or more people in the room, more trickling in each minute. The white men were from the mayor's office, but I didn't see Mayor Stone among them. A few minutes later the police chief, who was Caucasian, showed up with a small entourage of mostly black officers; followed by the fire chief, also white, flanked by two African-American deputy chiefs. It was around then that I realized I might be there merely as wallpaper and also that I was mentally dividing the room into black and white, segmenting everybody into groups in just the way we're taught *not* to do in Sunday School—an infraction I'd wager most people commit on a daily basis and then, if challenged, deny.

Horst, Chief Smith, the two deputy chiefs, and Estevez performed the obligatory handshakes, Chief Smith ignoring me. Chief Douglas moved next to me and spoke conspiratorially. Douglas was a man who clearly wanted to be the next head of the department and who knew that any further racial strife was likely to squeeze Smith out and propel one of our black deputy chiefs in.

"Smith's still sore at you for the awards thing," Chief Douglas said.

"I figured."

"You got a clue what's going on here?"

"They're putting together a committee. You guys see the pickets at Twenty-third and Jackson?"

"No. You see the freeway on TV?"

"We had a patient from there."

"Not the gal who got her foot run over?"

"Somebody else. You don't think there's a chance they'll ask me to be on the committee, do you?"

"They'll want a chief."

"So why am I here?"

"Couldn't tell you. The vice president was over an hour late getting into Seattle. We were told the Secret Service came close to turning him around and flying him out of town."

"Trouble in River City."

Chief Douglas, who had cinnamon skin, hazel eyes, and a buttery line of patter, was considered a ladies' man by those who knew him better than I did. He'd been in the department almost twenty-five years, most of it at a desk. Some fairly reliable scuttlebutt circulating among black firefighters (but not among white) had it that he'd gone through several years of heavy cocaine usage, but if true, he'd come through unscathed.

Unlike some police and fire departments around the country, and despite the rather heated conversation I'd had that morning with Winston, there was surprisingly little overt racial disharmony in the Seattle Fire Department. Historically there had been problems, but to be honest, most of the heavy stuff had died down long before I got into the department. I'd had a white instructor in drill school who I thought was out to shitcan me for no good reason, but then, we all had at least one instructor in drill school we thought was out to can us.

I edged away from the group and studied the room while Chief Douglas began flirting with Estevez. My suspicion and hope was that this committee, after bringing Estevez on board, would be supplementing the panel with either Douglas, Lennox, or both: two black fire department officers with solid qualifications.

My absence from the awards ceremony had, by all accounts, brought a good deal of embarrassment to Chief Smith, who'd touted my so-called heroics at the Z Club to the local press for many long minutes before he realized I wasn't going to show. It wasn't that I'd tried to embarrass anyone by not showing; it was more like I was trying to keep from humiliating myself. A week after the Z Club, I barely felt like going out in public to buy a tomato, much less collect an award.

A tidy but overweight black woman bustled into the room with a sheaf of file folders under one arm and a large purse swinging from the other. When she turned around to address the assembly, I recognized her as one of the sign carriers at 23rd and Jackson.

"People! People! We have to get started. We have to get started if we're going to get this off the ground today. I know you're all busy. If everyone who has a chair can please sit?"

Moving close enough that I could feel her shoulder brush my arm, Estevez whispered, "That's Miriam Beckmann. She's the chairwoman for the Z Club Citizens for Truth."

Estevez remained beside me, pressed close by clusters of people on either side, more citizens packing the room every minute until there were seventy, maybe eighty of us. I didn't mind that Estevez had made a quick and easy alliance with me in the way that new acquaintances in a room full of strangers sometimes do; in fact I rather liked it. Beckmann took an informal roll call, shouting out names as she recognized individuals, asking for group leaders to introduce the members of each contingent. When the fire department was invited to step forward, Chief Smith introduced Chiefs

Lennox, Douglas, and Horst, but skipped me. Estevez gave me a gentle nudge. "That's the second time. What was that all about?"

"He must have got mixed up and thought I was Denzel Washington," I joked.

After she'd introduced herself and the other members of the Z Club Citizens for Truth—Reverend Morgan, three other ministers from local churches, and two parents of Z Club fatalities—Miriam Beckmann said, "Why don't we all bow our heads while Reverend Morgan says a prayer to get us started?"

A tall man, Reverend Morgan was darker than either Estevez or me, regal in appearance, with a patch of hair under his lower lip and a voice low enough to sound like the beginning of an earthquake. "Lord, thank you for bringing us together here in your temple on this solemn occasion. Lord, we're here to make peace in a community that's been torn apart by suspicion and anger over the demise of thirteen of your precious angels. We pray we will have the wisdom to do as you see fit and that all of us can agree on a steering committee that will look into the catastrophe and reveal the truth to us. Lord, grant us the wisdom to proceed with this undertaking, and from the actions we take here this morning, help us bring healing to a disrupted community. God bless the families of all who died, and God speed their souls into your grace and into the arms of the Lord Jesus Christ. Amen." The room rumbled with a chorus of amens.

"To order," said Beckmann, slamming a small gavel onto a wooden block she'd taken out of her coat pocket. "First of all, I would like to thank the chief of police and the chief of the fire department for coming to this forum. I would like to thank the mayor's office for sending along the deputy mayor, although I understand the mayor cannot be here. Now, let me give you the situation in a nutshell. We've lost thirteen young people. As you know, there have already been several self-serving statements made by the city about the fire department's actions—or inactions—at the Z Club, and now this report has come out and basically given us a version of what happened that many of us have a hard time swallowing, especially in light of that nine-one-one tape. The way I see it, we can march on the freeway, we can send our young people out to throw rocks at fire engines, or we can commission a new report—one that we all know will be unbiased."

"We're not going to take this lying down," shouted a woman who'd come in with Beckmann. "They passed by our people and left them in there. We heard it on the TV."

"I'm sorry," Chief Smith said, stepping forward. "I can't let that go by."

"Sit back, please," said Beckmann. "Sit back."

I liked this woman, who by all accounts had been an unemployed bakery worker until three weeks ago and who wasn't afraid to tell city officials to get out of her face.

"No, I'm sorry, but have you read the report?" said Chief Smith.

"I've read enough to know it was a perversion and a whitewash. Saying it was those poor babies' own fault that they died in that fire. They don't put the 'white' in 'whitewash' for nothing." There was a loud chorus of amens after that.

"I know the people who wrote it did so in good conscience. Nowhere in those pages did it say those people died because it was their fault. And that tape didn't surface until after the report came out."

"If it wasn't the fire department's fault, whose fault was it?" somebody shouted.

"Yeah. Whose?"

A chorus of voices chimed in. Beside me, Estevez edged closer. Given what had happened elsewhere in the city over the past few weeks, it wasn't outside the realm of possibility that violence would break out in this room.

Eyebrows like cattle burs, Chief Smith stepped alongside Chief Douglas against the far wall. "We're here to help," Smith said by way of surrender. "We're here to do whatever it takes to heal things. That's all."

"Maybe you should heal up your fire department," yelled a woman from the back of the room. Several others shouted along with her.

"Now, now! Let's not get ourselves outraged all over again,"

Beckmann said, slamming her wooden gavel on the table and displaying the attitude of someone who didn't get center stage often and wasn't about to give it up when she did. It tickled me that she'd brought her own gavel and wooden block to slam it on. "We've got a plan. We've decided to appoint our own investigating committee. Next time they wave that *white*wash in our faces, we'll have our own report.

"Let me introduce Jamie Estevez. Most of you already know who she is, but let me remind you that Ms. Estevez is the reporter who broke the story on the police scandal in Spokane two years ago. You all remember? Four police officers lost their jobs after they were found guilty of police brutality against three of our young men on their way home from a church picnic. It was just another arrest and beating until Jamie Estevez started digging into it."

"What about the mother of one of the victims getting her foot run over by the vice president down on the freeway this morning?" somebody shouted.

All eyes in the room turned to the chief of police, who said, "We're looking into it."

A minister at the front of the room yelled, "Like you looked into the Jones assassination?" Marvin Jones was the alleged rapist-hijacker whose death via police shooting caused an uproar four months prior to the Z Club.

"Now, wait a minute." It was the deputy mayor, a man named George David, with a three-piece suit and a bald head. "You're doing yourselves a disservice by linking these cases. Jones had a record for sexual assault and mental instability. If he'd lived, he probably would have spent the rest of his life behind bars. This fire is a completely different matter."

"It ain't no different if you're black," somebody yelled.

"Please, Mr. Officer. Just shoot me!" another man repeated.

Somebody else said, "Burn us up, Mr. Fireman! Burn us up!"

"This is different," repeated the deputy mayor.

"It ain't *no* different if your children are dead," came a voice from behind Reverend Morgan.

Beckmann banged her gavel loudly for half a minute before the room grew quiet. "Brothers and sisters, listen to our plan before you get all distressed. Ms. Estevez has the experience to dig into this and find out what happened. Does anybody here really think she won't get the truth?" The room went silent. "But she can't do this by herself. In the same forthright manner in which this committee has struggled to embrace these issues, we've decided to ask the fire department to give us a representative to help her."

"Not *this* fire department!" shouted one of the ministers.

Slamming the gavel down, Beckmann said, "Hear me out before you go spouting off. Two days ago Chief Smith gave me a list of officers who might assist Estevez. But after talking to rank-and-file members in the department—several, by the way, who are members of the Mount Zion congregation—we decided to forgo the fire chief's recommendations and nominate our own adjunct. We're asking Captain Trey Brown to serve with Ms. Estevez."

All eyes in the room followed Chief Smith's murderous look toward me. Even Estevez, who was standing next to me, turned and stared. Chief Lennox glared daggers while Chief Douglas simply looked stunned, as I'm sure I did. "You want an answer right here in front of everybody?" I said.

"We want you to say you'll do it," said Reverend Morgan. "We are asking you for help. We understand you spent several years as a fire investigator. Your expertise will be invaluable."

"I was at that fire."

"That's a good part of why you're the perfect man for this job," said Reverend Morgan.

"Nobody who was there should be involved in the investigation. I will never be an objective observer, sir. I cannot be. Nor does this make sense from your point of view. If it doesn't represent a conflict of interest, it gives the appearance of a conflict of interest. You want a separate investigation, and that's an idea I can understand and support, but you'll be advised to take my name off the table."

Beckmann said, "Chief, I thought you said you would give us the services of anybody we selected."

Chief Smith's face began to turn red in the way that only a heavy drinker's face can. "Captain Brown will do this if I tell him to. But he does have a point. He will not be regarded as a dispassionate observer. Not by the papers and not by the—"

Reverend Morgan stepped forward. "Not by the what? The white community? We're not here to satisfy the white community. We're here for justice. And we're not looking for lack of passion, Chief. Passion is exactly what we want. Along with answers." He turned to me. "Son, the very fact that you don't want to do it makes you all the more perfect. I'll tell you something else. I'll tell you *all* something else. We spoke to a lot of people in the fire department, and we didn't have very many conversations where this man's name did not come up. Everything that everybody tells us about you points to you finding those valuable answers that so far have been eluding us. Why did those young people die? What was the fire department doing that led to this tragedy? Was there willful misconduct? What's going on inside the city, and specifically the fire department, that we in the African-American community need to be aware of? We've considered over a dozen candidates for this post, both inside and outside your department, including retired investigators from San Francisco and Baltimore, and Captain Brown is our man."

Resignation clouded Smith's voice. "Okay, but I'd like to place somebody else on the committee for balance. Chief Douglas here—"

"Screw the balance," said a man who hadn't spoken until now, storming up and down in front of the police and fire department members as he spoke, the veins in his neck standing out. He was dressed in a shabby sport coat with no tie, and if he'd been walking down the street I would have been tempted to hand him a dollar. "We're not looking for balance. We're looking for truth. Captain Brown saved my niece's life. As far as I'm concerned, that clinches it." Several others shouted in concurrence.

"Can I say something?" I said.

Beckmann slammed the table with her gavel. "You've got the floor, Captain Brown."

I took a moment to organize my thoughts. "I will gladly work with Ms. Estevez and whoever else you put on this committee. But I want to make certain you're hearing me clearly. Whatever I find, I report. I can't guarantee *anybody* will be happy."

"That's how I feel, too," Estevez said. "If what we come up with settles grudges or reinforces biases, so be it. If it doesn't, we're not going to tailor it."

A chorus of amens and hallelujahs burst forth from a significant population in the room. The angry man in the tattered sport coat spoke. "You just tell us how it came down, and we'll go home satisfied."

"We want something we can believe," shouted a woman in the back of the room.

Beckmann slammed her gavel down and said, "Estevez and Captain Brown, you're hired. Meeting adjourned."

A few minutes later in the foyer of the church, I found Estevez with Marvin Douglas, his black dress uniform impeccable, his smile dazzling. Estevez looked like a cat cornered by a stray dog.

5. STONE CARMICHAEL SHOWS UP AND THERE'S SOMETHING WRONG

JAMIE ESTEVEZ

In his usual way, Mayor Carmichael came rushing through the front door like a freight train. A small man, he was dapper in a tailored suit, a walking advertisement for the most lavish tooth brighteners. He cultivated an intellectual image, but local political cartoonists drew him with a huge head, gigantic ears, and oversize glasses. He was courteous and rarely contentious in public, a charming family man with a socialite wife and two children who appeared frequently in photo ops, yet he ran a disciplined administration from which there had been few leaks.

All in all, he was a politician's politician, and most of the time he had the city council eating out of his hand. Before running for mayor, he'd been a private attorney for several large multibillion-dollar enterprises run by his well-heeled family. He could charm the devil, and I liked him. So did most people, which is why Captain Brown's reaction shocked me. Brown who had only moments earlier shanghaied me from Marvin Douglas with the most delicate of lies. "Sorry to interrupt," he had said, "but the committee people need to be somewhere else in a few minutes."

When Brown had accompanied me back to the meeting room, nobody seemed to be in any hurry. I said, "Captain Brown, were you rescuing me?"

"You looked like you were in trouble."

"Actually, I can take care of myself."

"I was trying to make it easier for you to extricate yourself from what looked like a difficult situation. If you want, I can go back and get Chief Douglas."

He was purposely trying to irritate me for some reason. "No, thank you."

"You did look like a cornered rabbit."

Now he was really irritating me. "I certainly did not."

"Oh, you most certainly did."

Moments later when Mayor Carmichael entered the meeting room, Captain Brown's reaction was almost visceral, as if he'd been punched in the stomach, yet it passed so quickly that if I hadn't been standing next to him, I might not have noticed. Carmichael smiled at me and then did a double take when he glimpsed Captain Brown, but kept moving across the room toward Miriam Beckmann.

"You know him?" I asked.

"He's our illustrious mayor."

"But do you know him?"

"We've met once or twice."

"Your tone of voice makes me think you don't like him."

"I don't."

"Why not?"

"Because he's a shitbird."

"Watch your language. He's your boss. And he's the one who ensured the city would fund this investigation."

"You don't want my opinion, don't ask for it."

Mayor Carmichael spoke briefly to Beckmann and then Pastor Morgan. A few minutes later when the mayor and Beckmann approached, Carmichael was all flashing teeth and tight cheeks, although I noted his smile didn't reach his eyes. I'd never seen Carmichael lose his composure like this before.

"Ms. Estevez," Mayor Carmichael said, covering my hand in both of his, which were freezing. "I haven't run into you in a while."

"It's been a year at least."

"I was the one who suggested your name to Miriam Beckmann for this project. I hope you don't mind."

"Not at all. Thank you."

He turned his attention to Captain Brown. "Trey?"

"Stone."

"Is it still Trey, or did you change your *first* name, too?"

"It's Trey. I didn't have any compelling reason to change that one."

"It's good to see you."

"Is it?"

"I've thought about you, Trey."

"Funny. I haven't thought about you at all."

"I guess you've been in my fire department all along?"

"Just the last fifteen years."

"I'm glad you landed on your feet. It's . . . good to see you. It really is. And I'm glad you're going to be part of this new report." And then a thought struck him. "You don't happen by any chance . . . you aren't the Captain Brown in the original Z Club report?"

"I'm the only Captain Brown in the department."

"Well. This *is* interesting." He reached out to shake hands with Brown, who pretended he didn't see. "You think it's a good idea to work on this report?"

"I don't see as I have much choice," Brown said.

Carmichael pulled his hand back and looked at Pastor Morgan and Miriam Beckmann, who was beaming. "Yes, well, I'm sure Mrs. Beckmann and Pastor Morgan know what they're doing." He turned to me and smiled. "Jamie Estevéz and I have worked together on other projects. We're old friends, aren't we?"

"Yes, I suppose we are," I said, though I didn't regard a twenty-minute interview as working together or being old friends.

"I can't get over it," Carmichael said. "It's just so strange seeing you again. And wonderful. I mean that." Obviously Brown was supposed to reply in kind, but he said nothing, and after a few moments the silence grew to be too much for Carmichael, who stepped back and embraced me in his look. "I look forward to your report."

A few minutes later, as we were preparing to leave, Miriam Beckmann approached and said, "Tomorrow night there's a black-tie charity function for the Central Area Leadership Council's reading project. All the movers and shakers in the white and black community will be there, and I think it would behoove you to be there, too. I'll have tickets for the two of you waiting at the door. It's the Mikimoto Mansion on Capitol Hill. Eight o'clock. Can you make it?"

"Of course we can," I blurted, earning a glare from Trey.

"I'll have to check my calendar," he said, which made me feel silly, like an overeager puppy.

"I'm sure you'll find a way to make room in your schedule," Beckmann said. "And Jamie? I want to thank you for going through our list of candidates and selecting Captain Brown. We had it narrowed down, but we didn't really dare make the final choice until you saw the list. I think the two of you are perfect for each other."

Trey gave me a sour look as I surreptitiously wiped my perspiring palms along the hem of my blazer. I'd known him less than an hour and had already been caught in a lie. This was going to be uphill all the way.

6. BLOCKING THE DOOR, STANDING MY GROUND

JAMIE ESTEVEZ

I'd had quite a few people ride with me in the Lexus since I got it last summer, but none of them seemed to fill the car the way Trey Brown did in his large black military-style work boots and navy-blue uniform. I was well aware he was in a foul humor, partly from his interaction with the mayor and partly because he knew I'd chosen him to be on this committee but had been deceptive about it. I should have followed my own instincts and been up front with him from the beginning, instead of following Chief Horst's advice. Too late now.

We were a couple of blocks from Station 28, sitting at a stoplight, when I broke the silence that had enveloped the car since we'd left Chief Horst at Station 13. "So," I said, my throat dry, "you and the mayor seemed to have known each other before?" For over thirty seconds he didn't respond. "I'm guessing you haven't seen each other in fifteen years."

"Where do you get that number?"

"Oh, good. You speak."

"Is this whole thing between us going to be about sarcasm? Because if it is, I'm pretty good at it myself."

"I'm sorry. I *was* asking a serious question."

"Where did you get that figure?"

"It's the amount of time you've been in the department. The mayor didn't know you were in the department."

"The last time we saw each other I was seventeen. He'd just gotten out of law school."

"How did you know each other?"

"What do you want from me?"

"You don't have to snap."

"I'm in a bad mood. I snap when I'm in a bad mood." His voice grew softer. We were beside Station 28 now, parked in the visitor slot next to the front door. "What is it that you want?"

"I just want to know what was going on between you and Stone Carmichael."

The question appeared to be unanswerable, at least by Trey Brown, because he got out of the car, went to the front door of the station, and was thumbing the combination lock on the door by the time I caught him. "Stone was my brother," he said finally, opening the door and stepping inside.

Trey Brown was African American and Stone Carmichael was a blue-eyed Caucasian, so I wondered for a moment if he meant fraternity brothers, but that wasn't how I heard it. *Brother,* he'd said. I followed him inside and trailed him down the narrow corridor to the engine officer's room, where Kitty Acton sat at the desk filling out some paperwork.

"I've got some news," Trey Brown said to Kitty. "Maybe you can get Clyde and the others together in the beanery."

"Sure, Cap. Hey, Estevez," she said to me as she squeezed past.

I stepped into the room and closed the door, leaning against it so that I'd effectively trapped Trey. The tiny office contained a desk, some tall lockers, and a bed in the corner. After he doffed his coat and draped it over the back of the chair, he took a step toward me, but I didn't budge. "What?"

"You can't just tell me he's your brother and then walk away."

"It's personal."

"It's not personal if it affects what we're doing together. I'm not going to tell anyone, if that's what you're afraid of."

"It's complicated."

"I'm not smart enough to understand? Is that it?"

We locked eyes until I blinked, though I didn't look away. It was hard to know what was going on behind that slab of granite he called a face. "You're tougher than you look," he said finally.

"Anybody I've ever worked with could have told you that."

"Sit down."

"Thank you, but I prefer to stand."

He stepped back and considered me for a few moments. "When I was four, I was adopted into the Carmichael family. Shelby Junior was fourteen at the time I was adopted, twenty-seven when he died in a car accident. Stone was seven years older than me, and Kendra was the baby of the family, a year younger than me. The old man had political aspirations, and it doesn't hurt when a politician adopts a child of color. At least that's what Stone told me four or five thousand times when we were growing up."

"It was a fairly rare occurrence for a white family to adopt a black child back then, wasn't it?"

"It's still rare."

"But your surname isn't Carmichael. It's Brown."

"After the Carmichaels disowned me, I took my mother's maiden name."

"This is going to take longer than five minutes, isn't it?"

"It isn't going to take any time at all, because you've heard everything I have to say on the subject. I was Trey Carmichael. Now I'm Trey Brown. It's that simple."

"And you haven't seen your brother in fifteen years?"

"Nineteen." I did the calculations quickly. Nineteen and seventeen; he was thirty-six, six years older than I was. He folded his arms across his chest and waited for me to step away from the door. The story was probably as complicated as it was personal, and even though I desperately wanted to hear the rest of it, he was bent on guarding his privacy, and I had to respect that.

"Does anybody else around here know this?"

"No, and that's the way we're going to keep it."

I couldn't help thinking about it all through our first interview, which was with a firefighter named Justin Hinkel, a tall, thin man who'd done a lot of joking around earlier when Chief Horst and I were waiting for Captain Brown to return from the alarm. Brown told me that Hinkel had been in the department for four years and was assigned to Ladder 12, which worked out of Station 28, but on the night in question had been riding Engine 33, stationed just down the road to the south. Hinkel had a prominent Adam's apple and a cowlick over his forehead; he appeared nervous when he came into the room. I expected them all to be nervous.

7. SPLATTERFEST

FIREFIGHTER JUSTIN HINKEL, ENGINE 33, C SHIFT

The fire came in at 2230 hours. Dowd had already gone to bed, and the lieutenant was in his room on the phone to his wife. Me and Harrington were out in the beanery watching a movie called *Splatterfest.* Cowboys and werewolves.

So we all bunk up and we're screaming down Rainier Avenue, weaving in and out of traffic, and the lieutenant turns around to me and Dowd and says, "It looks like we're going to be first in."

Harrington says, "I'll pull the preconnect."

"Unless we see something different when we get there," says Lieutenant Smith.

The club—well, you know where the club is: two blocks off Rainier, down in Columbia City. It turns out we *are* first in, just like we thought.

It was an old wooden building. Right away I figure balloon construction with a lot of old pipe chases and crap like that. We'll get it out, but we'll be chasing spot fires in the walls all night. The front doors are on fire, actually burning pretty good, with a lot of black smoke and heat flowing into the building. That's the strange part. While there's plenty of smoke and shit—excuse the language—coming onto the street, and there's smoke on the sidewalk, there's also a lot going back into the building, like this funnel effect. We figure out later that somebody left some back windows or doors open, and there's a breeze blowing the fire right through the first floor.

Dowd parks in front of the building—I mean, smack in front of the doorway that's on fire—and when we get a good look at it, you can tell a preconnect isn't going to be big enough, but the lieutenant's busy talking on the radio giving a report and a size-up, so me and Harrington, we go behind the rig and pull out two hundred feet of two-and-a-half. Dowd comes around and helps us, then takes couplings and wrenches across the street to the hydrant.

By the time Harrington and I get all that hose into loops on the sidewalk in front of the building and get our face pieces on and air flowing, we have water. Harrington hits the doorway real good, water splashing us, and then, thinking he's put out most of the fire on the porch, we head inside. Ideally, with the fire in the front of the building, we should be laying lines through the building and coming out the front door instead of going *in* the front door.

That's when all these little Mexicans started busting around the corner of the building yelling there are people inside. So now we're not sure how to proceed. By this time Harrington is in the doorway. There's this big old foyer, and there's fire everywhere. I mean, on the walls, the ceiling, even the floor. And he's hitting it with a two-and-a-half, which should put it out in an instant, only it's not going out. Meanwhile I'm behind him pulling hose. That stuff is heavy when it's full of water. Harrington crawls into the foyer, and he's hitting the ceiling, and he's really going at it because we both know there are people. It's a big building, and we know if we can't put the fire out right away we're in trouble.

We're stuck in the doorway, Harrington using that nozzle like it's a jiffy hose. Then after a few minutes have gone by, he gets tired and we switch off. I get most of the first room knocked down, but by now it's dark and smoky and we can't see anything. About that time some truckmen come up, but they don't have hose lines and don't get very far. They're using the thermal imager and telling us where there's heat in the walls. They keep telling me it's up high, so I hit it with a straight stream thinking I'll bounce it around on the ceiling, but the stream goes right through the wall and there's a ton of fire up in there. I mean, it's boiling inside that wall.

I'm getting tired, so the two truckmen take over the line and I go out the front door, where Harrington's pulling hose, and it occurs to me that there's another set of doors on the front porch. Only these doors are on the other wall, facing kind of into the building toward the north. I try one of the doors and it opens up a couple of inches, and then it kind of shatters and the top falls off, and there are flames leaping out in my face.

That's when we get the line back from the two ladder guys and we aim it up the stairs, but it's like pissing into a hurricane, because absolutely nothing happens. After a while, Harrington looks at me and says, "Are we supposed to go up?"

I'm thinking those stairs are rotten with fire and they're going to collapse if we put any weight on them. "Are you kidding?" I say. "We're staying here." Lieutenant Smith is just coming up to join us. He asks me what I'm doing, and I tell him we have fire in the stairs. We pour water up those stairs like crazy, but there's a ton of fire just around the corner and we can't get to it because the lower part of the stairway is already falling apart.

Meanwhile, Engine 30 shows up and parks across the street on the hydrant, and they bring another line off our rig. They're fresh, so they go inside while we stay in front holding the fire in the stairs. But by now the fire's built up a little bit on the first floor, and they don't get more than fifteen feet inside the front door.

We never do see any civilians come out. Don't see them and don't hear them.

Whatever is in that big hall, it takes off and is boiling. It was Chief Hillbourn's order later to line up the dead people under the canvas tarp. I guess some of the media didn't think that was cool. Like if you're on a drinking binge and you line up all the dead soldiers on the windowsill or something.

The worst part is the crowd. The Hispanics are one thing, but we get this crowd of black folks, you know, in their late teens or early twenties, and they start to get angry. They all have cell phones and they are calling their friends, getting more people to come down, and the cops can't handle them. Then they start yelling things like "Put the fire out!" and "If this was a white neighborhood, you would be saving the building!"

One guy tries to tackle Harrington when he goes to get a fresh bottle, tells him he's going the wrong way. They arrest five or six people near us. I mean, by then fire is starting to come out every crevice on the front of the building. Finally they send some black chief—I think it's Lennox—around the crowd to explain what we're doing and why we're doing it. In the end, the cops have to come and pull Lennox out of there to save his butt. I think that's where the rumors start, right there that night on the fire ground, people standing around with bottles of malt liquor and flipping us shit. In the end we don't get to help with the bodies. They were having truck companies from the north end do that, guys who are fresh and haven't fought the fire, guys going in with ropes and stuff.

8. SUDDENLY TREY BROWN LOOKS WHITE

JAMIE ESTEVEZ

Hinkel's voice was actually quivering during parts of his testimony. I let him talk without interruption, and when he finished, asked if he had anything to add, then turned to Brown, who thought about it a while and said, "Did anybody call out to you for help from inside?"

"No, sir."

"And you didn't pass anybody in there?"

"No, sir. Not that I knew of."

We shook hands, and Hinkel left. I shut off my recorder and looked at Brown. "This is going to be tough."

"Yeah."

"The fire seemed to spread pretty fast."

"In the old days, builders didn't put fire stops in the walls. A fire stop is a simple two-by-four, usually, nailed in crossways between the uprights. You get a fire in a building as old as the Z Club, it's easy for a basement fire to travel all the way to the roof running right up through the walls. In newer buildings, fire stops hold the fire back for a while."

"Hinkel said they should have gone in the back door and worked their way to the front, instead of the other way about. Is that right?"

"Generally when you hit fire with a hose line, you want to work from the uninvolved portion of the building to the involved portion. Otherwise you push the fire to parts of the building it might not spread to on its own. A water stream pushes the fire, just like sweeping a pile of debris."

"So this might be the mistake that underlies this whole situation?"

"There was no way they could have been sure they would have gotten in on the other side of the building, and the wind was blowing the wrong way. On the other hand, it might have been a mistake."

"And then there was the door to the upstairs. Don't you think if they'd found that sooner they might have saved the stairs?"

"Nobody can say for sure. But if they had, a lot of people could have come down those stairs."

"Okay. A few more questions. What's a jiffy hose?"

"You really took notes, didn't you?"

"I always do."

"A jiffy hose is a standard garden hose. We carry them for cleaning off our gear after a fire."

"And a thermal imager?"

"It's a handheld camera that shows heat. Like infrared. It sees through smoke and through walls. We've got one on the truck right outside. I'll show it to you."

Trey took me out to the apparatus bay, where he climbed into the truck and came out with what appeared to be a handheld camera the size of a tiny portable TV. "Truckies carry this into a fire, and it can essentially see through smoke. It senses heat and has a scale along the side here that tells you the temperatures you're looking at." He turned it on, and a small black-and-white screen lit up. Then he pressed his palm against the side of the ladder truck for a few moments, and when he removed it, the camera showed the heat from his palm print on the sheet metal of the truck. Everything warm in the camera was white. His face and arms were white.

9. SHOE SALE

FIREFIGHTER HERBIE SCHMIDT, AID 14, C SHIFT

We help Ladder 7 put up their aerial on the B side of the building, but just as we're getting ready to go to the roof, somebody asks for the aid car on the C side, so me and Alan Francher drive the aid car around the block and park. I look up and there's a ground ladder going up to this smoky window on the second story, a good twenty-five feet to the window.

There's four or five civilians crumpled on the ground at the base of the ladder, all kind of lying there like they're hurt. Another guy's limping toward me. There's a woman coming down the ladder and one just getting off at the base. And there's a firefighter trying to go up the ladder while these civilians are trying to get down. There's only two firefighters there, and from what I can see, it's a mess.

It's pretty clear that the second floor is full of people, that the fire's about to flash over, and that we need six ladders, not one. Francher talks to the first person we see limping toward us. He's African American and dressed pretty nice, except he doesn't have any shoes. It turns out his ankle's broken. Francher takes him to the triage area and I move ahead.

I find two women on the hood of a car. The hood's all bashed in. They're kind of dazed, and there's smoke oozing out the walls next to them. The first is heavyset and she's got a broken tib-fib. I'm trying to figure out if I can carry her by myself, because, like I said, she's heavyset. The other woman, I'm not sure what's wrong with her. I do a scoop and run on the first one, picking her up like a kid, and just as I get her off the car I look up. There's a firefighter in the window, and he's dangling a woman out the window by one arm, and before I can say beans she lands on the roof of the same car. Boom! They're throwing them out the windows! I've never seen anything like it.

I yell up at him. "What the hell do you think you're doing?"

He yells back, "Clear some space. Get those people out of there!"

About that time another engine company throws up a second ladder a couple of cars to the left of us, but there's a shitload of flame coming out that window. I cart my first victim maybe thirty feet, set her down in the parking lot, and start ferrying the others out as fast as I can. They're flying out the windows. Hitting the cars. And that first car is just getting more and more pancaked.

We set up this relay. Me and Francher and some other firefighter whose name I never get. We transport the victims away from the building as fast as we can, most of them with broken legs, a few with no injuries except smoke inhalation. We're moving as fast as we can so we won't get hit by the next falling body. It's like some game thought up by a maniac.

After a while the bodies stop coming out of the dark so quickly, and then not much later they aren't coming out at all. If the firefighter who's been throwing people out gets out of there, I don't see it. I don't know what happens after that, because Francher and I both get drafted to help splint leg fractures. We have four broken femurs, one bleeding out pretty good. I think her blood pressure was something like eighty palp. Twenty-three broken legs, they told us later. Only a couple of people coming out of that window didn't get hurt. But hell, better a broken leg than another funeral, wouldn't you say? If they'd lined up inside that window and waited until the ladder was free, we would have lost another ten people, easy.

Six hours later, when it's winding down and we're thinking about going inside to look for bodies, somebody notices all these shoes in the parking lot. More than two dozen shoes lying all over the place.

In the middle of it all, Francher wears himself out and decides to have a heart attack. He's a smoker, so the worst part for him is they wouldn't let him have a fag in the hospital, you know. So later we go up there with a pack of Marlboros on the end of a fishing line with a pole and everything, and throw it into his room and reel it out into the hallway a few times. It was about the only fun we had out of the whole thing.

10. KITTY TALKS AND TALKS AND . . .

JAMIE ESTEVEZ

"What did Schmidt mean when he referred to the B and the C sides of the building?"

"Wherever the command post is," Trey said, "that becomes side A, which at the Z Club fire was the south side of the building. The other three sides are lettered in a clockwise direction from side A, so that Ladder Seven and Aid Fourteen started out on side B. C was in back on the north side, where the parking lot and alley were, and the doors where Engine Thirty-three stopped initially and began fighting fire was D, to the right of the command post. The designations all depend on where the command post is."

"So people were being dropped out the second-story window over the cars parked behind the building," I said, pointing to the sketch he'd drawn earlier.

"Right."

"And that was because there was only one ladder up in the back and all those people couldn't have gotten down it quickly enough?"

"Right."

"Why was there just the one ladder?"

"The only other windows back there weren't accessible because of the parked cars, and even if they had been, we didn't have enough manpower early on to get them laddered and unshuttered. There were just the three of us in the beginning."

"Unshuttered?"

"They were all boarded over except a second window that a woman had fallen out of."

Next we spoke to Brown's crew, but after we'd concluded with Garrison and were almost finished with Kitty, they got an alarm and left us like a puff of dust. Clyde Garrison was a big man with a boyish haircut and a tuft of hair he constantly had to throw out of his eyes, a slight hunch in his back, and a twinkle in his eyes. He was a little taller than Trey. He gave a matter-of-fact rendition of the events on September third, delving into the details seemingly without emotion, though I noted that from time to time his voice cracked. He was the oldest firefighter we'd spoken to so far, in his early fifties, and had been driving Engine 28 the night of the Z Club fire.

Garrison stated that Captain Brown had been assigned as C division, which put him in charge of the C side of the building, but had abandoned his post to climb a ladder and crawl inside the building. "I don't think the division commander should be making rescues," Garrison said, staring at Captain Brown. "I've told the captain before. It's no secret. I told everybody who spoke to me after the fire. But that's just my take on it. Maybe my nose is out of joint because he bumped me out of the way. Not that it does any good to be sore. I mean, in the end, he's the captain and I'm just a driver. I could have made those rescues as easily as he did. He was basically just dropping people out the window."

"So *you* were the one throwing people out the window?" I

asked Brown, somewhat astonished by the revelation. Why hadn't he said so earlier? And why hadn't the official report mentioned it?

He gave me a look. "I wasn't *throwing* them. I was *lowering* them and then dropping them. I would have walked them over to the escalator, but we didn't have one."

"Okay, whatever. Is that why the department wanted to give you the award that you threw in their faces?"

"I didn't throw anything in anybody's face. I didn't want the whole ceremony thing. Okay?" Again, the look.

"Okay. Sure."

Yikes.

Tall, angular, and a whirlwind of constant motion, Kitty Acton was a different creature altogether from the slow-moving Clyde Garrison. Kitty was near tears at the beginning of her interview; then she teetered away from her emotions as she veered off topic and approached tears again when she returned to it. The upshot was they'd gone to C side and put up a ladder, and then the captain went up and began throwing—uh, lowering—people out of the smoke.

She talked for almost an hour, backtracking willy-nilly, diverting her narrative off that night to other calls they'd been on, hogging the spotlight while she had it, a ballerina dancing on top of a music box. After Engine 28's station bell hit and she ran out of the room to climb onto the fire engine, I turned to Brown. "Is she always like this, or is she just nervous?"

"She's always nervous."

"Hmm." I took a deep breath. "Do you want to tell me your story while we're waiting?"

"Everything I have to say is already written down."

"Everything *everybody* has to say is already written down."

"I'd rather wait."

"Sure. Just one question, though. Clyde says you shouldn't have left your post as Division C commander. That he could have handled the rescues as easily. What's your response to that?"

"When it started, there were only three of us back there. Me, Clyde, and Kitty. Kitty isn't strong enough to yard anybody out of a window, and Clyde was moving like molasses. We only had a few minutes to act, and even as it was, we didn't get them all out. I didn't want to take a chance that somebody wouldn't get out because Clyde wasn't strong enough or was moving too slowly."

"And you knew you were strong enough?"

"I know for a fact I got more people out than Clyde would have."

"He doesn't want to acknowledge that, does he?"

"Nope."

When Engine 28 hadn't returned forty minutes later, I realized Kitty Acton's testimonial had degraded into speculation and sidetracking anyway, along with all the trivia about her love life, which Brown told me she was in the habit of talking about endlessly. She tapped into the guys for dating advice, as if they were all her big brothers.

"Oh, I guess I thought she was a lesbian for some reason."

"She is," he said. "The dating advice thing can get kind of weird sometimes, like the time she was making out with Miss Ballard behind the station." He grinned at me.

So, I thought, Trey Brown has a lighter side after all. I grinned back.

11. FOUR WEEKS EARLIER

ANDREW WASHINGTON, SPURNED LOVER/ARSONIST

It takes me freakin' forever to find two empty bottles. I finally snag a couple out of some old lady's garbage with all the bacon drippings and shit—wiping them off on my pants—and then I can't find no gasoline nowhere. I try a couple of garages for lawn mower equipment and shit, but I can't get into the first two, and the third has a motherfriggin' dog the size of a Seahawk barking his fool ass off at me and snapping at my kicks as I high-hurdle over one fence and then the next fence because there's another motherfriggin' dog in the next yard. Piss me off. Garages are out. Change of plan.

As it happens, I take out my blade and custom cut some old grandma's motherfriggin' garden hose, slash me out a five-foot section, just about as long as my unit. Ha! Now that's funny. That would make even Gerard laugh, if he got any laughs left after I finish with his sorry ass. Yeah. I got a five-foot unit—tuck it into my sock to keep it warm.

With the bottle in my coat pocket and the hose all stuffed down my overalls, I walk past the club—twice, just to make sure they're in there—after spotting Gerard's little Honda parked a block away. Soon's I see his car, I key the driver's side door, writing "dumb nigga" on it.

You can't hear no music outside the club 'cause they got the walls soundproofed, but once I get in the stairs and the dumbster asks for money, I can hear the hip-hop and I know they're dancin', too. I think about Gerard and LaToya, and Gerard getting all up on her, and then I think about bustin' past the dumbster and checking the place out, but he tells me on no account can I go up them stairs without a ticket. He's just pissing me off, which is more bad news for LaToya and Gerard and any other cats hangin' wid them. And this dumbster, too.

So now I got me a couple bottles and I got me a hose, but I'm running around the whole business district of Columbia City looking for some way to fill the bottles with what my grandpop used to call Ethel. And I'm having no luck, and there are cats walking 'cause it's a nice night, and a couple of cats give me a " 'sup, bro?" but I keep on walkin' 'cause I'm in a nasty mood and I gotta stay focused.

I get out my screwdriver and find this Mustang maybe two blocks from the club, and I jimmy the gas flap, and once that's off, the cap unspins and I put my face up in there and smell the gasoline. We used to sniff it, me and Gerard, in the hood, back when we was kids. Paint thinner, gas, lacquer, airplane glue, back when we still thought we was friends, huffing the night away listening to that fairy Michael Jackson and Prince and talkin' about bitches, pimpin' it up. Later Gerard gets this fat-ass job with City Light and thinks he's hot shit 'cause he's got some change in his pocket, the rest of us out here in the cold livin' with our grandfolks and dodgin' the po-lice. Nothin' worse than a nigger thinks he's better than all the other niggers. Gerard's got his own crib and his own wheels and he walks around with that 9 millimeter under his driver's seat like he's a special bullshit motherfucker.

So I put the hose into the Mustang's gas tank, but the other end won't fit in the bottle 'cause it's like a small-dick bottle and it's a big-dick hose. If you can believe this, I'm standing on the street maybe twenty minutes jackin' off with this hose and finally some white cat comes by on a motherfriggin' bicycle and yells something at me and keeps on pedaling like he knows what he's talking about. This cat's gone maybe a block when I realize what he said. "You gotta suck on the end." Like, I gotta suck on the end of the hose? No way I'm going to suck on this hose, I tell myself, and then the next thing I'm sucking gas and it's in my mouth and I'm pouring it into the bottles, spilling it all over my kicks and my hands.

I jam two bandannas down the necks of the bottles and carry them in the crook of my arm. It stinks worse than I remember. It's warm out, but I'm wearing my big Raider coat, so that makes it easier to hide the bottles.

They're having some sort of beaner party on the first floor, a bunch of Mexican chiquitas running around in white dresses and shiny black shoes, Gerard and LaToya all up in the club on the second floor, where you can't go unless you got a ticket. The first floor's a big hall like a Mason lodge or something. There's another set of doors on the front porch leading up to the club. You go in them double doors and go up this wide wooden stairway that creaks, and you turn the corner and go up another stairway just as wide. You wouldn't even know the club was there unless somebody told you. They say Jimi used to play his white guitar there with the

Rocking Kings back when he went to Garfield. There's bullet holes in the walls from the FBI raid in the sixties when the Panthers was holdin' meetings.

I open the doors that lead upstairs, and the dumbster's not in his usual position. My guess is, he had to take a piss. A car passes slowly, and for a minute I think it's a cop, but it's a couple checking the place out, going to go in, a man and his squeeze. They drive away and I pull the bottles out and go to light 'em. Only I forgot to bring a motherfriggin' match. Can you believe that?

I stand there with my bandannas stuffed down the bottles and my hands all cold from the gas, and I'm sick to my stomach that nothing I do tonight is going right. I wait any longer and the motherfriggin' dumbster's going to come down the stairs and I'm going to have to cap him. Then one of them Mexican kids comes out on the front porch and I look at the kid and say, "Hey, muchacho? You got a match?" He's about seven, with his shirt all pulled out of his cords. He runs back in and comes out with a box of matches. Can you believe that?

Balancing all the shit in my arms, I light the first bandanna and it goes poof. I'm not sure how long I can hold the business before it explodes in my hand, so I look down at the kid, who's staring at me, and I say, "Hey, kid. You better get back inside. I don't want you to get hurt." He turns and runs back inside real cute like. Can't be leaving no witnesses.

Just as I cock my arm back to pitch my shit into the stairwell, dumbster comes around the corner at the top and sees what I'm doing, yells something I don't hear, and races down the stairs toward me, but I pitch the bottle, and to my surprise the bottle doesn't break against the wall, it just bounces, but then it hits the stairs and cracks and spills gas out, and before you know it we got fire all over the stairs, not going too hot at first. Then the flames jump up.

Dumbster comes to a halt and stares at me, his face all glowing in the light. "You gonna pay for this, motherfucker."

"I didn't pay for no ticket, and I ain't payin' for this," I says.

"I'm gonna go get my piece."

"Go get your piece. Then we'll both have one," I say, pulling out my John Henry and pointing it at him.

"You better not shoot. You already in a heapa trouble."

"I'm in a heapa trouble, it don't make no difference, does it?"

"Just don't you shoot me, motherfucker."

By now the fire's starting to climb, and he's got his mitts in front of his face 'cause of the heat, and he turns around and runs up around the corner out of sight. One of them Mexicans comes out of the first floor, an adult this time, looks at me and turns his head until he can see inside the stairway, at which point he goes flyin' back inside with all that mariachi music.

I strike a match, light my second bottle, and throw it inside the front door behind him.

Just as I'm starting to leave, the wind picks up and rips up them stairs and blows on the fire, and I can hear it making this purring sound. Dumb bastards. Fix that old Gerard for messing with my woman. And LaToya, too. You can't trust a woman, there's no point in keeping her around.

Now I'm heading down the street, and I'm thinking, Mission accomplished, you know. That's when I notice this Caucasian cat angling across the street from the other side, headed straight at me, white hair and everything, got a little wiener dog on a leash. I keep a grip on my piece in my pants, but for a number of reasons I don't want to use it, the foremost being it makes a shitload of noise, and noise ain't something I want to be putting out just now. This white cat comes all up in my face and says something like "I'll testify against you."

"Fuck you!"

"No, you have to do something. You can't just walk away from that."

"Watch me, motherfucker."

We're on Rainier now, this long-legged freak walkin' side by side with me. I keep my cool until he goes too far and yanks on my Raiders jacket. I can't have no white motherfucker pulling on my coat, so I slip out the piece and point it. "What are you going to say about this?"

"There's no call for that," he says.

I can't believe this honky. When he reaches out to touch my coat again, I give him a coupla taps and down he goes, his glasses all broke. He's not dead, just kind of twitching, and his legs are trying to move, and I'm thinking to myself, why did he have to touch the jacket? He might as well have pulled the trigger his own-self.

I'm walking away now, and the deal back there at the club and capping this piece of shit: overall it makes me feel bad. Real bad. Fact is, I haven't felt this bad since the time I got arrested for scrapping with Chumley over on Orchard Street. First Chumley kicks my butt, and then the cops arrest me and kick my butt, and then I get in the tank and run into Shivers, and he thinks he owes me behind somethin' happened back in tenth grade, so *he* kicks my butt. This is almost as bad.

12. ESTEVEZ IS HOT

TREY

We were sitting in an office on the fourth floor at Station 10, the heat turned too high: me, Jamie Estevez, and Chief Frederick Fish, who was fidgeting at his desk as if making time for us had seriously imperiled his workday. For two years, prior to the Z Club fire, he'd been our chief in Battalion 5, but he'd been promoted after the fire, which was unfortunate, since the promotion had drawn unflagging criticism from the minority communities of Seattle.

Jamie Estevez sat opposite Fish in the only other chair in the room while I leaned against the wall. I took off my foul-weather coat and hung it on a hook, and Estevez stripped off her navy blazer and draped it over the back of her chair. The pink blouse didn't have to work too hard to make her look good. I turned away, thinking that if you're going to be working with somebody for a couple of weeks, it's best not to lust after them on the first day.

I'd been in a funk ever since running into Stone Carmichael and had been trying to shake it without success. We had a long history, and not much of it was pleasant, nor was any of it worth thinking about. It didn't help when Estevez turned to me, as she'd done twice already, and said in that chirpy voice that was part of what made her such a charmer on the tube, "Is something wrong?" Something *was* wrong. I didn't want to see my brother again and I didn't want to be digging up dirt on the Z Club, but I didn't want Chief Lennox or Chief Douglas handling it, either. Partially because I didn't trust them to come up with an objective report, but also, I had to reluctantly admit, because I didn't want Douglas drooling over Jamie Estevez for the next few weeks. Not that she was my type. She was hot, all right, but too aggressive and too much of a go-getter for a guy like me, who's always been drawn to the homemaker types.

All morning she'd been taking potshots at me whenever she had the chance: I was "throwing" fire victims out the window; I was ungrateful for the damned award. On the good side, she was empathetic with each individual we spoke to and put them at ease, so each of the interviews had gone without a hitch.

Chief Fish, in his fifties, a slight, timid-looking man with heavy black-framed glasses, was the last chief I would have nominated to lose fourteen people at a fire.

13. A FISH STORY

DEPUTY CHIEF FREDERICK FISH;
FORMERLY BATTALION 5 CHIEF, C SHIFT

Look, I have to leave in about twenty minutes to meet my daughter, so I'll cover as much territory as I have time for now, and if we don't finish, you'll have to come back at some later date. I find it best to go through that night with the run sheet and computer printout in front of me. The printout contains the time of the first unit's arrival, their radio report, the time we got water on the fire, the results of the initial search, all that.

I arrive just in front of Engine 13, park across the street from the south side of the building, and establish the command post there because I initially think this is the front of the building—but later I discover the main entrance is on the east side where Engine 33 has set up. When I first arrive, the smoke seems to be blowing away from us, but as the night progresses, the wind switches directions and there are times when it virtually engulfs us. At one point we're using flashlights to see the status board.

Lieutenant Smith from Engine 33 comes over shortly after I arrive, and we do a face-to-face. While Engine 13 begins setting up lines, two of the Latinos who've been milling around outside run over to the building. There is a fair amount of smoke pouring out the doorway on my side of the building, and I can tell from the color of the smoke and the force with which it's coming out that we have a good fire. Both these Latino guys are overcome almost immediately. I mean, they just go down. That's when this guy from Thirteen—I think it was Voepel—walks over and gets them out.

I find out later they were having a wedding reception. Not my idea of a primo spot for a reception, but to each his own.

What do I know? They'd done a head count in the street and realized one of their little girls was missing. I'll give them two points for guts, and I think we should take away one point for stupidity.

I have Ohman and his crew take a line through that same door, and then I send Ladder 12 in behind them to do search and rescue with a thermal imager. I ask Ladder 12 to ventilate the building, which they accomplish by putting up a gas-powered fan in the doorway. The fan turns out to be a disaster, because it isn't up a full minute when I get a call on the radio from Engine 33 saying the fire is coming out the front door onto them and is pushing them into the street, so I have somebody shut it down. Of course that doesn't help Engine 13 or Ladder 12 doing their search, because as soon as we shut the fan down, the smoke and heat just slam down on them.

About that time Ladder 7 shows up, and I have a face-to-face with the lieutenant and tell him we need some ventilation, but tell him what happened with the fan. Now we're in a bind. We put the fan up where it was, we'll burn Engine 33's crew. We go around and put it up where Engine 33 is posted, we'll blow the fire onto Engine 13 and Ladder 12 and maybe that little muchacha who's missing. It's a pretty big building with a lot of smoke in it, coming out around the windows and in the pipe chases in the bricks on side A. What we probably should have done, in retrospect, was put the fan back up and have Engine 33 go defensive, pull them out of the building. But then they give an additional report. Yeah. Here it is right here. "Command from Engine 33. We've found fire in a stairway leading to the second floor. We're going to need another crew and more lines."

I ask if they are separate fires, and he says they appear to be. I know then we have an arson, and with so much fire on their side, I'm reluctant to use a fan on my side.

I have Ladder 7 ventilate the roof. Fire in the stairs, I figure rooftop ventilation is the way to go. Of course, it wasn't going to do much for the conditions on the first floor, where Ladder 12 and Engine 13 were searching. Then one of the members from Ladder 3 comes over with a couple more Latinos, and they tell me there's two additional kids missing. A couple of little boys. I give that information to Captain Ohman on Engine 13, and he radios back that they're not making any headway inside, that it's really hot and smoky, that there are a lot of spaces to search.

About this time the entire Latino contingent more or less swamps the command post. I mean, there's thirty of them—kids, too. They're chattering a mile a minute and crying and getting in my way, and I can hardly understand a word any of them are saying. The cops see what's going on and start clearing them away, but by then I've missed a couple of radio messages, so I have to backtrack with the dispatcher. It turns into a real mess.

About this time Engine 33 is reporting that they've tried to go up the stairs on side D and the stairs are untenable. Engine 13 is reporting high heat and zero visibility on side A, unable to find the fire and unable to locate any victims. Unable to complete the primary search because of the heat. I try to call Ladder 12 inside but get no answer. Right about that time some of the bricks on side A start falling onto the sidewalk from about thirty feet up, and I'm thinking if we're not careful we're going to lose firefighters here.

Then this woman cop comes over, and she's got three kids with her, and they turn out to be the missing kids. They've been outside the whole time. This takes a while to figure out, because, I mean, none of these people are speaking good English, but finally I get them to agree that everybody is out.

At that point Engine 33 reports a loud explosion somewhere inside the building. And I'm thinking this is the Mary Pang fire all over again. So I ask Captain Ohman on Engine 13 if he doesn't think we should declare this a defensive fire, and he radios back that they're not doing any good inside. I ask Ladder 7 on side B how they're doing getting to the roof and they report that they've had to reposition their rig because of power lines, but they're working on it.

God, I hate to turn anything into a defensive fire. So I walk around the building to side D, thinking I'll take a look, maybe view the second and third side of the building, and when I get around the corner, there's this hellacious fire burning in the stairwell. And another one inside the doorway to the first floor. And they've got two two-and-a-half-inch lines going, but the water's not making a dent in the stairs. There's a crowd of Latinos on the corner watching, so I have some firefighter ask if there's anybody upstairs, but they say there's nobody up there, that the wedding reception was all on the first floor.

I call Engine 13 and Ladder 12 out of the building and declare a defensive fire. I go back to the command post, and it is about this time Engine 28 shows up. I make Captain Brown Division C. While I'm doing this, another group of civilians comes up to one of our officers and says they think there are people inside. They don't know, but they think so. Our officer tells them that we've already accounted for everybody inside.

A minute or two later, a group of African Americans comes to the command post and begins screaming that there are people inside. The police come over and there's some scuffling. I tell them we already had somebody inside searching. That placates a couple of them, but more keep coming. I believe this was the time . . . yes, this was when Captain Brown said he wanted to ladder the building. I told him no. My thinking at the time was you don't declare a defensive fire and then put up ladders.

By this time Engine 13 and Ladder 12 had come out.

Now, I know later on, a week after the fire, the papers found a bunch of people who claim they told us there were people inside and we blew them off, but this is how it happened. We were told by the Latinos in the wedding party that the building was empty.

So the cops disperse the blacks who are mobbing the command post, but they start to gather at the corner, and they're getting louder. Finally they're throwing bottles at my firefighters, and what we have basically is the beginning of a riot. More and more young black men and women showing up every minute, chanting, "Get 'em out! Get 'em out!"

I can tell the police are not ready for this—maybe for traffic control, but not a riot.

Then two things happen at about the same time. Captain Brown here gets on the horn and says they have a ladder up to a window and there are victims on floor two. At the same time, two young men come out the A side onto a small fire escape on floor two and start yelling for help through the smoke.

I tell Ladder 12 to put up ladders to the fire escape. They get those two down, and then two more and then two or three more, and I'm thinking, Holy Christ! How many people are up there? It becomes clear there is some sort of party on floor two, because all these people are dressed for a night out. We rescue eight or ten, and that's when I learn we have a missing firefighter somewhere inside on the first floor.

Listen, I hate to do this, but I've gotta go now. My daughter has this appointment I can't miss. There's more—obviously—but you've got the beginning.

14. ARE WE GOING TO DANCE OR NOT?

JAMIE ESTEVEZ

"Just a quick question before you leave," Trey said.

Chief Fish, who had already snatched a coat off a hook on the wall, did not appear pleased to be detained. "What is it?"

"You knew how bad the African-American community felt about the Z Club. Surely you must have guessed people would take issue over the fact that you accepted a promotion a week after fourteen people died there."

"My promotion didn't have a thing to do with the Z Club."

"*We* all know that. You work hard, and you've been around a long time. You deserve a promotion. That's not the issue. The question I'm posing is, Did it not occur to you or Chief Smith that people in the community would question the timing?"

"You said yourself I deserved the promotion."

"I'm asking if you had any second thoughts in view of the fact that it took place a week after the Z Club."

"It didn't have anything to do with the Z Club."

"That's not the perception in the black community."

"It didn't cause any uproar."

"Oh, but it did. Your promotion is one of the key points brought up when people suggest the fire department is callous and dismissive of the black community."

Trey was correct on that front. People were outraged that Chief Fish had been promoted, instead of reprimanded or even fired.

"I didn't do anything wrong at the Z Club, and I resent the implication."

"You preside over a fire in which fourteen people die, and a week later Chief Smith says, 'Hey, I think I'll make you a deputy.' And it doesn't occur to either one of you to put it off even a couple of weeks? That he maybe could have placed you in an administrative assignment in the wake of the Z Club, the way cops work at a desk after they're involved in a shooting?"

"Listen, I didn't shoot anybody, and my daughter is waiting."

Captain Brown stepped aside and Chief Fish stalked out, slamming the door. I said, "That certainly went well."

Trey turned and gave me a look with the barest hint of amusement. "Don't you think it odd that they didn't think about it?"

"It doesn't make any difference to how the fire was run. Why did you even ask?"

"Because it bugs me."

"He's going to have a chip on his shoulder next time we talk."

"No, he won't."

"You seem a little put out with Fish. I mean, other than this beef you just had over his promotion."

"What makes you think I was put out with him?"

"While he was talking I was watching your reflection in that window over there."

I saw Trey check out the window, which because of the light was acting like a mirror, and watched him realize with a start that I must have also seen him looking at me when he thought I wouldn't know. All day he had pretended not to notice I was a woman, but I'd caught him noticing, and I could tell it bothered him.

"I worked with Fish for two years, and his superior attitude toward people less fortunate than him always rubbed me the wrong way. Did you catch his snide comment about the Z Club not being a primo place for a wedding reception?"

"Not having seen the Z Club when it was standing, I don't have any idea what sort of place it was."

"Think firetrap. It had siding that was different colors and foundation problems, and nobody'd bothered to paint it in thirty years. Those people were there because they didn't have the money to go anywhere else. Fish knows that."

"Is that why you jumped him about the promotion?"

"I don't know. Maybe."

Earlier in the day at the Mount Zion Baptist Church, Miriam Beckmann pulled me aside and indicated she had collated a list of rumors that had been circulating about the fire. One rumor was that they'd been "pushing" victims out the windows. I still needed to talk to Trey about his part in the rescues, because he seemed to be the one doing the pushing or dropping or whatever it was—but he wasn't ready to talk about it yet. And then of course there was the phone call to the dispatcher from the man who claimed to have been bypassed by firefighters inside the burning building when he pleaded with them for help.

I pulled out my copy of the Z Club report the Seattle Fire Department had commissioned, a binder notebook with a black plastic spine and bold black lettering splashed across the front: *Seattle Fire Department Report on the Z Club Fire of September 3, 2005.* "You might want to study this in your spare time."

Taking it out of my hands, Trey said, "You've had this all along?"

"Yes."

"Why didn't you show it to me earlier?"

"I didn't think of it."

"I could have been going over this while we were driving around."

"Well, I didn't think of it."

"You realize the people who did this report were conscientious and that most likely we're on a wild-goose chase here?"

"What about that nine-one-one call?"

"We'll see."

"There are a lot of people with questions. If we do nothing more than verify the department's report, we'll be doing them a favor. But it needs to be verified."

"Or refuted."

"Right."

"You know what's really going on, don't you?" he said.

"You mean the rioting and all that?"

"All of it. You got a brother sets fire to a hip-hop club, kills a bunch of black people. Now we've got a community that wants to find a white guy responsible."

"That's absurd."

"Is it?"

"You're a cynic. Did anybody ever tell you that?"

"What do you think's going to happen if our report is identical to this?"

"If it's the same, we turn it in that way. By the way, I'm going to be busy all day tomorrow, and I have a wedding on Sunday. One of my best friends is getting married to her girlhood sweetheart. I'm flying to Spokane on Sunday morning, but I'll be back that night."

"I don't suppose it would do any good for me to do some digging on my own over the weekend?"

"Not unless you want me to replicate your work when I come back. I'm going to talk to everybody, and I want you there while I do it."

"That's what I thought."

"By the way, are you planning to attend the party Miriam Beckmann invited us to? The Get Out the Readers Project Ball."

"I don't believe I am."

"Why not?"

"I don't have anything to wear."

"That's cute. What's the real reason?"

"I don't like to dress up. I always feel like a penguin stuffed into a shirt and tie. It makes me itchy." Trey moved to the door and put his hand on the knob. "So we're done until Monday?"

"I think it's a good idea for us to go. If the community leaders have seen our faces and met us, it will help establish the integrity of our report. Trust me on this. There's a lot of indignation floating around, and having some political alliances isn't going to hurt either of us."

"You go. Talk me up to everyone you meet. That'll make it a win-win for us both."

"Is there another reason you don't want to go?"

"What are you getting at?"

"Maybe you're afraid you'll run into some of the family you've been estranged from all these years? It's not good to keep this stuff buried for so long."

"Is that right?"

"That's absolutely right."

"When did you get your degree in psychology?"

"Any fool can see this is eating at you."

"If you knew anything about me or the family or why I got kicked out, you wouldn't be saying this."

"I'm sorry, but I want you there with me."

"So it really isn't for me, then? It's for you?"

"It's for both of us."

He opened the door, took a couple of steps into the corridor, spotted Marvin Douglas across the hallway, then turned back to me. "I'll pick you up at seven."

15. SPYING FOR THE ENEMY

JAMIE ESTEVEZ

We'd left Station 28 in separate vehicles, and even though the weather was supposed to hold for the next couple of days and I could see traces of sunshine off to the west, it began raining on Rainier Avenue. I wondered if I'd made a mistake arranging to go to the ball the next night with Trey. We'd gotten off to a bad start as soon as he discovered I'd selected him for this investigation without asking him prior and then lied to him about it. Then his encounter with his estranged brother—the lily-white mayor, of all things; who could have guessed—only put him in a worse funk. In addition to his brother, there was a good chance the ball would resurrect other ghosts from his past. The Carmichael family was well known in the area for their philanthropy and community service. It might prove to be an unpleasant evening for Trey. And it might prove interesting.

Alone for the first time all day, I put on some Luther Vandross to mellow me out and tried not to think about the ball. At a stoplight I picked up my cell phone and punched in a number written in my address book. From the background sounds, I guessed his car stereo was on and that he was also driving home in Friday-night traffic. "Stone Carmichael," he said.

"Mayor, this is Jamie Estevez."

"Jamie. I was hoping to hear from you earlier this afternoon, but this is terrific."

"We just now finished for the day. Did I catch you at a bad time?"

"Not at all. I'm taking my boys out to dinner and a movie. Their mother's busy with last-minute preparations for tomorrow night's shindig. I'd help, but she claims the best thing I can do is stay out of her hair. I'm more of a concept guy, anyway. You coming tomorrow night?"

"I'll be there."

"Good. Arrive early and leave late. Save a dance for me. I hope I told you how pleased I was the committee took me up on my suggestion and selected you. I was reviewing your résumé again this afternoon and I'm impressed."

"Thank you."

"So. How is the investigation proceeding?"

I told him whom we'd spoken to and gave him a brief overview of what I'd learned, providing the broad outlines of the fire and the confusion, the harassment from the crowd, and the mixed signals as to whether everybody was out.

"I don't know Chief Fish well, but he seems conscientious," Stone said. "What was your impression?"

"Conscientious is a word I would use."

"And how are you and Captain Brown getting along?"

It was hard to know how Trey and I were getting along. He certainly wasn't pulling any punches when it came to letting me know how much I annoyed him, and so far he hadn't missed an opportunity to purposely nettle me in retaliation. I was willing to chalk it up to his being in a foul mood over the circumstances under which we were thrown together, and sensed that he was secretly enjoying the bantering between us, but I couldn't be sure of anything with him. By the middle of next week we might be getting along famously or we might not be speaking, though I wasn't going to volunteer any of this to the mayor. "To tell you the truth, I believe he was taken by surprise when we asked him to participate, but so far he's been invaluable. He certainly knows this fire department inside out."

"Yes. I suppose he would."

There was an uncomfortable silence while I tried to think of additional positives to put forth concerning Trey, as if I were his proxy and it was my job to patch up the family rift. It had always been my inclination to smooth things over, but you couldn't smooth over conflicts if you didn't know what they were about or how they originated. I said, "Yes. He's great."

"I would prefer it if Captain Brown didn't know you and I were in touch."

"I don't think I should keep secrets from him."

"I understand, but there are a lot of lives riding on the decisions I make downtown. You're my confidential informant on this, Jamie, and I'd appreciate it if we kept it that way. So far the civil unrest hasn't resulted in any fatalities, but I already have one police officer with a fractured shoulder, and last night somebody took a shot at a couple of paramedics."

"That's horrible."

"People don't realize it yet, but we're close to a state of siege here. I would hate to think something might happen to one of our city employees or a civilian when I was missing an essential piece of information because Trey felt intimidated that you were talking to me and failed to tell you something crucial. I know it goes against your grain as a journalist to be checking in daily, but this isn't journalism: This is a city investigation into an event that has already cost too many lives. Do you think you can work with me on this?"

"Of course, sir."

"And call me Stone, would you?"

"Sure, Stone."

"So where are you heading next?"

"I'm on my way to a meeting with Pastor Morgan and Miriam Beckmann."

"Good people. Are you hearing anything that's going to dispute . . . I guess what I'm asking is, have you heard anything that's going to lead you down a track the SFD report didn't specifically travel?"

"Not yet."

"If you do, be sure and give me a buzz. To tell the truth, Jamie, this has been the most challenging three weeks of my term. And the vice president running into those protesters, and then having the videotape played over and over again on the networks . . . it's turning into a public relations disaster. By the way, the vice president's an interesting man. We met with a trade delegation from China. Some fascinating developments coming out of it. When this project is finished and you're doing television again, I'll give you an exclusive. How would that be?"

"I might take you up on that."

"I'll insist. One more thing."

"What's that?"

"I'm wondering if Brown said anything about me after we met this morning?"

"Not that I recall." For some reason I found myself telling more lies in one day than I had in the entire past year.

"If he does, I'd take it as a personal favor if you would fill me in. I guess it's only fair to tell you Trey was adopted into our family. When he was in high school, he managed to get himself in some trouble with the law. We haven't really been in touch since. To tell you the truth, I'm not particularly thrilled that he's part of this inquiry. The last thing we need around here is a loose cannon, but I'm sure you'll keep an eye on him."

"Of course I will."

I would call him with updates, but I wasn't about to spy on his brother. Whatever was going on between them, I didn't need to get in the middle of it. The two of them clearly despised each other, and the more I thought about the restraint they'd both shown that morning at what was undoubtedly their first meeting in almost two decades, the more remarkable I judged it to be. I had a feeling whatever was going on made my nuclear family with its minor quibbles look like a sewing club.

16. THE SURPRISE PARTY

STONE CARMICHAEL, NINETEEN YEARS EARLIER

It's after midnight, and we're stumping along in the dark, with only the spotty moonlight illuminating our path. It's a secret, she says, leading me out into the darkness. I have a vague feeling, mostly because I haven't seen India in over two hours, that the girls have hatched some sort of grand surprise for me. India's little sister, Echo, is leading me out here in the darkness. Fifteen years old. Just a kid.

A surprise party would not only explain India's disappearance for the past couple of hours but might also be her way of making up for being miffed with me lately. Heck, I've been gone almost three weeks, and I know India is irked that I didn't call more often. True, they get a new movie every night and have every toy known to man at the estate: boats, scuba gear, all-terrain vehicles, dirt bikes, the underground pool for lap swimming—but being stranded on the island has to get a little stifling for someone of India's temperament. I wouldn't put it past her to spring a surprise party for me out at the gardener's cottage, where the old folks wouldn't know about it. Too bad I'm too drunk to appreciate it.

"Come on," I urge Echo. "Tell me what this is all about."

"Can't tell," replies Echo. When the moon disappears, I can barely see her walking alongside me in the dark, but when it comes out, I see her pale hair float alongside her head like the sheet on a ghost.

"This has something to do with India, doesn't it?"

"Yes. Maybe. You remember what I was saying the last time you were here?"

"No. Echo, it's been three weeks."

"I was saying the last time you were here that India and you aren't really that well matched. Don't you remember?

We were in the pool. Your mother had just left, and we were alone."

"That's silly. We're a perfect match. All my friends say so. And you're still trying to break us up, aren't you?"

"I'm not trying to break you up. I just sometimes think . . ."

"What do you think, sweetie?"

"Well . . . I just sometimes . . . Stone? Let me ask you this. And I'm not talking about anybody we know. How much of an age difference is too much? If a guy's going to be older than his . . . girlfriend, how much of an age difference would you say is too much? I'm only asking out of curiosity."

I'm trying to do the math in my head, knowing the beer sloshing around in my stomach isn't helping any, trying to figure out how to tease her even though she's asked for a straight answer. I'm twenty-six and Echo is fifteen.

"Let me see. The cutoff point would be ten years. Why do you ask?"

"My mother and father are still very much in love, and they've been married almost twenty years. And my mother's fourteen years younger than my father."

"Sure your mother's telling the truth about her age?"

"Oh, Stone. You are just so . . ." She pushes me playfully and I push her back; then we continue walking.

"Where are we going?" I say.

"The old cottage."

"What's happening out there? You're not going to try to seduce me, are you, Mrs. Robinson?"

"Of course not. Don't be gross."

She gets quiet and we keep walking. If it wasn't dark, I would be able to see her blushing. It's no secret that Echo has a childish crush on me, just as it's no secret her sister India and I will someday be married. While we haven't made it official, everybody knows we're destined to tie the knot. And now here I am walking across the island with her little sister in the middle of the night. It's August and warm, though a breeze is coming up over the bluffs from Puget Sound to discourage the mosquitoes and lift my spirits. It is only when I stumble and fall to my hands and knees that I realize how truly drunk I must be. And why not? I'm on the island with friends. At the family summer estate. Why can't I get a little tanked?

"Are you all right? Stone? Are you hurt?" She's helping me to my feet, touching me a little longer than necessary, just as she always does when she gets the chance. I begin to get the feeling she really is trying to seduce me, that the surprise we're headed for doesn't involve anybody but her and me. If so, it will *not* be good.

India and Echo. Exotic, rare, almost goofy names, though I've come to love the name India. Daughters of entrepreneur Harlan Axelrod Overby, who got more than a handful when he married that Nordic model ex-hippie, who ended up nearly bankrupting him. Not that Harlan couldn't bankrupt himself with his own bad investments and lack of business sense. He's done it twice that I know of, Father bailing him out both times just because they've been best chums ever since their school days, which both of them go on about ad nauseam—as if we haven't heard all their ancient tales of glory a million times. I know he comes from good stock, and maybe he was a big shot back in the dark ages when they were in school, but Overby's been playing out of his league ever since. I wonder if he'd have any money left at all if it weren't for the opportunities Father throws his way.

Mother once told me Elaine Overby called herself Freedom until she decided to go for the big money by marrying Harlan. She'd raised India and Echo with all sorts of bizarre notions. Playing eight musical instruments each. Caring for the poor in Bangladesh. Can you imagine, exposing her daughters to all that disease in the third world?

India and Echo, both clones of their mother. Blond hair. Blue eyes. Pale skin. Echo, more coltish; India, a little taller and more graceful. But different from each other, too. Echo, the chatterbox you can read like a grade-school primer; India, the silent one, full of mystery.

I excuse myself, leaving Echo alone on the path while I blunder through the tall Scotch broom to a place where I can relieve myself. I've had too much beer tonight by anybody's standards. What I need to do now is go back to the big house and hit the rack. It's been a rough night. First India pretends to be sick, which is her way of avoiding me, and then I get into that fevered political discussion with Renfrow, the aide-de-camp Father and Overby keep around to take care of all the most unpleasant chores. And the whole thing is, Why is he even here? Father knows none of us like him. And we like that girlfriend of his even less. Both of them riffraff. Renfrow so uncouth he doesn't even have the good grace to take his flatulence outside—or maybe she's the one filling the room with farts that smell like something dead that washed up on the beach.

After we regroup, Echo says, "I've been meaning to tell you how sorry I am about your brother. I've been thinking about you a lot, because I know it must be horrid for you to lose your brother and his girlfriend like that. I can't even imagine."

"Thanks, Echo." Six weeks ago—is it six weeks already?—Shelby Junior crashed his Porsche. It still breaks me up to think about it. Nobody knows for sure how it happened. Middle of the night on the twisties on Mercer Island. Raining. New car. Tires not broken in yet. Probably showing off for Melissa. They didn't even find the wreckage until late in the afternoon of the next day. The car upside down in a ravine, both of them with broken necks. And now Mom is beside herself and Dad's immersed himself in work. Kendra's been in shock since it happened. I guess Trey has been some comfort to her, which means the little bastard's good for that, even if he's good for nothing else.

We're headed for the old gardener's cottage in one of the gullies on the island, almost invisible until you're right up on it. For years I suspected the cottage was the old man's hidey-hole, where he parked his lovelies so Mother wouldn't find evidence when she came out to the island. Shelby Junior used it for the same thing and used to call it the sex shack.

We crest a rise in the road, and the moon comes out so we can see the sweep of the rutted Jeep road as it sags down to the cottage, and I think to myself, if they're planning a surprise, they've messed things up because they left the lights on in the cottage.

"We need to be quiet," Echo says.

"Okay," I say, playing along.

As we get close, Echo stops me by the old chopper pad and says, "Wait here." And then it's the dangdest thing, because she doesn't knock at the door or walk in the way you think she might, but creeps up alongside the wall where the light is spilling out of the main room and peeks in the window. I should never have come out here in the middle of the night with her.

She stares through the window, and then she turns and runs back through the broken yard and bumbles headlong into my arms. I straighten her up and she clings to me, her head against my chest, and I realize she's bawling like a baby. "This wasn't how it was supposed to be. You and I have to leave this place. Forget I ever brought you here. I'm so sorry. I didn't mean . . ."

"Wait here," I tell her.

"No," she says, grasping at me. "Don't go. This was a mistake. I wanted you to like me. I thought . . . Please don't go over there."

Her desperation only fuels my desire to see what she's talking about. I shake her off and creep up through the overgrown yard. There's some music in the cottage, which explains why they didn't hear us talking outside. Two lamps are lit. There is a couch in the living room, and there are two people on the couch. A man and a woman. The first is my little brother, Trey. The second is the woman everybody knows I'm going to marry, India. They're naked.

I watch for a while, perhaps too long, and then I blunder back through the dark, where Echo collapses against my chest again, and together the two of us walk off a ways in the dark and fall to the earth, sitting side by side in shock. Echo continues to weep while I turn my head away so she cannot see the look on my face. Trey, you little black bastard.

"I didn't mean for this to happen," Echo says. "I thought . . ."

"You must have known something was going on or you wouldn't have brought me out here."

"I didn't think it was this."

"Has it been going on all summer?"

"I don't know. They've been . . . flirting. I thought they were . . . like, just making out."

"They're making out, all right."

"I'm sorry, Stone. I really am."

We sit for ten minutes, and then the lights go off in the cabin, and a few moments later India comes walking along the path and passes not fifteen feet in front of us, walking toward the big house. Trey is nowhere to be seen until I turn and spot him heading in the other direction, a tall shadow in the moonlight. He makes for the bluffs along the path that zigzags down to the beach.

I head for the cottage with an insatiable need to see evidence: the rumpled couch, the drinking glasses, whatever.

"Where are you going?" Echo asks. "Don't go. Don't leave me. I'm scared."

I stop and she clings to me, her budding breasts against my chest. She folds her head against my chest, but I push her away and walk off. I've never been this angry in my life. I have no idea what I'm going to do. She follows, clasping my arm, and I keep thinking the little fool is in love with me. The wrong sister is in love with me. She brought me out here thinking we'd find India and Trey playing spin the bottle or some other innocuous game, thinking I'd see how India doesn't deserve me, and then like magic I'd be in love with her instead. What a little idiot. I could kill her for this.

17. THE FUNNIEST THING EVER

TREY

There are times when I can be an unapologetic jerk. It doesn't help that my best friend thinks it's funny when I disgrace myself, or that he encourages it by cooking up stupid stunts that for some reason I feel compelled to execute. Nor does it help when he reenacts them to endless gales of laughter from my brother, Johnny, milking the entertainment value out of them for months afterward. It almost makes the personal humiliation I suffer worthwhile, as if it's somehow more honorable and hilarious to be a jerk than to be otherwise, and of course that contrarian attitude appeals to my basic nature, which is part of the reason Rumble is my best friend. Like me, Rumble spends a lot of his life cutting against the grain.

Advice is only that, advice, and nobody twisted my arm to take Rumble's. I certainly don't act on any of his investment suggestions, which if I had, would have pushed me to the brink of insolvency more than once.

There was no reason to follow Rumble's suggestion and take Estevez to a formal ball on a motorcycle. Maybe in the back of my mind I was nervous about seeing so many people from my past, stressed at the prospect of coming face-to-face with the family that raised me and then banished me. I'd read in the paper that they'd all be there. When it came to the family, I never really knew how deep my feelings ran, because I'd been doing my best to bury them for the better part of two decades. You'd think I'd have the common sense to make the evening perfect for the woman I was escorting, so that I would have at least one ally when all the pitchforks were pointed in my direction, but when in trouble, I try always to alienate *everybody* around me equally. It probably has something to do with being ditched by virtually everybody I was related to in one fell swoop.

Rumble worked the same shift I did, C, but he'd been on disability with a neck injury since the Z Club and hadn't been back to work yet. Although he hadn't fought the fire, he'd been there the next morning, and the Z Club had shaken him like nothing else ever had—seeing those bodies lined up on the sidewalk, knowing we'd lost a firefighter inside. The fire had broken the spine of his ambition in a way I suspected could never be fully mended. My silent prediction was that he was more or less finished in operations, that he would grab one of the office jobs the department offered. He wouldn't do it right away, because he wouldn't want people making the connection between the Z Club and his taking a desk job, but sooner or later he would do it.

"A woman like that," he said. "On TV all the time. Thinks she's hot shit. There's no way she's not playin' you. You told me yourself you didn't want to go to the ball. Why are you going? 'Cause she's leading you around by the nose. You two ever get married, you'll be wearing skirts and vacuuming the house."

"We're *not* getting married. I'm taking her to *one* function, and after that I'll never see her again socially. Trust me on this."

"She's a fine-looking woman. You told me that your own-self."

"Yeah, well, looks aren't everything. She lied to me. She roped me into this bullshit investigation without asking me first. And she's got a tongue that's sharper than a snake's fang. I can live without all of that."

"Woman like that, the only thing for you to do is put her in her place at the beginning. Yeah. Pick her up on the hog. Pretend that's how you pick up all your dates. Don't even let her know you got that Infiniti." Rumble almost rolled out of the easy chair in my basement laughing. He laughed, and so did Johnny, and in the end so did I, the three of us convincing ourselves that the funniest sight ever seen on the streets of

Seattle would be Jamie Estevez riding the back of a hog in a formal gown while I motored along in my tux.

I went along with Rumble's gag, believing all along I'd pick her up in my car, that there was no way I'd go over on the Harley; yet for some insane reason on Saturday evening when it came time to fetch her, I went out to the garage and fired up the Harley. God only knows what I was thinking. Or *if* I was thinking.

18. CINDERELLA RIDES A HOG

JAMIE ESTEVEZ

For a moment I considered the possibility that he was drunk and was going to kill us both showing off. Trey was straddling the bike, cranking the throttle as we spoke, drowning out my words with the roar of the engine so that I had to repeat myself, peering at me through dark glasses he refused to take off, his helmet resembling a Nazi tank commander lid. I was angry for a few moments, too, and then I began to see the dark humor in it. It was a nice night, and the trip wouldn't be more than two miles, and I liked bikes, something he couldn't possibly have anticipated. In another world, where he didn't abhor me so much, it might even turn out to be a story we would tell our grandchildren. Our grandchildren. What a laugh. This man detested me. If I didn't know it before tonight, I certainly knew it now.

I crossed my arms and stared at him, waiting for him to shut the bike off so we could hear each other. Under my palm I could feel my heart beating, and for a couple of seconds I feared he was going to leave the motorcycle running and wait me out over the earthquake of noise, but suddenly the street was bathed in silence.

"Thought it would be an adventure for you," he said. "You ever ride a bike before?"

"Of course."

"Like this one?"

"Why? Did it used to be a pumpkin or something?"

"Pumpkin? That would make you Cinderella. What does that make me as your driver? A rat?"

"I believe the coachmen were mice."

"Oh, I'm a coachman now?"

"I didn't say that. I said mouse."

"I guess I'm dressed like a coachman."

"On the other hand, I think maybe they *were* rats." He stared at me, apparently unable to come up with another riposte. "Are you drunk? Because if you've been drinking, I'll ride up front and you can take the sissy seat."

"Like you could handle this . . ."

"Care to make a wager on it?"

"No way I'm letting you kill yourself trying to prove a point. You'd really ride it, wouldn't you?"

"Try me."

"I haven't had any alcohol in twenty-four hours."

"So where's my helmet?"

"Beans. Forgot the spare. I could go home and get it, but by the time I got back to ride you over there, we'd be late. Tell you what? You take a cab. I'll meet you there."

"I'll tell *you* what. You go home and get the helmet, and I'll wait here."

He hadn't been expecting an argument, had apparently thought I would turn down the bike ride so we would arrive at the ball separately. It was hard to believe he could be this rude and not be drunk. "You could take a cab. I'll pay."

"Not after you've offered me a ride."

"Your problem is you want to run everything."

"Look who's talking. I'm not the one picking up his date for a black-tie ball on a motorcycle."

"I would have called and warned you, except I lost your number."

"Hardly possible since it was written on the same piece of paper as my address."

He stared at me and I stared back, and I could tell he was going to brave this out, even though somewhere behind those black riding glasses he had to be embarrassed by the enormity of his faux pas as well as the crudeness of his attempt at sabotaging the evening.

"Tell you what," I said. "You wait here."

"You going to sneak out back and call a cab?" he asked. "Leave me in the lurch?"

"Why? Is that what you would do?"

I gave him my most withering look and went upstairs, picked out an old Bell helmet that was more spacious than my new one, then carefully worked my hair into it in a manner that would do the least damage. I threw a brush and a can of hair spray into my purse for repairs, and when I emerged onto Lenora Street wearing heels, a formal dress with wrap, and a motorcycle helmet, Trey Brown looked astounded. It was almost worth the discomfort to see the look on his face. He hadn't been expecting me to return, and he certainly hadn't been expecting me in a helmet.

We attracted a fair amount of attention on the streets of Seattle, a man in a tuxedo and a woman in a formal dress riding a chromed Harley-Davidson with an engine that sounded like bursts of cannon fire.

As we rode, I hugged him from behind—his torso as hard and knotty as a tree—and realized that no matter what my brain was telling me about this man, my insides were telling me something else. Like I said before, I have a long and sad history of falling for bad boys, and in spite of my best intentions, it was beginning to look as if Trey Brown might be next in line.

As we drove from the north end of downtown to the Mikimoto Mansion on Capitol Hill, I reviewed what I'd learned about Trey during the past eight hours. Earlier that day at KIRO, I ran into a researcher named Ferdie Miller, who'd heard about the project I was working on and told me Trey Brown had been a linebacker who played for the Huskies seventeen years ago.

"Nice kid," Ferdie said. "Quiet. One of the fiercest competitors I've ever seen. You see a lot of guys play hard and hit hard, but you only see a few who you think are actually trying to kill the opponent. During his sophomore and junior years for the Huskies, he devastated the opposing teams, one of the best linebackers ever in college football—like he'd stepped right out of the pros and was out here picking off these kids for the fun of it. If he hadn't blown out his knee, he would have been a top draft pick. Whenever he got pulled out of a game, you could hear an audible sigh of relief on the other bench. I saw him once . . . well, I'm getting off on a tangent here."

"You know anything about his family?"

"I know his last year in high school he was living with his coach. I gathered he'd been in some sort of trouble."

"Did you know his last name used to be Carmichael?"

"All I know is he came out of nowhere in the Central Area and played at the U."

A computer search brought up torrents of information about the Carmichael empire, about various business dealings over the past thirty years, but almost nothing on a lost son named Trey. There were a couple of articles mentioning Shelby Junior, who died in a car accident nineteen years ago, listings of the surviving siblings as Stone, Trey, and Kendra, but no mention after that of a Trey Carmichael in any of the articles about the family. I wondered if Trey's exclusion didn't have something to do with the car accident that killed Shelby Junior. I had a feeling I would find out tonight.

Built in 1903, the Mikimoto Mansion had once belonged to one of Seattle's founding families but ten years ago had been purchased by a wealthy Japanese businessman, who had restored it to its former grandeur and renamed it after his own family. Used often for business and community events, it was situated on John Street, sitting like a maiden aunt at a high school graduation in the middle of a block of high-rise condos, a gargantuan Victorian even by today's standards.

Trey rode across the sidewalk, scattering the parking attendants like chickens, and then when one of the attendants put his hand out for the keys, Trey slipped them into his jacket pocket, grinned, and said, "In your dreams."

"That was fun," I said as we dismounted.

"The fun hasn't started yet."

19. REMEMBERING THE STEPHEN KING NIGHTMARE

KENDRA CARMICHAEL

I wonder how many women can say they haven't seen their crazy brother in almost twenty years. I'm not even sure he's still legally my brother, because I never had the nerve to ask Father if you can disadopt somebody, or what else he might have done to make certain Trey didn't have any claim on the family fortune. I'd always affectionately called Trey "my crazy brother" until that last summer when, for the first time in memory, other people started referring to him as "your crazy brother." And I guess he did go crazy . . . just that once. At least I hope it was just that once. My feelings about him have been conflicted for nineteen years, and tonight, when I saw him step through the doorway in a tuxedo, I knew my feelings weren't going to sort themselves out easily.

Trey was always a little wild, or as Mother used to put it, a tad adventuresome. And yes, adventuresome was probably a more accurate word in his youth, because he was bold in a way nobody else in the family was except for Shelby Junior, who, when he jumped off that ledge into the tidal pool in Jamaica on spring vacation, was followed almost immediately to everybody's stunned surprise by nine-year-old Trey. Forty feet, I think we figured it later. Trey knocked himself out on impact when he flubbed the entry but wanted to go right back up and try again, as soon as Shelby and the others pulled him out of the water and revived him. Both my wild brothers . . .

what a cruel shock to lose them within six weeks of each other, Shelby to the Grim Reaper and Trey to that Stephen King nightmare that unfolded and then revealed aspects of his personality that none of us could ever have guessed.

Trey, I've missed you so much over all these years, wanting so badly to hear what you were doing and to catch you up on my life and somehow to see you clear your name—or failing that, at least redeem yourself. When we were kids and even into high school, we talked in a way I'd never been able to with Shelby Junior or Stone. Shelby was simply too much older, and Stone never seemed to have any time for me. But there you were, only a year older and actually interested in what was going on in my life. I always appreciated that, and despite the fact that you all but admitted to that hateful crime, I still find it hard to fathom.

Now, tonight, I'm near the main entrance to the mansion, having just come in, when I turn around and spot a beautiful young black woman in a pale pink dress with a flared hem, matching heels, and pearl earrings, patting her hair into place as she walks through the entranceway alongside a man I recognize with a start as my long-lost brother. To say I am startled is an understatement. I can actually feel my heart beating below my breastbone.

Trey has filled out, and he may even be taller. His face is more mature and handsomer, though I'd always thought he was recklessly handsome as a youth, but he still exhibits that inner calmness I've admired since the first day I laid eyes on him. I was three and he was four when he was brought home one rainy afternoon with a shabby little suitcase and a one-eyed teddy bear and introduced as my new brother. I clearly remember eleven-year-old Stone saying, "But he's black. We don't want any—" Before he could finish the sentence, Father slapped him across the face, one of the few times he struck any of his sons. None of us ever forgot it, and it was the last time Trey's ethnicity was ever mentioned. "He's going to steal my toys," whispered Stone under his breath, which was ironic, because later it was always Stone stealing

Trey's things or purposely trying to subvert Trey's relationships with girls.

Trey's inner calmness hadn't been shaken by his introduction into our household, or the radical overnight change of lifestyle he must have undergone, or seemingly, the loss of his original family—his grandmother having passed away only a few days before we met him. None of it had shaken him, and neither did getting knocked out cold in high school football games, or getting chased by a shark on that vacation in Jamaica, or much of anything else until the very last night he was with us.

In the first few moments we confront each other, I can tell Trey doesn't recognize me, and then when he does, that he doesn't know whether to hug and kiss me or shake hands or just stand with his mouth gaping. At first I'm not sure what to do either, but then all those years as brother and sister come back to me and block out that last night, and I launch into his arms and almost knock him over, hugging him until I can't squeeze any harder. I hope he can't tell how soft my three babies have made me, how flabby I feel despite the personal trainer and the nutritionist, and I hope he doesn't reject my friendship. Guilty or innocent, I at least want to know what's happened to him over the intervening years.

"You look terrific," he says, holding me at arm's length.

"Liar. But *you* do look terrific."

"You're a beautiful young woman. I'm overwhelmed."

"Young? I'm not young anymore, either. I have a husband and three kids and cellulite, and I'm starting to look like my mother, and oh, Trey, I've missed you. You did know Mother was gone?"

"I heard."

He hugs me again, more gently than I hugged him, and I sense how deeply he's missed me, and how much it must have hurt to be ostracized for so long and to miss his mother's funeral service—even if it was his own doing. It is hard to know if there is any way to remedy all the scars on both sides. In some ways it would have been so much simpler if he'd just stopped denying it and gone to jail, atoned for the crime, and afterward maybe some of us could have forgiven him and moved on.

"It's so good to see you, Kendra," he says. His gray eyes are as focused and as inviting as ever. His voice is deeper. "This is Jamie Estevez. Jamie, my sister, Kendra."

"Glad to meet you, Kendra."

"Me, too. I was admiring your gown."

After a few moments of chitchat, I begin towing Trey and his date through rooms packed with people, making introductions, working our way ineluctably toward select members of the family. As we wade through the party, I turn back to him and say, "Did I tell you I'm married?"

"Yes, and three children, you said."

"Three girls."

"I'd love to meet them." And of course, in the back of my mind, I realize I have to reevaluate whether or not I actually want Trey to spend any time around my girls. I push the thought off, vowing to think it through later.

"So," I say, turning to Jamie Estevez a few minutes later, when we are both elbowed out of the conversation by a Bank of America executive holding forth about the Z Club fire. "Have you known Trey long?" I've learned a few things already, that Trey's a firefighter in Seattle, a captain.

"I only met him yesterday. We're working together on the Z Club report for the citizens' group."

"Oh, my gosh. Does Stone know Trey's working on the report with you?"

"The three of us got together yesterday for a few minutes."

"So they've met? Stone and Trey?"

"Yes."

"How did it go?"

"Stone was guarded. Trey was . . . distant. Apparently it didn't go as badly as it might have."

"He's here, you know. Stone and his wife. And some other people Trey might not care to run into."

After Trey rejoins us and we work our way through the rooms, I wonder how Echo will take to seeing Trey again, how India will react, or Father. This isn't the ideal setting for a strained family reunion, and Father hasn't mentioned Trey in years, so when I escort Trey and Jamie to a sitting room where Father is holding court for a group of politicos, I'm apprehensive to say the least. Spotting Trey, Father halts the conversation with a wave of his hand, and after a moment walks over to him and speaks quietly. "Trey? Good God. What are you doing here?"

"Yeah, well . . ."

"How long are you here for?" Father asks.

"Until we feel like going home, I guess."

"No, I mean, how long are you in town?"

Trey pauses. "I live four miles from here."

Father seems taken aback, as if this newfound proximity is a threat and as if he might be able to tolerate a onetime visit, but not this other. Then Father says, "It's good to see you."

"Is it?"

"I would give my right arm to have had things turn out differently, I so regret what happened."

"Which part?" Trey asks, his tone sharpening.

"All of it, son. Every bit. I've never stopped loving you."

For a moment I think everything is going to be all right and all will be forgiven—though both men have valid reasons not to forgive—and Trey will be welcomed back into the fold like a lost lamb and we can all forget what happened. But then the room begins filling with people who want to talk business with Father, and because we all know this is a night for doing business, Trey makes noises as if he's leaving, and Father makes him promise to get back to him before the evening ends. Trey agrees, though reluctantly. As we leave the room, I strain to read Trey's face, but he maintains that blank look he used to get when he was brooding.

Once again we make our way through the mansion, mingling. Jamie seems like an intelligent, good-natured woman, and a whole lot of the people I introduce her to already know her from television. Things are going well until somewhere near the kitchen we run into Renfrow. Barry Renfrow is a hulking man with dark circles under his eyes, gray hair thinning across the top of his head, and a perpetually greasy face that makes him look like he's been eating oily potato chips. He's a man who's come more and more over the years to resemble a giant hard-boiled egg. He is just the tiniest bit uncouth in all things, smacking his lips when he eats, double-dipping in the cheese dip, and making covert sexual innuendos at the oddest moments, a sleazy habit that I first noticed when I was sixteen. I'd avoided him my whole life and virtually shunned him after Trey left. Aside from being part of the apparatus that ejected Trey from the family, I have no idea what he does for Father or how his affairs are entangled with the Overby empire.

Before I can think of a way to salvage the situation, Renfrow, looking bored and unflappable, puts his hand out to shake with Trey's, who ignores the hand and says, "I was hoping your fat old ass would be dead by now."

"That's no way to talk to your superior, son."

"I'm not talking to a superior."

"Mind your manners or—"

"Don't threaten me. I'm not some high school kid you can push around."

"None of us are who we were, dear boy."

The ripples of silence initiated with Trey's insults spread until people in the next room grew quiet, maybe twenty guests, many with grimaces of fear on their faces—somebody, anybody, there's an angry black man in the building!—staring at the confrontation even as these men glare at each other. What they see are two men in dinner attire, one overweight and out of shape and looking like a nominee for a heart transplant; the other with the look of a heavyweight prizefighter wanting to do some serious damage to an opponent. In light of their physical differences and Trey's obvious antipathy, it is rather amazing how self-confident and lethal Renfrow manages to sound.

As this is going on, I catch a glimpse of India gliding past the doorway, stopping as her eyes catch the utter stillness of the room, while we're all standing like a flock of sheep cornered by a rabid dog. India scans the assembly until her eyes stop on Trey. Her family has known ours forever and she's known Trey since they were kids. As she halts at the edge of the doorway, her long blond hair flowing past her bare shoulders, the strapless gown moving like a theater curtain that hasn't quite settled, she notices me, regains the glacial composure she is noted for, and vanishes as quickly and silently as an eel in a lagoon. Whether she is avoiding Trey or simply eschewing an unpleasant scene, I have no way of knowing.

20. THE NEWS LADY MEETS ANOTHER CHICKEN THIEF

JAMIE ESTEVEZ

Earlier I'd watched a young woman, a ballet dancer with the Pacific Northwest Ballet, trying to extricate herself from a lengthy conversation with Shelby Carmichael, realizing that if she couldn't beat his footwork, nobody could. For the last half hour the patriarch of the Carmichael clan had flitted from one woman to another, gabbing, flirting, and holding forth, a proclivity I sensed was borne of a lifelong passion for the opposite sex and a need to dominate all conversations in his vicinity rather than an old man's loneliness. Kendra's father was in his mid-seventies, wrinkled like an old dog, wearing a brown suit where everyone else was in a tux or a black dinner jacket. Once he started talking to me, I could see something of Stone Carmichael in his eyes, something of Kendra in his voice and choice of words, and perhaps a bit of Trey as well—Trey no doubt having adopted a handful of the family mannerisms even if he didn't have their genes. "So, young lady," the old man said, approaching me. "What does Trey tell you about the family these days?"

"I'm afraid I don't know him that well."

"Haven't I seen you someplace? You're the newscaster, right?"

"That's right."

"How would you like to come work for me?"

"I already have a job. Thank you."

"We're building an organization that has opportunities a young woman like you could run to the bank with. Stone's not going to be mayor forever. In fact, just between you, me, and the hatbox, a dollar against a dime says he'll be our next governor."

"There were rumors last year he was gearing up for a run at governor, but I thought he squelched those."

"Sometimes it pays not to let the opposition in on your plans. Governor of any state, if connected in the right way—and I assure you, he will be connected in the right way—can act as a springboard to national office. How would you like to get in on the ground floor? Meet me for lunch Monday and we'll talk."

"I'm sorry, but that won't be possible. I *have* a job."

"This isn't a job, honey. This is a career that will let you stop reading nonsense off teleprompters and start helping a band of revolutionary thinkers move national policy in directions it hasn't moved in a long while."

"I like reading off teleprompters. And for your information, I write mostly what's on them."

"You know where the vice president spent last night? In one of my guest rooms. Think about living in D.C. in ten years. Maybe eight. Think about that real hard."

"Father." It was Stone Carmichael coming out of nowhere, clasping my elbow, walking me away through a gaggle of people near the food tables. "Let me borrow Ms. Estevez for a few moments," he said over his shoulder. "I'll give her right back."

"You be sure and do that, son, because I don't know when I've seen a prettier little gal." I noticed he was staring at my bottom as we walked away.

In an alcove near the rear of the house, Stone said, "I'm glad we found another opportunity to talk, Jamie. I want to be sure you know that if we work together we can come up with a report we'll all be proud of. Last night was relatively free of street activity, but tonight I've received a report of rocks being thrown at cars outside the Paramount Theater, and the fire department tells me they've had three nuisance fires near the Convention Center. But the main thing is for you to know whichever way this comes out, you have my backing."

"I appreciate that, Mayor."

"Please call me Stone."

"Stone."

"There is one more thing."

"Sure."

"It concerns Trey. To be honest with you, I didn't realize he was in our fire department until yesterday, but I've talked to some people in the department about him. We both know about his participation at the Z Club fire, but there was another fire where he lost a partner under what I gather were suspicious circumstances. He didn't happen to mention that, did he?"

"This is the first I've heard of it."

"Yes, well. Something about a fourteen-story fall. He's got a past, that's for sure, and it causes me just a little worry. I'm wondering if he's going to be a good fit for you and for the investigation. He hasn't done anything that you would call . . . I don't know how to put this . . . I guess *irrational* would be too strong a word, but has he acted strangely at all?"

"I'm not sure I know what you mean."

"It's probably nothing. Anyway, I'm not sure we could get him off the inquiry if we tried. He does anything . . . odd . . . I want you to call me first thing. I mean that. I don't want to take any chances on this investigation getting derailed. It's important."

"I understand, and I assure you everything is on track."

"What have you learned about Trey in the short time you've known him?"

It was a question I wasn't sure how or even if I should answer, and before I could reply, Kendra approached the alcove. "There you are, Jamie. I have some more people I want you to meet. By the way, what *have* you learned about Trey?" She gave her brother a disgruntled look.

"I guess the most surprising thing is that you three are related."

"Adopted," Stone quickly inserted. "He was adopted."

"Adopted and then thrown out of the family," said Kendra.

"How did that come about?" I asked.

"Listen," Stone said, as he left the alcove, "you might want to avoid the old man. He gets a little grabby after that first glass of wine. He'll probably offer you a job. That's his standard MO, but there's usually no job. At heart he's just an old chicken thief."

"I figured that much out."

"About Trey being excommunicated from our family?" Kendra said after Stone had left. "See if Trey feels like telling you. I don't want to talk out of school."

"I gather it's a little touchy?"

"It's a lot touchy. But it was a long time ago, and I hope most of us are willing to forget it, at least for tonight."

Over the course of the next hour, Kendra shuffled me from one group to another, making introductions, smoothing out the small talk whenever it flagged, displaying a down-to-earth quality I liked. I could tell she wanted me to like Trey, and I could tell also that it was a major life event for her to see him again. Later I spotted Trey engrossed in a conversation with India Carmichael, Stone Carmichael's wife, a conversation so intense and obviously personal I was afraid to interrupt.

21. SEEING HOW THE SISTERS TURNED OUT, OR BURNING CASH FOR HEAT

TREY

It was spooky being reintroduced to this stratum of society after so many years away, to be consorting once again with the sort of wealthy folk whose idea of a bad year was finding the family stock down a quarter of a point or adding a stroke to their golf handicap. I remembered as a child having senators and their families over for Sunday dinner, vacationing with the children of old money and sometimes even the local nouveau riche. Taking a week off to jet to New York City to shop for school clothes and view the latest plays, museums, and operas—all of the latter was my adopted mother's way of exposing us, or me in particular, to culture. It was wonderful knowing anything that could be purchased was within our grasp, whether it was the latest dirt bike or a small plane like the one Shelby Junior received when he turned seventeen, or tailored suits that cost more than the average dockworker made in a week. Knowing any legal trouble we got into could be smoothed over with the aid of America's brightest and best-paid attorneys, knowing that if we got caught shoplifting or speeding or kicking a dog, we would be coddled by professionals and excused by experts. I hadn't thought of myself as spoiled or even particularly privileged. Not at the time, anyway.

Because until the time I was four I'd lived in poverty with my grandmother, and because I'd been the only black kid around the Carmichaels and thus automatically experienced their cushy world somewhat differently, I had a different take on things than my siblings. Yet for the most part I adapted readily enough to their patterns of ease, overconsumption, and entitlement.

Being a Carmichael was knowing you would never want for the best table at the trendiest restaurant, that any travel you could dream up was as close as a phone call to the family travel agent, that a job paying obscene amounts of money was waiting for you after graduation no matter what your grades or how many young women you'd knocked up—Shelby Junior had knocked up two that I knew of. It meant having a family chef. It meant having ski instructors who were former Swiss National Ski Team members. Spending three weeks every August in the San Juans on an island your family once owned pretty much in its entirety.

A kindhearted woman in the main, my adoptive mother felt compelled to ever so gently point out the differences between Carmichaels and middle-class America. Her attitude left a lasting impression I did not quickly shed after rejoining the rest of society. African-American culture was never talked about in the Carmichael household, but I'd had clues, lots of them, from their pronouncements on white culture. According to Helen Carmichael, the common man was to be pitied for his obsessions with cheap baubles, sex, expensive toys he couldn't afford, drugs, big ugly four-wheel-drive trucks, and obscenely large television sets that dominated tastelessly decorated houses. It didn't occur to me until years later that deep down she was afraid I would eventually return to my poverty-stricken roots and embarrass the family, which of course in her mind is exactly what happened in the end.

My mother would have been the first to deny she was an elitist, but she made it abundantly clear what the attitude of a Carmichael should be. We were separate. We were better. We were special. The rest of the world was playing catch-up but never could or would equal our elite prestige.

Of course, having been adopted, I had to dismiss a fair portion of reality in order to buy into this worldview, but nevertheless, until I was fourteen, buy into it I did. After that, I decided the advantages of being a Carmichael outweighed the sin of snobbery, and when I did have qualms, I let Kendra voice them instead of stepping up to the plate myself. Kendra fought my mother tooth and nail—never a mother and daughter who fought more than those two—from before I entered the family when Kendra was three until the day I left when she was sixteen.

I knew that after a few years of dips the Carmichael clan had increased its wealth substantially since I was booted out, that before entering politics with the promise to be the voice of the common man, Stone had worked first as a corporate lawyer and then as a CEO for a series of family-controlled companies. And that, had I remained in the family, I would have worked there, too, regarding a captain's pay in the fire department as pocket change. No true Carmichael would ever have considered a career in the fire service. Only peasants risked their lives for monetary gain. A Carmichael male might expose himself to danger, but he would do it climbing a mountain for charity, racing a car that cost as much as your average house, flying a private jet, or pursuing any number of the other activities peculiar to people wealthy enough to burn cash for heat.

What made my renewed proximity to all this money and exclusivity frightening was the fact that I knew I could once again adapt to it in a heartbeat, and the recognition of that weakness made me almost physically ill.

If I sucked up to the family in the appropriate fashion, there was a chance I could be forgiven and accepted back into the fold. I could have an income of six, seven, eight hundred thousand dollars a year, plus substantial bonuses, instead of my puny captain's pay, settling back into the fold that had ejected me like a hacking, humped-up dog getting rid of a chicken bone in its throat. But then, there was revenge in my soul, too—I could feel it heating my brain like a fever—and a Mercedes-Benz full of money wasn't going to quench that primal need for blood. Stone knew me well enough to realize what I was feeling, and it was part and parcel of why he was kissing my butt tonight. He and I both knew if they took me back in, sooner or later I'd fling a goober into their collective faces. Or a brick. Or a report on the Z Club fire that would be disastrous for his city administration. I knew him well enough to know he was afraid of me.

I knew Stone might be here and that it was almost a certainty his wife, who was one of the organizers, would be here, but the thought of running into Kendra simply hadn't occurred to me. I was glad to see her but was also watchful and leery, trying to deduce what she was thinking. Since she hadn't reached out to contact me in nineteen years, I had to believe she thought I was guilty of the crimes of which I'd been accused. But once we began talking, she was the same little sister I'd fought to protect in school, the same unaffected soul with the same teary blue eyes that I'd last seen weeping on the family island all those years ago, sweet, sensitive, and a bit ingenuous.

And then we met the looming, bombastic authority figure of my youth, the master of resolve, our father, who had grown jowls since I last saw him, and who was pontificating to a group of men using all the bluff and bluster that had been his stock-in-trade. I'd thought about this moment for almost twenty years, but the emotion I'd counted on was not the emotion that overwhelmed me as we came face-to-face.

Here was the father who'd drummed me out of the family with the finality of a hanging judge, but instead of a hateful man he was the saddest human I'd seen in a long while, a man who in his life had seldom tried to do right simply for the sake of doing right, and who, when he finally lifted his hand in charity by adopting me, found everything unraveling in one ugly episode. I'd always dreamed of a dramatic showdown where I came out triumphant and vindicated, where I somehow not only gained a consummate revenge for the evil visited on me but was also welcomed back into the family in a manner that made twenty years of exile almost worthwhile. But in the end we made small talk and I left.

I caught a glimpse of India, who, in the brief moments I saw her, appeared to be even more beautiful than the scattered photos I'd seen of her over the years. Moments after she disappeared, my gut was filled with yearning. But then, that had always been India's magic over the male species and her transcendence over the female: Her ability to make men ache for her.

As we worked our way through the party, trying to meet, greet, and then sideslip the African-American community leaders who wanted to give us advice, pump us for information, or lecture us on what they thought was wrong with the fire department and the city, I couldn't keep my thoughts from wandering back to India. I recalled how on that last horrible night everybody had congregated in the living room in the big house, and how they wouldn't let me see Echo. Though the room had been full of people who knew me well and supposedly, until that night, loved me, nobody had taken up the cudgel in my behalf: Neither of my adoptive parents, nor India, nor even my little sister, Kendra. The worst part came when I tried to stand up for myself.

As I thought about that night, I had an epiphany of the sort that doesn't seem possible because it's so late in coming and yet so painfully obvious. I realized with a shock that since leaving the Carmichael family I'd had relationships with African-American women, Hispanic women, Asians, and a Native American woman I nearly asked to marry me, but never anybody white. Now as I mulled it over, it was so obvious as to why that was the case, I couldn't believe it hadn't hit me before.

When I approached India, she stiffened momentarily, then quickly recovered her trademark composure, stepping forward to kiss the air next to my cheek as if we were casual acquaintances from the tennis club. "Trey. It's been a while."

"Yes, it has."

"To tell you the truth, I didn't expect to see you again."

"Don't worry. I have a ticket and a date and everything. I've already spoken to Kendra and Father and Stone, and so far nobody's called the police. Although I think they might be poisoning a batch of Gruyère cheese puffs in the back room."

"I didn't mean it that way."

"No, I guess you probably didn't."

We conversed warily about everything but what was uppermost in my mind and probably in hers, too, and then when the interruptions became too frequent, we retreated to the small herb garden outside the patio doors on the first floor. It was there in that warren of relative privacy that her demeanor softened, and I began to get the feeling she had no more forgotten the best parts of that last summer than I had.

"I guess I should warn you. Echo's somewhere on the premises with her husband. John's a little unpredictable."

"I was hoping you would be here. I wanted to see you again. But I wasn't looking forward to running into her."

"No, I wouldn't think you would be."

"She lied about me. You know that, don't you?"

"I don't know anything."

"Does she ever talk about it?"

"Never."

"How is she?"

"They're getting by. They've got two boys, same as Stone and me. It's a challenge with John, and she's completely absorbed in her music. She always has been. I think she'll be okay seeing you, Trey. It was a long time ago."

"The question is, will I be okay seeing her."

"What is that look? Why are you looking at me like that?"

"I'm just wondering why you didn't stand up for me that night. I've been wondering for nineteen years, and now I'm standing here talking with you, I can't help myself. Why didn't you tell your father where we'd been?"

"I wasn't your alibi, Trey. I couldn't account for the time when it happened. I couldn't get you out of it."

"You mean all you could do was embarrass yourself if you tried to defend me."

"Yes."

"You must have known I couldn't possibly have done what they said."

"It was between you and my little sister, and I had to take her word over yours. Besides, you don't want to drag all that up. Not here. Let's talk about pleasant things. How's your job going?"

"Sure. That's pleasant. Let's see. Four weeks ago I was at a fire where fourteen people burned to death. I got burned myself, and now I'm being asked to investigate the conduct of the fire department at the fire in an effort to stop the longest series of marches and rioting this city's seen in decades. I just tonight insulted the woman I work with, so she probably won't be speaking to me next week, and now because of my job I'm running into the five or six people in my life I never wanted to see again and who never wanted to see me again, and we're all pretending it's hunky-dory. Work is going fine."

"I'm sorry you feel that way about me."

"I didn't mean you. I've thought about you a lot over the years. And forgive my sarcastic answer to your question. I'm bad that way."

"You were sarcastic as a kid, too."

"It happens to be a family trait. My real mother has it. So how are you doing?"

"How am I doing? I have two kids I love to death and a husband who works too hard and wants to be president of the United States. Honestly. President of the United States."

India's sister, Echo, didn't take my unexpected reintroduction with the same equanimity India had—which because of our history, I expected. But then, she'd never been in the same league with her older sister when it came to public appearances or glossing over the disagreeable aspects of life. Echo more or less stuttered, "Trey? Is that you?" then began going on and on about some avant-garde music project she was involved in. Oddly enough, India had evolved into a more mature version of her eighteen-year-old self, while Echo had journeyed out of her teens in the opposite direction, her hair dyed black and cut in irregular notches, her ears and other visible soft tissue filled with metal studs, her arms and the side of her neck peppered with tattoos. She was more gangly than she had been as a teen, walking across the room after we spoke as if she had a rock in her shoe.

22. JUST LIKE OLD TIMES UNDER THE LYNCHING BRIDGE

TREY

It was shortly after midnight, and most of the guests had gone home. I should have had the good sense to leave, too, but Kendra was clinging to me as if she was afraid I would disappear for another nineteen years, and I didn't have the heart to depart. In the sitting room where I'd first encountered my father, we were gathered together: the Carmichaels, assorted spouses, Jamie Estevez, and me. Behind Shelby Carmichael stood his nurse, a woman named Lonnie, whose skin was the color of black coffee and who dutifully remained part of the wallpaper. It occurred to me that the old man had never been without black help, always a driver or cook or gardener, the darker the better.

Echo was there with her husband, John Armstrong. Stone and India Carmichael were beside the old man at the head of the table. Kendra, tentative and leery of the new family dynamic, stood next to me with her husband, Cal, a stocky man who had a genial air about him.

"I guess we all know why we're here," my father said. "The shindig tonight was a success financially. Raised what? India?"

"Something over half a million."

There was some polite clapping, and then he said, "And of course Trey is back. As it happens, he's a captain in the fire department right here in town. He's working on the minority community's report on the Z Club fire."

"I for one am so glad to see him," said Kendra.

"That's right," said Stone. "People make mistakes. They turn their lives around. And the past is the past." Echo, who was staring at her shoes, displayed no emotion one way or the other.

Before anybody else could break the silence, John Armstrong stepped forward and said, "Are you people all demented?"

"Please, John—" Kendra began.

"You're all pretending as if this son of a bitch didn't rape my wife when she was fifteen. You're all pretending she didn't lose her virginity to this black bastard." The room lapsed into a stunned silence, like the quiet after a cannon burst, and it was apparent that nobody had any idea what to say, including me. I thought the best thing would be to turn around and leave the room, take Estevez home, and try to forget the evening, but when I made a move to leave, Kendra grasped my arm and held me in place. She was not going to let go. In a sense, I had to applaud her for that.

Finally Kendra looked at Armstrong and said, "Pipe down, John. There's no call for that kind of talk."

"I'm not going to pipe down. This bastard raped my wife. He shouldn't be here. He should be in prison."

"I think—"

"Rapist motherfucker!" Armstrong said, standing directly in front of me and staring into my eyes.

"All I can say is I didn't do it."

"Now you're calling my wife a liar?"

"Yes, I am."

"Bullshit. You're the liar." From the front of the mansion we could hear the string ensemble putting away their instruments and murmuring among themselves. "I don't believe you people," Armstrong said, moving around the circle. A heavy man an inch or two shorter than me, he had a bulky chest, ruddy cheeks, and thick-knuckled hands. He looked as if he could take care of himself. Earlier in the evening India told me he was a painting supervisor for one of his father-in-law's construction companies. "Have you people forgotten your own family history?"

"You weren't even there," my father said, "so how would you know?"

"I know Echo hasn't been able to sleep for twenty years. I know she needs to see a therapist twice a week."

"Quiet, John," Echo said.

"I won't be quiet. This man ruined your life, and they're all acting as if it never happened."

"They're just trying to get through the evening like reasonable human beings," Echo said. "Let it go."

"It's not like there was a trial or anything," said Kendra, straining to say something that made sense of this conflict.

"A trial? Screw the trial. You had enough proof to banish him from the family for nineteen years. Enough for a half-million-dollar settlement between the Carmichael and Overby families. There was enough proof that none of you people has seen him since it happened. And now you welcome him back as if he's been on a two-week cultural exchange to Canada? Get him out of here. Get him the hell out of here."

Armstrong was as angry as I'd ever seen anyone, and when he stopped in front of me, I knew he wasn't nearly as drunk as he pretended. "You goddamn bastard," he said, fists clenched at his sides, the blood vessels in his thick neck and along one eye bulging. I noted his tie as a possible point of leverage, even as I unknotted mine. Kendra let go of my arm and stepped forward, but Armstrong brushed her off roughly. On the other side of me, Cal, Kendra's husband, knocked over a lamp in his rush to put distance between himself and the possibility of a physical confrontation.

"You're right," I said. "I am a bastard. A circumstance of birth over which I had no control." I tossed a look at the old man. "And I may be damned, too, but I never touched your wife."

"Liar! She'll never be the person she could have been, and it's all your fault."

"I *am* the person I could have been," Echo said weakly, although I'm not sure her husband heard.

"That was all a long time ago," said Shelby, standing shakily. Lonnie, the nurse, stepped forward and took the old man's arm to keep him from toppling, holding it against her ample bosom.

"What you need is to get your black ass out of here," Armstrong said at the same time that he took a wide, looping swing at me. He was powerful enough to hurt me if he connected, but he was just a little bit drunk and a whole lot pissed, and it took the edge off any skill he had. He threw two more quick punches and stepped into me, trying for my gut. I dodged the first blows and stepped inside the last. Neither Cal nor Stone, the only other able-bodied men in the room, made any effort to stop it.

His fourth swing was wider than the others, and because we were bumping up against each other now, it threw him off balance and he knocked over a chair.

"Let's you and me go outside and settle things," Armstrong said.

"John, stop it," said Echo. "I mean it. We have to go home."

"Why are *we* going? *He's* the one who doesn't belong here."

"He's right," I said. "I'm the one who should go."

"Don't you dare leave like this," Kendra said.

At that point John Armstrong took another lunging swing at me. I stepped aside and gave him enough of a nudge that he slammed into the wall and made the chandelier rattle. Echo said, "Enough, John. Stop it. Can't you see he could beat your brains in if he wanted?"

"Fuck that. And fuck you all," said Armstrong, barging out of the room.

Echo kissed India good-bye and followed her husband. With the assistance of his nurse, the old man sat heavily, caught his breath, and proposed a toast to the successful fund-raising project, though by now the bloom was off the rose and the only person who hoisted a glass was Stone.

23. CONFESSIONS OF A SHUNNED SON

JAMIE ESTEVEZ

After I refused his offer of a cab, Trey, amid a flurry of apologies for his earlier behavior, took me home on the Harley. It seemed that even if the family reunion hadn't exactly been a rousing success, the affair had burned off some of his excess nastiness. If I'd had a lick of sense, I would have taken him up on the cab, because the late-night breeze was bitterly cold.

By the time he shut the Harley off in front of my building, my watch said it was just after two in the morning. I was feeling a little woozy from the wine and maybe also from the bizarre revelations of the evening. "I'm a little, uh . . ." I said.

"I'm guessing you want an explanation for that scene back at the mansion?"

"It sounds complicated and . . . ancient." He'd been accused of rape. He was embarrassed talking about it and so was I. But I did want to hear his side.

You could tell the thought of revealing this story was as harrowing for Trey as facing John Armstrong must have been. I'd watched Trey turning to his father and later his brother for intercession while he was being cursed and accused, and couldn't help but see the heartbreak in his eyes when he realized they weren't going to intervene. Echo must have been easily as mortified as Trey had been.

"When I was seventeen and Echo was fifteen, she and her sister were invited to stay at the family vacation home in the San Juans for a few weeks. India was eighteen and had just graduated from a private school back east. I had one year left in public school. Kendra and Echo were both sophomores and great friends. The adults came and went that summer as their business demands allowed: India and Echo's father, Harlan Overby; my father, Shelby; our mothers."

"I'm sorry," I said. "I'm cold. Would you like to come upstairs and talk where it's warmer?" I couldn't believe I was inviting someone up to my apartment who was by recent accounts a sex offender. I should be locked up for my own protection, just like Mama always said.

I had a small condo on the fourth floor with a partial territorial view between two buildings to the west so that I caught a glimpse of the sunsets. The small kitchen was buffered from the living room by a counter island. I seated Trey on the sofa while I ditched my helmet, scooped up a photo of myself on my bike before he saw it, and went into the bedroom, where I dropped my wrap onto the bed and checked my makeup in the mirror. My hands were trembling. "Can I get you anything? Coffee? Tea?" I asked as I came back into the living room.

"No, thanks." He sat on one end of the sofa while I turned on the gas fireplace, then sat on the other end, tucking my knees and bare feet up. Even though I had an early flight in the morning, I was glad we were doing this. Maybe it would make working with him easier. Or at least tolerable. I couldn't help thinking about him and Stone Carmichael's wife, the way they'd talked alone in the parlor and then disappeared, the way they'd looked at each other. I didn't know whether they'd been allies in the past, enemies, or what, but I would have expected Echo's older sister to have had some protective instincts when her sister's erstwhile attacker returned to the scene.

I'd watched Trey all night and saw the strain in his relations with the family, especially his father, but I liked the way Trey spoke to the nurse, because he was the only man in the room who treated her like a real person. He was the same with the waitstaff, which gained him A grades in one of my major tests: treating waiters, receptionists, and ticket attendants like people instead of hirelings. Having worked as a waitress all through college, I felt this attribute to be important. Who would have thought I'd have to add not being a rapist to the list of qualifications I looked for in a man?

Staring at the flames, Trey seemed reluctant to return to his story. "You were in the San Juans for the summer," I prompted. "You and some others."

"Actually, just the last part of the summer. All the Carmichael boys worked summers—character building was big with my mother. I had a job at a lumber mill, but they closed down, so I joined the group late. It was basically an open house for friends and family, as it was every summer in August. Echo, India, Kendra, and I were the mainstays, along with my adopted mother, who has passed on now. I'd worked all through June and most of July at the mill, so it should have been nice to be on the island with nothing to do except lift weights for the football season and play croquet with the girls." He stopped and thought about that summer for a few moments. "But the week I got laid off, Shelby Junior and his fiancée, Melissa, were killed in a car wreck on Mercer Island. As you can imagine, it was devastating for us all.

"But we all put on a brave face, because that's what Carmichaels do, and it was good to have Echo and India there, since they both needed to be entertained and it kept Kendra and me from drowning in grief. Then one night I come back to the house after taking a walk, and they're all staring at me like I'm some kind of monster. It turns out Echo had come in all beat up and accused me of raping her. I didn't even see her out there. I've never understood why she would accuse me."

"Did they take her to the hospital?"

"I have no idea. As far as I know, the police were never called. The Carmichaels and the Overbys both go to great lengths to keep their personal problems out of the public eye."

"You talked to India for quite a while tonight."

Trey's gray eyes swung from the flames to me. "She was updating me on the family."

"So all these years you've been hoping Echo would tell the truth?"

"Or get found out."

"Did she have a grudge against you for some reason?"

"Not that I knew of."

"Or maybe it was dark and she actually thought it was you?"

"Doubtful."

"What were the Overbys like?"

"They'd lived on the East Coast most of their lives. My father did a lot of business with their father. They'd been friends since school. Like us, they were quite well off. Their mother was a reformed hippie type. Note their names, India and Echo. India told me tonight that her mother left their father not long after this happened and is now married to a guy on the East Coast who builds private jets."

Trey lapsed into silence and stared into the gas fireplace. I watched the emotions flicker in his eyes with the flames.

"What did you say?"

"I told them I didn't do it." He sighed and leaned back. "My father told me I was to cease all contact with the family. I couldn't believe my ears. I was being drummed out of the family. They'd made some sort of deal with the Overbys not to prosecute if I was banished. My father told me he was doing me a favor by saving me from the greater damage of prosecution and life in prison. Nothing I said could convince them I was innocent. Remember Renfrow from the party?"

"The man you were so rude to?"

"He worked for my father and Overby both—still does, I guess. He was there that night. He always looked at me like he expected to catch me stealing the family silver. To add insult to injury, it was Renfrow who drove me down to the ferry that night, neither of us saying a word, but him sitting there with a smug look on his face. There was no ferry until morning, so I waited by myself until the commuters started lining up at five."

"You must have been bitter."

"Assuming I was innocent, I must have been bitter? Isn't that what you mean?"

"I'm assuming you're innocent."

"Thanks," he said and seemed to mean it. "I *was* bitter. It's tough being the black sheep of the family, you know."

"You think color had something to do with it?"

"You think it didn't?"

"I couldn't say. Kendra spoke up for you tonight. She seems to be on your side."

"A few years too late. Oh, I don't blame her. She was in shock, too, and Echo was her best friend. She didn't know what to think. She was only sixteen." He stood up and said, "I think I should go. It's getting late, and I have a history of being dangerous when it gets late."

"Don't make jokes like that. You can't be disappointed with the way your life has turned out? I mean, if you'd been a Carmichael, we both know you'd be doing something else for a living, but you've got a great job as it is."

"It's a job I love. My grandmother lived two blocks from Six. When I lived with her, she would take me there and the guys would sit me up in the driver's seat. Then she died, and I went away and was rich for a while. And thirteen years later I was back in the Central Area, and a few years after that, I was sitting up in that fire engine for real. It's an amazing job a lot of people want and very few get a crack at."

"You wouldn't go back to that family if you could?"

As he opened the door, he gave me a fleeting look. "It's a moot point, isn't it? Because they're not going to ask me back. Tonight was a onetime deal."

"I'm not so sure about that."

"Oh, yeah. I'll never hear from any of them again."

"One last thing."

"What?"

"What's really going on with you and India?"

"We were friends once. Actually, more than friends. I guess you could say we have some history."

"You've got a lot of baggage."

"I'm a black man. That's what we do. We carry baggage. Or didn't you know that?"

24. SETTING THINGS RIGHT

STONE CARMICHAEL, NINETEEN YEARS EARLIER

"Echo, come back. For God's sake, come back. Jesus. Wait up."

But she doesn't wait. She is running in the moonlight in a ragged gait, running and sometimes limping, and all the while holding her arms across herself as if she's made of straw and about to burst apart, and I guess she is still crying because she was sure as heck crying before. Hard to tell from back here. I can't keep up with her at the best of times because she is the star on the cross-country team for her school, but especially tonight when I'm drunk and so incredibly pissed off about India and my little bastard so-called brother. Jesus. You'd think of all the people under the stars your brother would have some allegiance to family and nameplate and tradition; you'd think your own brother could keep his hands off the woman you've vowed to marry. But then, he was never my *real* brother, was he? My real brother is dead.

"Echo?"

I trip in the path and stumble forward, dancing like a three-legged goat to keep my balance, and by the time I regain my equilibrium and get my stride back, she's dashed up the porch of the big house and vanished through the front door, light spilling out through the doorway behind her. Somebody reaches out and closes the door, but it doesn't seal completely and a knife blade of light slices out across the porch. As I climb the steps, I try to catch my breath and rearrange myself, smoothing my hair back, wiping my face. I'm drunk, and they are inside waiting to judge me. I can hear them jabbering excitedly, Echo's entrance stirring them up like a stick in an anthill.

But most of all I can hear Echo sobbing. She's still crying, for God's sake. Who would have thought she would have taken this so badly? Who would have thought a couple of feuding brothers and a faithless sister could upset her this much? Or that the simple misunderstanding we had together in the cottage could be so blown out of proportion?

Her mother says, "What happened, Echo? My God! Who did this to you? Darling? You're hurt."

"What the hell happened?" This, a man's voice.

"Goddamn it!" It's her father now, no mistaking the booming Harlan Overby baritone that's convinced so many people to invest with him despite his wretched history of losing money. "Who've you been with?"

I slip quietly through the door, and at first I'm noticed only by India, who's in a long white robe, her hair swathed in a matching white towel, clearly just out of the sauna downstairs, her skin flushed from the residual heat. Everyone else is staring at Echo's bloody face and black eye, but India is looking at me studiously as I slide over to slip my arm around Echo's shoulder, her mother on the other side. My mother is rushing from the kitchen at the far end of the house with a wet rag, presumably to dab at the splotches of blood under Echo's nostrils. "There, there," I tell her, patting her narrow shoulder.

"Who did this to you?" her mother asks.

"It was in the old gardener's cottage, wasn't it?" I say. "I have to confess I was outside, too. Just taking a walk."

Echo hears my voice and realizes for the first time I'm the one standing on her left side, and as the recognition dawns she tenses up. She speaks through the damp cloth her mother is using to swab her face, weeping so frenetically we can barely hear her words, much less form intelligible sentences out of them. "We were in the cottage. Me and—"

"I saw Trey leave the cottage," I tell them, "but I couldn't figure out what he was doing out there in the middle of the night. Then I saw Echo leave and I followed her up the path. I tried to call her, but . . . well, you can see how she is."

"Trey?" Kendra says. "Echo, that can't be right. He wouldn't hurt you. That's not like Trey at all."

"No, it isn't like Trey," says India.

"Was Trey in the cottage?" her mother asks, shaking her by the shoulders. There is something frantic in her mother's questioning, and I know it has to do with the unsettling thought that a black boy has besmirched her daughter. "Was he?"

"I know he was in there," I tell them. "Because I saw him leave. He was in there, right?" Now, bawling more than ever, she nods and looks even more confused, glancing up at me as I pat her shoulder and kiss the top of her head. "Poor dear Echo," I say. "What a terrible night for you. I bet you didn't plan this." She shakes her head. No, she didn't plan *this.*

"What happened?" asks her father, standing in front of us, his hands on his hips. Despite the fact that he looks something like a cartoon in his smoking jacket and jodhpurs, Harlan also looks like the rich and powerful man he is. "He didn't force you, did he?"

At the word *force* Echo becomes even more hysterical, crying even louder and of course everybody in the room draws the conclusion that she was raped. "Was it that black thug?" her father asks. Harlan always thought Father had made a mistake of Olympian proportions in adopting Trey. It is one of two traits I have in common with Harlan Overby: distrust of Trey and an undying love for his eldest daughter.

"Had to be Trey," I tell them. "I hate to say this about my own brother, but I saw him leaving the cabin." She says nothing. "It's okay. I know you're afraid it will be your word against his, because that's how it always turns out in a situation like this. And you know the victim is almost never believed, but that won't happen tonight, because I'm on your side. We're all on your side. It won't be just your word against his. I swear to you on that. I'll stand alongside you. I'm your witness. I saw him leave the cottage. Come on, Echo. We need to get this settled. But we can't do that until you admit it was Trey."

"I don't want to . . ." she says, her words muffled as she buries her bloodied face between her mother's breasts. She is so slim and small, still a child really. I would give anything if we could reverse course and start the evening over.

"If it was Trey, you have to tell us," her father says. "There's no point in trying to say it was anybody else. Stone saw him leaving the cottage."

Echo tilts her head and gives me a look so filled with broken yearning and shattered trust, so salted with confusion and erosion of hope it almost breaks my heart. She is a wilting flower, an innocent in the process of losing her innocence.

"Goddamn that Trey," says Harlan. "You swear he did this?"

Once again, Echo looks at our faces, then at me, and our eyes lock for a few seconds, and she looks away and says, "Who else could it have been?"

"Goddamn him," says my father. "Goddamn that bastard."

"What happened?" asks India, speaking for the first time. "How did you come to be out at the cottage after midnight?"

The two sisters look at each other, and then Echo begins crying again and covers her face with her hands, and she and her mother walk awkwardly out of the room together. "No more tonight," her mother says. "That's the end. I shouldn't have let it go this far. This is private now." They head toward the rear of the house and disappear into the main bathroom. Soon we hear the shower running while Elaine waits outside the door, as if standing guard. Echo is under the running shower for a long time.

I look across the room to where India has dropped into a chair, her face blank. Everyone in the room is running through their own version of shock, trying to digest why Trey, the adopted son and gifted athlete, has done something that not only disgraces the family but will no doubt rupture relations between the Overbys and Carmichaels for years to come. Off in a corner Harlan and my father confer, Harlan as angry as I've ever seen any man, Father defensive and calming, some sort of deal being worked out by two deal makers who've been working out property and investment agreements for twenty years. Everyone else is silent except for the misfits, Renfrow and his girlfriend, who continue to play backgammon as if nothing has occurred, laughing to themselves, popping peanuts into each other's mouths at every toss of the dice.

At one point Harlan strides over to the massive stone fireplace and grabs an iron poker, swinging and slashing at the air, mad with grief and furious with the urge to make things right—a man seeking retribution if not blood. For a few moments I feel a twinge of regret over the fact that Trey is probably in the worst trouble of his life. But then, I didn't ask him to start banging the Overby girls.

When he notices Harlan waving the poker, Renfrow gets up from his game, and together he and Father calm Overby down. Not much later Renfrow is dispatched to the cottage to scout the scene of the crime and to look for Trey, who according to Renfrow is probably hiding somewhere in the knowledge that he is guilty and will have to pay the piper. Renfrow has a law enforcement background, having worked for the FBI, so he is the natural choice to investigate and apprehend the malefactor. He returns twenty-five minutes later without Trey but with an object wrapped in a handkerchief, which he deposits on the coffee table in the great room and which we all eyeball apprehensively until finally Father walks over and unwraps the handkerchief to reveal a Corum, the diving watch Father gave Trey on his seventeenth birthday at the beginning of the summer.

It's perfect.

25. A COMPLAISANT MEETING ONLY LEADS TO ANOTHER SQUABBLE

JAMIE ESTEVEZ

Monday morning at the prearranged time, I found Trey at the long table in the beanery at Station 28, sipping coffee from his personal mug amid the hustle and bustle of the fire station. A different shift from the one that handled the fire was working today, so I wasn't certain how much we would get done, though we were likely to find at least a few people to interview.

When I entered the room, Trey was reading the official fire department report on the Z Club fire, which was half an inch thick, a black plastic spiral binding holding it together, with dozens of diagrams and schematics. He pulled out a chair for me and offered me coffee. "How are you this morning?" he asked, his tone solicitous if not downright friendly.

"A little tired," I said, wondering if he wasn't still trying to make amends for the motorcycle ride Saturday night.

"That's right. The wedding. How'd that go?"

I told him about Patti and Howard, leaving out the part where I cried on the flight home because I was despondent after the beautiful ceremony. My mother was in typical form during the reception, pointing out in a beleaguered voice to anyone who would listen that I still didn't have a man in my life, and that she wasn't likely to see any grandchildren before she left this cruel world and was gone to glory. It didn't help that, truth be told, I *had* been feeling low over the lack of candidates in my pool of prospective boyfriends. Who would have guessed Seattle would be a place where all the men were either just out of prison, committed—usually to white girls—or so full of themselves you were mad at them before they even asked you out? I didn't need to be married, but it would be nice if there was somebody I could go to a movie with, or somebody I wouldn't be ashamed to take to a friend's wedding.

I sat directly across the table from the dark television, put my bag on the floor, and sloughed off my coat. Trey wore black wool uniform pants and an official white shirt with captain's bars on the collar, the pleats in his clothing razor-sharp. His coppery skin was a perfect contrast to the white, and as he brought the coffee mug to me, the sunlight from the windows brightened his shirt. As he sat and looked into my eyes, Trey seemed warmer, friendlier, less antagonistic, more at home in his own skin and more at ease with me. Maybe it was the fact that we shared a secret now, the story of how and why he'd left his family at seventeen. Or maybe he was getting used to me. He seemed altogether relaxed, which stood in contrast to how I felt being this close to him again, my stomach filled with butterflies, my palms damp. Only a few men in my life had affected me this way, and it was annoying to realize I wasn't beyond irrational juvenile crushes that took hold with a first look and wouldn't let go.

"Where would you like to start today?" Trey asked.

"With Chief Fish. We never finished with him."

"He called in sick today. Dependent care. His daughter's got the flu."

"You already checked?"

"I already checked."

"How old's his daughter?"

"Thirteen, I think. Fourteen."

"She must be pretty sick if he has to stay home with her."

"There's just the two of them. His wife died in an automobile accident a few years back. The day it happened he was in the garage working on the CV joints in his wife's Acura, so she borrowed his truck to drive to the store. While she was getting groceries, a freezing rain started coming down and the roads turned into ice rinks. On the way home she slid off the roadway and went down an embankment and turned upside down in a culvert. Nobody saw the accident, so by the time Fish got worried and launched a search, several inches of snow was covering the roads. It had to be about the hardest thing he's ever done, walking down that hillside knowing there were no footprints leading away from his truck, the roof all crushed in. She was dead by the time he found her. He'd been putting off work on her car and blamed himself for the accident. Now his daughter's the center of his life."

"I can understand that."

"He was a good chief while we had him. Never got rattled at fires, always remembered the basics, and looked out for his guys. He's one of the few chiefs who hasn't forgotten what it's like to be a firefighter. On the other hand, on a strictly personal level he's hard to figure."

Except for us, the room had emptied, and now the two fire trucks in the apparatus bay had their engines running. "Where are they going?" I asked.

"Inspecting. Every year we do building inspections on businesses in the city. Looking for fire hazards. After you've been at a station a while, there aren't too many buildings in your district you haven't seen inside and out. You get a fire and find yourself stumbling around in the smoke, it helps."

"Had you been in the Z Club? Did you know the layout?"

"I remembered it was a tinderbox. I remembered there was an upstairs and a downstairs, that they weren't connected through the interior. I forgot about the door in back at the northeast corner of the building."

"They found people inside that door, didn't they?"

"Ladder One found them."

"But *you* might have found them if you'd remembered?"

"What are you getting at?"

"I'm not trying to accuse you of anything. I just . . ."

"This is why you should have a different partner. This is why I'm no good for this."

"Do you feel bad that you might have rescued those people if you'd remembered the door?"

"No, I feel great that three more people are dead because in the middle of the night I couldn't remember a building inspection I'd done three years earlier."

"I didn't mean—"

"I don't like being the subject of an inquisition."

"It isn't an inquisition. I was only trying to get a sense for how you were thinking."

"Okay. Here's how I was thinking. I was thinking I could forget this whole thing and move on with my life until you came along and drafted me to be your helper. That's how I was thinking."

"It has to be done, Trey. You know that. The community is never going to relax until they get an independent investigation."

"How can this be independent when I'm in the department and was at the fire?"

"I'm the one who's writing it. You're my technical advisor, nothing else. Listen, I'm sorry if you're not happy about this assignment, and I know I should have asked you before I went ahead and planned out your next few weeks."

"You would have nixed me the first time I opened my mouth."

"Probably."

"That's okay, because I would have nixed you, too."

"Nice start to the morning."

We glowered at each other for a few seconds before I broke it off and stirred some cream into my coffee. He sighed and said, "I jumped on the computer and found three people on shift today who were at the fire. Also, I thought we should talk to the guy who owned the building. His name is McDonald."

"Why do you want to see him?"

"It's a hunch, mostly. That club on the second floor was supposed to be for members only, but they were charging admission to the public. Also, the row of windows along the north wall had been boarded over. The fire department report mentions it in the configuration of the building, but they don't say whether it was legal under the fire code. I'm wondering why they did that. And when."

"What was the building like?"

"Downstairs was basically a huge hall, big enough to play basketball in, with a corridor and offices and restrooms on the north side. That's where the wedding reception was. At the front door there was a separate entrance, wooden steps ten feet wide leading up to what used to be a small theater on the second floor with a stage and dressing rooms and so forth behind it, bleacher-type seating at the east wall. A runway up above with balcony seating. If we contact the building owner, we might be able to find some recent photographs."

"I don't know. It's going to take forever just to see all these firefighters. Plus, there are victims we need to talk to."

"Humor me."

"Who's in charge here?"

"You are, sir."

"I thought we were going to be Trey and Jamie?"

"Jamie, sir," he said with a twinkle in his eye, the antagonism evolving into a joke.

"By the way. I went down the list and found another name this morning, spoke to a Frank Putnam on the phone." Putnam had resigned from the department after the Z Club fire.

"Why did you do that?" he asked. "Jesus, just when I thought we were going to be buddies. Now you're talking to people without me?"

"I knew he'd left the department and was only trying to locate him, but then when he answered the phone in B.C., he said he wouldn't be around for a few days, so I started shooting questions at him. I didn't think about it."

"Obviously not."

"You knew he had resigned from the department?"

"I heard."

"He said he didn't quit because of the fire. Said he'd been thinking about it for some time."

"He only had two years in the department. How long could he have been thinking about it?"

"I'm only telling you what he told me."

"What else did he tell you?"

"You're really mad, aren't you?"

"Two sets of rules, lady. One for you and one for the rest of us. I could have been interviewing people all day yesterday while you were at your wedding."

"I told you how this happened."

"So what'd he say?"

"You really think I have two sets of rules?"

"Absolutely." He glared at me for a moment. "So what *did* he say?"

"You don't have to be like this."

"No, I don't. But I am."

"He said he was on Ladder One. That they had been assigned to place a ladder to the roof on the north side of the building so Ladder Seven would have an alternate means of egress if they ran into trouble. Putnam said the four of them were carrying some ladder that was apparently huge."

"A fifty-five. It's only forty-five feet now, but we still call it the fifty-five. It has tormentor poles out to the side to brace it when it's upright, and it weighs over two hundred fifty pounds, so it's a four-person ladder. Aside from the aerial, it's the only thing that would have reached the roof."

"They were carrying the ladder when they heard some feeble pounding that sounded like it was coming from inside a pair of painted-over doors. There weren't any handles on the outside of the doors, so they got axes and broke in. I don't know where they got the axes."

"Truckmen carry axes on their person."

"Putnam said when they got the doors open there were six victims at the base of a stairwell. One of them was on his back and had been kicking at the door. Could barely lift his leg by the time they got to him. They dragged all six out and got help. Turned out two were already dead. The other four were semiconscious from smoke inhalation. They helped work on the victims for a few minutes, then were assigned to take a line up those back stairs. He said it was pretty disorganized on that back side."

"Are you accusing me again?"

"I'm just repeating what he told me. Where were you?"

"Probably inside the building by then. I don't recall seeing those doors being opened. I remember them open, but I didn't see it happen."

"Does the person in charge generally go inside?"

"You're thinking about Clyde accusing me of taking over his job? No, the division commander does not generally do any work. But when we arrived there were only three of us, and I couldn't sit on my hands while people were dying. I knew neither Clyde nor Kitty would be as capable at carrying out victims as I was, and we had no other help back there. There wasn't time to wait around for more manpower. Jesus, they were jumping. The first one broke his neck."

"Okay. Putnam said after they got the victims out they were told to work a hose line up the back stairs. He seemed to think that wasn't a job for a truckman, but his officer was from Engine Ten and wanted to use some water. They didn't make it even halfway up the stairs. He said it was roaring. That it was hopeless by then. He said he was never so happy in his life than when they were told to pull their lines out."

"Not even when he quit the department?"

"You resent him quitting, don't you?"

"Not as much as I resent you judging my performance when you haven't heard my story."

"Listen, calm down. I'm not judging you or anybody else. Besides, you can tell your story any time you want. Right now would be fine with me."

"Did any of Putnam's victims say anything while they were bringing them out?"

"I don't know. We have the names and addresses of the survivors. We can talk to them later."

"What they say now, after the whole community has been in an uproar, and what they may have said that night might be two different critters. Or didn't you think about that?"

"I'm sorry. Next time I'll be sure you're along so you can ask the really important questions."

"I didn't say it was important. Just somebody should have asked."

"You want me to call him back?" Angrily, I pulled my cell phone out of my bag and found Frank Putnam's number, dialing it before Trey could stop me. It rang unanswered.

Half an hour later our first interviewee was a member of Ladder 12 working at Station 25 for the day. We drove Trey's ten-year-old Infiniti to Capitol Hill and met him in the engine officer's room.

26. NO POINT IN KNOCKING YOURSELF OUT

ACTING LIEUTENANT WILLIAM RUDOLPH,
LADDER 12, C SHIFT

I was walking alongside the north face of the building next to the parked cars when something heavy hit the pavement in front of me. Fell out of one of the upper windows. If I'd taken two more steps, two hundred pounds of woman would have driven me into the pavement like a spike. She was staring up at me when I put my flashlight on her, making these gurgling sounds. Agonal breathing, we call it. She was dead, of course.

We were supposed to report to Division C, but we couldn't find him, so after we hauled the jumper away, we helped put Ladder 1's fifty-five up to the roof. There was already a thirty-five up with some firefighters working off it, getting people out, so after we got the fifty-five up, we grabbed a third ladder off Engine 33 and threw it up to the window the woman jumped out of. There wasn't much hope of getting anybody else out that window, though. There was a lot of flame coming out of it. We were getting ready to go up and try anyway when we heard the Mayday. Lost firefighter.

Me and Nash ended up going back around to side A and being one of the two teams going inside, which turned out to be ironic, because the missing man was Sweeting, our number three guy that night, only we didn't know it at the time.

What happened earlier was we all went inside with Engine 13's crew looking for the little girl who was supposedly still in the building. Then they realized she was already out and we got called back outside. I got out onto the porch with the crew of Engine 13 and my partner, Nash, and I saw McMartin coming out behind us through the smoke, so I said, "Is your partner coming?" And he says, "He's right behind me." So I didn't think anything more of it.

I found out later that McMartin turned around right after he said that, and no Sweeting. He should have called out his name, you know, oriented Sweeting by voice contact, and he should have told us 'cause we were on our way to get fresh bottles, but he thought it was a simple thing to just step back into the smoke and grab him. So without telling anybody, he went back in. It was a fatal mistake for Sweeting and almost fatal for McMartin. Meanwhile, I'm thinking him and Sweeting were outside behind us.

McMartin made a couple of wrong turns in the smoke, and all of a sudden he was lost, too. Right then he should have got on the radio and called a Mayday, but he was convinced the door to the building wasn't more than a few steps away, so he kept wandering around until his low-air bell started ringing, and then before he knew it, he was out of air. Somebody at the command post heard the bell and put out a call for all units on scene to check their manpower, make sure everybody was accounted for, but I didn't hear anything. I had two guys lost inside the building and I didn't even know it.

At this time the aide from the command post goes over to the front door, standing in all this smoke without a mask, and shouts that the door is right there, you know, orienting McMartin by the sound of her voice, and McMartin finally comes out, having run completely out of air. We used to think we could take all this smoke, that if our bottles gave out, we had two or three minutes to get out, maybe even five if we were tough. But the fact is, with all these new components in building materials and the gases they give off when they're burning, a lot of times we take one breath and we're down. But McMartin gets out, and they get a medic and put O_2 on him, and after a couple of minutes he regains his senses and asks if Sweeting is out. That was the first anybody knew there was somebody else in there.

So we go back around the building, and me and Nash get assigned to go inside and do a right-hand search for the missing firefighter, who we still don't know is Sweeting. We do two small rooms on that second search, but then the captain on Ladder 6 calls the search off, says conditions are untenable. We sure as hell don't want to leave, but maybe it was a good thing. The thermal imager is registering 1300 degrees on the ceiling. Our worry was that the whole first floor would flash over and burn us alive.

We got out and went to rehab, where McMartin told us it was Sweeting who'd gone missing.

About ten hours later we found him in a back room on the first floor, where for some unknown reason he took off his gear and was sitting against the wall. They let us haul him out—the body, I mean. They usually do that, let the crew haul their own guy out. Engine 13 helped. He looked peaceful, actually, the way he was sitting. Of course he was dead from the smoke long before any fire got to him.

Did we pass up any civilians while we were searching for Sweeting? Hell, no. I didn't see or hear anybody except my partner, Nash, and most of the time I couldn't see him.

Do I feel bad about losing Sweeting? You bet. Everybody on the fire ground felt bad. I feel bad for his wife and kid, too, but we can't turn the clock back, can we? There's no point in knocking yourself out over it.

27. A MISTAKE WE'VE ALL MADE

TREY

After Rudolph left the room, Estevez finished scribbling her notes.

As far as I was concerned, an officer, even an acting officer, had one job on the fire ground that was paramount to all others: ensuring his or her men were safe and accounted for. True, Rudolph didn't stand in as an acting lieutenant often, but he'd been in the department sixteen years and had seen a good deal of action. You simply did not take a new assignment and walk around a fire building without verifying that your crew had secured from the previous assignment. Did I want to tell this to Estevez so she could write it in her report? Not any more than I wanted to tell her about missing that painted-over door in the back of the building, but I didn't see any way around it.

The official fire department review of the Z Club had glossed over the disappearance of the firefighter but went on to depict the search for him in intricate detail. It was typical of an official report when covering a fatality to skip over details that might finger individuals, the operative theory being that there was nothing to be served by publicly skewering one person for a mistake anyone could have made.

The dead firefighter, Vernon Sweeting, had only been in the department a year and a half. Twenty-six years old, shuffled from one station to another at indefinite intervals, he landed at Station 27, where he'd been two months at the time of his death, not long enough for anybody to really know him or to grieve for him. He'd been riding Ladder 12 the night he died, and none of those guys knew him at all. We all found out from newspaper articles following his death that he'd been writing a novel. His young widow said he'd had literary ambitions since he was ten, that he'd viewed the fire department as a temporary job to put food on the table until he made his bones in the writing world.

Estevez and I were alone, sitting in the two straight-backed chairs in the Engine 25 officer's room. "I have a couple of questions," Estevez said. "Rudolph was an acting lieutenant. What does that mean?"

"Even though he's only a firefighter, he was riding in the officer's spot on the rig, performing the job of the officer."

"But he's *not* an officer."

"No."

"I would gather some of the blame for Sweeting's death hangs on him."

"Probably. Sweeting's partner, McMartin, didn't help things."

"But doesn't it seem pretty basic at a fire to keep track of your people?" Estevez asked.

"Sitting here in this room, it does. You put on fifty pounds of gear, sweat until you feel like you just stepped out of a sauna, and inhale a mouthful of poisonous smoke on the street, and you might feel differently. Especially after you've already put in a fifteen-hour day. Plus, there's a lot of confusion at any fire."

"If Rudolph had called a Mayday, do you think Sweeting would have been found in time?"

"It's hard to know for sure, but there's a possibility. McMartin was lucky the aide went up there and called out to him and that he was close enough to the doorway to hear her, or he would be dead, too. But if he was out of air, by that time Sweeting was out of air himself, which means Sweeting was probably dead before they even launched the search."

"Correct me if I'm wrong, but wasn't it this incident that set the stage for the rest of the night? Because the IC was busy looking for the missing firefighter, he couldn't concentrate on victims?"

"The IC was swamped, but as far as he knew, we were removing victims successfully from side C. If they hadn't been looking for Sweeting, they might have had more people looking for civilians, true, but it was bad any way you looked at it."

"One last thing? Early this morning at the station I heard somebody mention a Lieutenant Hogben. They said he'd inspected the Z Club before the fire. Wasn't he at Station Twenty-eight this morning?"

"Yes, but he wasn't at the fire, so he's not on our list. You want to see him?"

"I was about to suggest it."

28. YOU CAN'T ASK THEM ANYTHING

LIEUTENANT LOUIS HOGBEN, ENGINE 28, D SHIFT

I admit I'm not the most perspicacious building inspector in the department. Is that the right word? Perspicacious? I mean, let's face it. The department doesn't give us any training on how to inspect buildings. They used to present a measly two-hour class once a year, but they don't even do that anymore.

And you have to realize, we're squeezing all this building inspection in along with our other duties: drilling, physical fitness, equipment maintenance, endless classes, our alarms. I ride Engine 28, and if we're not the busiest engine company in the city, we're close. Sometimes we get fourteen, eighteen alarms a shift. There've been times I didn't touch the sheets all night. Eight or ten runs after ten o'clock. Don't get me wrong. I ride it because I like the action, but trying to squeeze a regular workday in between all the emergency stuff can get silly.

I inspected the Z Club this year. The guy in charge is named Chester McDonald. The place is locked up the first time I go around in late March. It's locked again the two times we go by in April. So I finally get this McDonald on the horn, and he wants to meet me next shift, but the next shift we have an all-day class, and the shift after that is a Sunday, so I set up a meeting in two weeks.

Two weeks later he doesn't show. We leave messages, but he doesn't get back to us. I can't remember the whole timeline, but we finally get hold of him on the phone two or three shifts later and he says he's on his way down, so if we can go right that minute, he'll meet us. So we meet with this Chester McDonald, and there are holes in the walls and open electrical boxes, and extinguishers are missing, and he doesn't seem to be able to find his public assembly permit—though at the time we don't think he needs it, because he's telling us this place is a private club, just members. So I call downtown to the fire marshal's office and ask if he needs a public assembly permit, and they say he's had one in the past but it's up to me to decide if he needs one now. I write him up a permit application and an NOV for all the violations.

The trouble with this whole thing is I'm writing the Notice of Violation for the first floor only. We never get into the top space. McDonald says he's got it rented out to some group and the guy in charge is impossible to get in touch with, and he doesn't have a clue what they're doing up there. I find this hard to believe, but it was hard enough to get into the lower portion of the building. So McDonald gives us a cell phone number for this guy who supposedly is renting the upper floor. Only he never answers and doesn't return our messages. So one day we just happen to be driving past on our way back from an alarm, and there's people there. So we stop, introduce ourselves, and meet this John Chaps. The upstairs was worse than downstairs. So we make a list of all the stuff they need to fix. It's actually more than I think we can let them get away with, especially since they're telling us they are going to be having a hundred and fifty paying customers there in two nights. So I call up the fire marshal's office and ask what to do, because this guy John Chaps is telling me they're hanging by a shoestring, and if we don't let them open Friday they'll go out of business.

It happens we're working Friday night, so I tell him we'll be back. So we go see them Friday night, and they've made a good-faith effort. I mean, they've got eight new extinguishers. They've put up exit signs. Almost everything we asked for. And here's the kicker. They tell us Franklin from the fire marshal's office was there looking at things the day before. Only Franklin never said a word to us about it. But that's how they get down at the fire marshal's office. They're like gerbils trying to power a tractor—overworked. I mean, the only reason we even know he was there is because the occupants told us.

I need to know if those boarded-over windows on the second floor are legal or not, so I leave a couple more messages at the fire marshal's office, and they still don't get back to me. Meanwhile, I'm having trouble with McDonald. He's not cleaning up the place and it's rented out almost every weekend, and when I try to get hold of him, he's in the hospital for another operation on his leg. Then our crew gets a whole series of classes, and we get into May and June, and we're so damn busy I don't get back to the place.

At the end of June I get a note from a lieutenant on the other shift telling me the cops are watching the place because they think there's drug activity. So we go by the next Saturday night, and there's a party going on. And they're charging fifteen bucks a head to go upstairs. No permit. No clearance from us. Nothing. We go up and the place is jamming. Music. Maybe a hundred and fifty people. I found out later the building department had already condemned this place. In fact, they'd condemned it two weeks before our first inspection, but nobody told us. They put a yellow letter on the front of the building, which somebody just tore off. So I call the batt chief, and he doesn't know what to do, either. We call the fire marshal's office and get Franklin off shift. He's on a pager. He says we can go home. He'll take care of it. That's the last we hear for another two weeks. What's bothering me is that the back exit is blocked. There's all these people and only one exit down the wooden stairs in the front. The rear exit behind the stage is blocked with a table and a pile of boards. We had them unblock the exit, but I had the feeling they were going to put everything back the minute we left.

By now we're getting real close to September. The fire was September third, right? What we didn't know was that Franklin never got down there at all. He got prostatitis and almost died and was off three weeks. And the fire marshal's office didn't have enough people to cover for him. I didn't know the building department had condemned the place, and the building department didn't realize they were still holding parties.

They told us they never actually got in touch with anybody, that they simply wrote to the owner and posted a letter on the front of the building. In fact, when it burned down, I still didn't even know who owned the place. The one time I tracked the tax records through the assessor's office, they listed Silverstar Consolidated as the owners. When I called McDonald and asked about it, he said *he* owned it. And the guys running the club upstairs, Chaps and Campbell, both died in the fire, so you can't ask them anything.

29. THE ONE-LEGGED LIAR

TREY

After Lieutenant Hogben left the room, Estevez looked at me and said, "Did you know any of this?"

"Just at the end. About a week before the fire, we got a memo from Franklin and his captain at the fire marshal's office stating that the address had been closed down by the building department and that any public assembly on the premises was illegal. I wrote a memo for all shifts to drive by every Thursday, Friday, and Saturday nights we worked to make sure nobody was there. Preferably late, when these parties would be going on."

"The fire was on a Saturday night. Did you check it that night?"

"Not yet. The fire came in at ten-thirty. But they checked it the night before, and it was dark."

We were back at Station 28, using the engine officer's office, Estevez sitting alongside me. Lieutenant Hogben had been bouncing around nervously in the tilting swivel chair. A pasty-faced man with a good-size belly and a uniform that looked as if he'd been wearing it ten years, he was more nervous than anybody we'd interviewed so far.

"Hogben seemed nervous," Estevez said.

"If you did the last building inspection on a place where fourteen people died, you'd be nervous, too."

"Do you think he did his job properly?"

"You'd have a real hard time making a case against him. The department's asking him to perform a task he's never been trained for. None of us have. He asked for help any number of times, and the fire marshal's office more or less ignored him."

"Why would they do that?"

"Overworked. Just like us. We never saw a letter on the front of the building. Somebody took it down. My money would be on Chaps and Campbell. It would have helped if the building department had mentioned it, but we don't work that closely with them. There's no doubt in my mind that either McDonald or the two guys running the club upstairs removed the letter."

"It's not likely anybody's going to admit they saw a letter."

"No."

Estevez had seemed high-strung on Friday when I got roped into this gig, and at the time I'd attributed it to nervous strain over the fact that people were rioting in the streets and she was being placed at the center of it all. Or maybe she was jittery because she'd lied to me. But even after all this time together she was tighter than a wet fiddle string. Oddly, the only time she had seemed to relax was when I was in her condo Saturday night telling her how my family had disowned me. She was relaxed around other people, but other people weren't as hard on her as I had been, and I know they weren't as sarcastic. For reasons I couldn't put my finger on, Estevez brought out the worst in me. The funny part was that I was starting to like her.

Chester McDonald lived above Seward Park in a split-level house that, in today's rising real estate climate, had to be worth a small fortune. The house was built on a knoll with a view of Lake Washington, Mercer Island, and a slice of Seward Park. I parked behind a ten-year-old Cadillac in a circular driveway, noticing bits of eggshell on the rear window of the Caddy.

The woman who answered the door was a light-skinned African-American woman around forty. She looked as though she'd been pretty once but had gained some weight in her face and midsection, her legs like sticks. She wore green polyester pants and green fuzzy slippers. After we told her who we were, she yelled, "Chester, people here to see you."

She invited us into a large, well-kept living room and left us to our own devices. After a moment or two, an elderly man hobbled into the room on crutches, one leg missing from the knee down. He was short and shaped like a toad, his face a mass of circular growths, one of the ugliest men I'd ever met.

"What can I do for you?" he asked, sizing up Estevez and ignoring me. I had to admit, Estevez had been the highlight of the day for most of our interviewees.

She explained who we were while I used the free time and lack of supervision to wander the periphery of the room perusing photos on the walls. He'd been in the Navy. Then he'd worked for some service industry, as evidenced by a line of photos, a gas station maybe, judging by the brown uniform. The woman who answered the door was younger in the photos and clearly proud of the man she'd bagged, and he of her. There were earlier photos of McDonald with other women, all of them pretty. Rumble would have labeled him a sugar daddy. I wondered why his current woman, wife or whatever, would let him display pictures of former girlfriends so prominently on her walls.

"I'm glad you're here," McDonald said, hobbling across the room and into a den, plopping into an old wooden swivel chair. There were more photos in there.

"I'm just so damn glad you two showed up. Our pastor was on the news with that Beckmann woman. She goes to our church, don't you know? Her cousin married our neighbor here. Always was a firebrand. I'm glad she's looking into things. Too many people blaming this on me. All I did was rent the place to those scoundrels. And here I was in and out of the hospital. You see all the problems I have without people running around egging my car. Everybody knows Chester

McDonald owned the Z Club. 'Course, nobody called it that until after the fire."

"Mr. McDonald," I said, "The King County tax assessor's office has it on record that somebody named Silverstar Consolidated owns that property."

"Oh, I think that was something the lawyers cooked up. I'd forgotten all about it. What I'm trying to figure out is how people can think it's my fault when some crazy nigger goes and throws a Molotov cocktail into my building. I didn't even know who he was until I saw his name in the papers."

"So you still own the building?"

"Yes, sir."

"They were having club parties upstairs, Mr. McDonald," I said. "Did you know about that?"

"Chaps and Campbell are dead. I can't remember what all they told me."

"Do you have any paperwork with their names on it?" Estevez asked.

"Paperwork?"

"A rental contract. Something in writing between you and them?"

"We done business on a handshake. They paid on time, and that was all I cared about."

"Where'd you meet them?" I asked.

"Don't recall."

"How long were they renting the space?"

"Now, that I would have to think on. I been in and out of the hospital so many times this year, I'm not remembering the way I should. You know we've had people out here throwing white paint in our rockery? Oil-based. Trying to mess up my things. All I know about these two guys is they changed the locks on me. Said people was stealing stuff. I raised a fuss, but what could I do?"

"Did you know the building had been condemned by the building department?" I asked.

"The fire department never told me that."

"In the beginning the fire department didn't know, but you

should have. It was the building department. You never saw the notice?"

"No, I never knew. Musta happened when I was in the hospital. I got mail I ain't opened piled from here to Timbuktu."

"This picture," I said, holding up a photo I'd found on his desk. "When was it taken?"

"When we first rented the place to them guys upstairs. Before they changed the locks."

"Who's this in the background?"

"That guy there?"

"Yeah."

"I think he worked with the guys upstairs."

"You don't know his name?"

"I mighta met him. I don't remember names very well anymore."

30. IN THE MIDDLE OF THE THIGH

JAMIE ESTEVEZ

On the way out of Chester McDonald's house I got a call on my cell phone from one of the Z Club Citizens for Truth members, explaining that a pair of deacons wanted to meet us in fifteen minutes at the Mount Zion church. We got into Trey's car and he began driving toward the church.

"They think we're going to drop everything and run to them whenever they have a question?" he said.

"How long could it take?"

"The point is, we're either doing this investigation or we're at their beck and call."

"Oh, I think we can manage both."

"Do you? This is Monday. We've been at this exactly two days, and this'll be your third meeting with them."

"Actually, my fourth."

"Good God."

"You're kind of a whiner, aren't you, Trey?"

"Tell you what. You meet with them. I'll go talk to the next guy on our list."

"I thought you wanted to do this together?"

"You're the one who went off on your own."

"I told you how that happened. It wasn't as if I planned it that way. And stop whining."

"I'm not whining. I'm bitching."

Neither of us spoke as he drove. In my case, I wasn't speaking because I was so angry I could almost spit, but in his case, it was hard to tell what he was thinking. I wasn't sure he didn't grouse just to be grousing. At one point he smiled at something on the road, and I got the feeling from his erratic change of mood that he really wasn't in such a foul humor at all.

I wasn't sure how much we'd learned from Chester McDonald, though I quickly began to get the feeling most of what he told us was embellishment if not outright prevarication. His vaunted cooperation with the fire department didn't match Lieutenant Hogben's recollections. During the interview, Trey had acted disinterested and began walking around the room, casually picking up an item or a photo, motioning behind McDonald's back for me to keep him chattering—which wasn't hard, because McDonald had convinced himself we were flirting. Meanwhile Trey wandered around the room and finally snatched one of the photos from the desk.

"So what's the deal with the picture?" I said.

"What picture?"

"The picture in your right-hand trouser pocket. The one you stole off McDonald's desk."

"Borrowed."

"Borrowing is when you ask somebody and they give it to you. Stealing is when you just take it."

The snapshot was still warm from his body heat when he handed it to me, a photo of the Z Club taken before the fire, Chester McDonald and three hapless young women in the foreground. "So?" I said.

"There are three people in the background, two workmen

in hard hats with their backs to the camera and one man walking toward the camera. Check out the guy walking."

The figure was blurry but looked vaguely familiar, a heavy-set Caucasian male in a long black leather coat. "Who is it?"

"Remember the person I was rude to at the party Saturday night?"

"Were you rude to only one person? Oh, you're just counting the men?"

"Real funny. Barry Renfrow. What do you think he was doing at the Z Club three weeks before it burned down?"

"It resembles him, but are you sure?"

"It's Renfrow, all right."

"Okay. Maybe it's him, I can't tell for sure. What makes you think it was three weeks before the fire?"

"The date on the side of the picture. And it's not *that* blurry."

"Even if it is him, could it be some sort of coincidence?"

"Renfrow works for the Overby family, but he works for the Carmichaels, too. India confirmed it Saturday night when I generously offered to throw out all the freeloaders, starting with him. She said we couldn't throw him out because he still worked for Stone and her father."

"When you showed it to him, McDonald said he didn't know who the man was. You didn't really offer to throw Renfrow out, did you?"

"I said I did."

"You think McDonald was lying?"

"Absolutely."

We were silent for another mile or two. It took me a while to work up my nerve, but finally I said, "I have a question, but I don't want you to be offended."

"Shoot."

"May I look in your personnel file at headquarters?"

"What for?"

"It's a matter of making sure there aren't any surprises when we come out with this report. Even if what we write isn't controversial, there's going to be a degree of scrutiny on both of us, and it's my standard practice to clear the decks before going into battle. I do this with all my sources. I need to know the sorts of background stories that might crop up."

"You consider me a source?"

"I was thinking about the man who fell out of the fourteenth-floor window."

"Bernie Withers? Who told you about him?"

"Blame it on my profession. My concern is that this will come out somewhere along the line. The papers are going to find out you're the brother of the mayor, too. None of this is going to work to our benefit."

"I told everybody I wasn't the one for this job."

"It's not that. I just don't want any surprises."

"You want to look in my file, look in my file."

"Thank you. If you'd like to tell me the story first, that might help."

"Sure. I don't mind. We were called to a fire downtown in a condominium complex on Boren Avenue. I was working on Engine Six, where I was assigned at the time. Somehow Withers and I managed to get on the first elevator. We were going to scout the fire unit and give a report, maybe tap it with pump cans if we were lucky. As per procedure, we got off the elevator on floor twelve and hiked up the two flights to fourteen. Bernie was running, afraid the guys from Engine Twenty-five would beat us."

"Does that happen often? Racing somebody to their fire?"

"Often enough. When we got to fourteen, we could see the light from our flashlights in the smoke, but that was all. The apartment was vacant. A string of tiny lights above the patio doors had overheated and set the wall and the drapes on fire. There was an overhead sprinkler that had gone off, so we encountered a huge spray of water along with smoke. Withers found the patio doors and slid them open. Then I heard his pump can working. He was in deeper than me, and after a moment I heard this noise and called out to him but he didn't answer. I couldn't hear his SCBA anymore, either. I was feeling my way in the smoke, and all of a sudden I was smack up against this railing that hit me in the middle of my thigh. I almost went over it. Then the smoke cleared a little, and I realized I was on the patio, looking down fourteen stories at the street. Bernie had done the same thing, only he hadn't caught himself. He was sprawled out on the sidewalk. Until the Z Club it was the worst day of my career."

"That's horrible. Is there anything else about your background I should know?"

"Lots of things. I like children, but I don't like large dogs, bowling, long bus trips, or slow drivers who hog the passing lane. I like fried chicken and mashed potatoes, but I don't like cheese, and I'm not partial to people who spend a lot of time talking about wine."

"I meant anything pertinent."

"All of that is pertinent, but Bernie's the only firefighter who ever died on my watch, if that's what you want to know."

"At the Z Club, weren't you on the side of the building where Sweeting died?"

"Okay, Bernie and Sweeting. Maybe one or two others." When I looked at him, he said, "Just kidding."

"You weren't involved with Sweeting at the Z Club, were you?"

"On that one, I got lucky. I was on the side of the building where we lost thirteen civilians."

31. RIDING IN A CAR WITH THE ICE QUEEN

TREY

On the drive to the Mount Zion church, Estevez seemed to be reinvigorated. I couldn't tell whether it was because she'd caught me stealing the photo off Chester McDonald's desk or because she'd learned I'd lost a partner at a fire. I'd spent the whole morning trying to figure her out. I'd thought at first Estevez was one of those women who had been coasting on her good looks all her life and thus didn't know how to deal with real people. I know I'd made things difficult for her, but

I was still irked at some of her presumptions, the worst being that I didn't need to be asked about being on this committee. One of my specialties, though, was being difficult, and knowing this, I was beginning to regard our clashes less as irritation and more as entertainment.

The photo *was* a trifle blurry, and there was a chance it might not have been Renfrow, but with fifteen deaths to be accounted for, I wasn't going to write it off to coincidence the way Estevez seemed inclined to do. I had been virtually certain of my identification until Estevez sowed seeds of doubt, but then, that appeared to be her subcontract in our arrangement—to cast doubt on any thoughts I had that weren't based on fire department technicalities.

We were almost at the Mount Zion church when Estevez said, "While we have a minute, would you explain how a normal fire operation works. Or is there such a thing as a normal fire operation?"

"Seattle adopted an incident command system maybe ten, twelve years ago. We use it on every fire call now, the same basic system that's utilized in a lot of places around the country. The same plan for every fire call. One person, the incident commander, essentially runs the show. He or she gives the orders, makes the decisions, and delegates. Everybody works as a unit, because there's one brain driving things. The weakness is that if the IC is disorganized or forgets something important—or worse, if he chokes—any fire can go to hell in a handbasket. Another problem is that the IC generally doesn't go inside and often doesn't get around to the back side of the building, so he knows only what he's told and what he can see from the command post. If the reports he's getting are garbled or inaccurate, things can go south in a hurry.

"Also, there's a span of control we try never to exceed. One individual should have no more than five to seven people reporting to him or her. The IC will have four to seven divisions reporting, and each division commander will have no more than that number of company officers under him or her."

"Every fire has the same basic command structure?"

"Yes."

"That's good to know. And thank you for coming to this meeting."

"My pleasure. I'm sure I'll enjoy it. I'm going to take notes and put them in my journal."

"You keep a journal?"

"I'm going to start one tonight."

"You are so sarcastic."

We parked in front of the church and walked to the main entrance, where we found the front doors locked. There were lights on in the back, so I pounded on the doors until a smallish woman with a red-haired wig let us in.

"They're waiting in back," she announced.

Just as I suspected, it was two deacons from separate churches who'd joined the Z Club Citizens for Truth just today, each insisting they wanted to pick our brains, though it quickly became apparent that what they really wanted was to complain about the fact that half a dozen young people were arrested Saturday night on charges of disturbing the peace, and another dozen were detained last night for throwing rocks and bottles at a fire engine. "You gotta get this report out so we can put an end to all this," said the larger of the two men.

"How about telling people to behave?" I said.

Estevez gave me a harsh look and then listened patiently to their concerns, which was more than I could manage, knowing that the more time we wasted here, the longer it would take to complete our task. Forty-five minutes into the confab, my cell phone rang and I stepped out of the room to answer it.

"Can you meet me?" I recognized the caller immediately.

"Where are you?"

"Downtown."

"Whereabouts downtown?"

"Right now I'm in the Georgian at the Four Seasons Olympic."

"I'll be there in twenty minutes."

I stepped back into the room and caught Estevez's eye. The two men liked listening to themselves talk and didn't stop even when she got up to speak to me. "What is it?" she whispered.

"Something's come up. It's personal."

"Now? We're almost finished."

"Yeah. Sure we are. And after that the four of us are going to start a rock band and turn out a hit single."

She glared at me for a moment. "When will you be back?"

"Sometime this afternoon."

"In the meanwhile, what do I do for transportation?"

I handed her a twenty-dollar bill. "If you ever finish up here, take a cab. I'll call your cell phone when I'm free."

"I hope this is important."

"It's at least as important as all this pissing and moaning."

"Shhh, I think they heard you."

"Tell them I send my love. See you later."

It was with a rising sense of anticipation that I parked in a garage off Fifth Avenue near the Four Seasons, then walked across the street, throwing on a jacket to cover my white uniform shirt and badge.

I found India Carmichael seated at a table for two in the restaurant, looking both casual and elegant in a simple white blouse and blue skirt, hair pulled into a loose ponytail; the woman I'd fallen madly in love with the summer I turned seventeen. You know the one—the one you never forget. And here she was, married to Mayor Stone Carmichael, my ex-brother, having already given him two children, a pillar of society, while I was a lowly unmarried captain in the Seattle Fire Department, subject to the whims of every nutcase who got the itch to dial 911.

When I sat across from her at the table I was starkly aware of the contrast in our social positions, and not just from the five-thousand-dollar watch she wore or the silk blouse. The rich also project an air of privilege the rest of us can never quite exhibit. I know; I had been one of them.

She looked at me coolly. "How are you?"

"Fine. You look good."

"I was surprised to see you Saturday night. Pleasantly surprised. I really didn't know you were going to be there."

"Nobody did. I gate-crashed."

She smiled, indulging me. "I know they gave you tickets. It's been so long. It seems like forever."

"Does it?"

"Do you ever think about that night?" She asked it as if we were a couple of geriatric patients in a nursing home, as if there couldn't possibly be an ounce of passion left between us, but I knew she was talking about the two of us making love in the gardener's cottage and not about what happened later.

"I think about it once in a while," I lied. I thought about it all the time, both parts of the night.

"Do you know I've never talked to Stone about it."

"He still doesn't know?"

"He's never had a clue. Not that I haven't been tempted occasionally in our worst fights to blurt it out just to hurt him. You still don't like him, do you?"

"He hasn't done anything to change my opinion, but that's okay, because I think the feeling is mutual. You have two boys. How old are they? Or did I ask Saturday night?"

"You did, but I'll tell you again. Seth and Marshall. Eight and ten. Marshall's a sports fiend. Seth wants to be a musician and already plays the guitar and piano."

"I bet they're adorable. It's too bad how it turned out the other night."

"John has a habit of making a jackass out of himself. I felt sorry for my little sister. And for you."

"Don't feel sorry for me. I rather enjoyed being called a rapist in front of my date."

"I really am sorry."

"No, don't be. Everybody should be taken down a peg or two once in a while. It helps us keep perspective. I mean that."

"That's a good philosophy. I'll have to remember it."

"She's changed enormously, Echo. More than any of us."

"I suppose she has. I've been close to her all along, so

maybe I haven't noticed the way others do. But then, we've all changed."

"Not so much that anybody stood up for me when Armstrong teed off."

"Kendra did her best."

"Yes. I've missed her spunkiness. In fact, she's the one part of the family I've really missed."

"I hope you're going to keep in touch. She's talked about you a lot over the years, wondering where you were and what became of you. Do you hold that against us? That nobody stood up for you that night?"

"Kendra was only sixteen and in shock. My mother never voiced an opinion contrary to my father's, so I didn't expect much out of her. Stone always wanted me out of the family, so as far as he was concerned, it was perfect. And my father . . . I've thought about this a lot, and he must have truly thought I was guilty or he wouldn't have done what he did. You were the one I was waiting for. But you never let out a peep."

She sat back and appraised me, her wide blue eyes cooler than a drink of cold water. "Yes. Well. What did you want me to say? My sister told a room full of people you were the one. Later, I tried to talk to her about it, but she wouldn't talk."

For a few moments watching India watch me, I was like a junkie going back on the juice, thinking she'd surely called me here to see me—ME—and that she was sending signals that she wanted to renew the relationship we'd had so long ago, that she might even want to go upstairs right here in the Olympic Four Seasons and take a room. Crazy thoughts. Until now I'd lived what I thought to be a moral life, taking care of my family, doing my job, staying away from women married to close relatives, but I could see the facade crumbling in one long lunch if she made the right moves. I had the feeling for part of the time that we spoke that she was working through some of the same feelings, that we were both sitting there battling our worst instincts, sensing Eden just over the ridge and fighting not to venture toward it. It was a fantasy, of course. She hadn't sent out any signals.

She said, "I've had conflicted feelings about what happened that summer."

"The part with you and me, or the part where my family called me a rapist and said they never wanted to see me again?"

"Being friends with the brother of the man I was eventually going to marry was a good thing, or so I thought. Having sex with him probably wasn't such a good idea. You were always a very nice guy, Trey. You had a good instinct about you. That was why I found it difficult to accept the fact that you'd hurt my sister. We all found it hard to accept, but there it was staring us in the face. She said you did it. She obviously didn't want to finger you, but she did."

"And you accepted that even when I denied it."

"I did at the time. I've called you here to tell you I've changed my mind. I no longer think you did it. I know I'm late, but I believe you're innocent, and I needed to tell you and offer you whatever my support is worth—if it's worth anything at this point. I needed to get the words out and I needed you to be in front of me when I said them. I'm sorry you were falsely accused, and I'm sorry your family disowned you. I'm sorry about all of it. I truly am."

"So what you're saying is, your sister lied and you know it."

"I'm saying I believe you're innocent."

"Why this sudden change of heart? Because of our chat the other night? Did I seem so reasonable and normal that you decided to reevaluate what happened? Or did your sister tell you she lied?"

"I'm not at liberty to say anything about my sister. I can say I'm sorry you got kicked out of the family and I'm sorry you didn't get to see your mother before she died. I wish none of it had happened. It must have been awful for you."

"Echo talked to you, didn't she?"

"I think if perhaps you spoke to her, you and she might come to some sort of understanding. I think she might be . . . I don't want you to tell anybody I'm the one who told you, but I think if you spoke to her . . . things might rearrange themselves. I can't guarantee that, but I have a feeling it might happen that way. You should at least give it a try. And please be gentle with her."

"You're asking me to be gentle with the woman who essentially ruined my life."

"I think . . . yes. I think you should talk to her and be nice. She's not as stable as some of us."

"Somehow the thought of seeing her again doesn't seem very appealing, especially after meeting her husband."

"Promise me you'll get in touch with her."

"I'll think about it."

"I should have spoken up for you that summer. I should have told everyone why Stone saw you leaving the cottage and how your watch happened to be there. You deserved to have all the facts out on the table. Now that I know you were innocent, I feel sick about it."

"Speaking up for me might not have changed anything."

"At least I wouldn't have had to live with this feeling of cowardice all these years. And you would have had the satisfaction that one person wasn't afraid to speak the truth on your behalf."

"Apology accepted."

"Thank you."

We had lunch and talked about more mundane matters during the meal. Afterward, we paid the bill and she gathered up her coat and moved toward the restaurant entrance. I followed her into the hotel lobby, where a well-dressed, middle-aged man and woman on one of the davenports watched us as only two disapproving white people can watch a black man with a white woman. She asked for a ride to the Monorail terminal, which I gladly gave her. We were strangely silent on the walk to the car and during the drive, but then, India had always been a woman of silences.

I'd had all those empty summer weeks to win India's affections from Stone. Whether I'd done it on purpose or whether we'd simply fallen into a trap of proximity and hormones, I was never certain, but over the years I had to live with the sick fact that sleeping with my brother's girlfriend had given me almost as much satisfaction as throwing me out of the tribe must have given him.

32. HOMECOMING

TREY, NINETEEN YEARS EARLIER

It's been a long night, and even though an hour ago when I was with India I felt about as good as any man can ever feel, I'm pretty miserable right now. Leery of crabs and wary of sucking tide pools, I've been pacing the beach in the moonlight, standing still and thinking hard when the moon moves behind the clouds, walking and thinking even harder when it comes out and forms a tall shadow in front of me as I dodge slimy rocks and holes near the waterline. The tide is out and the beach is wide and broken and rocky. Even though Stone has either sabotaged or tried to sabotage every relationship I've ever had with a girl, I feel like a total rat for what India and I have been doing behind his back.

We've been thrown together most of the summer because Stone's been off gallivanting for Father's companies, and while Kendra and Echo have been here, too, they're younger and in many ways have nothing in common with India and me. Then there's been the issue of Shelby Junior's car crash and the way I've been handling it, or not handling it, including the afternoon I broke down out in the boat and wept in front of India—just the two of us in the sunshine, as she scooted over and pulled my head into her lap. She'd been comforting me, and then we shared our first kiss, and everything was different from that moment. We'd been distant friends since we were kids, and lately she'd been my brother's girlfriend, the woman whom by all accounts he was fated to marry. But after our lips touched, we were something else to each other and we both knew it—saw it in each other's eyes at the dinner table and when we were goofing around with our sisters, although it was still a week before we kissed again, and another week after that before we drifted out to the gardener's cottage late one evening.

No telling whether it was her plan or mine, though we both felt guilty afterward and said as much, talking for hours about what we'd done and why. And then, predictably, we did it again and then went back to the big house to our respective bedrooms to spend the rest of the night mulling things over. I've always been wary of Stone, probably because he has always treated me shabbily. Shelby was the oldest, and it was Shelby who took me under his wing; Shelby who was my mentor, guardian, and coach throughout my grade school years; Shelby who in fact had at times been more of a father to me than his father had been to him. His death struck the family like a tornado taking off a roof.

India would have been a temptation to any male on the planet, so I didn't have much of a chance against her allure: seventeen, overloaded with testosterone, stranded on an island in the San Juans with nothing to do but keep her and her sister amused for the better part of the summer; my adopted mother urging me to take them out on the boat, to the wreck off the north end of the island for diving, waterskiing, crabbing, fishing. Often, neurotic Echo would opt out, and Kendra, suffering from her usual overblown sense of duty, would stay with Echo and read or listen to music while India, the more adventuresome of the sisters, would go with me.

As I walk back to the house the clouds loom darkly over the night sky. I can see all the lights are still on in the great room, and through the windows I watch figures moving about the rooms. Harlan Overby is visible, gesticulating like a wild man, unnaturally agitated in a manner I don't think I've seen before. Everybody's still awake, which is unusual for this time of night, past one in the morning. When I reach the house, I'm startled to discover Renfrow's girlfriend sitting in the dark on the stoop smoking a cigarette, the only clue to her presence the orange glow of her cigarette tip. When I say hello, she stares past me as if I don't exist. Even though I've known her only a few hours, it's not the first time she's ignored me.

When I open the front door and step into the foyer, my father and mother are sitting near the tall stone fireplace in their accustomed chairs. Kendra and Stone are by the tall window overlooking the dark Puget sound and the distant glow in the sky provided by Seattle's skyline. Renfrow is hunched over a backgammon board rolling the dice and scoring against an imaginary partner. Harlan is strutting back and forth in front of the dead fireplace, and Elaine is beside him with her arms folded tightly across her breasts, lips pursed. India is all by herself in a far corner curled up in the window seat with her eyes closed. Only Echo is missing.

As I enter the house, everybody in the room stops whatever it is they've been doing and looks up at me. Suddenly I feel like a kitten in a room full of mad dogs. If I didn't know better, I would guess they all hate me, all except Stone, who actually does hate me but who gives me a look I can't figure out until later.

"What?" I say, turning to close the front door behind me, only to find Renfrow's girlfriend staring at me. "What?"

Harlan jogs across the huge room, but stops ten feet away, his face tinted with rage, the veins under his eyes standing out. He looks like a man who's just lost a diamond ring down a drainpipe and believes I'm responsible. "Were you out in the gardener's shed with my daughter?"

I swallow hard and glance across the room toward India but cannot judge by the blank look on her face what the climate of the room is or what I should say. I have no idea what she might have told them. Whatever it is, it's made Harlan angrier than I've ever seen him. Elaine, too, who is behind him glowering at me.

"It's not a shed. It's the gardener's *cottage,*" I say stupidly, trying to remain calm and gain time to think. I've had sex with three girls in my life, but until now I've not been confronted by any of their fathers. It's unnerving, especially with my whole family watching.

"Were you out there with my daughter?"

"I . . . Yes." I see him coming at me but don't realize he's going to release all the fury in his tightly coiled body until it's too late and he's struck me across the face with the back of his hand. I've been hit harder by brush while riding my dirt bike around the island, but I back off anyway, worried he might do worse. He tries to strike me again, but I sideslip, and then Father flounces across the room and takes hold of Harlan's arm. Neither man looks at the other; all eyes in the room are on me.

"She already told us everything, but we want to hear it from you. Did you have sex with her?" my father asks.

"Yes, but . . ." Overby wrestles my father for a few moments, two middle-aged men engaging in the roughhouse behavior of their youth, and then Renfrow approaches and together they hold Overby at bay. "It wasn't like that," I say.

"Oh," says Elaine, her voice curdling with disdain. "Just how was it?"

"It was . . ." I glance one more time across the large room to India, looking for a clue or for some help, for some hint of how she wants me to respond. I feel as if I am betraying her as badly as the two of us have already betrayed Stone. When she doesn't give any sign as to what she might have told them, I glance at Stone to see how he's taking this, but instead of a look of injury on his face, I am surprised to see triumph. Or am I imagining it? Why would he be amused that I slept with his girlfriend? And why am I taking all the heat for this? There were two of us in the cottage.

Elaine walks over to a coffee table and picks up a watch, dangling it by one finger. "Is this yours?" she says.

"If it's a Corum, it is. Father gave it to me for my birthday."

"You bastard," Overby said. "You stupid bastard. You're going to prison. You're going to spend years behind bars, you bastard."

"She went down there with me. She wanted to do it."

Harlan practically explodes in my face. "You lying misfit! You raped my daughter."

"Now, now, Harlan," Father says, holding him firmly. "We made a deal. Remember?"

"He needs to go to prison."

"You know what we agreed. At least give me this."

"Rape? I didn't rape anybody. We were . . . together . . . she wanted to. Tell them," I say, looking imploringly at India, but before she can utter a word, her mother steps forward, my watch still dangling from her finger as if it were a dead reptile, and attempts to launch a gob of spittle at me. She isn't much of a spitter, and the saliva drops to the carpet between us. For some reason her efforts and the hate in her pretty eyes shock me more than anything else.

"How dare you say it was consensual. How dare you." She glares at me.

"But I . . ."

"I suppose she asked you to beat her up, too?"

"Beat her up? She's not beat up."

"Come now, big sports hero. We've seen Echo. We saw what you did."

"Echo? But I . . . Echo?"

"I saw you leaving the cottage, little brother," Stone says. "Sorry. I had to tell them. I saw you leaving."

"Sure, I left the cottage a while back, but . . . I never saw Echo."

"Liar," said Elaine.

"It's time to get this bastard out of the building," says Harlan. "Get him out of here. You're right. We made a deal. You go through with your portion of it before I call the police—or kill him."

It is hard for me to figure how this has all come about. Echo. India. Am I going crazy? I glance from face to face in the room and register looks I've never felt before, but which I know will follow me to my grave.

"How could you take advantage of a fifteen-year-old girl?" my father says, stepping forward until we're nose to nose. I haven't moved since coming into the house, am stuck to the spot as if I'd stepped into a glue trap.

"I didn't see Echo." India is refusing to look at me. "I never saw Echo. I saw—"

"Echo says you did, and you just admitted it yourself,"

says Elaine, stooping to mop up the spittle off the carpet with a damp rag she's had in her hand all along. "Echo says you did, and that's good enough for me."

"I saw you leaving," says Stone. "I mean, I'd like to lie for you, bro, but with something this serious and the Overbys being such good friends and all, I don't see how I can. I did see you leaving the cottage, didn't I?"

"I left it. But—"

"That's what I was afraid of," says Stone.

"Let me talk to Echo. She can't be saying I did anything, because I didn't."

"You admitted you had sex with her," my father says. "Stone saw you leaving the cottage. Renfrow found your watch. Echo said you were the one. What else is there to talk about? The subject is exhausted."

"But I never saw Echo."

"You just said you had sex with her."

"I said . . ." I glance around the room, my eyes lingering on India for just long enough to realize she isn't going to speak up and may not confirm what I want to tell them. Maybe she believes I actually did this, that I waited out there in the dark until Echo happened along and jumped her. "Why don't we bring Echo out here? Get this out in the open."

"Not on your life," says Harlan. "You're not going to lay eyes on her ever again. Not if I can help it. Not in this lifetime."

I glance around the room, and India finally gives me a look she might have given a small animal her school bus has crushed. We'd been in love for a few days, at least I'd thought so, and I expect her support. I suppose it's too much to hope she'll defend me when it would mean admitting we were in the gardener's cottage making love for an hour and a half. I wonder if she's sacrificing me because she thinks I'm guilty, or if she's merely trying to protect her own reputation. And what the hell did happen to Echo?

For a while nobody speaks. Kendra won't stop sobbing. My father appears to be the most shocked and possibly the most tormented of the lot. He is clearly shattered by this whole situation.

"But I didn't do it."

For a few seconds a white father looks at his black son as if he believes him, but at the end of the look the window of doubt closes and the father's eyes grow even more sorrowful and he takes on the mien of a man who is about to put down his favorite horse.

"What about the time on the boat?" asks Elaine.

By now I am in tears. I know what she's referring to and so does Kendra, but I had no way of realizing Echo had blabbed to her parents about the incident. Weeks earlier we'd been out on the boat looking at starfish on the bottom, maybe twenty feet down, when I took hold of the gunwale and started rocking the dory. Kendra thought it was funny because she was used to my humor and she was a good swimmer and we were all in suits, but Echo began crying, and even when I stopped rocking, she wouldn't stop. Her crying grew hysterical and was, I thought, out of proportion to what I'd done, and I knew Kendra thought so, too. After that I tried to treat her like the delicate flower she apparently was, but the damage had been done, and the story of my malfeasance had spread. "I admit I might have gone too far, but I was just teasing."

"She said she cried for hours."

"So what? I didn't rape her."

"Let's get this over with before we change our minds and have him jailed." Overby turns to Shelby. "I still don't understand why you adopted this black bastard."

"Let me handle this, Harlan. Son, we've made a deal, and in order to stay out of jail, you're going to agree to this. You'll go upstairs and pack whatever you can carry, and then you'll leave the house. You'll leave the house and you'll leave the family."

"And go back to the house in Seattle?" I ask.

"No. Don't ever go back there. Just leave and don't come back. Ever. We don't want to see you again."

"I do," said Kendra, weeping.

"If you think I did this, call the police. Because I didn't."

"You don't want that," Stone says. "Trust me. You don't want the police involved."

"You're getting a good deal here," Father says. "Don't throw it away, son. It's the best offer you can hope for. It wasn't easy, but we've convinced the Overbys not to press charges. We'll keep this inside the families. The stipulation is that you have to leave. Pack your belongings and move out. Tonight. Whatever you can carry. Anything else, we'll give to charity. Trey, you've shamed me and your mother, and you've done damage to a young woman who deserves only the best from this family. You've disgraced us all."

"Give me a polygraph. Give us all polygraph tests." India looks up, aware for the first time that she might get dragged into this. Stone doesn't look too happy about the prospect of polygraphs either, but I figure it's because he can't wait to see me thrown out of the house. He's wanted me out of the family since the night I was brought into it.

"You little shit," says Harlan. "You don't deserve the cost of a polygraph. You should be tied up and gagged and peed on like the rabid dog that you are."

The house grows quiet. Finally my father steps in front of me, touches my shoulder and says, "I've lost two sons this summer. I don't know why you did this or what you thought you were accomplishing, but I gave you the world and in one night you've thrown it away. Maybe you should be in prison, but I'm not going to let you do that to your mother or to me. You're leaving tonight. That's your legacy. No jail time. That's my gift to you. Good-bye, son."

"Trey!" Kendra says, running to me and hugging my arm. "I'm so . . . it's just . . ."

Kendra is still crying as I go up to my room and pack a bag. Strangely, I can't get myself to pack anything important; it's as if taking essential items will make this more concrete and trivial items will diminish the reality. I grab underwear, a pair of basketball shoes, two pairs of pants and a jacket. I have a small collection of gold eagles various family members and friends of the family have bestowed on me over the years at Christmas and on birthdays, maybe eight hundred dollars all told, and I slide these into a side pocket of the satchel. I tuck two books in on top of the clothing and zip the bag closed. Outside my bedroom door, my mother slips me four hundred-dollar bills, avoiding my eyes while she mumbles, "Good-bye, Trey."

Downstairs in the kitchen I pick up the keys to the Mustang I've been driving for the past year, but Stone snatches them out of my hand. "Uh-uh. The car stays. Just what you can carry."

"Where am I supposed to go?"

"I don't know, Trey. Just get out of our house."

"Jesus, Stone. You know I didn't do it." I am so scared I can no longer fight back. I feel as if somebody has injected my brain with Novocain.

"If you didn't do it, who did?"

"I don't know, but you know I couldn't have."

"Bullshit. We've been expecting something like this out of you for years."

33. COUNTING THE COCKROACHES IN ESTEVEZ'S PURSE

TREY

I caught up with a fuming Estevez in front of an apartment house just off Rainier Avenue maybe six or eight blocks north of Station 28. I'd been missing in action for almost three hours and had finally connected with her via cell phone.

"Where the hell . . ."

"Don't ask."

"I've been leaving messages for the last hour."

"I . . . uh . . ."

"Don't tell me you don't know how to take the messages off your cell phone?"

"They showed me, but I forgot."

"Is that the best you can come up with?"

"I had a meeting. What have you been up to?"

"Me? I had a wonderful lunch downtown while reading your personnel file."

"I hope you didn't get any mayonnaise on it. Mayonnaise turns brown and stains paper."

"Your account of the man falling out of the building was confirmed by the official reports."

"Thank you for believing me."

"I believed you. I just needed to get all the facts straight and make sure there weren't any contrary opinions floating around."

"So what are we doing here?"

"One of the victims lives upstairs and is expecting us. His name is Luke Roberts."

It was easy enough to tell by the absence of small talk as we traipsed up two flights of stairs that Estevez was furious with me. Estevez worked the metal rapper in the center of the door while I stood back and thought about the contrast between her dusky good looks and India Carmichael's pale beauty, trying to figure out why the contrast had even occurred to me. They were both intelligent, though their patterns of behavior were polar opposites. Estevez was a talker, full of nervous energy, and all her emotions played out on her face like some kind of movie. India preferred to let others do most of the palavering, was cool and less willing to mix it up with anybody who aggravated her; in fact her face rarely gave away any of her feelings. Estevez's coffee-colored skin was so dark and smooth and spotless, you wanted to run your fingertips over it just to see if it was real. I hadn't asked, but suspected that just as I was the result of a white father and a black mother, she was Hispanic and black.

Luke Roberts was a small African-American man in his early twenties, already balding, nervous at seeing me. Estevez said, "This is my partner, Captain Brown of the Seattle Fire Department."

Roberts invited us in, knocking piles of rumpled clothing off two chairs so we'd have a place to sit. There was a hole in the living room wall, a missing kitchen light, a carpet that needed shampooing, and walls that needed scrubbing. I counted five single shoes thrown in the hallway, along with socks and underwear. It was the sort of apartment where I might have counseled young firefighters not to leave their helmets lying around lest they pick up hitchhiking cockroaches, though when Estevez set her bag on the floor, I said nothing. If anyone could benefit from a cockroach in her purse, it was Estevez.

When we were seated, she said, "Captain Brown is most likely the individual who got you out of the club."

"You dropped me out the window?"

"If you got out on the north side second floor, that would have been me. I dropped a number of people out that window."

"Oh, man! I been meaning to thank you. Man, if you hadn't grabbed my ass, I'd still be in there." He leaped across the room and pumped my hand. "Me and my cousin Karl decided we'd go to this club. Supposed to be a happenin' place. Word got around they were going to be open on the weekend, so we got dressed up and went on down.

"I still can't hardly believe he's gone. Karl and me did everything together. Hell, he was living here, paying half the rent. Now I'm going to come up short this month. I'm hoping we get this lawsuit going and I can get me some money out of the old man who owns the place. What's his name? Freddy something?"

"I forget," Estevez said.

"Right. We got lawyers working on it anyway."

"You suing the fire department?" I asked.

"They're going to look into it this week. I think you guys are the greatest. I mean, sure, I had a couple of sprained ankles after that fire, but I'm alive. It weren't for you guys, I'd be with Karl. Still, if the department did something wrong, I deserve the money, don't you think?"

"What happened when you got inside?" Estevez asked.

"Me and Karl paid up. Fifteen bucks a head. Then we went up them stairs, but there weren't many people there yet. It was just after ten, and we were told the place didn't start hopping until midnight. So we were just hanging. At the top of the stairs you turned into this huge old hall, must have been a playhouse at one time. They had electronic music and a DJ, spinning lights. We were just getting ready to go over and talk to some fine-looking bitches when somebody yelled fire. No shit. Just like in the movies. They yelled fire and Karl and me turned around and this big sheet of black smoke had already filled the doorway and began filling the hall. It was moving, man.

"We thought about running back down the way we come in, but a couple of dudes in front of us tried that and came right back coughing their fool heads off. They were only in the smoke a few seconds before they'd turned around. Karl started heading for the stage. I guess he figured there was an exit back there or something. Time we got halfway across the big open dance floor, so much smoke had come in we couldn't see the stage. And if there were any doors anywhere, we couldn't see them, either. I turned around, thinking once more maybe we should head out the way we'd come in, 'cept I couldn't see anything but a bunch of people running from this smoke. So now we're maybe a minute into it and we haven't moved thirty feet."

"How many people were inside when the fire broke out?" I asked.

"The TV said fifty. I didn't stop to count, but there were a lot of people, more than fifty. I still hadn't got myself a good breath of smoke, but everybody who had was coughing, and a couple of dudes was standing in the middle of the floor puking. So Karl says, 'This way,' and heads up these stairs past all these seats. I held my breath until we were on the level above the dance floor. Then all of a sudden Karl was gone. He was there one second and the next second I was by myself. I couldn't hold my breath no longer, so I took a big gulp of this hot smoke I'd been feeling all on my face. That's the last thing I remember, man, until I woke up outside."

"Where outside?" Estevez asked.

"Actually, I was on top of this fat chick on this car. I kind of looked up wondering what the hell happened, because all I could remember was we were getting ready to go to the Z Club, and then this fat chick is saying 'Get off me! Who you? Get your ass off me!' I couldn't move. I was dazed. Finally these two firemen came and picked me up off the car. Got the chick, too, who was still yelling at me. Carried us over in the dark, where they had all these medics and people. Next thing I know I'm in the hospital. Whole thing, from the time we walked through the door until I was in the hospital, couldn't have been thirty minutes. We never even spoke to anybody in the club. I didn't find out until the next day Karl was dead. That's no shit. I came home in the morning expecting him to be here, but he wasn't."

"You see any firefighters inside?"

"Just the guy put me out that window. I guess that was you."

"No other firefighters?"

"Not until I was out in that parking lot."

As he walked us to the door, Roberts gave me an apologetic look. "It's just the lawyers, man. I gotta do what they say. The Z Club committee people got people looking into that fire. They're going to dig out the truth."

"That's what I heard," I said.

Estevez and I went downstairs, where I walked her to my car. "You didn't tell him who we were?"

"I just told him I was with the news."

"How'd you get here?"

"What do you mean, how'd I get here. I took a cab. How do you think I got here?"

"I was just trying to make conversation."

Once we were in my car, she said, "Do you recall Roberts from that night?"

"No."

"But you're the one who saved him?"

"I was the only one lowering people out windows. I remember this woman . . ."

"Yes?"

"Nothing."

"I thought maybe you were in the mood to talk finally."

"I was feeling around for bodies, and this woman grabbed me around the neck. She knew she was going to die if she didn't get out. I was bending over, and I guess she heard me and grabbed me around the neck, pulled my face piece off. I tried to get her to let go so I could get over to the window, but she was fighting me. Hey. I don't want to see this in print."

"You won't."

"I tried to pull her arms off me, but she had that biblical strength people get when they're in a panic. So I head-butted her with my helmet. It was the only thing I could do."

"What happened?"

"She let go and I dragged her to the window. The ladder was full, so I lowered her out by her arms and dropped her like the others. I remember finding this big guy in the smoke right after that. I have a feeling the big guy might have been Roberts's cousin."

34. WATCHING TOO MUCH TELEVISION AGAIN

JAMIE ESTEVEZ

"You were a hero. In fact, just about everybody in the department mentions it. Whatever else you were before that fire, you're a hero now."

"If a civilian with no equipment and no training had run up that ladder and made those rescues, *he* would have been a hero," Trey said. "I was only doing my job."

I didn't want to argue with him, but I couldn't see anybody else accomplishing what he'd accomplished, certainly not a civilian. As a reporter, I'd been in training fires with the Spokane Fire Department, and it was impossible to describe how terrifying it was to be wearing all that heavy gear so that your mobility was restricted, or to know how hot and confusing it actually was inside a fire building until you'd been there.

Once in the confines of Trey's car, I smelled traces of a woman's perfume, a fragrance that definitely hadn't been there earlier. Another woman had been in his car. I was certain of it. I'd smelled that fragrance only one other time in my life—on Stone Carmichael's wife Saturday night. Why is it that men always think they're getting away with something when they're fooling around with somebody else's wife? My boyfriend out of college cheated on me, and even though he swore it hadn't happened and tried the standard male defense of insisting I was crazy, I knew inside twenty-four hours I was right. It was the first but not the last time I'd run up against the fact that where women are concerned, all men have the capacity to become morons.

"I don't know what your history with the mayor's wife is, but if you're planning to do anything her husband doesn't know about, you're playing with fire."

"What are you talking about?"

"I'm just going to say my peace, and then I'll be quiet. If you're doing anything that could bring the mayor's wrath down on you, I want you to stop."

"What I do and who I do it with are none of your business."

"It's very much my business if you compromise this investigation by acting stupid." I watched him for a few moments while he stared at the raindrops splattering against the windshield. It had been cloudy all day, but this was the first rain.

"You don't know what you're talking about."

"Just remember, plenty of men have been killed fooling with other men's wives." He gave me a look like I was crazy—classic guilty male behavior! Then, as if he hadn't already convinced me I was right, he looked away from me, shaking his head and chuckling under his breath in a manner that infuriated me. My guts were churning all out of proportion to the offense, and I was forced to admit to myself that my anger was a product of personal jealousy rather than concern for the investigation. This man was doing more than accusing me of being crazy. He was actually *making* me crazy.

Half an hour later after we went downtown to the fire marshal's office to study the inspection history for the Z Club, I said, "Would you like to have dinner? I mean, maybe we should continue this. There are other people we might interview tonight. They're all in the stations until tomorrow morning, right?"

"I've got someplace I need to be."

There it was. I'd invited him to dinner and he turned me down practically before I had the words out of my mouth. Of course he had things to do. He had people to meet and friends to take care of, women to have affairs with, while I was the workaholic who spent weeknights languishing alone in my condo trying not to watch too much television.

35. FIGHTING FOR YOUR SANITY, LOSING YOUR TEETH

TREY, NINETEEN YEARS AGO

I spent the two loneliest days of my life in a seedy motel in Georgetown across the street from a concrete factory. When I wasn't watching truckers and hookers passing in and out of the adjoining units, I was watching television, surviving on crackers, canned tomato juice, and old sitcoms. I called on an attorney in an office not far from the motel and was given a list of options, none of which offered the salvation I was looking for. He kept telling me a rape conviction could put me away for quite a while. I called my football coach, who *believed* my story and graciously offered to let me sleep on his couch until my affairs were settled.

I kept wondering how my parents could have thought me capable of such a crime.

What I needed, I decided, was to approach family members one at a time and convince each of my innocence.

Having borrowed the rusting Pontiac that was my coach's second car, I drove to the ferry and took it to the island, thinking I would talk to Kendra first. Or India. Convince one of them. Then the other. With allies in tow, I would use the leverage to gain another believer, and then another. It was a harebrained domino theory of resurrection, thwarted by Renfrow's better plan.

It was still August, breezy on the island and now cool enough for a light jacket after dark. I waited until nightfall, parked the borrowed car down the road, then walked toward the estate. At night on the island, things grew quiet quickly.

As I approached the house through a copse of evergreens I didn't see anybody. On the far side of a grassy field, most of the lights were on in the house, and after a while standing in the field by myself, I saw movement in one of the downstairs rooms. It was India, walking past the window, her long blond hair brilliant in the light from a nearby lamp. She appeared to be talking to somebody in the room.

For most of my life I'd been the only black person in any group, and for years it had worked to my benefit. Once I got into athletics and began to excel in a way that drew the attention of sportswriters and college scouts, I became even more of a trick pony, but that evening trying to defend myself against Echo's accusation, I realized race had worked to my detriment. There had been assumptions made about me because of my color that never would have been made about a white boy. Standing in the breeze, I wondered if I hadn't turned a corner; my skin color had worked for me in the first seventeen years of my life, but it might work against me the rest of it.

"You thought we were kidding when we told you to stay away?"

I turned around and saw Barry Renfrow coming out of the evergreens behind me, Renfrow, greasy, rotund, and smug. Beside him were two rough-hewn men in workmen's clothes and work boots. From the way they were standing, I got the feeling these men had been boxers, perhaps retired professionals, and guessed they probably worked for the Overbys in some menial capacity or other.

"Mr. Renfrow?"

"They don't want you here, son. You must know that. Just go away and everything will be all right."

"I came to talk."

"Sure you did, but the talking's all done, son. Just trot your ass out of here."

"Has Echo said anything?"

"I told you to turn around and walk out of here."

"I need to explain."

"You can explain to me, son." The two workmen, one black and one white, had circled me so that they were blocking my path to the house.

"I need to talk to my family," I said and turned around. Before I took two steps, the black worker stepped into my path and hit me on the shoulder. I'd been hit on the football field and occasionally had taken a slam playing basketball, but I'd never really felt anything like this man's fist, which came like a piston exploding out of an engine. "I don't want to fight," I said, holding my shoulder while trying to contain the pain.

"There's a difference between a fight and a beating," the white worker said, stepping forward and swinging on me. I saw it coming and ducked backward, though he caught me across the brow anyway. Unbelievably, the partial blow knocked me off my feet and into the long grass.

When I looked up, Renfrow was standing over me. "You can leave it at this, or you can take some more. Your choice, son."

"I need to go up to the house."

I started to get up, but before I was fully to my feet, the black man hit me hard with a downward motion, driving me to my hands and knees. It was pretty clear now that these men had fists like rocks and that their blows would come at me quicker than I could react.

Renfrow was behind me, the two fighters in front. I rushed the white fighter like a lineman rushing off the line, hoping to grab him around the knees and knock him down, but before I got to him, he hit me on the back of my head and I somersaulted onto the ground, dizzy and seeing stars.

When I looked up, the black guy was standing over me. "Don't do it, kid."

Out the side of my eye, I saw Renfrow walking across the field toward the house as if I didn't exist, tossing a last comment over his shoulder. "Just keep him away from the family." The audacity and assurance in his assumption that I would not make it to the house pissed me off.

I managed to get to my feet before either of them hit me again, dancing, holding my fists in the air as if I knew what I was doing. I'd never had boxing lessons, but I had a feel for it from horsing around in the gym at school. Or thought I did.

The white fighter stood back while I advanced on the black man, who appeared to be in his early forties, his face battered and lumpy, one scarred ear noticeably smaller than the other. I was taller and probably stronger, but his shoulders were wide and he hung his fists at his sides in a way I'd never seen.

I threw a quick punch, which inexplicably missed and then another, which missed, too. Then I threw a couple of combinations. Everything missed. Then, out of nowhere, his fist hit me above the eye and I staggered backward. It felt cold where the blood was running down my brow and into my eye socket. Then the white guy stepped in close and threw a flurry of blows at my head and stomach, six, eight of them, and I fell onto my back, the wind knocked out of me, my lip swelling. The teeth on one side of my face were numb, one eye beginning to swell shut.

"Go away, kid," said the black man.

"That's my family in there." I stood up and was put back down with a blow to my left cheek. I started to get up again and was hit in my back before I could get off the ground. And again.

Toward the end it was the black guy mostly. I didn't realize it at the time, but he was trying to end it with a knockout punch, nailing me with everything he had. I wasn't able to duck; in fact, couldn't see it coming from the left side and only a little from the right, my eyes puffing up badly now. One of them would hit me, and I would go down. Then I would get back up, take a paltry swipe, and somebody would hit me again.

The white fighter said, "Your family doesn't want you. Maybe you should take a hint."

"Who was it?" I said, my words garbled. "Stone?"

"The mother of the girl," said the black guy. "Mrs. Overby. She knew you'd be back. But you better stop getting up, because we don't want to kill you."

There was a smacking noise and the earth came rushing into my face. "Don't get up, kid. We'll drive you back to the mainland. Just don't get up."

Somewhere along the line I lost consciousness for good, because I remembered dreaming and I remembered being driven in a car. The police found me near the rail yards in Seattle and drove me to coach's house. We never did find the Pontiac I'd borrowed. Or the belongings that I had naively stashed in the backseat, thinking I would be going home. I stayed with coach my last year of high school and used the twelve hundred dollars of my savings to pay for the missing car. I couldn't play ball until October, and even then my ribs hurt on every play. It was the year I switched from quarterback to middle linebacker and began taking my aggression out on other teams.

I worked all the next summer in construction for a University of Washington alum who gave players summer work, and in the fall I took a scholarship and moved into a fraternity. Money was tight, but I made out okay. I studied and had girlfriends, though never white ones. I looked up my real mother and found a brother I never knew I had. I established a new life and began looking at white people differently.

36. THE DEAD DESERVE BETTER THAN ME

TREY

After dropping Estevez off at Station 28 and waiting like a gentleman until she was safely in her car, perhaps the only gentlemanly thing I'd done all day, I headed home. I had a lot of thoughts running through my mind, mostly personal, mostly not involving our investigation or the deaths of fourteen innocent people. It exasperated me that my problems were taking precedence over this investigation, that I was bewitched by my personal history and a woman I'd known as a teenager. Jamie Estevez was a hardworking woman who meant well and had taken our assignment to heart in a way that my distracted mental apparatus hadn't been able to. The city deserved better than me. The dead deserved a whole lot better.

It bothered me that Estevez had figured out I was with a woman today, and it bothered me even more that she'd guessed who the woman was. Still, neither of those guesses was as aggravating as her assumption that I was planning to have or was already having an affair with India Carmichael. Had the notion come out of thin air, or had she seen something going on between India and me Saturday night? If so, how had I missed it? And how had she found out about my meeting with India? Was I that easy to read?

Listening to the news on the drive home, I heard about the last memorial service for one of the Z Club fatalities, which like the other services had been attended by a small, uniformed contingent from the fire department. In the middle of the ceremony the brother of the deceased approached one of the firefighters and started cursing him out, then slapped a police lieutenant who tried to intervene. Unfortunately, the lieutenant was not a meek sort and struck back, which immediately incited a melee. According to eyewitness accounts, the police had been forced to use tear gas to disperse an angry crowd outside the church. Things were getting worse instead of better.

When I passed Station 6, a few blocks from my home, two SPD cruisers were parked on the sidewalk in front of the station. A bottle of blue paint had been smashed on the wall beside the front door. Surrounding the totem pole in front of the Douglass-Truth branch library catty-corner from the fire station was a crowd of about forty young people. Though no overt criminal activity was going on, all crowds have a signature, and I didn't like the earmarks of this one. You can tell when people are waiting for a bus by their passive immobility. And just as easily, you can tell when a crowd is spoiling for a fight by the way the players mill about. These kids were ready for combat.

It was all so meaningless. I wasn't sure if they wanted retribution or a sort of street justice only they could define the parameters of, but nothing was going to change the Z Club tragedy or bring any of those people back to life. And nothing the fire department could do in the future would make these people's lives any better.

My home was a few blocks east of Garfield High School in a quiet residential area that had been Jewish until World War II, African American in the fifties, sixties, and seventies. Now it was being gentrified by mostly white couples and gays buying up older homes and remodeling them, which was basically what I was doing, remodeling a home erected in 1913. My brother and mother—my real family—lived in my grandmother's former house eight blocks due west, and my brother walked between the houses several times a day.

My place was on an embankment with a small garage that faced the street, and a porch above that. As usual, Rumble's truck was blocking the driveway in front of the garage. It was a game he played, pretending he didn't think I would want the parking spot, offering to move the truck, all of this after I'd already carted my stuff into the house from half a block away.

I found a parking spot, got my things, and walked through the basement. The paint was peeling on the wall beside the door, just a reminder of things I needed to do when the weather warmed up next year. I left my jacket and boots in the mudroom before going into the family room in the basement. Rumble and I had set up a big-screen television there, where we watched sports, movies, and my old *Fawlty Towers* tapes, and where he and my brother watched porno when I wasn't around.

Rumble and Johnny were standing in the center of the room arguing. "I is too going," Johnny said.

"The hell you are. Trey, try to talk some sense into this knucklehead."

"What's going on?" I said. My brother wore his coat and earmuffs, which was common with him. I turned down the volume on the television.

"He thinks he's going to go out and get himself a new scooter," Rumble said.

"What?"

"A scooter. You know. A Vespa. He's planning to steal it."

"No, I ain't," Johnny said, speaking with so much animation I could barely understand him. "When you get into a riot condition, everything is fair game. I get me a scooter, it's fair game. That's what they said."

"Who said?" I asked.

"Gerald and Randy."

"I told you I don't want you hanging around those two, Johnny. They take advantage of you."

"No. They ain't takin' advantage. I had to beg practically to go with them."

"Where are they going?"

"Going to riot. Leaving right now. All of us going to riot against the man. Time to show the man we ain't takin' this shit no more."

"Ain't takin' what shit?" I said.

"Ain't takin' *this* shit. Ain't takin' it no more. No, sir. Them people in the Z Club wasn't doin' nothing."

"Johnny, you steal a scooter and I'll turn you in myself.

You don't even have a driver's license. You know how many times you've tried to pass the written."

"I ain't takin' no more bullshit from the man."

"You keep up this nonsense, I'll call Mom right now."

"Don't do that. I don't want Mom mad at me."

"You go out and participate in a riot, you'll have the whole city mad at you. Me, Mom—even Rumble here."

"Rumble and me's buddies."

"That's right," Rumble said, sitting in the leather easy chair he'd claimed for himself years ago, picking up the television remote and turning the sound back on. "But we're not going to be buddies if you go out and start throwing bricks with Gerald and Randy. You know both of 'em already spent time in the joint."

"But they said—"

"I don't give a shit what they said. They're going to take that scooter for themselves, and you're going to get arrested."

"I won't get arrested. I'll run."

"You're going to riot better on a full stomach," I said. "Let's have dinner first, huh, Johnny?"

He thought about it and finally said, "Okay, but I still want a scooter."

"You in, Rumble?"

"What? The riot or the dinner?"

"What do you think?"

"What are you making?"

"You want the menu, or are you in?"

"I'm in."

"You two do the salad."

The three of us ate upstairs. During the meal I sneaked away and phoned my mother, explained what was going on and asked her to come get Johnny after dinner. She said she'd been meaning to take him shopping at Southcenter Mall for some new clothes and this would be a good excuse. Before we finished the meal, Mother showed up and after I slipped her three hundred dollars, dragged him whining out to her car. Even though he was over thirty, Mom and I ruled

Johnny—who was developmentally disabled—with an iron hand, a good cop/bad cop routine we'd been honing for years. We switched roles, sometimes two or three times a week, but since our most recent trip to Las Vegas she'd been the bad cop.

After they left, I changed clothes and walked through the TV room on the way out the door past Rumble, who was already planted in front of a football game. I gave him a withering look.

"You're leaving anyway, aren't you? It's not like football's going to contaminate your TV."

"Back in a couple of hours."

"Okay. I might go home and see if the dog's still alive."

"Good idea."

If there were riots in the Central Area when I left Seattle, I didn't see any evidence of them, though police cruisers were everywhere.

I headed toward Tacoma, the next port city south of Seattle and the second largest city in the state. During the hour of freeway driving I listened to CDs of Ray Charles and Patti LaBelle when I wasn't listening to the news broadcasts advising Seattle-ites to stay indoors.

India's sister lived in a shabby area in south Tacoma, two blocks off Pacific Avenue just shy of Parkland, an indication that Echo and her husband John Armstrong were clearly not doing as well as the rest of the family. According to India, Armstrong had worked at five or six businesses and had run several into the ground, then had gone through personal bankruptcy, and was now running a crew of illegal immigrant painters for his old man's real estate operations. A lot of Overby operations skirted the precise letter of the law one way or the other.

It was dark by the time I got to Tacoma, and it took a while to locate their place, a ramshackle house in need of paint, planted in a yard full of tall weeds.

37. KISS EARTHLING!!! HEE.HEE.HEE!!!

TREY

There were a lot of possible reactions that Echo might have had seeing me in her doorway, but she chose the one I would not have guessed in a million years: nonchalance.

Stepping back onto a worn carpet, she waved me in as a dog barked in the rear of the house and children squealed behind a closed door. Echo gave me one of those half smiles you're not quite sure actually is a smile and turned her head toward the dog. "Bertrand, shut up!"

I wasn't sure what to say. I should have planned something.

"Let me go quiet the kids. I'll be right back."

Echo stepped down a corridor to the rear of the house, opened a bedroom door, and spoke in hushed tones to children who'd been shaking the walls with their rampaging. The house was shabby, the carpets threadbare, but it was immaculate.

Coming back into the living room, Echo invited me to sit on the sofa and took a chair nearby, crossing her legs in a way that reminded me of two pieces of licorice wrapped together. She wore baggy paisley pants that could have been mistaken for pajamas and a midriff-revealing sweater. She was thin and full-breasted like her sister, although she had lost any trace of the elegance she had been growing into when I last knew her at fifteen. Back then, Echo and India looked and moved like tall, coltish sisters, yet these days you'd be hard-pressed to believe they came from the same town, much less the same family.

She had six or eight studs or rings of various sizes and shapes in each ear, a square stud in the tip of her tongue and probably more metal in places I didn't want to think about, tattoos on her slim stomach, and a large blue-and-red devil ran down her left ankle like a dripping candle. Saturday night her hair had been a calculated mess, but since then she'd shaved half her head and colored what was left blue and orange. There were a lot of ways to conceal the fact that you had slipped into the bowels of the lower middle class, but playing at being an artist was one of the most time-honored. Echo had fallen almost as far from her family's social rung as I had from mine. It was hard to imagine she'd at one time attended private schools with an annual tuition greater than my yearly salary.

On India's recommendation I'd looked her up on the Internet and found Echo had been mentioned on numerous websites devoted to performance artists around the world. She'd put out several CDs and had traveled to England and Australia, where she performed in clubs, playing flute, tambourine, bongos, and tenor sax, and putting on shows with slides, nude dancers of both sexes, magicians, fire-eaters, and other assorted gimmicks, including a trio of shaved dogs. I'd read about a contest where a private concert by the World Famous Echo Armstrong was awarded as a prize. The winner wrote a narrative on the Web explaining how Echo Armstrong had sung down his throat for twenty minutes, a new form of music she'd invented that she called a "kiss from another galaxy," wherein she fitted her lips around the lucky winner's mouth and sang music into his lungs and diaphragm. It was, I was fairly certain, an experience one probably had to endure in order to fully appreciate. The Echo I remembered had been timid, easily amused, and remarkably insecure, and the thought of blowing songs down a stranger's throat would have sent her fleeing.

"Tea? Beer? You want a joint? We have some dynamite grass."

"Uh, no, thanks."

"It was interesting to see you Saturday night, Trey. We heard a rumor you played football, and then we heard another one that you were a bouncer in a nightclub in New Orleans. Later somebody said you were in Angola for killing a pimp in a fight."

"Never been to New Orleans. Never been to jail, either."

"We, uh . . ." For the first time since my arrival I realized my presence was making her jittery. "We don't really have the money to attend a party like the one Saturday night. We got in free."

"So did I."

"I mean, most of those people paid five thousand dollars to get through the door, as if that was even possible on our budget. I wore one of India's old dresses. She only wears stuff once." She looked around the room, trying to see it through my eyes.

"John at work?"

"He has a friend who owns a security company, and he subs when people call in sick. He's usually back by midnight so he can get up at six and plan his day with the paint crews. The worst part on Saturday night for John was how bad you made him look in front of the family."

"I tried not to hurt him."

"I noticed that and I appreciate it."

"I never hurt you either, Echo."

"Okay. Sure. Great. If you came here to talk about that, I guess I'll come right out and say what I have to say. I could have looked you up to tell you this, but I just haven't gotten around to it. You and I both know you never hurt me. I admit that. I should have admitted it a long time ago. I don't know why I ever said you did, and I've felt ashamed for blaming you ever since the words were out of my mouth. I came so close to retracting them that night. But I didn't. We both know you didn't hurt me. I just wish the whole thing had never happened. Any of it." She started crying and then grew quiet, and for the first time since I arrived, her soft blue eyes, which had been flitting about, fixed themselves on mine, as if begging me to stare into her soul and recognize the need for absolution. "Can you ever forgive me?"

"You weren't raped?"

"No, I was. But it was somebody else."

"Why did you lie?"

"It's a long story, and to tell you the truth, I'm not even sure why."

"Because I'm black?"

"No, no. It was never anything like that. I am just so sorry."

"Sorry enough to tell everyone it wasn't me?"

"I'd like to, but I can't. There are considerations you don't know about."

"Tell me about them. Help me understand."

"I can't."

"Considerations such as who really attacked you, and what he has over you that made you lie in the first place?" When she didn't respond, I continued, "I don't expect you to take out a full-page ad in *The New York Times* or anything, but it would be decent of you to tell a few specific people. I don't expect to see her again, but it would ease my mind to know your mother didn't hate me. And my father."

"And my father?"

"I don't give a damn about him."

"It must have been so awful for you to be alone for all these years."

"I wasn't alone. I found my real mother. And a brother I didn't know I had. And then I joined the fire department, where I have nine hundred and fifty brothers and sisters." Before either of us could say anything else, two small boys came screaming into the living room, the smallest diving into his mother's lap, the second boy hot on his brother's heels. They looked remarkably similar to Echo's husband. The boy in her lap sat up and ran a plump hand across the shaved portion of his mother's skull wonderingly, and then she took them back into the bedroom while I waited.

The mantel was thick with photos and awards. She'd won awards in college for playing the violin. There were photos of Echo performing in small clubs, two trophies for pistol marksmanship bestowed to John Armstrong, and a ribbon one of her sons had earned in first grade—trophies that proved these people had lived and had passions and cared enough to collect the residue of their days.

"I'm sorry about that," Echo said, returning to the room, where she sat in the same chair, wrapping her legs together again in the same manner. "It's bedtime and they're getting cranky. It's . . . my life has gone in directions I didn't think it would, but by and large I'm pleased with it. I hope you are with yours, too. I hope I didn't ruin too much of it."

"What you did mostly was demolish my faith in human nature."

"Yes. Well, human nature's never been much."

"Are you going to tell my father I'm not guilty?"

"I have to think about it. This isn't easy for me, you know."

"If it was, you would have come to me before I came to you."

"Exactly."

"You're not going to tell me what really happened that night, are you?"

"It's too embarrassing. And it would hurt other people."

As I drove toward Seattle on the freeway, I found myself in a kind of time warp. Seeing Echo so far removed from the past, where she'd been stuck in my brain all these years, was bizarre to say the least. She had a story to tell but wasn't telling it, just as she hadn't told it nineteen years ago.

38. DOWNSTAIRS UPSTAIRS

COOPER HENDRICKSON, Z CLUB SURVIVOR

We're in the Z Club maybe an hour when Limogene decides to go outside and have a smoke. I don't use tobacco products, but she does, so we're headed down the stairs when Limo meets these two chicks she knows from beautician school. We start rapping, and then the cat who was guarding the door and collecting tickets comes running up past us. I told all this to the cops a million times already.

I'm standing with my back to the stairs when he runs past and we hear the sound of glass breaking. The girls start waving at me to turn around, and when I do there's smoke flowing up the stairs. They're telling me to go down and see what's happenin', so I walk over to the stairs and peek around, and just about the time I get there this big ball of flame starts rising up the stairwell, burning up all these old posters and billboard sheets on the walls. I can feel the heat on my face. I still got no eyebrows. Check it out.

So I turn around to run, and that's when I realize I'm having a hard time outrunning it. This shit is just roaring up the stairs at me, flames coming around my ears and black smoke racing in front of me until I almost can't see where I'm going. I didn't know fire could move that fast. Faster than I was running. Burns all the hair on the back of my neck and melts my jacket to my shirt. I race past Limogene and her friends so fast I'm ashamed.

Anyway, they catch me up, and the four of us are running into the main hall shouting "Fire!" and there's a bunch of cats standing there looking at us like we're nuts. One of them saunters toward the stairwell to see for himself, you know, like he's going to make me look bad by going back the way I came, even though you can already see this black smoke coming through the doorway. For some reason I can't explain to this day we stop to watch him. Maybe because his reaction is so cool and he's so certain we're dumb shits that for just a few seconds there, I am beginning to doubt my own sanity, you know, like, maybe there really isn't any fire. Or maybe I just want to see him get his ass burned. So this cat gets maybe five feet past the doorway toward the stairs, and the next thing I know he's running to save his ass, too. Runs clean across the dance floor, past us, past the DJ, and into the back behind the stage. Leaves all his friends. Turns out later he was one of the dead cats they found at the bottom of the stairs.

Limogene and I don't know what to do. You can see this

big orange ball of flame poking out the top of the stairs, the whole place filling up with smoke. Limo's girlfriends split, so we didn't have them to think about. They both make it out, too. We kind of run around looking for somebody who knows what's what, but there isn't nobody. Everybody coughing. The girls screaming. A couple of guys shouting orders that don't make sense.

It doesn't take but a minute for the hall to fill up with this black smoke. In less than a minute—I think it was less than a minute—it's banking down so we are breathing it. And then it starts to get real hard to see.

Limogene says, "Let's follow him," meaning the guy who ran behind the stage. So we follow the cat onto the stage, both of us thinking there must be an exit behind the curtains, else in the old days how would the actors get in and out? It's smoky up on the stage, but we end up going down this dark flight of stairs. Go down so far I'm afraid we're going into the basement. It's pitch-black, and the only lights we have are from cigarette lighters, and this guy has an Indiglo watch he's using to see his way. Somebody says careful with that cigarette lighter, bud, you don't want to start a fire. Everybody laughs, and we all feel like we know each other after that. Not too much smoke down there at first. When we get to the bottom there are about ten of us. The doors are locked.

We think we're going to have time to figure it out, but after a couple of minutes nobody is figuring out shit. A couple of people call out on their cells, man, but what good does that do? This girl talking to her grandmother, telling her to call 911 when she could have called it her own-self.

Then the smoke starts banking down the stairs. Somebody who works there—one of the owners, I think—says the door is locked because people used to sneak in without paying. A couple of people go back up the stairs to try their luck, and we start to do that, too, but it's smokier than shit, and halfway up, Limo—well, she has asthma from when she was a kid and she's a little heavy and I suppose her tobacco use doesn't help—so her getting back up them stairs is about impossible. I tell her to stay there and I'll go look for another way out.

So I go back up them stairs with Limo telling me not to leave her and me telling her it's going to be okay, and we're both knowing I'm talking out my butt. If I could live anything over in my life it would be the moment I decided to leave her.

I go up them stairs, and it is so smoky on the main floor now I can barely tell where I'm walking, and it's starting to get real hot. There is nobody around. I mean, nobody. It's spooky. We go down and there is a shitload of people, and when I get back up, I'm alone. After a while I hear some people moving and coughing, but they were a long way off and they sound like they're crawling or something.

I go across the back of the stage, and there is this door which I figure is a closet or a dressing room or something, and I try to open it but somebody is pushing on it from the other side. Finally I jack it open, get my leg in there and force it, and there are like six or eight people in this tiny room, and they are all yelling out this window for the fire department to come and get them, and somebody slams the door behind me because they don't want all the smoke to come in.

After a while the fire department puts a ladder up and starts helping us down. Some girl firefighter up there helping us onto the ladder one at a time, everybody pushing and shit. For some reason I'm the last one out. After I get to the street, I start telling them about Limogene, and they ask me where the stairs are, but by that time I'm so turned around I don't have a fuckin' clue.

So they take me to some chief, and he tells these two firefighters to take me around the building to look for the stairs. Big crowd at this point, talking shit to the firefighters, grabbing at the two guys I'm with. I have to tell cats to leave them alone, these guys were trying to help me find Limogene.

So we go to the back side of the building, and there's firefighters and ladders and people with broken legs laying on top of cars. And there's Limogene's friends from beautician school, and I ask if they've seen Limo, but one of them's got a bone poking out of her leg and doesn't want to do anything but wail. I can't blame her.

When we find the stairs, the doors are open, and Limogene and everybody else is gone. So now I'm thinking she got out and she's looking for me while I'm looking for her and we're in this circle-jerk thing. So I go around the building the opposite of the way we came, and I see a couple of chicks who got out, but I don't see her. I remember where we parked, and I go look at the car to see if maybe she's been there, but nothing seems disturbed. I'm starting to get frantic. Limogene is the person who kept me sane when I was in Lompoc.

After about a half hour of watching the fire and using my cell to call her home and her mom's home, I call the hospital, where they say they won't give out names. So I'm talking to some fire officer, and he tells me a couple of the people they found at the bottom of the stairs are dead. He don't know which ones, but a couple. By that point I'm starting to go nuts, so I get with my friend Jarvis and we head down to the hospital. They tell us, yeah, there's some dead folk ain't been identified, and we can look at 'em if we think we know them. So we do. These are the first dead people I ever saw. Limogene's the last one. It's like she's asleep or something, just laying there in her blue dress with her eyes closed, a little bit of soot around her nostrils.

39. HAND TO MOUTH

JAMIE ESTEVEZ

Trey has been so pleasant and easy to get along with all morning, I'm beginning to wonder why I lost sleep last night worrying about him. It's my turn to drive, so I've been ferrying us from one firehouse to another as we interview firefighters. I'm hoping my nervousness will go away and that I don't snap at him as I have so many times over the past few days, because I'm beginning to get concerned at what he could perceive only as my unremitting foul humor.

Today we've managed to talk to four firefighters who were at the Z Club, but we covered mostly old ground. They were all working as hard as they could fighting the fire and none had been involved in any rescues or seen any civilians inside. After finishing with the firefighters, we spoke to Cooper Hendrickson, who told us how his girlfriend died. Cooper is twenty-eight but still lives with his mother, along with two grown brothers and a sister and her two children, in a falling-down house between Rainier Avenue and Lake Washington—a house just far enough down the wrong side of the hill to depress its real estate value. Judging by the way his mother and sister were dressed, cash was in short supply. When we showed up mid-morning, Hendrickson and his sister had been glued to the TV watching *The Price Is Right.*

Hendrickson's grief over his girlfriend seemed genuine. He had the attitude of someone with less education than street time and the mien of a man who'd spent some years in stir: a man determined not to let society co-opt any more years of his life. From his testimony I got a hint of the panic and hopelessness of those inside the Z Club, and I realized it was a miracle more people didn't die. Unless some court deemed the fire department negligent, it was unlikely, I thought, that he would collect any money from the city for his girlfriend's death.

Now we were on our way to Mercer Island, where the housing prices were as elevated as they were depressed in Hendrickson's neighborhood.

As Trey sat beside me in the passenger seat, he appeared almost as relaxed as I was tense, a contrast that for some reason made me see red. I didn't enjoy the constant tension between us. It made me furious that he didn't seem affected by it while I could barely squeeze an intelligent word out of my mouth and that he was casually commenting on the traffic around us while I had a death grip on the steering wheel.

"What did you think of Hendrickson?" I asked.

"I used to play ball with him at the Garfield Gym."

"He didn't mention it."

"He gave me a little head nod when we came in. A couple

of years ago he stopped playing, and a little later he and his brother knocked off a couple of grocery stores for drug money and got caught. I don't think he's been out long."

"Were you friends?"

"Not so you would notice. He hung with a pretty tough crowd. Having attorneys ask him to join in a multimillion-dollar lawsuit against the city must have been a dream come true."

"You don't really believe that?"

"You didn't see his eyes light up when he talked about it?"

"He lost his girlfriend."

"I don't doubt he feels bad about that, but that doesn't change the fact that if things go well, he'll probably end up with a good chunk of change."

"I'd forgotten there were rescues from the A side of the building. Ten victims, I believe. That's the side he went out. His girlfriend must have died at the bottom of the stairs."

"If I'd remembered that staircase, she'd be alive. It was tough facing him knowing that."

"That's not what I meant."

"Whatever you meant, I felt like crap looking into his eyes and knowing if I'd given one simple order his girlfriend would be alive."

"It was dark. There were doors with no knobs on the outside and they were painted the same color as the wall. It was years since you'd been inside. Others at the fire had inspected it, too, but none of them remembered the doors. You'd already been working fifteen hours. You can't expect miracles. It wasn't your fault. Besides, nobody in the Seattle Fire Department had ever done anything quite like what you did at the Z Club. I've heard that over and over."

We were halfway across the Mercer Island floating bridge when I said, "Do you think Fish hasn't been showing up for work because he doesn't want to talk to us?"

"I think his daughter's sick."

"Or maybe it has something to do with your snide comments about his promotion."

"You want me to leave that out of the conversation today?"

"That would be nice." Trey grinned. A moment later, I added, "Do you think he's planning to retire?"

"My guess is somebody who presides over a fire where fourteen people died doesn't want to hang around any longer than necessary."

"I hope you don't feel that way. That the rest of your career is tainted?"

"What? Do you have a blank space in your notes where my story is supposed to go? Your obsessive-compulsive nature beginning to get the best of you?"

"I'm not obsessive-compulsive."

"Why are all your paragraphs numbered?"

"I do that for . . . okay, maybe I'm a little—"

"Why does the inside of your purse look like it just passed a military inspection. Why are all the CDs in your car in alphabetical order?"

"Okay, okay."

Chief Fish lived on the east side of Mercer Island in a plush neighborhood of homes on big lots, most with views of the Cascade Mountains, which had not received their first dusting of snow yet this year. Below, we could see a slash of Lake Washington and a hill across the East Channel dotted with housing and commercial property. Fish's house was sprawling, two and a half stories with a three-car garage and a workshop. The yard was low maintenance, beauty bark and junipers.

"You been here before?" I asked.

"No."

"You going to be good?"

"Maybe."

"No, I mean it. Because I don't want this to turn into a wrestling match."

"You're in charge."

Chief Fish met us at his front door, looking just as slight and vitamin-deficient in civilian clothes as he had in the oversize white chief's shirt I'd seen him in on Friday. His hair was limp but his handshake was warm and friendly. "Beautiful home," I said.

Fish looked around the yard and said, "I had to take out most of the garden. Joyce did the yard work, but I couldn't keep it up after she was gone."

We went inside, where he seated us in a sumptuous living room overlooking the Cascades. There'd been a riot in the Central District late last night, and Fish wanted to talk about it. Trey told him a series of gangs had been running through parts of the Central Area throwing rocks, breaking windows, spray painting slogans onto the walls of businesses and city properties. Eighteen youths were arrested, scores more injured in conflicts with police, a Honda dealership looted. There'd been talk of a curfew, but it hadn't yet been instituted.

"I heard Medic One's vehicle had rocks thrown at it while they were treating a cop on Cherry," said Fish.

"I heard that, too. Somebody threw eggs at Engine Twenty-eight, but that's becoming an everyday occurrence."

Fish said, "Maybe they should egg it themselves at roll call just to confuse the natives."

Trey didn't respond. It might have been Fish's reference to "natives." Some people were supersensitive to word choices like that, though I didn't have a handle on whether Trey was one of them.

After an uncomfortable silence, Trey said, "Last night around midnight, Engine Twenty-eight went out on a false alarm and somebody threw rocks at them. Garretson chased some kid two blocks through backyards, and when he finally collared him, the kid wanted to fight. He was about thirteen. A bunch of the neighbors heard the commotion and came out in their pajamas. Garretson said he thought they were going to beat the hell out of him. While this was going on, some other kid broke the windshield and one of the side windows on the engine with a baseball bat."

"Jesus," said Fish.

"Maybe we should get this moving," I said. "I don't want to take up any more of your day than we have to, Chief Fish."

"Sure. Why not? I've got my notes here, so I know where we left off. I've been thinking about this since we spoke, and what it boils down to was we had three different operations going on at the Z Club. The first was fighting the fire. The second was a series of rescues: the Hispanic kids, which turned out to be bogus, the partygoers on the second floor, ten of whom came out the window on the A side and twenty or so on C, and then the attempted rescue of Vernon Sweeting. The third operation was the handling of the patients. The multiple casualty incident.

"What happened after Captain Brown here put up the ladder on the C side and started making rescues was that we got word Ladder Twelve had left Sweeting inside. Right away we organized a group to back them up and sent crews in on A. I wasn't comfortable with that, because the fire was going pretty good, but in the end it didn't matter, because the rescue team came right back out. It was just too hot. I still wonder what happened that caused us to lose a man. I've talked to Acting Lieutenant Rudolph at length. You come out of a building with your crew, you count heads.

"At twenty-three seventeen hours we declared it a defensive fire for the second time. I sure as hell didn't want to do it since Sweeting was in there and there was the possibility of making more rescues, but I wasn't about to lose more firefighters, either. When I got word from Captain Brown that he'd been forced out of the second floor, I knew it was time. We set up monitors and every ladder pipe we could get and did our damnedest to drown the thing. We didn't have any hope of getting more people out by then. We knew it had ceased being a rescue situation and turned into a body recovery. Between the medical group and all the units we were calling in for the fire, we had half the city on site. We drowned it pretty good, but in a building that old, there are lots of hidden spaces.

"We declared a tapped fire at zero three hundred hours. Started taking bodies out at zero five hundred. I had one group climbing through the rubble marking dangerous spots and bodies with glow sticks and ribbon, and another group removing the corpses under the supervision of the police department and our fire investigators.

"By that time we had newspeople from all over the city. They were beginning to show up from the national news outlets, too, stringers for NPR and ABC and all of them. It turned into a three-ring circus. You get that many dead at a fire scene . . . it's just . . . well . . . I had three firefighters assaulted that night. That's where it started, really, I think. All this anger we're seeing. It started at the fire, and it's never really gone away. Anyhow, that's my statement. Questions?"

"I have one," I said. "If you had to do it over again, what would you do differently?"

"I wouldn't come to work."

Trey laughed and it broke the tension, causing Chief Fish to smile at his own lame joke. I said, "How about the dispatch tape from the man on the cell phone saying firefighters were bypassing him?"

"I'm willing to bet that was somebody who was so panicked he didn't know what he was seeing. Either that or he actually got rescued and now isn't coming forward to acknowledge the fact. You know the cell phone was stolen, so they can't trace it to the owner."

"Chief?" I said, after we'd all been silent a few seconds. "How much of the manpower used on Vernon Sweeting was diverted from the rescues on the second floor?"

"I know what you're getting at, but we had ten people looking for Sweeting, and while they were inside, they would have brought out any civilians they found, too. But they didn't find any civilians. And they didn't find Sweeting, either. Besides, the whole thing folded up inside of a few minutes. In fact, I have the timeline right here. The log of the dispatch tapes. The Mayday was called at twenty-two forty-seven hours, and the rescue group was withdrawn at twenty-two fifty-seven hours. Barely ten minutes."

"The thing of it is, Chief," I said, "you have one company making rescues and two or three companies searching for Sweeting."

"And?"

"And Vernon Sweeting was white. The victims on the second floor were black."

Fish turned to Trey Brown and for a few moments it was as if I ceased to exist, all their years of working together in a violent and dangerous profession providing them a bond I was not part of. "Is that how they're looking at it?" Fish asked. "Is that really how the black community is seeing this?"

"I'm afraid it is."

"But they know we don't operate that way, don't they?"

"They don't know anything," Trey said. "Not now."

On the drive back into Seattle, Trey and I were quiet until we drove into the tunnel that extended from the west end of the floating bridge. Inside the tunnel, I said, "Didn't he have ten men looking for Sweeting and only you and two helpers to drag out twenty some victims?"

"It's more complicated than that."

"Explain it to me."

"To start off with, we were on the back side, sure, pulling people out, but I'm not so certain more firefighters back there would have made much difference. They put a ladder up to one other window, and all they got was flame. And the rest of the windows couldn't be laddered because of parked cars. We had people breaking into vehicles and trying to roll them away so we could get another ladder up, but it took . . ."

"What? Manpower?"

"Yeah."

"And all the manpower was on the other side of the building?"

"I still don't think we would have saved anybody else. That's just my opinion."

A few minutes later Trey suggested stopping for lunch at Borracchini's, a long-standing family-owned bakery and deli, a reminder of when this area was mostly Italian-American and known as Garlic Gulch. We ordered from the deli and took a small round table in a corner of the crowded shop. Within minutes I'd picked a fight about whether the Republicans had an effective national political strategy. Fortunately, or unfortunately, depending upon how you looked at it, he got a call on his cell phone and went outside to talk privately. I had the feeling it was India Carmichael. Call it intuition.

40. IT'S STILL IN MY LOCKER IF YOU WANT TO SEE IT

CAPTAIN FRANK ZIMMER, ENGINE 13, C SHIFT

I hope you don't mind if I smoke, because I really don't think well without a pipe in my hands. The guys say it's Freudian, but they say that about everything I do. As I was saying, we're going to miss Chief Fish. It took a while to figure him out. He's always been kind of an odd duck. Even back when he was a firefighter, the old guys tell me he never quite fit in. He admitted once he barely knew his wife when she was alive, that he spent all his spare time in the basement shop and he'd never met half of her friends and didn't pay attention to the other half. All I know is he treated us like kings. He worked here almost five years, and I don't think I saw him angry once.

As far as the Z Club goes, Engine 28 was out of service when the call came in, so Engine 33 was first in and we were second. Engine 30 showed up behind us. First thing, he had us mask up and go through the doorway on side A. We went in, but there was too much smoke to see much, and Voepel and I got tangled up in all this wire. Must have fallen out of the ceiling, is all we could figure. That was scary, because for a few minutes we were really tangled. We were looking for this Mexican girl who, it turned out, was outside the whole time.

Ladder 12 was in there with us, and that was when Vernon Sweeting went missing. We left the building first, so I don't have any idea how that happened.

After the first search, we were assigned to set up two lines on the A side. It took us a while to stretch the lines and get water to them.

It was about then that Fish asked me to do a three-sixty of

the building. So I go around to side D, where Engine 33 is. Engine 30 has come in behind them and is setting up. Three guys are on Engine 33's line. They're in the foyer of the building, and the whole thing is orange. They've got their line on straight stream, and nothing the line hits seems to have any effect. We know the arsonist used Molotov cocktails, and we know he threw at least one on the main floor through the front door, because Marshal 5 found the telltale char pattern on the floor afterward. Man, it was really burning. I went around to the C side, and at that time—I think Engine 28 was just arriving—it was all dark back there. Just a row of cars parked up alongside the building. No windows that I could see. Hardly any smoke.

When I get back to the A side, there's these two trees on fire on the parking strip next to the building, but my guys are getting water on them. And I'm hearing some civilian saying there are people inside. We ask them how they know, and they say they just know. No reason. Well, we'd just established that there wasn't anybody inside. Right about then McMartin comes out the front door alone. I think, like a lot of firefighters in that position, he couldn't quite believe he'd really lost his partner.

So flame is coming out of the lower windows along the street on side A, and we're pouring water through them when some guy up on the second floor flags us down. Turns out there are people inside after all, but they're on the second floor. We put up a ladder and take ten victims out the window. That was when Voepel and I thought we'd better take a line through the window and look for more victims.

We get the line up, and you know how much work it is to take a charged line up a ladder. Me and Voepel go through the window, which puts us in this little room, and we open the door, and it is just nothing but this really hot black smoke and fire. Melted my helmet shield. It's still in my locker if you want to see it.

We were only up there a few minutes before the chief made us come back down.

Losing Sweeting goofed us all up. Sweeting . . . Jesus.

41. WHEN YOU READ PEOPLE LIKE I READ PEOPLE

VINCENT TULLEY, Z CLUB FIRE WITNESS—
NOW DECEASED

It's Friday night, and I'm getting ready to take Barney Fife for a walk when I spot a man loitering across the street in front of the old dance hall on the corner. Sensing trouble, I grab my cell phone and give the cat a little pat before hooking up Barney's leash. It is a beautiful night, and if I'm heedful, we can get back before the start of the *Frontline* piece they're doing on airline safety.

Sure enough, down on the corner the young man continues to loiter in front of the old dance hall. Barney's watering a maple tree, and then I look up and the guy's talking to some kid on the front steps of the dance hall. I don't know what this guy's game is, but I didn't work the ferries for thirty-five years without cultivating the ability to read strangers at a glance. In my sixty-two years I've witnessed several crimes and been to court to testify against people twice, so I'm always on the alert for nut jobs.

Barney's doing his business, and all of a sudden there's a fire across the street, by golly, right in front of the young man, who just stands and looks at the flames, and then pulls out a cell phone and starts waving it around.

Except, when I get closer, it's not a cell phone after all. I'm pretty sure it's a gun. Probably a toy. I have a sense about these things. So I get on my cell and call 911 and finally get put through to fire, and they ask me a bunch of questions, and by this time he is walking away, and I'm thinking, What the bejesus. You're a witness. Get back and do your civic duty.

You let people get away with the little stuff, next thing you know they're up to their eyeballs in the big stuff. I don't let people cut in front of me in checkout lines, and I don't let people talk during the opera, and I'm not planning to let this young man get away without giving a full report to the fire department.

So Barney Fife and I do a quick jog-trot across the street and intercept him in a spot where it's particularly dark because not all the streetlamps are working, even though I sent in a complete list of the outages in our neighborhood more than six months ago. I catch him quickly because his pants are halfway down to his knees, like they wear them these days, and hobbled like that, he can barely walk, holding up his trousers with one hand.

I find it best to get right to the point with malefactors. If you're as tall as I am, you stand close, too, because that intimidates them. Especially the young, who are easily intimidated by my deep basso voice.

"Hey you, mister. You've committed a crime leaving the scene," I say.

"Fuck you!" he says.

"Go back and make it right. You can't just walk away."

"Watch me, motherfucker."

"That's just . . . you know, that kind of talk . . . that's just not necessary."

There's a busload of witnesses in front of us when I tug on his jacket trying to get him to stop, and he turns around and whips out the toy gun and sticks it in my chest. "Outa my life, motherfucker."

"That language is just . . ."

And then there's an explosion and something hits me in the face, and as I lie there I realize the object that hit me in the face is the sidewalk. And that's when I hear the bus drive past. It just drives away as if I'm not lying here on the germ-laden sidewalk with Barney licking my ear. Could it be that I've had a minor stroke like my brother, Ambrose? I'm going to need a shower before *Frontline,* because there are millions, if not billions, of germs on your average sidewalk.

I don't know how many minutes have gone by, but I'm trying to get up when I hear the siren. A vehicle door opens and closes. I hear what sounds like a police radio. A man is next to me on the sidewalk, his voice laced with command. In a small way, it helps cut through the confusion. "You awake, buddy?"

42. TREY SPILLS NO TEARS

JAMIE ESTEVEZ

Somehow, miraculously, Trey and I have come to the conclusion that the best thing to do tonight is to dine at my place over a plate of pasta while we talk things over. He's drawn a series of maps and graphs, intricate scenarios of the building and the fire ground on Mylar sheets so that one sheet can be laid on top of another: a timeline of sorts, each sheet in ten-minute increments in the beginning, and then thirty-minute increments for the duration of the fire. It's incredible work and gives me a picture of the fire as it unfolded, and as I glance at it in the car, I wonder if he might not have made a good living as a graphic artist. Along with the Mylar drawings, he's composed a list of every firefighter who was at the fire and carefully charted their positions, as far as we know them. All I can figure is he's been up all night working on this, because much of this information we gleaned only yesterday. And I thought he wasn't taking our work seriously.

Wednesday night we visited the partially demolished Z Club, a pilgrimage I'd been putting off almost as sedulously as Trey, for we'd been passing within two blocks of it every day. The Z Club was in Columbia City, a multicultural neighborhood, originally a mill town, which had fallen into disrepair by the seventies but had recently been undergoing extensive renovation and rebuilding.

As would be expected, all that was left of the Z Club was a mere shell, the tallest standing walls on the west and north sides. The east side, where the front door and the stairs had been, was leveled almost to the street, so that it resembled a burned-out garage rather than a building that had once been fully enclosed. The only intact portion of the roof was tilted at a crazy angle. Astonishingly, even after three weeks the area reeked of smoke and char.

The parking lot was filled with pyramids of debris and three enormous Dumpsters heaped with charred wood, burned furniture, and artifacts from the fire. Yellow crime-scene tape surrounded what was left of the building, as did a temporary Cyclone fence. What really surprised me, even though I'd seen the news reports, was the plethora of flowers, cards, and beribboned trees. Offerings of teddy bears, dolls, carnations, helium-filled balloons, handwritten notes, gift cards, and other paraphernalia overflowed the site like an infestation, filled up most of the small parallelograms in the Cyclone fencing, and even showed up a block away on telephone poles, trees, and parked cars. Everywhere, we could smell flowers along with the char.

We got out of Trey's car and stood looking at the rubble, neither of us moving. Finally Trey said, "It's overwhelming, isn't it?"

"I thought you might feel differently, since you were here when it happened."

"Why would that be?"

"I just thought there might be something else in your head."

"My head is full of dead bodies. That's what my head's full of."

"Hard to believe so many people have visited." Even as I spoke, a large Ford cruised up the narrow street, the occupants craning their necks to view the wreckage of the Z Club. They stopped in the intersection for a few moments, noticed us, and moved on. They were white. We were black. Maybe that had something to do with their leaving. Everybody we'd spoken to in the past two days had mentioned the black-white thing. Every morning in the papers there were angry letters to the editor on both sides of the issue, and the local radio talk shows were buzzing with it.

It had rained, and the sky was damp with clouds.

Trey walked me around the building, showing me where the command post had been, where Engine 33 came in and set up the first hose lines, where Engine 13 parked, and where Engine 28 had ended up in the rear behind the parking lot now filled with debris.

"We came in from Rainier," Trey said. "Clyde was driving pretty fast. Usually we do a search, but on one side of the building they couldn't get through the flames and on the other they were driven out by the heat. Then there were all those parked cars behind the building. I wasted a minute or two trying to get some cops to get the civilians out of our hair. They'd been harassing Engine 33, but the smoke started coming out that door and it pushed all the civilians toward us. Finally I told this one guy it was a federal offense to hinder a firefighter at a fire scene."

"Is it?" I asked.

"I don't think so. He thought his brother was inside. He said he was either in Wenatchee or in there. I called the IC and asked if anybody'd searched the second floor, but I couldn't get through on the radio. Too much air traffic. That's the way it is at a big fire. One person gets on the air for whatever reason, nobody else can use the channel. It's like a big party line where only one person can talk at a time."

"What'd you do?"

"You want it all now, standing here in the dusk, maybe rain coming on?"

"If you're ready to tell it."

43. THE DEAD MAN IN THE WINDOW

CAPTAIN TREY BROWN, ENGINE 28, C SHIFT

I'm working with my regular crew, Clyde Garrison and Kitty Acton. The bell hits at 2225 hours, an aid call a few blocks north on Rainier Avenue: man down.

When we arrive, bystanders are staring at a man on the sidewalk, a yapping dog next to him, a large puddle of blood under him. I kneel beside the man, white, in his sixties, Kitty and Clyde behind me with the aid kits. Nobody seems to know what happened to our patient, although several onlookers thought they heard gunshots.

I radio the dispatcher to send us a medic response.

After we put a cervical collar on him, we roll the patient over, cut off his shirt and expose two bullet wounds in his chest; we find no other wounds except for a hematoma on his forehead, probably from falling to the sidewalk. He's moving good air but only on one side. We assume one of his lungs has collapsed.

As we load our patient onto the stretcher and trundle him into the back of the medic unit, Engine 33 comes roaring up Rainier Avenue and turns west half a block behind us. The two men in the crew cab are dressed for action, in full bunkers and masks, which means it's a fire call. It should be ours.

A police car pulls up, and one of the officers looks at my captain's bars and asks what happened. I tell him it's a shooting, two holes to the chest. He tells me they may have the shooter in the backseat, just as Engine 30 comes racing up Rainier from the north. I hear more sirens in the distance. Clyde yells that they have a fire around the corner.

From the medics I get the okay to go in service, and as we roll, Kitty is already masking up in the crew cab. A fire. A shooting. An arrest. All within blocks of each other. It's crazy.

I contact the dispatcher and they add us to the fire call.

We drive around the block and arrive at the fire building, where Engine 33 is scrambling to get water on the fire. Two firefighters have masked up and are trying but failing to fight their way into the entrance.

I announce to dispatch and Chief Fish that we're on scene. The street is full of men, women, children, none with coats, all looking as if they've evacuated the building. On channel 1, Chief Fish orders us to go around to the rear of the building and establish Division C. At the back of the building, I dismount and throw a backpack and bottle onto my back, though as a division commander I probably won't use them. There's nothing showing on the face of the two-story wall in front of us. No fire. No visible windows or doors. Just a row of cars parked below the wall. Above us smoke is being pumped from under the eaves of the roof.

I spot a row of boarded-over windows on the second floor painted the same color as the wall. Although the parked cars are blocking access to most of the windows, I tell Kitty and Clyde to throw up a ladder between a pair of cars where there's enough room to squeeze one in.

I give a report to Chief Fish, telling him we've got no fire on this side. Heavy smoke out the eaves. No access.

While Kitty foots the ladder, Clyde climbs up and pulls the plywood off the window with the axe. Black smoke boils out the window frame, and Clyde climbs back down the ladder, coughing. He's halfway down the ladder when a man appears in the window above him, blind from smoke and panic. Despite my shouts for him to wait, he climbs up onto the window frame and steps into space. He catches a foot on the ladder and plummets to the ground, doing half a somersault and brushing Clyde, who is still on the ladder, so that he lands on his head at the base of the ladder.

"Backboard and C-collar?" Clyde asks, but by this time there's another man in the window, and I tell Clyde to go back up and get him. The broken man at our feet is in semiformal clothes, good shoes, and an expensive watch, and it worries me. He's dressed for a party. People don't usually go to parties alone. I call for a medic unit and more manpower for rescues, but I can tell by the bonking tone my portable radio makes that my transmission isn't getting through. I wait and try three more times before my transmission is received. The delay makes me crazy.

By the time I get the message across, Clyde has helped a heavyset young man onto the ladder and I've spotted two more heads in the smoky window, each of which disappears. Now I'm wondering how many people are up there. And then deep inside the building, I see the oily dark orange express train that signals heavy flame. It will roll across the ceiling until it builds up, and then it will descend and wither everything in its path.

To my left, another window pops out and another body falls toward a parked car with the jagged motion of a bird that's been shot out of the sky, almost striking two firefighters who are probably on their way to report to me. I don my face piece, activate my air supply, put on both gloves, and race up the ladder just as Clyde and his victim clear the bottom rungs. Clyde is hacking from the smoke, and the victim is limp from it, a male dressed as if for a night out—gold chains, a gold watch, and his best Nikes. Kitty is examining the man in the heap at the bottom of the ladder, who I suspect is dead.

"I'll pitch, you catch," I say to Clyde as I scramble up the ladder and dive inside the window, landing on a pair of soft bodies. I'm wearing full turnouts, rubber boots, and a mask with forty-five minutes of compressed air in the bottle on my back. I can see the space is heating up and about to flash over. If memory serves me right, we are in a huge space with a high ceiling, so there is plenty of room above me for hot gases to build and produce a flashover larger than anything I've ever encountered.

"Fire department!" I yell so people can find me by my voice. "Fire department!"

I see nothing but smoke and some flame maybe twenty

feet above my head and the dim outlines of the window I've just come through. I find a woman on her knees almost directly below the window. I encircle her torso with my arms and lift. I get her to the window and help her out. She is semiconscious, and I suspend her over the ladder while Clyde, still coughing, climbs up to assist. Even with Clyde's help, it's touch and go getting her out safely. I can hear the flame ripping behind me, can feel the superheated smoke blasting out the window. Can feel another body on the floor bumping into me repeatedly like a trapped bumblebee slapping the sides of a jar.

I reach down for the victim at my side just as somebody else crashes into me. "Where's the fire department?" she says, and continues on.

"Back here," I call out. "Right here."

The body I've got in my hands now is a male, but he's too big to lift. He's probably too big for two people to lift. I try, but it's like trying to pick up a three-hundred-pound bag of Jell-O. He's been crawling but has collapsed in place. Meanwhile, the woman comes back and embraces me. I help her to the window and she's saying, "Thank you. Thank you. Thank you." I put her on the ladder just behind Clyde and the first victim, who have made little progress.

"Move it!" I yell. "This place is loaded with customers." Behind me I hear women screaming.

"Over here!" I yell at the two screaming women, now three screaming women, now four. "Up here! Fire department." The screams are coming from a lower level of the little theater. I hear footsteps on the wooden floor, lots of footsteps. There are more people than I expected. I can't hear any firefighting efforts, only a dull roar from a rapidly approaching fire overhead. I've never been in a situation with this much potential fire above me or so many people to rescue, but I know this: the larger the space, the larger the flashover, so that the puny residential flashovers I've survived in the past by flattening myself on the floor will seem like nothing when this thing melts me into a puddle of wax and teeth.

"Up here!" I shout.

A woman crashes into me, mumbling, and without stopping to think, I hoist her out the window. She shrieks with the suddenness of it. There are already three people on the ladder, and they're moving slowly. "Get another ladder," I shout to a firefighter who's shown up in the parking area below us, even though I have no idea where he might place another ladder, and even though it will be too late for the woman in my arms.

The woman begins to slip from my grasp. I lean out the window and lower her as far as the combined length of our arms can reach, so that her toes are only seven feet or so from the hood of a Honda. I let her go and hear the crumpling of sheet metal as she slams into the car. Another woman is at the window beside me. I pick her up and drop her onto a second car.

I call out, grab a man shuffling past in the smoke, manhandle him out the window, and drop him as delicately as you can drop a man out a second-story window. It is starting to get really hot.

I drop another victim. And another. I begin to lose track. I am breathing heavily with the work, sweating so that I'm soaked in my turnouts. Some of them resist, but they are blinded and incapacitated by the smoke. Somebody grabs me in a stranglehold the way a drowning victim grabs a rescuer, but I head-butt her to the floor, readjust my face piece, which she's knocked ajar, and drop her out the window. She lands on the hood of a car, where her head cracks the windshield.

Feeling around in the smoke, I listen to footsteps pounding on the wooden floor in distant sections of the building. We have less than a minute before I will be forced to leave. Maybe less than thirty seconds. I'm taking a risk just being here. I don't want to be here when it flashes. But then, neither do these people.

I call out and then fumble for more bodies and sling them out the window as quickly as possible, placing only one or two on the ladder, which seems to be full each time I need it.

And then I find myself engulfed in flame.

I've timed it badly and have been caught in the flashover, and I'm curled up on the floor below the window, at least I think I'm below the window. I'm disoriented. The only sound is the roar of the flame as it descends on me. Slowly I scoot backward, trying to wedge myself into the corner under the window, but the farther I scoot, the more I begin to suspect I'm moving in the wrong direction. Everywhere I look I see orange and black and nothing else. I'm being burned through my turnouts. Baked like a potato.

I crawl to where I hope the window is, reach up, but grasp only smoke, not even the wall. Now I've lost the wall and don't know which direction to go. I crawl another foot or two and bump into a body on the floor. For all I know, I'm heading deeper into the building. A quick touch tells me the body is the obese man I've been bypassing, the one who's too heavy to lift. He groans, "Help me." Ironically, the position of his body acts like the needle on a compass, because I remember his legs were pointing toward the window. I follow his legs.

"Get up, buddy," I yell, but he doesn't stir, and he's too big for me to move without his assistance. Flame comes down like a sheet blowing in the wind, and I can feel it through my turnouts, and then in one swift movement I squirm over the windowsill like an otter sliding into a pond and ooze down the ladder face-first, gripping the beams on either side and braking with my gloved hands, sliding two stories to the parking lot, a technique we've practiced in training.

When I get up off the pavement, flame is shooting out the window above me. I've got some minor burns under my turnouts, but I'll survive, which is more than I can say about the man I've been forced to abandon upstairs. How many others are up there with him won't be known for hours.

44. CAPTAIN BROWN FINDS CAUSE TO REEVALUATE ETERNITY

CAPTAIN TREY BROWN, ENGINE 28, C SHIFT

The night is nothing but confusion. I don't want anybody to know about my minor burns, through my turnouts, because once they find out, I'll be relieved of my post and sent to the hospital. By now everybody realizes there are still people in the building.

I keep thinking about the man I left inside. I'll never forget those few minutes in the smoke or his words, "Help me," and somehow, whether I want it to or not, I know it will forever affect the way I think about the world and life. But for now we're still on the fire ground, still humping hose and working the logistics of which crews will do what, cycling firefighters through rehab and back to the trenches.

The ground and the hoods of cars are littered with broken bodies, shattered windshields, and civilians who've escaped the building limping through the melee, shouting out the names of missing friends who have not. Sweaty firefighters in full turnouts are helping the injured, ten or twelve of them now, trying to move the battered victims away from the fire building before they get injured by falling debris.

One or two citizens shout at me angrily. When they get close and realize I'm a brother, it takes the wind out of their sails. There is talk of the fire department not caring about black lives. Talk that white firefighters are letting blacks die. I keep thinking about the man I left upstairs. I keep telling myself, Another five seconds in those blowtorch conditions and I wouldn't have made it out either.

We soon have a team shooting water from a two-and-a-half-inch hose line through the open windows, but it's like pissing into a hurricane. The water streams penetrate the window and disappear from sight. The ladders are removed, and later we learn ours was soldered to the wall by heat and will be retired from service.

Some of the citizens in the parking lot are screaming for their loved ones inside the building. One man tries to drive his car out of the lot, a feat which will involve running over charged hose lines, our equipment, and perhaps firefighters. Clyde stops him, removes the keys from his ignition, and throws them off into the darkness. The man wants to fight, but the police show up moments later. The car is now in everybody's way.

Within minutes I have crews working monitors on this side of the building. At first they shoot through the two open windows, but then part of the roof burns through and they pour water into that gap. All the while civilians tell us we should be going inside, that there are people in there. No shit. I turn up the collar on my bunking coat, hoping to conceal my burns for as long as possible. I don't want to go to the hospital until this is over.

Now I realize there is a door at the right-hand corner of the base of the building, black smoke pouring out. I walk over and examine an interior stairway and see several shoes and one lost purse. I pick up the purse and hand it to a nearby policeman, who is transfixed by the spectacle. It shocks me to find these doors. Like a lot of firefighters, I pride myself on remaining calm at emergencies, and it worries me that I may have missed them because of adrenaline.

Later I learn six people were removed from the stairs. Four alive and two stone dead. A third dies in the hospital. I feel nauseated. In a moment of relative quiet, I notice there are castoff shoes scattered all over the parking lot.

At midnight a meeting of the division commanders is called, and Chief Fish looks at me and says, "What happened to your ears?" I am driven to the hospital in the safety chief's vehicle, the safety chief excitedly narrating what he saw of the fire as if I hadn't been there. At Harborview a burned firefighter is always treated immediately—head of the line. I tell the doctor there must be more critical patients, but she keeps working on me anyway. The ER waiting area is flooded with the friends and relatives of victims from our fire. The place smells of antiseptic and smoke.

An hour later the safety chief drives me back to the Z Club, where much of the roof and walls have caved in, though the fire continues to rage.

At three in the morning the fire is declared tapped. At five in the morning we form body recovery teams and begin working our way into the mostly collapsed structure. Because of my burns, I am not allowed to take part. They begin finding bodies immediately, but Vernon Sweeting isn't carried out until nine-thirty the next morning, after a crane is brought in to remove sections of the walls and after photographs are taken of his position and his equipment. Ironically, he is not far from the door he used to enter the building.

45. BEDROOM MUSINGS

STONE CARMICHAEL

It was one of those talks that come out of the blue late at night while you're both in bed trying to get to sleep after a party, and the buzz of the wine and the reverberations of a dozen conversations are keeping you awake: The type of lethal bedroom chatter that begins with a seemingly inconsequential question and builds like a thunderstorm until the very foundations of your marriage seem at issue. I could sense the thunder and lightning as soon as the first words crept out of her pretty mouth. She liked to sleep on her back, so when I glanced over I saw only part of her face in the darkness, the back of her head buried in the pillow.

"Stone?"

"What is it, honey?"

"You ever think about the time Echo got raped?"

A question like that required some consideration, though I was too tired to really think it over. "No."

"Never?"

"Never."

"Why not?"

"A lot of water under the bridge since then."

"I think about it."

"You shouldn't. It's not something you should be thinking about."

"It was the last summer I was ever really good friends with my sister. I've been thinking about it a lot. We got to know Trey and Kendra pretty well while we were out there at the island, and I'm not sure Trey was guilty."

"Your sister claimed otherwise."

"I'm not so sure."

"Of course he was guilty. I saw him leaving the cottage. His watch was found out there. Echo said he was the one. He wouldn't have left like he did if he wasn't the one."

"He left because he got thrown out. What if he wasn't the one? What if Echo was lying?"

"If she was, she's stuck to her story all these years. Why would she do something like that?"

"I don't know."

"I *saw* him leaving the cottage."

"I know you did, but what if he left the cottage *before* she was attacked? What if he was never in the cottage with her? You never said you saw *her* leaving. You just said you saw him leaving. So you didn't see them together, did you?"

"You know she's been seeing a shrink practically forever."

"Just bear with me."

"I don't know why you're even thinking about this. He left the family and never came back. That was acknowledgment enough for me. Anybody who was innocent would have tried to come back. He didn't try because he knew he was guilty. Besides, what difference does it make now—I mean, even if you are right?"

"That's not the issue."

"Okay. Who else could it have been?"

"What else did you see that night when you were out there?"

At that point we both knew we were talking about something much more involved than whether somebody committed a crime two decades ago. We were talking about the lies our marriage was built upon, the misconceptions and deceptions we'd laid brick on brick on both sides. I've never confronted India over the fact that Echo and I saw her having sex with my brother, never mentioned it, never brought it up even in the middle of our most phenomenal battles, and until now, as far as I knew, she wasn't aware that I knew. But it seemed now as if she was working up her nerve to talk about it.

I hate it when these conversations start in bed. I hate it when they start on a night when I've been up late and have to get up early. I hate it that neither of us is going to get any sleep and that tomorrow I'll be dragging through the day. I hate it that she has a habit of waiting until just before I fall asleep, when I am at my weakest and most exposed, to initiate these kinds of subtle but unrelenting onslaughts. The moment she wanted to talk I knew my night was ruined. Trying not to let my voice give anything away, I said, "Has your crazy sister said something?"

"I wish you wouldn't call her crazy."

"Her hair's a different color every time I see her. She plays that weird jazz. She married a loser. What do you want me to call her?"

"Call her Echo, like everybody else does."

"I don't know why you would listen to her at all."

"Maybe because she's my sister. That night Trey said he didn't do it. But nobody would listen. What if it was one of the Mexican gardeners? Weren't they in the habit of staying the night when they'd worked late?"

"They didn't stay over that night. We checked into that later. Trust me, it was Trey. Now, maybe he was drinking and that contributed to it, or maybe he had some other excuse, like she was teasing him or something, but it was him."

"Echo told me she lied."

"What?"

"I talked to Echo, and she said it wasn't Trey."

"When?"

"After the ball."

"Why on earth would she say a thing like that?"

"I assume because Trey showed up in our lives again and she felt guilty."

There is a stillness in the bedroom, palpable, deadly, and heavier than air, and it is so relentless and chilling I have no doubt it can be measured by scientific instruments.

"She say anything else?"

"Just that it wasn't him. She wouldn't tell me who, though. I knew it couldn't have been your father or Renfrow because they were accounted for all evening. Now you're telling me the gardeners were off island. Who else was there? Nobody. And she swears it wasn't Trey."

I stilled my breathing and tried to think. I'd had too much wine and wanted to sleep almost as much as I wanted this to go away. Why do women have to analyze every little event? And why can't they ever forget anything? "You know I didn't do it."

"Do I?"

"Are you saying your sister accused me?"

"She didn't accuse anybody. She wouldn't tell me who it was. All I'm saying is if it wasn't Trey, and I've thought for a number of years it wasn't, then it had to have been one of the gardeners. But you tell me all the gardeners left the island. That leaves one male in the vicinity and unaccounted for."

"Are you accusing me of raping your sister?"

"I don't know. Am I?"

"I might be mistaken about the gardeners. It was a long time ago. Now that I'm thinking about it, I'm pretty sure I am mistaken. I think they were there. Yes. They were there."

"You said you saw Trey leaving the cottage. What else did you see?" When I didn't reply, she waited a few beats and then answered for me. "You saw *me* leaving the cottage, didn't you? You and Echo were spying on us."

"Were we?"

"Oh, come now. Trey went down to the beach and I went to the big house, swam some laps, took a sauna and then a shower. I'd just gotten back upstairs in the living room when Echo showed up. It makes sense that the two of you saw us at the cottage. It's the reason she lied. She didn't want to put herself in the middle of our relationship by admitting she'd spied on me or that you hurt her. Once she lied, she was trapped. She's kept this to herself all these years to preserve our marriage. But then when Trey showed up, she realized how badly she's treated him and she had to speak up."

"If you're intimating that I had anything to do with what happened to your sister, you're crazy."

"First my sister's crazy and then I am. Good. I'm glad to hear that. In the morning I'll ask Echo who really did it. I'm sure she'll be happy to clear your name."

"Oh, for God's sake. It was a long time ago. People's memories don't—"

"What? Don't last that long? I remember how you came through the door right after Echo and how your face was flushed the way it gets when you've been running and how you put your arm around her, and I remember the way she flinched and looked at you as if you were a stranger. I remember all the times she didn't want to come to our house for Christmas, how she didn't want to let her boys stay overnight. She's been protecting me all these years. Or thinks she has."

"You're so accusatory, and yet you and Trey were the ones who ruined everything. You and Trey."

"So you did see us?"

"Yes! And don't try to use my knowledge of your infidelity as proof that I'm some sort of criminal. I saw the two of you, and I've never forgotten it. You were out there screwing that bastard."

"Then why did you marry me?"

"I'm beginning to wonder."

"So you punished your own brother by framing him for something he didn't do?"

"Don't ever call him my brother. And what right do you have to criticize me?"

"We made a mistake. We got carried away. But what happened between you and my sister?"

"I didn't rape her, if that's what you mean."

"What happened, then?"

"We had sex, that was all."

"You had sex with a fifteen-year-old?"

"She wanted to."

"That's why she was all bloody? You were twenty-six years old! I don't know a state in the union where that's not rape."

"It wasn't rape. Your sister . . . We had sex, yeah. But it wasn't rape. She wanted to. She—"

It was at that point that my lovely wife picked up her pillows and a robe and left the room. I was used to grand exits by the ice queen. She'd done it before. She would do it again. And she would get over this. I was sure of it.

46. PHONE CALL FROM ANOTHER WOMAN

JAMIE ESTEVEZ

I've been working with Trey for six days and have grown to know his moods in a way I will never know the other subjects of our interviews, and his mood now is melancholy. It's as if he has taken off his clothing for me, emotionally and spiritually, and laid bare his soul. It is oddly endearing and even a little erotic. Nobody else's story has affected me in this way, but then, no other firefighter has affected me the way Trey Brown has, either.

We've circled the building and are standing where we started in the debris-laden parking lot on the north side of the Z Club. In front of us are four crushed cars that remain half buried under a crumbled wall. Trey has been calm while reciting his tale, and he struggles to appear unemotional. I am wrung out and feel as if I've lived through the fire with him. In the evening chill he wears his department foul-weather coat, and it makes him readily identifiable as a fire department official to passersby. A car with a single black male in it slows, and the driver gives Trey a hard look that I've seen often over the past few days. There is a lot of public disgruntlement directed at black firefighters, whom some in the community see as having been traitors to their race. A few minutes later though, another car passes and two African-American women give Trey smiles and big waves.

The community is breaking up. Last night two parked cars in mostly white neighborhoods were torched by a group of roving youths. A curfew has been instituted for all neighborhoods south of the canal. Anyone under eighteen caught on the streets after midnight will be subject to arrest. The governor and mayor have agreed on this action, and it has made national news, as have the arrests of fifty-seven young blacks over the past four nights. Although most have been released to their parents or guardians, eighteen have been charged with felony mischief and assorted misdemeanors. The local NAACP chapter vows to fight the curfew in court.

"Can you handle a few follow-up questions?" I ask.

"Go ahead."

"Did anybody call out to you while you were in there, anybody you had to bypass?"

"Just the man by the window."

"Do you recall his exact words?"

" 'Help me.' "

"Just like that? Just like the tape that was released?"

" 'Help me' is all I remember."

"So he might have been the person on the cell phone to the dispatcher?"

"I didn't see a cell phone, but then, I didn't see him in the smoke, either. I just felt him. I passed him several times, so it's possible he thought he was being passed up by more than one firefighter. Are you going to write this in the report?"

"I'll have to. People in the community are particularly upset about that cell phone call. You've known this all along, haven't you, that you might be the firefighter the caller was complaining about?"

I expected him to snap at me again, to remind me once more that he wasn't the right person to help with this investigation, but he looked at me with utter sadness in his eyes and said, "Of course I have. I've replayed it all a hundred times in my mind."

"When you got around to the back of the building, you had nothing but a blank wall in front of you, but you put up a ladder. Did you hear or see something? Or is that standard operating procedure?"

"I saw those boarded-over windows and wanted to know what was inside. Also, the cars in the parking lot didn't seem to match the Hispanics in the street who usually drive older cars or small trucks that serve double duty in their jobs. Yeah, I know that's stereotyping, but sometimes stereotypes can be useful."

"If you hadn't had that intuition, a lot more people would have died, wouldn't they?"

"Are you trying to be a cheerleader now?"

"I know you feel bad about what you failed to do, but think about what you accomplished."

"I don't need a cheerleader."

"I'm not saying you do. All I'm saying is there were a lot of other people who might have spotted those doors and didn't."

"I think about it every day."

"You didn't want to tell me this, did you?"

"I thought I was through telling it, that's all."

"Okay. Sure. I'm sorry if I—"

"What else do you want to know?"

"Has that ever been taught to you in training, to drop people out windows?"

"Of course not. But right now I'm sorry I didn't drop them all out."

"Why?"

"Because every one I dropped lived. Every one I didn't get to is dead now. There were ten who died up there. Three died at the bottom of the stairs, but besides the man who was just too heavy for me to move, there were nine more somewhere inside that I never got to."

We were both in a somber frame of mind by the time we got to his car. As we drove, we listened to the local news on the car radio. Leaders of the African-American community were suggesting the city's investigation was tainted and that the Z Club Citizens for Truth "special team," meaning Trey Brown and myself, would tell an appreciably different story from the official one. I wasn't so sure they weren't going to be disappointed. From the beginning I'd been aware of the irony of the City of Seattle paying a citizens' group to do a study the city had already done, when the point of the second study was to rebut the first. Commissioning this study had bought Stone Carmichael a great deal of cachet in the minority community. The police chief was in trouble. The fire chief was in trouble, but Mayor Carmichael was golden. Each of the warring groups—police, fire, civilian—believed Carmichael was on their side. It was quite a trick.

We were downtown working our way through rush-hour traffic when Trey's cell phone rang. He took one hand off the steering wheel and handed it to me.

"It's *your* phone," I said.

"I'm driving."

"Hello," I said.

It was a female voice, the eventuality I feared most, since I was certain Trey was having a fling with the mayor's wife, or at least flirting with the idea. "Hello? Who's this?"

"Jamie Estevez."

"This is Carly Smith with the Seattle Fire Department." I hoped this wasn't what I thought it was. I hoped he wasn't having an affair with a fire girl as well as the mayor's wife.

"He's right here."

"May I speak to him?"

We hit a stoplight and Trey took the phone from me. "Hello? Yeah? How is he doing? Is he making sense?" He listened for a moment. "You get vitals?" The light changed as he flipped the phone closed and said, "I can drop you off or I can take you with me. I'd rather take you with me. It'll be quicker."

"What's going on?"

"Engine Six has my brother again."

"Stone?"

"My other brother. I need to make sure he's okay. Then, if you can wait, we're still on for dinner."

"I can wait."

47. JOHNNY BROWN, THIRTY-FOUR, SPITS OUT A COP

TREY

Johnny was sitting on the sideboard of Engine 6 at 20th Avenue and East Fir, a hematoma over his right eye and a swathe of cling bandages holding down a stack of 4x4s above that. Somebody had set his Environmental Defense cap on his head at a cockeyed angle he never would have chosen himself. A block away on Fir, I saw blue lights and cops and heard a bullhorn sounding off in the twilight as light rain began falling out of the evening sky.

I pulled up far enough behind Engine 6 so the officer and I could talk without Johnny hearing. My brother had diabetes and was also subject to epileptic seizure disorder, and because he frequently forgot to take either his Dilantin or his insulin or both, was prone to collapsing in the street and later waking up to what he'd once told me was a "whole new world," usually with a crew of local firefighters standing over him. Johnny was both the bane and the hub of my mother's existence, as well as the unique link between her daily rituals and mine, and Engine 6 had picked up Johnny more times than I could remember.

Men like Johnny generally had a look you could spot: the

the four-block drive to my mother's house, the same house I'd lived in with my grandmother until I was four. I parked in front, opened the door for Johnny, and glanced at Estevez. "You better come in," I said. "My mother finds out I left you out here, she'll skin me alive."

"Sounds like *my* mother."

48. TREY'S MOTHER'S WILD LIFE

JAMIE ESTEVEZ

While I was in the kitchen fixing spaghetti and a salad, I watched Trey's muscular shoulders as he hunched over my coffee table in the other room, arranging his schematics and the Mylar presentation he'd prepared. I thought about serving wine with the meal, but decided that would be too much. I considered candles but passed on those, too. I put a jazz album on the CD player, early Miles Davis, and saw Trey, without looking up from his work, give an appreciative little smile to himself when he recognized it.

I'm not sure what I'd been prepared for, but Trey's mother did not fulfill any of my expectations. To begin with, she used a mannered speech sprinkled with constant references to blessings and Jesus. There were pictures of Jesus on the walls and several Bibles lying about. The house was tidy but spartan, the television an old console that would require four men to move. Her house had been built in 1906, his mother told me, but had been remodeled a section at a time by Trey.

Johnny, Trey told me on the drive to my condominium in Belltown, had been a crack baby, with some fetal alcohol syndrome mixed in. "You want the whole story?"

"Well . . . I don't want to pry . . ."

"Of course you want to pry. Until I was four, I was raised by my grandmother. The week my grandmother died, my mother showed up strung out on malt liquor and crack. At the time all I knew was that there was something wrong with her and she was arguing with the official from the Department of Social and Health Services. In the middle of it she telephoned Shelby Carmichael and told him to come and get me. It wasn't until years later that I figured out he was my real father."

"Shelby Carmichael is your biological father?"

"That's what I said."

"Does the rest of the family know?"

"I'm not sure. It was certainly never mentioned when I was part of the Carmichael clan. I was the adopted son as far as everyone, including my father, was concerned. It was kind of scary, going off with this white guy—not that going away with my mother, who I barely knew, wouldn't have been scary. I remember I had this little suitcase with a few clothes inside, and a teddy bear under my arm. That was it."

"How did Shelby Carmichael come to be your father?"

"When she was sixteen, my mother got a summer job as a maid at the Carmichael estate on the island. By the time she got home and started school again, she was pregnant and wouldn't tell her mother who the father was. She'd gotten straight As until then, but she dropped out of school that autumn and started hanging out with a bad crowd. Shelby Carmichael gave her ten thousand dollars, which he thought would take care of things and which my mother promptly used up on a string of low-life boyfriends and a car that one of them wrecked the first week she owned it. Fortunately for me, she didn't start in with the drugs until after I was born. It was the drugs that spurred my grandmother to kick her out of the house when I was six months old.

"When Shelby got that phone call, he picked up his lawyer and they came down to the DSHS office and saw the shape my mother was in. I don't know if he copped to being my father right there or if my mother signed some papers that released me to him or what, but he took me home, and then some time during the next year I was officially adopted and they changed my last name to Carmichael."

"That must have been an adjustment for everyone concerned."

"Shelby Junior took me on as a project, and I followed him around like a puppy. Kendra was a year younger than me. I took care of her the same way Shelby Junior took care of me. I remember beating up some kid who was messing with her in school and going to the principal's office for it. The odd man out was Stone, who was seven years older than me and never really accepted me. He used to tell me I was adopted because it would look good for a politician to adopt a 'colored boy.' At that time Shelby was a state representative."

"Was it confusing to be the only black child in a white family?"

"Not as confusing as you might think. The tough part was later, going back to the black community with my tail between my legs, accustomed to all the money and clothes and travel, and not having it anymore. It's a lot harder to be poor when you were rich once."

"And you went to the UW?"

"On a scholarship until my junior year. We were playing Arizona. We were up by fourteen when I took a hit from behind and blew out my ACL big-time."

"When did you reunite with your mother?"

"A year after I separated from the Carmichael family, I was walking through the old neighborhood and recognized my grandmother's house. I went up and knocked, and my mother answered. I hadn't seen her since I was four, but when we looked at each other, we both just knew. By then, she'd cleaned up her act and was working."

"Did your mother ever tell you what happened between her and Carmichael?"

"Well, I think they had sex."

"That's not what I meant. She was sixteen. He was her employer. There's nothing right about that."

"The one time we spoke about it, she called it an affair. I do have to say this for him, as busy as he was, he worked hard at being a father to me. And any time he caught Stone giving me the business, he let him have it with both barrels."

"How could your family believe you were capable of what they accused you of?"

"I still don't know. If there were doubts about my guilt, I never got to hear them, because I never got to talk to any of the family after that night."

"Did you try?"

"About a week after my ouster I went back to the island determined to convince someone I was innocent. Renfrow was waiting for me with two thugs. They beat me up pretty good."

"This is the Renfrow I met Saturday night?"

"The same man we saw in the photo I took from McDonald's place."

"Why would he have somebody beat you up?"

"Maybe you forgot he was working for Harlan Overby, Echo's father."

"Oh."

After dinner we began to review our findings. The fire department report on the Z Club concluded that the department made small mistakes, which included some of the incoming units being on the wrong radio channel for a few minutes and an inability to get the main floor ventilated. There were miscues when Ladder 12 left Vernon Sweeting inside. Additional mistakes when his partner, McMartin, went back to look for him instead of calling a Mayday. The report stated that most of the civilian fire deaths could be attributed to the lack of windows and secondary exits on the second floor. While there had been several cell phone calls to the dispatcher from individuals trapped on the second floor, all of those calls were received after Captain Brown had already announced there were victims on the second floor and begun rescue operations. The cell phone call that had caused all the ruckus had been placed around the time crews were inside looking for Vernon Sweeting as well as civilian victims. My personal hypothesis was that it was the man Trey couldn't lift and that Trey had passed him several times, causing him to believe he was seeing multiple firefighters pass him by.

A paragraph at the end of the fire department report read:

> Throughout this incident, firefighting and rescue efforts of the department were hampered by individuals harassing and at times physically restraining fire officers from effectively pursuing their tasks. The crowd quickly grew to unmanageable proportions. Had the fire ground been clear of civilians, there is every reason to believe all victims would have been retrieved from the building before the IC was forced to declare a defensive fire.

This paragraph had been criticized by black leaders and agitators because it essentially said the victims died because of the crowd outside. "Do you believe that?" I asked. "That the crowd was the reason you didn't save more people?"

"Hell, no."

"Why not?"

"They weren't bothering us that much. One thing the IC should not have done was believe the Hispanics when they said everybody was out of the building. Fish assumed they'd been on both floors, but they'd only been on the first floor and were unaware of what was happening on the second."

"Anything else?"

"Fish knew we were making rescues from the second floor on side C, but he didn't get a ladder up on side A until they spotted people in a window. They should have laddered it right away."

"Why do you think they didn't?"

"I think the mob pestering them might have delayed him some. And there were two trees on fire right in front of the fire escape."

"So the crowd did have an effect?"

"Some. But the central issue was the boarded-over windows and two blocked stairwells, one blocked by fire and the other locked by the owners."

"So maybe we should be talking to Chester McDonald about that."

"I don't think McDonald really owns the property. I did some tracking the other day after we called it quits. Tax on that property was paid last year by McDonald, but there's a notation at the assessor's office that it will be paid in the future by a company called Silverstar Consolidated. I can't find anything on them, but I do know the light-rail line is going to be built through that part of town, and I wouldn't be surprised if somebody isn't buying up land cheap in the belief that it's going to be worth a lot more in the future, somebody who's studied where the rail line is headed. I did some more checking and found quite a few land sales to Silverstar Consolidated in that neighborhood."

"McDonald is still listed as the owner on the paperwork we've seen having to do with permits and fire inspections. And we talked to him ourselves. Why would he claim to own the building if he doesn't, especially in light of the minority community being up in arms about the fire?"

"What are these?" Trey asked, uncovering a stack of glossies on the coffee table, all photos of the Z Club.

"Just some photographs from the original investigation."

When he came to the last one, he stared at it. It was a photo of the Z Club prior to the fire, workmen setting up scaffolding on the north wall, a man in the foreground, the same man we'd met Saturday night, the same man in the photo Trey had filched from Chester McDonald's place, and the man who'd had him beat up nineteen years ago: Barry Renfrow. The date on the photo was three weeks before the fire. "You had this all along?" Trey asked.

"I got the material Monday, but I didn't get a chance to look at it until last night after you and I had finished."

"This is Renfrow. Renfrow works for Overby and for the Carmichael family. You should have shared this with me before."

It was hard to argue. Perhaps I thought if he saw it, he'd go off on some wild conspiracy theory and neglect the rest of the interviews. Perhaps . . .

"You just have to be in control, don't you?" Trey said.

"What?"

"That's what this is about. You let me lay out the case for going after the building owners as if I was some sort of two-twenty conspiracy fruitcake, and all the while you were sitting on a piece of evidence that bolsters my theory. Two-twenty is fire department code for 'crazy person.' "

"I know what a two-twenty is, and I never thought you were a fruitcake."

"That's not what I said. I said you let me go on like I was, when all the while you had this photo."

"I was going to show it to you."

"When? Next summer? This is Renfrow. *This* is Renfrow," he added, holding up the photo from his briefcase.

"I'm sorry if you think I've been hiding things."

"I think you've been hiding things because you *have* been hiding things. I thought you wanted to get to the bottom of this."

"We *are* getting to the bottom of this."

"What else are you hiding?"

I knew how angry he would be if he discovered I was calling his brother, the mayor, every evening with updates. I didn't feel great about the phone calls, but I'd promised Miriam Beckmann I'd make them, Beckmann having forged a deal with Stone Carmichael when he agreed the city would finance this second investigation. She'd traded away total secrecy for solvency. We stared at each other and then eventually arrived at a truce, yet as he helped me clear the table and put the dishes into the dishwasher, a strained silence lingered. Afterward, Trey went to the living room window to look out at the western skyline. "Nice view," he said finally.

"Yeah."

Using the Mylar representations Trey had drawn up, we began going over the events of September 3, piecing the timeline into a coordinated whole the way I'd been piecing Trey's life together in my own mind. About an hour into it, he excused himself to use the bathroom, and while he was gone, his cell phone on the coffee table rang. I picked it up and answered without thinking. In the newsroom we were always answering each other's cell phones, unable or unwilling to let a possible news tip slip past, and he *had* asked me to answer his phone earlier.

"Hello?"

"Hello?" said a voice I would not have mistaken in a zillion years. "I must have the wrong number."

"No, I don't think so. This is Trey Brown's phone. He'll be back in a minute."

"Oh. Do you mind if I hold?"

"Of course not."

"You must be Jamie Estevez."

"Yes."

"I guess you're working together. The two of you."

"I guess we are."

It was the blond goddess herself, making her daily call to lover boy.

49. IF IT'S AN EMERGENCY, MAYBE I SHOULD GO WITH YOU

JAMIE ESTEVEZ

When I handed the phone to Trey and busied myself in the kitchen, he lowered his voice and walked over to the window that looked out over a scrap of downtown and the Olympic mountain range on the horizon.

Despite Trey's cautious tones, I could hear everything he said.

"Yeah," he said. "We're working." Pause. "The woman you met Saturday night." Pause. "Yes, in the pink dress." Pause. "Okay. A little. I don't know why—" Pause. "If you say so. Okay, she *is* pretty. Hell, she's gorgeous, smart, too. But this is strictly business." If I'd had any inclination to leave the room, it vanished at that moment. "No. Not at all. She's just . . . I don't know. A little too aggressive. A little too perfect." Pause. "A couple of hours more. No. I told you. We're working." Pause. "Tonight? How about tomorrow?"

Without looking up from the counter, I could tell he'd

turned from the window and was directing his gaze at me. "I can't dump all this in her lap. There are people waiting." He turned back to the window, apparently thinking again that I couldn't hear him."Well, yeah. She's in the other room. I don't know. Cleaning up the kitchen or something." Pause. "Okay. See you in a few minutes." If I'd had any doubts about Trey and the mayor's wife, this conversation erased them.

How quickly one's universe can flip-flop from hopeless to full of possibilities to hopeless again. I was gorgeous and smart, but I was too aggressive and too perfect. What does that mean—too perfect? And now he was going to leave me so he could make love to another woman. The worst part was I had to smile and pretend I hadn't heard every word and that I didn't know he was on his way to pour the coals to the mayor's wife.

A moment later Trey approached me in the kitchen and said, "I've got kind of an emergency."

"Is it your brother? Is he in trouble again? Maybe I should come."

"It's something else. I'm sorry. We'll have to catch up on this tomorrow."

"If it's an emergency, maybe it would be helpful if I went with you?"

"It's not like that."

"That wasn't your sister, Kendra, was it? I thought I recognized the voice."

"It was an old friend. Well, I have to be going. "

"You mind if I keep the Mylars so I can look them over?"

"Keep it all," he said, opening the door. "I'll pick it up in the morning when I come to get you." On top of everything else, he was so busy chasing his peter, he left my door open.

Alone, I tried to collect my thoughts, yet found myself unable to concentrate. I went to the window where Trey had taken his call and picked up my phone and dialed. Stone Carmichael answered on the third ring.

"I hope I'm not bothering you," I said. "You're probably with your family."

"We're at a Mariners game, actually. We decided at the last

minute. We'll take them to school late, let them sleep in. What the heck. They're only kids once."

"You're lucky your wife likes baseball. A lot of women don't."

"Actually, she had a board meeting for one of her charities, so she's not with us. She's not a huge baseball fan anyway."

"It sounds as if it worked out perfectly for everyone. The game just start?"

"At seven."

Though I'd called Mayor Carmichael every evening as promised, I'd been keeping most of the salient information to myself, feeling I would be betraying the project and Trey Brown if I let the bulk of it out. On the other hand, it gave me a queasy feeling to be speaking to the mayor when I knew his wife was spending her nights with the same man I was spending my days with. Tonight I was on the verge of telling the mayor to go home and check on his wife. Maybe it was the eagerness with which Trey had rushed out that spun me out of control. Still, I didn't have any claim on Trey and had no right to feel wounded when he saw another woman. What a peculiar collection of feelings I was going through, I thought as I gave the mayor a quick rundown of what we'd been doing.

When Stone Carmichael spoke, the sounds of the baseball game loudspeakers and the stadium organ played in the background. "So let me get this straight. You're almost finished with the fire-ground interviews, and you're moving in two separate directions now. You want to pursue the department's handling of the building inspections, and Trey wants to—"

"Trey wants to go after the owners," I blurted, realizing as soon as the words were out of my mouth I'd said too much, especially if the Carmichael or Overby family had any interest in the property, as Trey seemed to think.

"The owners?"

"Uh, yes."

"I don't understand."

"I don't really understand it either," I lied. "Personally, I think he'll change his mind." Now, on top of all the other sick sensations roiling around inside, I had to deal with my own treachery.

"Maybe I shouldn't tell you this, but somebody saw the two of you at headquarters, and you seemed to be having a disagreement. Actually, what they said was, you were fighting like a couple of roosters."

"We . . . have had some vigorous discussions."

I was so close to telling him Trey was at that moment breaking speed laws to get to his wife that it's a miracle I didn't. At least I hadn't told him about the photos of Renfrow outside the Z Club; at least I hadn't told him Trey was thinking this whole ownership thing might lead to the Carmichael family. I'd said too much, but at least I hadn't told him that. Given all the personal stuff going on between the two of them, perhaps Stone would forget about the ownership angle, or perhaps, and this was the best of all possible worlds, it would lead nowhere.

After we hung up, I tried to work for a few minutes and then gave up and lay down in front of *The Hustler,* watching television for longer than I should have. I'd never seen the film before and found it riveting. I especially liked the part where they broke Paul Newman's thumbs. Now if only somebody would break Trey's thumbs, I thought, feeling a spark of guilt for even letting my mind wander in that direction.

50. A DUMB IDEA EXECUTED BY A NAIVE YOUNG MAN

TREY, NINETEEN YEARS EARLIER

Even as I sit here in the waiting room, I'm beginning to think this is a bad idea. I'm on the eighteenth floor of the downtown bank building, everyone in suits, me in a pair of jeans and a sweater, having taken almost no clothing with me the night I left the island. I've been sleeping in coach's basement on the couch and storing my meager belongings in a cardboard box next to the broken-down freezer that coach keeps down there. It's three weeks into the school term, and whenever I need a parent or guardian to sign forms, coach signs. He's got two small kids and a pregnant wife, so my presence is an imposition, I know, but right now I don't have anywhere else to go.

A few people have been kind, and I'm beginning to think from the looks they throw around, they are not doing it because they are drawn to me as an individual but because I'm a black kid who's been dumped on by whites. At this point I'll take what I can get. Last year I was the premier high school running back in the state, and as such, was showered with newspaper attention and back slapping from the alumni, not to mention admiration from girls at school. It must have gone to my head, because I turned into a bit of an ass. I know that now and I'm trying to reform.

Coach knows the whole story and has repeatedly urged me to set up a meeting with my father to "set things straight."

How I am going to set things straight is beyond me, but here I sit, running possible conversations and turns of phrase through my mind as if rehearsing for a play that has yet to be written. I know at his core my father is a good man, and I have faith in his doing the right thing eventually, my faith emboldened by the encouragement of coach and his wife. I trust that the truth will win out in the end, that my persistence will in itself be a persuasive argument for my innocence.

I grow nervous in the waiting room as visitors come and go, each seemingly more welcome than I. Perhaps I should have gone to my adoptive mother instead, but as sympathetic as she would be to my plight, Helen detests conflict, defers to her husband's judgment in most venues. Besides that, it would kill me to convince her and then wait on the sidelines while she failed to turn around the rest of the family.

I've always been a fast healer, and my physical wounds

from the beating have mostly knitted up, though I still have some dental work to be completed. For whatever reasons, whether charitable or accidental, I remain covered on my father's insurance policy.

Almost an hour after my appointment time, a secretary conducts me down a long corridor to the doors of a large suite. I am guiltless, and I've been raised in a world where people are not punished for crimes they did not commit, so I have high hopes.

As we walk, Stone shows up behind us, scurrying along as if he has a train to catch, arms full of papers. He is chipper. I had been hoping not to run into him. It is almost a month after my disbarment from the family, and at first Stone seems to have forgotten it, or forgiven me. "Trey! What are you doing here?"

In his vest and dress trousers, Stone looks every bit the corporate lawyer, just as I look like some high school dolt who's taken the bus downtown after being excused from football practice, which is precisely the case. We stare at each other. Stone is grinning wildly. He dismisses the secretary with that curt nod he uses on subordinates, and I can tell she doesn't like him. Once we are alone, his tone changes. "What the hell are you doing here?" he asks.

"I came to see Father."

"You came to try to talk your way out of this? Are you crazy, you little shit?"

"Get out of my way."

"I'm not going to block you," he says, although he *is* blocking me. "I just want to know what you're planning on saying."

"That I didn't do it."

"Jesus, you've got a pair of balls, little bro. You're lucky you're not in a cell. Why don't you leave well enough alone and get out of here before somebody calls the cops?"

"I have an appointment."

"Then go right in," he says, stepping away from the door. "I won't stand in the way of a man with an appointment."

As soon as I open the door I realize I've been had, that my

appointment was never okayed or even known by my father, that Stone must have intercepted the message and arranged this. It is a meeting room with a long table and maybe twenty-five high-backed leather chairs encircling it, all filled with dusty old men. I've interrupted some sort of meeting. At the head of the table sits Harlan.

I scan the room wildly, but my father is not here.

"What do you want?" Overby asks, his voice filled with loathing. Directly in front of me is a man I've always called Uncle Al. He's on several boards with my father and has been over to the house too many times to count. Over the years he has taken me sailing and to movies, and done many other things to make me feel special. He is married to a woman in a wheelchair and is childless. Of all the people in the room, I care most what Uncle Al thinks. He glances from me to Overby and back again.

"I . . . had an appointment to see my father."

"Your father's not here."

"Where is he?"

"Your father's probably some pimp down on Yesler Avenue."

"My father is Shelby Carmichael. I had an appointment."

"Shelby adopted you, but he's not your father. I told him it was a mistake when he did it, and I told him again after we found out what you did to my daughter."

People are staring at me so hard I feel like a bug pinned to a display board. "Sir, as long as I'm here, I need to . . . say . . . to tell you I didn't do it. That's what I came for. To explain to my father—"

"You son of a bitch. My daughter's seeing a psychiatrist just so she can get to the point where she sleeps through the night."

"I'm sorry about Echo, but—"

"Get the hell out of here. Get out, or I'll have my people give you another beating."

My face is burning. I'm sweating. Uncle Al says, "Trey? Is any of this true?"

I turn and look into his sad blue eyes, and as I do I realize that no matter what I tell him now, after I leave, Overby will convince him that I'm a rapist.

Without replying, I push open the door, speed down the corridor, dash out of the building, and hustle down the sidewalks of Seattle, knowing I will never again try to contact my father or anyone else in the family. Standing at the bus stop, I weep silently. Pedestrians make wide arcs around me.

51. SUITCASES, A TAPE, AND SOME LAST WORDS

TREY

It was pretty much the estate I would have expected Stone to live in, or any of the Carmichaels for that matter, the kind of grand place I might own myself had I remained on good terms with the clan: a sprawling lawn and garden area in front of a circular drive, low walls of limestone, the garages discreetly out of view around back, visitor parking in a brick area in front of the house, the house itself a three-story Georgian with a wing off to the right that was larger than my entire house. I knew this neighborhood from my days on the University of Washington football team, because the head coach had lived a block away, the president of the university on the other side of the street.

Alongside the house and running down to an inlet of Lake Washington lay a long and perfectly manicured lawn, beyond the lawn a dock and boat, the boat easily worth more than anything I'd ever owned, including my house.

Directly in front of the house sat a white Land Rover, the rear hatch open, the back filled with boxes, luggage, and a painting wrapped in brown butcher paper.

The door to the house swung open before I could knock, India Carmichael wearing jeans, deck shoes, and a pink sweatshirt, her hair pulled into a loose ponytail, staring at me with those widely spaced blue Overby eyes. She seemed slightly breathless, as if she'd been working and just happened to be passing the front door when she spotted me through the window.

"Come in, Trey. Thanks for showing up on such short notice. I know this is inconvenient for you, but I think it's about the only chance I'll have to see you again. Sit down. Would you like something to drink?"

"No, thanks. You taking a trip?"

"You might put it that way." I didn't sit down and neither did she, the two of us standing between the entranceway and a large sunken living room. Beyond her shoulder at the foot of the stairs were two suitcases, matching pieces to the luggage already stashed in the Land Rover.

"I want you to have this," she said, handing me a tiny black object. "Do you know what it is?"

"It's from a phone answering machine. I have one just like it. I don't take the tape out very often, but I know what it is. What's on it?"

"You'll know when you hear it. Do whatever you think is best with it. Just don't lose it."

"I won't."

"By the way, Echo called me after your visit."

"I want to thank you for setting that up."

"Nonsense. I didn't set anything up. I just knew she was hurting and probably needed to talk to you. That night has been preying on her mind for a long time, and she needed to deal with it. I hope she explained adequately and that you can see it from her point of view."

"I understand she was fifteen and hurt and confused, but it doesn't make what happened to me any easier to stomach."

"No. I guess it wouldn't. She's . . . been a different person since that night. I didn't realize it until lately. We were close growing up, but after that night we grew more and more distant. I always attributed it to the normal changes that occur with growing up, but it was all about that night."

"She wouldn't tell me who did it."

"She didn't tell me, either. But she told me enough that I

was able to figure it out for myself later. This morning I called her and she confirmed my suspicions."

"She was protecting you, wasn't she?"

"She told me when she was fifteen she thought she was in love with Stone and that she tried in her own blundering fashion to take him away from me. They were outside the cottage spying on us that night, Echo and Stone."

"I guessed something like that."

"All these years, and Stone's never said a word to me. After we left, they went into the cottage and she tried to comfort Stone. She may have kissed him. He was angry and drunk."

"And that's when he raped her, wasn't it?"

"Yes."

"It was always in the back of my mind, but like you, I couldn't believe it."

"I suppose he was trying to get even with me, but the fact remains that he raped my sister."

"Do you know that for a fact?"

"He said they had sex when I confronted him about it. She's always called it rape. I'm inclined to believe her."

"And now you're moving out?"

"Yes. We had the fight to end all fights. Not knowing the kind of man your husband is after all these years is a little off-putting. In fact, it's damned embarrassing to admit."

"I hope my showing up didn't—"

"It has little enough to do with you, other than the fact that he's been blaming his crime on you all these years."

"Why would Echo blame me, though?"

"She was still half in love with Stone, confused and vulnerable, which made it easy for him to manipulate her and put words in her mouth. She felt guilty for trying to break us up and even guiltier for the outcome, felt like the whole thing was her fault, and she wanted to protect Stone."

"She could have told the truth later."

"I guess it was just too hard for her to admit she'd lied. She somehow convinced herself that the consequences to you weren't all that bad, considering what she was accusing you of. What she lost sight of was that you were innocent and didn't deserve any consequences at all. She didn't say this, and I'm not really sure if I should either, because it's pure speculation, but . . . well, our father has always had some racist attitudes. He made it pretty clear to us when we were growing up that he disapproved of your being part of the Carmichael family, and I wonder if hearing that so often didn't make it easier for Echo to justify your banishment. Echo did tell me she's going to call Kendra and your father to make sure they finally hear the truth from her."

"So what about you and Stone?"

"Like I said, I'm leaving him. Stone and I have been heading downhill for the last five or six years anyway. Plus there's what I heard on that tape I gave you. This way at least the decision is made for me, so I won't have to be continually looking back and wondering if I did the right thing. I'm moving to Maryland. My mother's back there. She was diagnosed with cervical cancer last year, and for a long time I've been feeling we should be closer to her." In a contemplative mood, she traced a red fingernail around the edges of the badge on my foul-weather coat. "I could have guessed this for you."

"Could have guessed what?"

"Putting out fires. Rescuing people."

"Yeah. It suits me."

"Well, I've got work to do. I want to be out of here when he gets back. I'm going to pick up the boys at school in the morning. Stone will be downtown, so that'll keep the histrionics to a minimum."

She stepped out onto the porch with me and put a hand on either of my shoulders. India was close to six feet tall, and we fit together with the ease of two people who'd been fitting together for years. She stepped close and kissed me lightly on the lips, her face lingering a few inches from mine, and for a few moments I think we were both back reliving that summer. "I'm sorry about what happened, and I'm sorry I didn't have the brains or the guts to figure out what was going on and step in."

"It wasn't your fault."

"I feel like it was."

"Good-bye, India."

"Good-bye, Trey."

As partings between onetime lovers go, ours had been oddly bloodless.

52. THE TAPE

TREY

Rumble was half asleep in front of the big-screen television when I hung up my fire department coat in the hallway, took off my department boots, and padded in stocking feet past the TV and the little dojo I'd built into a corner of the basement. "Anybody call?"

"Not that I heard. You expecting a call?"

I picked up the remote and muted the television. "You seen Johnny?"

"No."

"Engine Six called. I had to go over there. He got beaned by some cops. I told him to stay home tonight and stay out of the rioting, so if he shows up, he's not supposed to be here."

"Fuckin' cops. He all right?"

"He'll make out. I think he was more embarrassed than anything. He's kind of sweet on Estevez."

"So am I. When am I going to meet her?"

"I'll set you up on a blind date right after she's through with Denzel Washington."

"Is Denzel in town?"

I went upstairs as the sound returned to the television, poured myself a glass of water, and inserted the small cassette that India had given me into my own machine. There was a message from a city councilwoman asking Stone about a meeting they were to convene next week and one from India's mother. Then I heard Stone's voice, and it took a few moments to realize he hadn't been calling from outside the house but had accidentally recorded an incoming call, as can happen when you let the recorder pick up and then change your mind and start speaking to your caller on a second connected line. India had intercepted the tape before it got erased. Near as I could tell Stone was talking to Barry Renfrow.

"Yeah. Thought I'd check in. I got that info. They're definitely going after the owners of the club. Yesterday he called the King County assessor's office and then the city attorney's office. He's already got Silverstar Consolidated's name. It's only a matter of time before he finds out Overby owns Silverstar and has been funding your gubernatorial campaign and getting special favors in return. The direction he's taking isn't good. And we both know this isn't some kid you can intimidate. He's a captain in the fire department. He comes up with certain facts and people are bound to believe him. The whole city's watching these two investigate, and the worst part is, I don't know what the hell he's going to do next. We've got to figure out some way to control this report so it doesn't make us look bad."

"Just keep an eye on Captain Brown, and let me know what he's doing."

"It might be too late by the time we see what he's up to. I think something needs to be done now."

"Something harsh?"

"You can't treat a guy like this with kid gloves."

"Don't worry about it. I have an inside source. When things start to get too scary, she'll let me know and then I'll let you know."

"But, Stone—"

"Christ, Barry, I'm late for a ball game with my kids. Okay. Have it your way. Stop him. Maybe you can distract him or something. Get him a white woman. A fat one. All the black guys seem to go for that. Overby has raised a lot of money so I can be the next governor, and we don't need some hero messing it up by digging up the truth about Silverstar and our connection to the Z Club. But keep my name out of it. Keep my campaign out of it. Keep Harlan Overby out of it.

Hell, Barry, you've been doing this for years. And I don't care if you have to hurt him. Listen, my boys are waiting with the bodyguard out at the car."

"Later, then."

"Yeah."

My guess was Stone Carmichael's very considerable political aspirations were finished. Nobody in the black community, or any community for that matter, was going to vote for the man on that tape. The particulars of the cover-up or even the reason for it had little relevance compared to the fact that Stone was involved and was actively talking about concealing information related to the Z Club. With one hand he was commissioning a second Z Club study, and with the other he was essentially putting out some sort of hit on me. It was the very fact that he was conspiring to limit our investigation that would finish him politically. Once this tape was made public, the media dogs would tackle him with bared teeth. Anything Estevez and I hadn't already uncovered would be dug up in a matter of days.

Now we knew Silverstar Consolidated was footing the bills for Stone's gubernatorial bid, and in turn, Stone Carmichael had done something, God knows what, to make certain Silverstar Consolidated didn't take any of the responsibility for those fourteen deaths at the Z Club. One thing they'd apparently done was use some prestidigitation to coerce McDonald, the former owner, to pretend he still owned it. Anything to keep the heat off the real owner. It seemed simple enough and even silly, but the first investigation had bypassed the question of ownership—with or without coercion by the mayor's office—and we might easily have overlooked it, too. It was a small thing unless you were Silverstar Consolidated. Or Overby, who owned Silverstar Consolidated. Or Carmichael, who obviously was in on some of the corner-cutting. Stone had mentioned an insider who was giving him information. I wondered if he was talking about Miriam Beckmann—or was it someone even closer to the investigation?

Unplugging my machine, I carried it downstairs and once

again picked up the remote so that I could silence the television. "What the hell!" Rumble said. "That's two times in five minutes. Have some consideration, would you?"

"Listen. I'm going to play something for you, but I want to swear you to secrecy. This is serious shit." Rumble sat up in the recliner, which for him was the equivalent of a cadet standing and saluting a general.

"What?"

"I'm going to play this in my machine and then make a copy. I want you to keep the copy at your place. I don't want to know where."

"Okay. You know where that—"

"Didn't I just say I didn't want to know where?"

"I wasn't going to tell you."

"The hell. You were already telling me."

"What's going on?"

I played it for him and watched his face change. When the tape was finished, he said, "Who's talking?"

"The first voice belongs to a man named Barry Renfrow. The second belongs to our illustrious mayor."

"Carmichael? You're shittin' me. How'd you get this?"

"You keep this tape under your hat, and I might let you in on the rest."

"Come on, Trey. Tell me."

"I would if you could keep a secret."

"Shit, Trey. The mayor would have to resign if this ever came out. And the bullshit in the streets we've been seeing? Hell, people'd be flying in from all over the country just to throw rocks at city hall. The situation in Seattle's going to be on *20/20* next week. Trey, you've gotta get this to *20/20*. You gotta—"

"We're doing this on our timetable, not by the *TV Guide*."

"Yeah. Sure. But Christ almighty. This is going to be explosive."

53. THE OLD MAN MAKES A TOUGH BUT NECESSARY CALL

STONE CARMICHAEL, NINETEEN YEARS EARLIER

I remember getting pissed at the old man when I was nine and throwing a rock through our living room window, playing dumb, conning him into thinking it was the neighbor kid. Funny how people can be blind when it suits their needs . . . yet it was the last time I ever conned the old man. Since then, he's learned to read me like a book.

So now Echo's come home and incited a near riot in the great room, and I've gotten here just behind her, and somehow I've managed to place the blame for all this on Trey, convinced everyone in the room Trey was her attacker, maybe even convinced Echo. But then after Echo and her mother leave the room, I sweep my gaze across the faces and for a fraction of a second I catch my father looking at me, and when our eyes collide I realize he knows somebody's been lying, and it injects a needle of fear through the center of my heart. I try to pretend I haven't noticed, and so does Father, who ignores me for a while, speaking quietly to Harlan in the corner, Harlan and Elaine, who are both ready to lynch Trey.

A search of the house is mounted for Trey, but his room is empty, and it's pretty clear he's still outside wandering around in the dark. As we wait for the confrontation in the great room, tension builds. A few think he's afraid to come in, afraid to face what he's done, while I'm getting more and more nervous because of Father. He knows part of it, but I'm not sure which part.

Renfrow, who's been sent out to scout the cottage and look for Trey, comes back alone and talks to Father in the hallway just outside the great room.

People are in various stages of disbelief, Kendra, my mother, Elaine, Harlan, India, and Renfrow's creepy girlfriend. Echo is off somewhere sedated and trying to sleep. Mother is trying to persuade Elaine that the attack must surely have been perpetrated by a stranger, but Elaine believes her daughter and is having none of it. Mother is good at papering over reality with her own view of the world, but it's not going to work here.

After Renfrow and Father confer, a red-faced Father steps into the great room and says, "Stone, can I see you a moment?"

I know that tone. I get up and follow Father into the library down the hallway, where Renfrow is already waiting. They remain standing but insist I have a seat on a sofa. I continue to harbor the faintest glimmer of hope that this isn't going to be what I think it is, that maybe we're here to talk about some bearded stranger or they are merely trying to confirm Trey is the guilty party. Portly, bowlegged, and dogged, Renfrow stands with his hands behind his back and looks out the window into the black night. Our little skiff bangs against the dock outside.

"Look at me," Father says. "Look at me when I'm speaking to you."

"Sir."

"You damn well better call me *sir.*"

"Yes, sir."

"You can tell whatever wild-ass story comes to your mind out there in front of the Overbys, but in here you're going to speak the truth. You understand? Echo lied, didn't she?"

"No, sir. She told the God's honest truth. I mean, I guess she told the truth. After all, I wasn't there. I just saw him leaving."

"One more asinine comment out of you, and I'm going to call the county sheriff and he'll do the rest of the questioning. What happened between you and Echo?"

"Nothing."

Father walks over to the telephone, picks up the receiver, and begins to dial.

"Okay. It was an accident. I was drunk."

"What was an accident?"

"We had . . . we had sex."

"Echo, the daughter of my best and oldest friend? She's only fifteen years old, for Christ's sake! What the hell is wrong with you?"

"I know. I can't believe it myself." When neither Renfrow nor my father says anything further, I add, "It seems like a nightmare. It really does, sir. I'm so upset over it, I can hardly keep a straight thought in my head. I don't know what happened."

"You don't know what happened?"

"No, sir."

"Well, you better tell me how it happened right now, or I'm going back to that telephone. Spit it out."

"This is kind of embarrassing," I say, glancing at Renfrow.

"Not as embarrassing as a rape trial. Spit it out before I come over and knock it out of you. Goddamn you!"

"I . . . India and I've been having problems. I came back early to straighten them out. You know I was supposed to work another week in L.A. Tonight I wanted . . . to spend some time with her, but she said she had an upset stomach and went up to bed early. Later, I sneaked in with a rose and a little glass of wine, thinking it would make her feel better. But she wasn't there."

"Finish the story, Stone. In case you haven't realized it, there are people out in the other room waiting to put a gun to your head."

"Yes, sir. Echo and Kendra were downstairs watching a movie, but India should have been in her room. When I went downstairs and asked about her, Echo said she had something to show me. That was when she walked me out to the old gardener's cottage. I thought Echo was trying to get romantic. She's had a crush on me forever. You know that."

"No, I didn't. Is that how all this happened? Because she had a crush on you?"

"It's more complicated."

"Go on."

"I don't know what she thought we were going to find at the gardener's cottage, but evidently she knew or suspected Trey and India were out there. We saw them through the window."

"Trey and India?"

"Rutting like a couple of dogs in heat."

"Trey and—"

"Like dogs in heat. I didn't know what to do. I was crazy for a few minutes there. And still drunk. We just sat in the grass, stunned. Then India left the cottage, heading for the house, and Trey went down toward the beach. Neither of them saw us."

"And that's when you saw Trey leaving the cottage?"

"Yes, sir. I wanted to go into the cottage. I don't know why. To see where they'd been. To look for proof so I could throw it in their faces. I'm not sure what I was thinking. Echo came with me. I didn't want her to, but she did. I was nuts really. And drunk, like I said. I'm still a little drunk. She started coming on to me. I'm not saying she wanted to sleep with me, but I'm not saying she didn't, either. Looking back on it . . . I'm not sure what she was thinking. But we started kissing. And then the next thing I knew, she was fighting. She popped me in the mouth a good one, and I got mad and then . . . well, you know the rest."

"Actually, I don't. Finish your story."

"Is he . . ." I say, gesturing at Renfrow.

"This is confidential. He won't repeat any of it."

"Echo and I . . . well, what happened . . . we had sex. Afterward, Echo got up and got dressed and ran out of there. I started chasing her. I was hoping to catch her before she got to the house so I could try to talk some sense into her. I don't think either one of us had any idea everybody was still up. I think she just stumbled into that crowd out there and then had a hard time coming up with a story."

"Unlike you. You didn't have a hard time coming up with a story, did you?"

"It was true. I did see him leave the cottage. What I left out was I saw India leave, too."

"Why didn't India say something? No. Don't answer that. She's not going to be anxious to announce to everybody she was out there getting sexed by Trey. Especially when you and she are practically engaged. You realize we're in a bit of a bind now, don't you, Stone?"

"You're not going to tell them it was me, are you?"

"They want blood. Right now they want the blood of my son."

"Give them Trey. He's adopted."

Father gives me a disappointed look. "For that comment I should drag you out there right now and help Harlan beat the living hell out of you. I can't believe you even said that. You're both my sons, goddamn it. And don't you ever forget that."

"No, sir. But—"

"Just shut up a minute."

"Yes, sir."

"Boy, what the hell were you thinking?"

"I don't know."

"You *weren't* thinking."

"No, sir. I was blind drunk."

"Don't bullshit me. I've been drunk more times than you've played with your pecker, and I can tell you right now, nobody's *ever* that drunk."

"Yes, sir."

"What the hell are we going to do? Harlan is out there expecting some sort of resolution, and I can't let him take all his anger out on Trey. All Trey's guilty of is seducing your girlfriend. Or maybe she seduced him. Hell, the only reason I got evidence before Harlan was I made a deal with Barry to keep whatever he found at the cottage confidential until he spoke to me about it. He said he found evidence there had been two couples out there. And probably not at the same time. But then, I already knew you were lying. I just couldn't figure out what happened."

Renfrow doesn't bother to glance away from the window. Standing there, he's looking like a pretty good imitation of a wooden Indian, getting paid twice for his dirty work, once from Echo's father and once from mine. Father is shouting now. "I asked you what the hell we are going to do now!"

"I don't know!" I shout back.

"Shit, Stone. It was bad enough we lost Shelby, but now you have to go and pull a stupid stunt like this. It's going to kill your mother. You know that, don't you? If it was Trey, like you said, it might not be so bad. It would be bad, but not *as* bad. She's resented Trey in her heart all along, but this is going to kill her, and it's going to kill me, too. You're her last natural son." Father sits on a stool in front of the sofa and drops his face into his hands. I've never seen him this distraught, not even when Shelby died. "Jesus, we have so much at stake. It's not only the family stuff. I mean, hell, we've been friends thirty years, but all the business we've got going together this year. Do you know how bad he could shaft us if this doesn't come out right? I know Harlan, and if he thinks we've hurt his family, he'll put the screws to all of us. It's the way his mind works. It's one thing if he thinks Trey did it. He's been against my adopting Trey since the beginning. But when he finds out it was blood . . ."

"We could—"

"Shut up! Let me think." I've never seen Father in such a foul mood, but this is nothing compared to the state Harlan Overby will erupt into when he learns the truth. "God, this is a mess," Father says. "I don't know what to do. Goddamn you, Stone. I cannot lose two boys in one summer. Your mother cannot lose two boys in one summer." When he looks up, Father is crying. I don't believe I've ever seen him cry. "Okay. Let's think this through."

Father keeps his face in his hands for a long time. I can hear the grandfather clock ticking in the corner. Finally he pulls a neatly folded handkerchief out of his jacket pocket, unfurls it, and mops his face. "I've got two sons left and I love you both. I do. But you, you son of a bitch, have put me in a position no father should ever be in. You're intelligent, and you've finished law school with honors, and you could have gone anywhere. Then there's Trey . . . everybody adores Trey." After another long pause, Father looks up and says, "I know you've never liked him. And I know in her heart your mother loves him but that some part of her wishes I'd never brought him into the house. I still remember that night I saw him at the DSHS office thinking he wasn't mine, and then seeing that little dimple when he smiled and knowing he was, and seeing how screwed up his life was going to be if I left him with that woman. I just fell in love with the little guy. God, Stone . . . I should take you out in the gravel and beat you half to death . . . putting me in this position."

"Yes, sir." Although I'd suspected it for years, it was the first time I'd had it confirmed that Trey was his biological son.

Renfrow speaks from his position at the dark window. "If I might make a suggestion?"

"What is it, Barry?"

"Why don't we go back out and wait for him to come back and then see how it plays?"

"You mean keep the blame on Trey?"

"If it works out that way, why not? You've already got a deal worked out with Harlan. It seems as if you're only playing with fire here if you change the players. He's come to terms with this in his own way. He agreed to let you throw Trey out and leave it at that. We both know how he'll feel about this new development. It won't be good."

After a few moments staring into my eyes, Father arches his head up at Renfrow and says, "Will you go along with it?"

"It'll cost you, but not nearly as much as it'll cost if Harlan hears the truth."

"What about Echo?"

"She's not going to change her story. She's cemented in."

Turning back to me, Father gives me a withering look and mutters under his breath, "Don't ever put me in a position like this again. You understand?"

"Yes, sir."

"And you," Father says, turning to Renfrow. "You breathe a word of this, and I will pay to have you killed."

"I know that," Renfrow says.

"God, I can't do this. I just can't. Jesus. He didn't do anything to deserve this."

"You're going to have to give up somebody," Renfrow says. "Harlan's out there waiting. Think of it as a business decision. In business you do what's expedient. Which choice does the least amount of damage to your holdings?"

"I'm in hell here," Father says, dropping his head into his hands.

54. MORE LIES FROM CHESTER

JAMIE ESTEVEZ

I began crying after I went to bed last night. It might have had something to do with the first guy I've been most attracted to in the last ten years having dinner at my place and being friendlier than he's been since I met him, and then watching him receive a phone call and rush off to have sex with his blonde while I took a bath and watched an old movie on TV. The whole thing was so damn depressing. I wish I could stop feeling this way, but it's one of those syndromes you can't stop once it begins.

And of course when I woke up in the morning, my eyes looked like I'd glued tea bags under them. Ice, a cold shower, and even a couple of dabs of Preparation H under my eyes didn't help, and when Trey showed up at eight, I was still putting the finishing touches on my makeup. Hard to know why I even tried.

I buzzed him up and met him at the door, searching his face to see if he could tell I'd been crying, but he didn't seem to notice my face, or me even. Not in those first few seconds. And then in a heartbeat everything changed. He took his briefcase off the counter and looked at me with those big gray eyes, and for the first time in our short but contentious relationship seemed to be looking directly at me. *Me.*

"How are you this morning?" he said.

"Fine. You?"

When we got into the car, I said, "What do you want to do today?"

Both hands on the steering wheel, he turned to me and said, "You're the boss."

"Not this again."

"Okay, I'll tell you what I would like to do, and you tell me what you would like, and we'll see if we even need to say anything else. Heck, maybe we're thinking the same thing."

"That'll be the day."

"I'll bet you a lunch we're thinking the same thing," he said. "If you're honest, I'll win."

"You're on. And I'm always honest."

He looked at me and smiled slowly with that contagious grin I'd seen him use on others so frequently. I smiled back limply.

"Okay, what's *your* proposal?" I said.

"I think we should catch Chester McDonald before he can get out of the house. Ask him why he's claiming to own the Z Club. Ask him about Renfrow. What was your plan?"

"That was it," I lied.

"It was?"

"That was it."

"So you owe me lunch."

"Right."

"I'll buy dessert."

"You have a deal." We both laughed. I believe it might have been my first shared laughter with Trey Brown, ever. I'd lied and it would cost me lunch, but maybe there was some hope for the two of us after all; hope that at least we might be friends before this was all finished.

The weather had turned balmy, which it does in the early autumn in Seattle, cumulus clouds threaded through blue skies, sunshine bleaching the clouds a blinding white. Trey drove in silence. I could see there was something on his mind other than our impending visit with Chester McDonald. I was hoping he'd had a fight last night with his girlfriend and they were history, but that was a lot to hope for. More likely they'd figured out a way to spend the night together, and she'd sent him off with a kiss and a pat on the butt just minutes before he showed up at my door. Whatever was on his mind, it caused him to nearly run a red light on Lenora Street.

Chester McDonald's drapes were drawn, and two windows on the north end of the house above the rockery had been boarded over with plywood, shards of broken glass under the camellias.

"Who you?" McDonald asked when he finally answered the door, ignoring Trey while staring me up and down. It was hard to tell if his eyesight was bad or if he was just being rude. I'd forgotten how ugly and frail he was.

"My name is Jamie Estevez. We spoke last week."

"Don't have time now. Too early. Just got up. No breakfast. Don't have time." He tried to shut the door, but Trey wedged his foot in the doorjamb so it wouldn't close. At first, McDonald couldn't seem to figure out what was happening.

"Mr. McDonald," I said, "Chester. Please let us in."

"Can't find my meds. Gotta find 'em. Feelin' sick."

"Then this is the perfect man to have at your side," I said, stepping in past McDonald. "He's trained in emergency medicine." Trey followed while McDonald remained in the doorway, flummoxed by our invasion.

"Can't be warming up the outdoors," he said, closing the door and shuffling through the living room and into the kitchen as if we weren't there. Dinner plates crusty with food sat next to the couch. In the kitchen, McDonald opened cabinets and drawers, leaving the doors ajar when he didn't find what he was looking for.

From the doorway, I said, "We noticed some broken windows at the side of the house."

"They threw bricks! I had the po-lice out here. It's them damn kids up the street. They claim their uncle was in the club, but I think it's bullcrap."

"When we were here the other day, you led us to believe you owned the Z Club."

"Can't find shit in this place," McDonald mumbled.

"You don't own the Z Club, do you, Chester?"

"I got blood pressure medication here somewhere."

"Chester? Who owns the Z Club?" He stopped scrounging through the kitchen and looked at me. "We're looking for the truth, Mr. McDonald."

McDonald squinted at me in the dim light of the kitchen. "I *owned* it."

"I owned a Buick once," Trey said. "Somebody else owns it now."

"I sign so much I can't keep track of it myself. That's what I got lawyers for. I buy and sell real estate. I make the calls, and they just come along and suck cash out of every deal. Used to have a good attorney, J.J. Pickles. I trusted J.J. Got himself"—McDonald began rummaging through a pantry near the other doorway to the kitchen—". . . got himself drowned in some river out east. Went out there to put his mother in a nursing home and got drowned trying to fish in some dadblamed river had fish you couldn't eat anyway. All polluted and shit."

"Mr. McDonald," I said, "who owns the Z Club? We have tax information that says Silverstar Consolidated owns it." McDonald's rummaging came to an abrupt halt at the name, then started up again, though more slowly.

After a moment he hobbled to the front door. "I'd like you to leave."

"You sold it to Silverstar Consolidated, didn't you?" Trey said. "Then after the fire, they asked you to pretend you still owned it."

"I signed papers. Signed lots of papers. Ever since J.J. died, my affairs have been in the shitter."

"You ever see this man?" Trey asked, holding up a photo of Renfrow. McDonald, who'd been looking more and more annoyed, suddenly became frightened.

"I don't have my glasses."

"We'll wait while you get them," Trey said.

"Was in the hospital four times last year. My life isn't as wonderful as it looks from the outside."

"Your life could get a whole lot worse if you don't answer these questions," Trey said.

Wearing a mask of anger and stubbornness, McDonald tried to stare him down. He was a little man, but he was tough, and at first I waited for them to finish the staring contest, but then I said, "Chester, who owns Silverstar Consolidated?"

"Look it up in the records."

"We've tried. They've concealed it pretty well."

"Okay. That's it. I didn't invite you in. Get out of my house." He pulled the door wide and stepped to one side, a slight breeze ruffling the flapping cuff of his flannel pajamas against the artificial leg.

"This isn't going away," Trey said softly.

Outside, we leaned against Trey's Infiniti, and for a few moments neither of us said anything. I could see Trey thinking hard. Finally he said, "Somebody's been telling the mayor everything we're doing."

I felt like I'd been slapped. "I don't know what—"

"I thought you said you were always honest."

"I am, but I made promises. When I make a promise . . . Trey, I'm . . ."

"Don't tell me you're sorry. I don't want to hear that."

"Beckmann asked me to give the mayor a daily update. I made the promise before I knew you, before I knew he was your brother."

"You tell him I was trying to track down the owners?"

"I'm afraid I did."

We drove wordlessly down the hill to Lake Washington Boulevard. He passed Seward Park and pulled into a parking lot alongside the water. Across the sun-dappled waves sat Mercer Island. To the distant north, the Mercer Island Floating Bridge. Trey shut off the motor, turned to me, and said, "Do you mind explaining why you've been spying on me."

"I wasn't spying. I don't like that word. He wanted a daily briefing. He had reasons. There are riots. He wanted to know how we were progressing, and . . ."

"He asked about me, didn't he?"

"He mostly wanted to know how we were getting along." Trey got out, slammed the door, and leaned against the driver's fender, his back to me. I walked around the back of the car, feeling vulnerable walking toward him in the open air. It was a small parking lot, one car at the other end, probably a homeless guy because the car was old and full of belongings. Arms folded, Trey stared out at the water.

"You were spying on me for my brother."

"I told you—"

"I can't believe you were doing this."

"It's not going to have any effect on our findings. It's—"

"You know the history we have together."

"You're the one running around with your brother's wife."

Trey glared at me, his eyes full of fury. We stood like that for a while until he relaxed and said, "How did you figure that out?"

"I deduced it. I'm not a fool."

"Okay, listen. I like you, Estevez. I really do. Maybe we should start again from scratch. You stop phoning the mayor, and I'll . . . I'll lead my life the way I please."

"If I stop calling the mayor, he'll think something is up."

"Something *is* up. He's got a connection to the Z Club he wants to hide. My guess is it was just a loose favor. Silverstar Consolidated was getting some income from renting the place out while they waited for the light-rail line to be completed. After that, they were probably planning to tear it down so they could put up something more profitable. From what I know now, Stone promised Harlan Overby and his minions he would keep the fire department off their backs to keep the costs down. I'm sure the promise meant nothing at the time he made it. So the guys at the club went ahead and played fast and loose with the fire regulations. Then the unexpected happened. And now we're in danger. My ex-brother has Barry Renfrow working on this. That means you and I are both in danger."

"How do you know all this?"

"I overheard a phone conversation."

"That's how you knew I was talking to Stone?"

"More or less."

I don't know why, but I began weeping, the tears pouring out like rain. I didn't want to smear my makeup by rubbing my face, and I might have climbed back in the car, but then he would have gotten in beside me and I would have been trapped, so I simply stood in front of him with my hands at my sides and wept, which of course was the most ridiculous thing I might have done.

And then, in a move as uncharacteristic as it was unnerving, Trey stepped forward and enveloped me in his arms. He didn't say anything, just held me until I laid my head on his chest, which felt like a slab of oak. "I'm so embarrassed," I said into his shirt.

"Everybody cries."

"Not in the middle of the day in front of . . ."

"It's been stressful. Besides, I'm an asshole."

"I *was* spying. I'm ashamed. And I'm sorry."

"Don't worry about it. We're doing fine. You and I."

"We are?" I asked, tipping my head to look up at him. He was smiling. He leaned down and kissed my forehead, my left cheek, and lightly brushed my lips with his.

I was ready for more, had closed my eyes, when he released me and said, "Feel better?"

"A little," I said, trying to get my bearings. "Okay. So . . . tell me exactly what you know and how you know it."

"Here?"

"I don't feel like going anyplace where people can see my puffy face."

"Here's fine. I was about to suggest it myself."

"Sure you were."

"Let's make a pact. We're both going to be completely truthful from now on."

"Okay. Fine. Were you really going to suggest we stay here?"

"No."

55. BAD THINGS, BARRY, BAD THINGS

STONE CARMICHAEL

Renfrow and I met at Ruth's Chris Steak House, just the two of us, Renfrow bringing his bourbon over to the table, while I studied the menu, breathing heavily as he sat down, a man unused to physical exercise—which was an odd trait for a self-confessed former soldier of fortune, college athlete, and onetime club-level boxer. After college and a stint in the Navy, Renfrow had worked for the CIA for eight years. Then, following a series of incidents involving the deaths of multiple low-level officials in a small South American country, he resigned and spent ten years freelancing for various U.S. spy agencies. When he decided to go into private industry, India's father hired him. Overby and my father had been using his services ever since. He's good. He's a pig, but he's good at what he does.

Renfrow was adept at maneuvering through the bureaucratic process wherever we encountered it, but he was also useful for all the ugly little stuff nobody else knew how to deal with—or didn't have the nerve to tackle. He'd maintained contacts in the spook world and seemed to know at least one man in almost every police department and prison in the country.

The restaurant was not crowded yet, and I was still a little annoyed that this meeting had forced me to cancel a meeting with my divorce attorney. Even though he denied it, Renfrow had been putting me off for a couple of days, so I knew there was something he didn't want to tell me.

It was like pulling teeth to get him to meet you where a free meal was not involved. His suits were always shiny because he'd been wearing them too long, and his shirts were dingy, and unless he was in a company vehicle, he rarely drove a car that wasn't fifteen years old. At home he had two cats, a pet lizard, a condo full of photos of a girlfriend he hadn't seen in ten years, and a seedy sex life he only hinted at. He was a blowhard, too. Had once claimed you could remove all the silverware from the table and he could still find six items to kill you with, two that could be used from across the room. My guess was he'd read about it in a book somewhere.

When his breathing settled down, he said, "So what's going on? You going to have the rib eye well done and a Caesar? You always have the rib eye and a Caesar. A glass of Indian Wells chardonnay? No dessert. A decaf."

"You've been avoiding me."

"Didn't I call yesterday?"

"No."

"Wasn't yesterday Wednesday?"

"Thursday. This is Friday. You didn't call either day. And neither did our little weather lady. I'm beginning to get annoyed."

"I thought she was a special features person? They have some blond chick doing the weather, don't they?"

"They've got that chubby black dude who makes jokes doing the weather. Right now I haven't heard from her in two days. Or you either. Can you tell me what that's about?"

"Same old, same old. You know. They're interviewing firefighters and witnesses. Had a picnic the other day. Spread their crap all out on a blanket down at the lake."

"They sweet on each other?"

"I don't think so. So what's this? Friday? Tell you the truth, they might be done with the interviews by now. I'll ask my people." He flipped open a cell phone, but I motioned for him to put it away.

"What's going on, Barry? And what do you know about my wife leaving me?"

"Your wife?"

"The day she left was the last day I heard from you. What do you know about my wife, Barry?"

"India? Why . . . nothing."

"There's something going on, and I have a feeling you know what it is. I'm not leaving until you tell me."

Renfrow sighed heavily. "She was with him the night she left."

"Who?"

"Your brother."

I hadn't thought of Trey as my brother even when he *was* my brother, but now that he'd been disinherited and footloose for years, it seemed an absurdity to think he was part of the family. Even though I'd reintroduced him to everyone, I was planning to ostracize him again as soon as they produced a satisfactory report. "Are you saying India and Trey have been seeing each other?"

"A couple of times that we know of."

"That's not possible."

"I'm afraid it is."

"Are they having sex?"

"I don't know. We're not watching him every minute."

"They're having sex. Goddamn it. I knew something—"

"I don't know that they are."

"I do. Who else knows?"

"Me. One other operative."

"How did you find out?"

"We've been following Trey and the woman. Monday around lunchtime we followed him to the Olympic Four Seasons, where he had lunch with your missus. They drove somewhere, but we lost them in traffic. He also was at your house the night when she moved out. They kissed at the door."

"Fuck! Why didn't you tell me?"

"I was afraid of how you would react."

"You had good reason to be afraid. Do you have any idea how much this pisses me off?"

"Mr. Mayor," came a voice, "I'd like to introduce you to my wife and her daughter. My stepson and his two children."

I looked up and found the table surrounded. An older gentleman I had no recollection of ever meeting was standing over us with a squadron of relatives. I nodded to my SPD bodyguard across the room that it was okay. The trouble with being recognizable was people recognized you. Fortunately, most of these people were from out of town and weren't impressed with a mayor they'd never heard of, so we were able to quickly dust them off.

Our meals came, and Renfrow began eating with a gusto I found sickening. I should have known something was up at the ball Saturday night when I noticed the way India was watching Trey. It just didn't seem possible that she would be attracted to him . . . again. "You sure about this, Barry?"

"I was going to tell you. I just didn't know how."

"This is a hell of a thing for me to have to drag out of you. After my wife has already left me."

"Marriage is tricky. You want the truth, I don't think it was meant to be."

"My marriage or marriage in general?"

"Marriage in general."

"Are they serious?"

"All I know is they've met a couple of times. The last time at your house."

"Oh, they're having an affair all right. Jesus, Barry, you should have told me right away. You know that call you made Wednesday, before I went to the game? The machine picked it up, so I think our conversation was recorded. I was going to check it when I got home, but the tape was missing. Along with my wife. And now you tell me he was there? You think she gave it to him?"

Speaking around a mouthful of a half-chewed lamb chop, Barry said, "I don't know. How pissed off is she?"

"Pissed off enough to move out and ask for a divorce."

"Then one of them has it. My money would be on him."

"Bad things are happening, Barry. Bad things. Okay. This is what we do. You get that tape back, and then you hurt him. Hurt him bad. Do you hear what I'm saying? I thought you were already going to hurt him. Why hasn't it been done?"

"Give me some time to set it up. Listen, Stone. It was probably just something they had to get out of their systems.

Why don't you go home and pretend it never happened? I'll get the tape. I've got people who can do that."

"I want somebody to beat the hell out of him."

"I can arrange it, but it's not right."

"It's exactly right. You don't know him."

"I think I do. I drove him for two hours in a car once and thought he was going to die choking on his own blood the whole way. He's a tough cookie. You ever see him play for the Huskies? The other teams were scared of him. I mean, scared . . . I went to every home game he played. He was something."

"Just do it."

"Listen. Once you get up in the governor's mansion, things will look different. Leave it until then. There's public focus on him now."

"You tell me some black guy . . ." I looked around at the other tables and lowered my voice to a whisper. "You tell me this black bastard is boning my wife, and I'm supposed to sit on my nuts and take it? Is that what you're saying?"

"He's not just some guy."

"Which makes it worse. He's the bastard my father brought into the house because he couldn't keep his hands off the upstairs maid. What I want is for somebody to mess him up."

"This is not a good thing, Stone."

"Tell you what," I said. "With all this rioting . . . why can't we have a Reginald Denny of our own right here in Seattle? Only a black one. What if some of his own people took him down? Huh? Beat him and maybe hit him in the head with a brick for good measure. He wakes up two weeks later and can't remember his name."

"We might use some coke, too. Drugs always remove any credibility a victim has."

"You're a genius. Tell you what. I'm going to Minneapolis for a conference. I want him in the hospital when I get back. Preferably the brain ward."

"I'll have to clear it with Harlan."

"You know how he feels. He'll probably give you a bonus for coming up with the idea."

56. IF CATS WERE AS BIG AS DOGS

TREY

Our materials spread out on a blanket on the grass, we worked for a little over three hours and then went to Café Flora, where Estevez paid for a leisurely lunch for both of us. Café Flora was in the Madison Valley neighborhood midway between my house and Stone Carmichael's mansion on the lake.

When I took her in my arms down at the lake, I knew in the blink of an eye that Estevez had feelings for me I hadn't noticed before. Like India, Estevez was one of those women most men assumed they didn't have a prayer with, and she'd been so damn snippy with me that it was a real ego boost to realize she'd been thinking about me in that way. For some reason, it changed the whole way I thought about her, made her more lovable.

At Café Flora we ordered Wu-Wei tea, and then I feasted on the Oaxaca tacos, roasted corn tortillas filled with spicy mashed potatoes served with black beans and wilted greens. Estevez nibbled at her organic wild greens salad. After the meal, she took out a notebook and said, "Let's talk about how it came about that people didn't get rescued."

My phone rang before we could go any further. It was Kendra inviting me to visit our father with her that afternoon. "Sorry, I can't make that. I'm busy and can't leave my partner hanging."

"What about Saturday? I could bring the girls and you could meet them. Father wants to see you badly. I think he wants to make amends."

"I don't know if it's such a good idea."

"I would love it if you and he could find some sort of resolution. I know this has been hard on you, Trey, but I would love it if we could work this out somehow. Please?"

"Okay, I'll do it for you. And I'd love to meet your kids. He at the same house?"

"No. Grandpa's old place across the lake. Saturday? Threeish?"

"Okay."

As Estevez and I saw it, the Z Club fire was confusing for a lot of reasons. There were civilians giving contradictory stories to the IC. There was what amounted to a secret club operating on the second floor, and it was a long time before anybody in that club got to a window. The only two exits were blocked. But so far I hadn't seen anything to indicate fire department personnel had knowingly bypassed victims.

On the north side of the building, Engine 28 put a ladder up and found multiple victims on the second floor. At the time firefighters had been assured everybody was out of the building, while many of the onlookers had concerns that this was not the case. It appeared to many of these increasingly angry onlookers that the fire department was deliberately ignoring their concerns.

Approximately twenty-five minutes after the first units arrived, it was determined that firefighting efforts inside the building had become too hazardous to continue, and all rescue operations were suspended.

We'd already spoken to every firefighter who'd been on the second floor, where all the victims except Sweeting were found and where the people in the stairwell had come from. The cell phone call was what is known in the movies as the MacGuffin. It kept our search going, but that was all it was good for. The fact was, I was the only firefighter who ran into civilians inside the building, and we were fairly certain the caller had seen me pass by in the smoke more than once, and thus thought he was being passed by more than one firefighter. If the man hadn't been so heavy, I would have gotten him out. In the report, we would have to explain that rescuing him would have required two or three men. The community could make what it wanted of our not having enough manpower on side C to accomplish this. What we were finding out about the building ownership, and my suspicions about Stone being involved in some sort of cover-up, went a lot higher than the original charge of firefighters bypassing victims in the smoke. This was going to bring down an administration and maybe put some people in jail.

When we left Café Flora, we headed downtown on Madison, the only street in Seattle that stretched uninterrupted from Elliott Bay to Lake Washington. I explained as much to Estevez, who said, "You're just a fountain of information, aren't you?"

"Have you ever considered the fact that if house cats were as big as dogs, they'd kill us and eat us?" She laughed.

At Madison and Broadway we stopped at the light while a group of marchers carrying signs, placards, and a toy fire engine crossed the street against the light and blocked traffic. They were chanting, "We want the truth. We want the truth." Instinctively I scanned the faces for Johnny, but he wasn't among them. One sign had photographs of Z Club victims under the words "We're not going to forget" written in red paint. I would have liked it if they'd included Sweeting's photo, but in all this conspiracy talk, his sacrifice went largely unmentioned.

We worked through Thursday and Friday, interviewing the rest of the people on Estevez's list. Nothing major came to light, and to my surprise, Estevez and I managed to keep our bickering to a minimum.

57. DADDY'S BOY

TREY

Palatial is the word the Sunday magazine used ten years ago when they profiled the Meydenbauer Bay estate where my father now lives—a brick-walled ivy-covered mansion with an English garden Kendra and I used to romp in as kids, and in which her children play now.

It was Saturday afternoon just before two o'clock when I pulled through the security gates behind a Lexus SUV, roared down the long driveway, and parked the bike in front of the main doorway near the portico and the wisteria I remembered from when we were kids. I twisted the throttle a couple of times just to make sure the neighbors knew the devil was in town, dropped the kick stand, and shut off the motor. I wore black leather chaps with jeans underneath, a beat-up black leather jacket, and a black helmet with sunglasses.

"Trey, it's good to see you again," Kendra said, hopping out of the Lexus. She wore a sundress and sandals.

"You, too. I thought you were bringing your kids."

"I, uh . . . they had a party I forgot about." It was a weak lie, delivered without conviction, and we both knew she hadn't brought the girls because of lingering doubts about my character—and because she was afraid of the possible fireworks when I met our father.

Father was tucked into his chair in the living room with a blanket around his legs. It was all a little formal and awkward, even for him. Watching Father watch me, I recalled that India had told me how he went to pot the summer Shelby Junior died and I was banished from the clan: how he began drinking heavily, how his business affairs began to slide and continued to slide for years, and in the end, how he and my adopted mother went through some sort of rift they never really seemed to recover from until those last few weeks of her cancer. It was almost as if the guilt for what he'd done to me had undermined his life.

We handled the awkwardness of the situation the way Carmichaels always handled such things, by pretending it wasn't awkward, by plunging ahead as if nothing untoward were happening. "So why don't you tell us all about the Z Club?" Father asked after the conversation fell into a lull.

"It's not something I talk about," I said.

"Stone tells me the investigation's gone off on a tangent."

"I don't know where he's getting his information."

"Is it going off on a tangent?"

"We're doing what needs to be done."

"Sometimes a man thinks something has to be done, and later it turns out it wasn't right. It can haunt you."

"Are you speaking from experience?" I said. The room grew silent. There were just the three of us, and we all knew I was referring to what had happened in the San Juans all those years ago. "You're not going to talk about it, are you?"

"Talk about what?"

"About why I was booted out of the family."

"We all know why you left. You left the family because I made a deal with my business partner to keep you out of jail."

"There was a lot more going on, and you know it."

"Can't we let this go? For your sake, can't we?"

"For my sake? I've already done my suffering. I thought it was time we spread it around a little. You ushered me out of that house like somebody sweeping a dead mouse out of a closet. Couldn't get me out fast enough."

"I wanted you out of Harlan's sight. He was getting madder and madder, and I was afraid of what he might do."

"I told you I didn't touch Echo, but you didn't believe me."

"No, I didn't. Because . . ." Father's voice was beginning to tremble. "Echo convinced us otherwise."

"Did she?"

"I didn't believe it at first, but I couldn't let you get away with it, either."

"Who *could* you let get away with it?"

"I don't know what you're getting at."

"Sure you do. Echo's phoned you by now, right?" Father was quiet. "Right?"

"I may have spoken to her."

"Oh, come now. How could you forget Echo calling to tell you she lied about who raped her, telling you the wrong son got pilloried? Or maybe it wasn't news to you."

"She's been under psychiatric care for years. I'm not sure if anything she says can be believed."

"You still don't want to admit you made a mistake, do you?"

"I made the best decision available to me at the time. It was a confusing night. If there were mistakes made, they were honest ones."

"You and I both know that's a crock of shit." The maid, who'd been heading into the room with a tray of lemonade, turned and scampered away. "There was nothing confusing about it at all. If there were, you would have come to find me after a year or two. But you didn't."

"You seemed happy where you were."

"How did you know where I was, and how could you possibly know whether I was happy or not?"

"I saw you playing ball."

"It was convenient, wasn't it? You had two sons left. One white and one black. One of them had to get booted out of the family or your fortunes were going to wane. You had too many deals going with Harlan not to be worried about his reaction. And he wanted the black kid thrown out, didn't he? So out I went like a bucket of trash. Without letting me confront my accuser."

"You have to remember the alternative was prison."

"The alternative was a fair hearing."

"Echo said you did it."

"And nobody's ever been falsely accused before? What killed me was you believed her over your own son."

"But why would she lie?"

"You know why." We stared at each other for a few moments. "Kendra, did Echo call you?" I asked.

"She left a message last night. I haven't gotten back to her."

"It's your lucky day, old man. You get to tell her. Go ahead. Tell your daughter what really happened."

"Tell me what?" Kendra asked.

Father coughed. "It was . . . confusing at best."

"A couple of nights ago Echo admitted to me that she lied," I said. "She called him and said the same thing. She's going to tell you, too." I glared at Father until he looked away. "They railroaded me. I got thrown out of the family so that the real perpetrator could run the family businesses and get elected to public office."

"But you said that night . . ." Kendra said. "You said you had . . . relations out at the cottage."

"With India."

The room was suddenly full of silence and autumn sunshine, the gas fireplace burning as it always did when Father was home. "I was only doing what I thought was right," he said.

"You knew the truth that night, didn't you?"

"There was so much going on, and Overby was crowing for blood. We had all those land deals intertwined, millions of dollars, and if he'd backed out just then it would have gone bad for us. Stone was thinking about asking India to marry him, and Harlan and I were like brothers back in those days. Helen and Elaine were best friends and had been for years. The whole thing was going to split the families apart like a suicide bomber."

"Wouldn't want to break apart the big happy family, would we? For a while there, you and I were almost like father and son."

"At least let me apologize."

"I'm listening."

But he didn't apologize. It wasn't the Carmichael way to admit having done anything wrong. Deny, obfuscate, and accuse others; but to apologize was bad form. Instead, he said, "I never look at Stone without thinking about that night. I knew he was lying when he was telling us about it by the little tic in his eye. Echo wasn't acting right, either."

"Oh, no!" Kendra said, apparently without meaning to open her mouth.

Father continued, "My life went to hell after that. We lost all those state contracts. Then Helen was gone, and our net worth went down by almost half."

"Could slice it up a few more times and still have more than most people see in a lifetime," I said.

"Don't worry. We're doing better now. You're in my will,

Trey. I never took you out of the will. You can rest assured of that. I never took you out of my heart, and I never took you out of my will."

"You can take me out now."

"Some day a third of this and a third of what I've got in the market will be yours."

"Somebody say it," Kendra whispered. "Say it out loud. I need to hear it in words."

The room grew quiet, motes of dust swirling slowly in the sunlight near Father's head. He said, "You're going to have to tell her, Trey. I've done too much accusing to do any more."

I turned, looked at Kendra, and said, "India and I were lovers. Stone and Echo went out to the cottage that night and found us, but they didn't make their presence known. After we left, Stone attacked Echo. Father knew it all along."

Kendra turned to Father and stood over his chair. "This is the real reason you never let anybody mention Trey? Because you felt guilty? You let Trey take the blame for what Stone did?"

Shelby Carmichael looked a hundred years old now, silent, staring into the plaid blanket on his lap, biting the inside of one cheek. If he didn't have so much money and so many creature comforts, I might have felt sorry for him.

"You're getting a third," Father said.

"I don't want it," I said, heading for the doorway.

"Can you at least understand there was your mother to consider? She knew who *your* mother was. And who your father was. And we'd already lost one son that summer. Can you at least understand that?"

"What I understand is that you sacrificed *your* innocent son for her guilty one."

58. RICKIE CARTER ERRS ON THE SIDE OF CAUTION

RICKIE CARTER, SOLDIER OF FORTUNE

We're riding in the back of the van, me and two guys I've never seen before, a couple of pugs from one of the boxing gyms. One of them has half an ear missing. I get the feeling they're from California because of something they said and because of the faded gang tattoos on their arms. Click and Clack. That's what they told us. They're going to do the work. Me and Jerome are the holders. Jerome's driving. Jerome's the only one I know. Was in Walla Walla with me on an armed robbery beef. Jerome's good people. He's the one who knew the fat man who's following us in the stolen BMW, the only one of us who is not a brother. Had to be brothers, Jerome said. All four of us had to be black.

Jerome's getting three big ones, and I'm getting two. Once we get the bike down, we jump out the back and we hit him so hard he don't know which way is up. Jerome says this guy on the bike is bad, and even the fat man is planning to err on the side of caution. I heard that phrase on the TV. *Err on the side of caution.* First I thought it was about basketball: "air on the side of caution." Then somebody told me.

The main thing is to make it look like he got caught in these riots. People see a bunch of brothers pounding somebody, they automatically associate it with the club burning down, 'stead of four hired soldiers of fortune. That's what Jerome calls us. Soldiers of fortune. I like that.

Ordinarily, I don't go around picking on strangers unless they're fronting me, but the fat man told us all about this guy. Seems he raped a kid. Got away scot-free. Laughed about it afterward. Jerome and I figure this guy deserves what we're going to give him and maybe a little more. Little white girl, he said, so scared afterward she hid in a closet for a week. Damn. Nothing I hate worse than a rapo.

It's just getting dark, and the fat man signals Jerome that the bike is here. We've been parked across the street from the Douglass-Truth Library, which been standing since I was a kid. I ain't never been inside, but someday I'm going to see what it's about.

The motorcycle flashes by and the fat man pulls out fast and flicks his hand as a signal for Jerome to follow. We're heading up Yesler, and I can see the BMW following the bike, turning left down one of the residential streets. Jerome swerves hard, following the BMW. In an instant the beamer has the bike tipped over and the rider is down. Musta tapped his rear wheel with his bumper.

The two Cs bail out before we're done rolling.

By now Click and Clack are walking over to him like they're offering to help. Nice touch. The fat man is sitting in his BMW with the engine idling, like he's waiting for his insurance agent.

They're walking toward the biker dude, asking if he needs help, and before the dude can answer, Click hits him in the face and he's on the ground and there's blood all over. I mean, all over. And for the first time I realize he's a brother. We're hustling over to get in on the action when I say to Jerome, "Hey, man. I thought he would be white."

"He's white enough, man. Let's get him."

"Man, I thought this was supposed to be some sort of riot thing."

"Don't worry about it."

"How do we know we got the right guy?"

"The fat man picked him out, didn't he? It's him."

They must have really smacked him, because he's not moving. Jesus, Clack hits him with those brass knuckles, he doesn't see it coming, and now he's probably dead. I mean, he's not moving a muscle. I'm not going up for Man One. I'll flip for the prosecution. Hell, I wasn't even near the guy.

The two Cs circle the downed man from either side, and

Click rears back as if he's going to kick the dude in the thigh, maybe test how bad he's hurt, but before he can kick him, the dude does some sort of break-dance move and boots Click in the nuts. Click goes down so fast he falls on the dude, but Clack is already working it and he's got his boot in the air coming down on the dude's helmet. Only for some reason I never quite figure, he misses, and then he's reaching down and there's blood coming out through his jeans, but if the dude's got a knife in his hands, I can't see it. I don't know where the blood came from.

With Click and Clack temporarily out of commission, Jerome and I glance at each other. We move around real quick, and Jerome goes in and there's a tussle, and the guy isn't even off the pavement yet, but they're wrestling, Jerome and this cat. Jerome lets out this squawk and I move in and all of a sudden my mouth closes like a clamshell and I've bit off half my tongue. No shit, my tongue is flapping.

I'm on my knees on the pavement, and my teeth hurt and my tongue is killing me and there's blood all down the front of my jacket. The bastard kicked me in the mouth. And then before I can get up, Jerome is lying on the ground real still, and the dude is up and kicking Clack in the head—Clack the only one of us still standing—with those motorcycle boots, kicking up high over his head like a dancer or something, and Clack goes down like a sack of steer shit. The dude turns, kicks down hard on Click until I know Click isn't going to be breathing easy for months. Just as the BMW tears out of there, he turns to me.

He takes a step forward, but I've been in brawls before and I have a length of pipe with me and I whip it out, but he's moving like a bird, and the next thing I know the bike has crushed my back. Like somebody threw it on top of me. Only I think it's the other way around. I glimpse a piece of the sky as it's happening, but it still takes a second to realize he's somehow thrown me over himself and I've landed on the bike, and damn, I think my back might be broken.

I hear sirens in the distance.

This was supposed to be a cakewalk. Easy money. Half an hour of work. Damn that Jerome.

Then the dude has hold of my jacket and is hauling me off the bike, dragging me away. I smell something burning and wonder if my clothing was touching the hot pipe on his bike. I don't feel burned. But then, I don't feel anything. The dude is looking at me like he feels sorry for me.

A moment later they're cuffing his hands behind his back.

As I lay there trying to figure out what happened, I know I'm headed for the hospital and from there to stir. There's no way around it. On the other hand, maybe if we get a good lawyer, maybe . . .

And then the fire department people are here. Two of them are putting something stiff and uncomfortable around my neck, and one of them says, "Is that Captain Brown over there? Hell, that is Captain Brown."

"One of these guys tagged his bike with a car. The rest was some sort of road rage thing, I guess."

"You're shitting me. Brown did this himself? There's four patients here."

"Brown's been studying martial arts since he was a kid. I heard he's even been to Brazil to study."

In the hospital they give me some dope and I am X-rayed, and then somebody comes in and tells me I have a spinal cord injury, and then some cops try to tell me Jerome already answered all their questions so I better answer, too, but I know that is bullshit because Jerome wouldn't turn over on me. And then I wonder if we're ever going to get paid.

59. BIKER CHICK STRIKES TERROR IN HEART OF SEWARD PARK NEIGHBORHOOD

TREY

When the phone rang at ten A.M., I was still in bed, nursing a fractured cheekbone and twelve stitches. My face had swollen so that I looked like a Frankenstein creature, but at least I hadn't needed surgery. I skipped the pain meds, but now that my head was clear and the junk they'd given me at Harborview had worn off, I wanted a hit of Vicodin so bad I could taste it. Still bandaged himself, Johnny had stayed over to nurse me—it made him feel important. The phone had been busy all morning and I'd been letting the machine pick up until I heard Estevez's voice.

"You all right?" she asked.

"More or less."

"What happened? You sound funny."

"A mouthful of stitches is what happened."

"Stone called here last night, but I was out. He's wondering why I haven't reported to him in three days. What happened to your mouth?"

"I had a little discussion with a few guys last night. Remember Renfrow? I think he was there, but the windows of his car were smoked over, so I'm not sure."

"Oh, my gosh, Trey. How badly did they hurt you?"

"I'll tell you about it later. There's one last interview I think we should do."

"I'll pick you up."

"I thought we'd go over on my bike. Is that okay? Wear something comfortable. A warm jacket."

"In an hour? I'll meet you at your place."

"Better make it an hour and a half. I have to bang some dings out of my bike." I gave her my address.

Ninety minutes later I was on the sidewalk in front of the house with a rubber mallet and a large chunk of metal when a motorcyclist rode across the parking strip onto the sidewalk and shut the motor off, walking a Harley-Davidson Sportster toward me with a leg on either side. The rider wore a white helmet and full leathers.

"You ready?" Estevez asked, removing her helmet and shaking out her voluminous hair.

It took me a few moments to believe what I was seeing. "You never told me you had a bike."

"You never asked. Does that hurt? You should be on medication."

"I'm saving the meds for later."

It was almost noon when we left. We took nonarterials. Estevez handled her bike well. I wanted to ask her how long she'd been riding, but as long as we were moving, neither of us could hear the other over the sound of the bikes.

I'd spent the morning on the phone and on the Internet, trying without success to track down any public information on Silverstar Consolidated. I couldn't find anything, but I knew who to ask.

Chester McDonald was in his driveway washing his Benz when I roared up the slope, skidding to a halt in front of him. I tipped the bike on its kickstand and shut off the motor. Behind me, Estevez shut off her bike. "You got some answering to do, Chester."

"I want my attorney. What right you got to come—"

"Talk, you bastard."

McDonald dropped his head, and I knew the combination of fear and being cornered had finally gotten to him. "You get me my crutches?" Estevez picked up the crutches and handed them to him. Once he had them under his shoulders, he said, "I sold it to Silverstar Consolidated last February. After that, all I did was manage the place. Before the fire they didn't want me to make it public that they were buying up property, and after the fire they didn't want people to know they were squeezing nickels out of the place. All they cared about was bringing in a few more bucks. Nobody thought it would hurt anything to skip some stupid regulations."

"What else?"

"The guys running the club . . ."

"Chaps," I said.

"And Campbell," Estevez added.

"They was trying to cut corners. Somebody from Silverstar Consolidated told me and them to go right ahead. He would fix it downtown. They weren't supposed to be having parties. The building department told them not to. But they came to me and I spoke to . . ."

"Renfrow? Barry Renfrow?"

"He said not to worry about it, that the owners were highly connected, and if we could squeeze some more rental money out of the place before it came time to tear it down, so much the better. It was all so stupid. It was only a matter of a couple hundred dollars a week. But that's how they were. Every little penny. Said that's how rich people stayed rich."

"Who were the owners?"

"Silverstar Consolidated."

"That's a holding corporation. The real owners."

"Renfrow told me the real owner was Harlan Overby. I remember the name because I read about him in a magazine the next day. When the light-rail came through, they were going to tear it down and put up something that would make some real money."

"You sure Harlan Overby was the owner of the building?" I asked.

"That's what Renfrow told me."

Estevez looked at me and said, "We need to talk."

We fired up our bikes and cruised down the hill to Seward Park, driving around the park loop until we found an outlook over the lake. A couple in an older Toyota left when they saw two black people on Harleys. I reminded Estevez about the tape India had given me, and she said, "We could give this information along with the tape to the TV station. Or the Z

Club Citizens for Truth. If they can connect Renfrow to the attack on you last night . . ."

"Maybe we should let things cool off before we drop a gasoline bomb on a campfire. You play that tape in public, there's going to be maximum civil unrest. This whole city has been on the verge of a meltdown. Even my brother got caught up in it."

"We write the report. We release it and you release the tape a little later. Keep them separate?"

"But soon. We have to do this soon."

A day later, when a prize pig flew out of an airplane and through a roof in West Seattle, the news guys forgot about chasing me around for quotes on the assault. A week passed in which I took a different route from my house every time I left, sometimes riding the Harley, sometimes taking the car, and more often borrowing Rumble's truck. Though I didn't believe they would try it again, I didn't need to get ambushed a second time. The swelling in my face subsided; I went back to work. I needed to ride Engine 28, needed the normalcy of the abnormal our job provided to feel like myself again. Over the course of several dinners, Estevez and I negotiated the wording in the report. We continued to squabble, though the tenor became less adversarial and more playful, and I realized that without meaning to, I was beginning to fall in love with Jamie Estevez.

60. GEE, I'LL HAVE TO GIVE A REALLY SAD SPEECH

STONE CARMICHAEL

"Jesus, Stone. You should have warned me your brother spent the last twenty years studying martial arts. And the clowns I hired—the doctors thought one of them was going to be in a wheelchair the rest of his life, but luckily he's starting to get some feeling back in his legs. I hate to see guys get hurt. One of the others lost a testicle, for God's sake."

"You're the one who's supposed to do the intelligence," I said. Renfrow was in front of me in my father's old office in the Key Tower, breathing heavily the way he always did. "A testicle?"

"I guess you could say I was the one who got him interested in martial arts all those years ago. Hated to do that to the kid. He was game, though. He just kept getting back up. I couldn't even watch. That's what scares me now. He's going to keep coming . . . I know he is. It's his nature."

"What are you planning?"

"I got somebody watching the house. It's only a matter of time before we get the tape, if he's got it. Beyond that, I'm not calling the shots here. You are. We should have Tasered him, but people start using Tasers, the cops get suspicious."

"Next time let's be prepared for every contingency, okay?"

"Like the contingency he's going to bang your wife and steal a tape out of your machine?"

"Hey, shut up! You're the employee here! Don't forget that!"

"Maybe so, but I work for Overby."

"Yes, and he's working this out with me. When I'm governor next year, you'll still be the employee. And Barry. Don't mention my wife again."

"Sure. Fine. No problem. Guy bones my bride, I guess I'd be a little touchy, too."

"Fuck you."

"Hey. It never happened. I doubt they even did anything. Geez. I was having a little fun."

Together we watched traffic on the street below. I said, "I didn't think it was that big of a deal. The club guy wanted to cut some corners with the fire department. The building's only going to be up a few more months. So when you came to me, I said, yeah, go ahead, we'll cover you. And then . . . just like that, fourteen people are in coffins and mobs are in the streets and Seattle's skyline is on the cover of *Newsweek*.

If people ever find out Overby owned the building and I was promising immunity from the fire inspectors, all hell will break loose."

"We can stop it right now."

"How?"

"I called an old acquaintance on the East Coast. He tells me there's nobody easier to eliminate than a professional firefighter. All you have to know is *where* they work and *when* they work. I hate to do something this drastic, but he's put us in a corner, hasn't he?"

"How would it work?"

"Firefighting is an inherently dangerous job. People fall in holes. Roofs cave in."

"And when might this happen?"

Renfrow pulled a small card out of his wallet and said, "I've got the fire department work schedule here. When would you like it to happen? My friend back east is free any time."

"Let's do it the night of the party. And don't make him into a goddamn hero this time, okay?"

"That's going to be a tough order. Dead firemen are always heroes. When it's finished, I'll swing by the party and inform you that the city's had another tragedy."

"Gee, I'll have to give a really sad speech."

"Your star always shines during a tragedy."

"Doesn't it, though?"

61. A FAST-RISING COLUMN OF BLACK SMOKE

TREY

Everybody in the department carries a portable radio into fires, and every portable radio has an emergency button that is capable of sending a signal to the dispatchers indicating the firefighter is in trouble, yet you can count on your fingers the number of people who've activated their emergency buttons even once during their careers. For the most part, emergency buttons are activated by accident. When they're activated purposely, it is usually done too late, because by the time your typical firefighter decides things are hairy enough to push the panic button, he or she is finished anyway.

Nobody wants to appear to have panicked by calling an emergency unnecessarily. Firefighters pride themselves on being cool in all situations, and even if none of us say it aloud, a person who panicked would know at least some of his coworkers no longer felt he or she was trustworthy. At most large fires, Seattle keeps a team ready for downed firefighters, so that in less than a minute at least five people come busting in with hose lines, pry bars, thermal imagers, and extra air, but even then it takes time to locate a person. The rule is, don't run out of air. When modern materials are exposed to the combustion process, the by-products are so toxic a firefighter without a breathing apparatus may have only minutes of consciousness. Or seconds.

The second difficulty with the panic button is that you have to take your glove off to activate it. You can pick up a hot ingot in fire department gloves, climb a ladder, or work a power tool, but you cannot activate the emergency button, which means you'll be taking off at least one glove in an environment hot enough to melt plastic. You will be immediately incapacitated for many of the other tasks at hand. The two dead firefighters I'd seen who'd activated their buttons never got that glove back on.

The third issue with using the emergency button is that the button automatically transfers the sender to channel sixteen, a channel nobody but the dispatchers monitor. The thinking is you will push the button, get switched to sixteen, and avoid all the fire traffic that clutters the fire channel, thus enabling you to converse with the dispatchers in a timely manner. The dispatchers will then relay information from the trapped firefighter to the incident commander, who will relay it to the troops making the rescue. That is the theory. In actuality, the more layers of respondents a message goes through, the more likelihood of a miscommunication. Also, your average trapped firefighter has a lot on his mind, so it is not uncommon for him to forget he's been switched to channel sixteen with access only to the dispatcher.

On Wednesday night when I pushed my emergency button, all three issues came into play.

By that morning a lot of things had changed. I still hadn't decided when to drop the hammer on Stone. I had physical proof that he was included in the shenanigans that made the two Z Club managers feel they had the right to sidestep the law and that he was part of a cover-up in the chain of events that resulted in the deaths of thirteen civilians and one firefighter. Yet putting the tape out in the public domain might not get him prosecuted, although I had no doubt it would certainly ruin him politically. I'd been told by a lawyer the tape most likely would not be admitted into a court of law, but it might be used to get a grand jury started.

The previous Sunday I had rode Engine 28 for the first time in over a week. That night from work I surprised myself by asking Estevez to be my date for a dinner I'd reserved a month earlier. I'd planned to ask somebody special but had never settled on whom until then. Or maybe I'd known for a week. So last night we walked from her condo in Belltown to Teatro ZinZanni, a dinner club with a full-scale vaudeville show between courses: clowns, singers, tumblers, jugglers, and a trapeze act. Oddly, our arguments were not only friendlier but downright sexy.

Estevez's report would be ready for me to read in a day or two, and as soon as we were in agreement on its contents, we would release it. The report would be released simultaneously to the mayor, the Z Club Citizens for Truth committee, and the media. Estevez expected the demonstrations to end when the report came out. I expected them to grow worse.

"Care to make a bet?" I'd asked.

"What do you want to bet?"

"How about you lose, you cook a four-course meal for me, my brother, and Rumble."

"And what are you going to put up against dinner?"

"I'll tune up your bike."

"What's wrong with my bike?"

"Nothing a little tune-up won't fix."

Anticipating an easy victory, she smiled. "You're on." When we reached the front door of her building, I kissed her lightly on the lips, then told her I had to get home and get some rest for the twenty-four-hour shift I would be working the next day. For an instant I thought I saw just the faintest glimmer of disappointment that I wasn't coming up.

As for me, my wounds had mostly healed. The facial swelling had gone down and the fracture to my cheekbone would heal on its own. It was good to be back at work with Clyde and Kitty.

Tonight the mayor was planning to throw a bash on the 100-foot level of the Space Needle, ostensibly to celebrate his fifteenth wedding anniversary, but in reality to announce his candidacy for the governor's race that was going to be held in a special election in February, to replace our current governor who was leaving to take care of a wife with Alzheimer's.

During the day, Engine 28 caught five aid calls and a resuscitation. My friend Rumble was working a rare overtime shift on Engine 30. He'd called me at the station several times that day, bugging me about various little matters mostly pertaining to the "date" I had with Estevez the night before and explaining ad nauseam how he'd already spent the overtime money he hadn't yet received.

The trouble started just as we were about to sit down to dinner at Station 28. It was an alarm for a building fire on Martin Luther King Way near where they were tearing up the streets for the new train line, maybe fifteen blocks from the station. We would arrive first, which made me responsible for the initial size-up, fire report, and tactics. By the time we were rolling up Graham Street, already several blocks in front of the slower, heavier ladder truck, we could see it was a good-size blaze.

The dispatcher's radio update said, "Engine Twenty-eight, this is a report of a warehouse fire. We're getting a lot of calls on it."

"Engine Twenty-eight okay," I said on the rig radio. "We're on Graham Street, and from here we can see a fast-rising column of black smoke."

"Okay, Engine Twenty-eight."

Although we'd had a small house fire on our last shift, this would be the first good fire most of us had been to since the Z Club. "Looks bad," said Kitty, who was a bundle of nerves at the best of times.

"Piece of cake," I said. "We'll probably lay a manifold. You stretch the line. I'll give my radio report and meet you at the front door."

"You got it," Kitty replied, choking on a dry throat.

Martin Luther King Junior Way was one of two primary north-south arterials running through our district. It was a characterless roadway lined with strip malls, small shopping centers, tire shops, take-out chicken joints, and Vietnamese grocers. The road was four or five lanes across, and this section of it ran through a residential area that was home to African Americans, recent Asian immigrants, East African immigrants, as well as a significant Hispanic and South Sea island population.

It didn't seem like much at first, a forty-five by sixty-foot two-story building that had once housed a restaurant, later had been converted into a small church, and for the last year or two had, according to what I remembered, been vacant. It had a flat roof and windows along the parking lot. The side toward MLK had a door and one high window. All the windows were smoked over from the inside, and a column of black smoke was rising out of a heating/air-conditioning duct on the roof. Greenish-tinged gray smoke was puffing out around the doors. Clyde parked close enough that I could see padlocks on both sets of doors.

There was a hydrant close by, but Clyde signaled he wanted

to park directly in front of the building on MLK, which we did. I told Kitty to forget the manifold and stretch the preconnect, two hundred feet of hose already connected to the pump.

On the radio, I said, "Engine Twenty-eight at Martin Luther King Junior Way South and South Lucille. Establishing King Command. We have a two-story wood-frame building with heavy black smoke showing from the roof. Engine Twenty-eight laying a preconnect through the front door. Engine Thirty-three, give us a supply. Engine Thirteen, lay a backup line. Ladder Twelve, use forcible entry on the front door and ventilate."

The dispatcher was repeating my report and the various units were confirming assignments as I stepped to the rear of the apparatus and slid open my mask compartment. People were stopping their cars on MLK to watch, and I quickly got on the portable radio and said, "Dispatch from King Command, give us SPD for traffic control."

"Okay, King Command. SPD for traffic control."

There were more occupancies nearby, a strip mall and some parking spaces and a small Buddhist temple, but I wasn't focusing on any of them. Smoke was coming out from under the door, and it looked to be under pressure. The whole area tasted like a melting boot might.

By the time I got masked up and joined Kitty at the front door, a man from Ladder 12 was breaking the lock off the doors, kicking them open. Kitty and I took the now-charged hose line inside and into a mass of black and greenish smoke. This was one of those times when we prayed the truck company behind us would get a fan running in the doorway or go to the roof and cut a hole, because as soon as we crawled across the threshold, it got hot. The farther inside we went, the hotter it got. Visibility diminished to nothing.

Listening to ourselves breathe through the noisy regulators on our masks, we found ourselves in a long corridor, crawling along the floor, feeling the left wall for doors. Still without having dispensed any water, we found a door and opened it into a cavernous room that had far better visibility than the corridor. The opposite end of the room was filled with junk, old chairs, pews from when this was a church, dining tables, and stacks of personal belongings previous occupants had abandoned.

In the far corner, high up, we could see a smidgen of flame. I was on the pipe and hit it with a burst from a straight stream until steam filled the room and obscured my face piece, which I wiped instinctively with a glove. Now that visibility was decreasing, we moved by the quick memory fragment we'd received upon entering the room, pulling the extremely heavy, water-filled hose line in behind us, gathering an extra loop so we'd be able to negotiate the room freely.

With the hose line shut down, I could hear the fire crackling in the far upper corner of the ceiling, and then, as I stood in the heat, I could see another dab of orange. I hit it one more time, knowing more steam would come down on us.

Instead, the ceiling caved in and ripped the hose out of my hands.

It started behind us, but came down so quickly I wasn't sure which direction to run. It was coming down in chunks, shaking the floor, various objects landing with metallic thunking sounds.

I pulled Kitty's coat to indicate she should follow me, and we high-stepped through the junk toward the doorway, then made our way to the main entrance. There was no point in picking up the hose, which weighed over a hundred pounds with all the water in it and it was pinned to the floor by debris anyway; no point in risking our lives in a vacant building. We needed to get out as quickly as possible. We would fight this from outside.

In the main entranceway it was noticeably cooler, but when I turned to mention this to Kitty, she'd vanished. "Kitty!"

I started back down the corridor toward the room we'd just exited. "What the hell are you doing? Let's get out of here." More objects crashed through the ceiling, large pieces of building material, judging by the sound. It was sootier and smokier than ever. I could barely see her, and she was only five feet from me. "Kitty, what the hell are you doing?"

"Getting the hose."

"Screw the hose. We need to move. Let the city pay for it."

But she wasn't going to let the city pay. She didn't want to write a letter explaining why we'd abandoned the line. Nor did she want to appear panicky by having run out of a building without every piece of equipment she'd hauled in.

I could hear her moving inside the doorway as more junk fell from the rooms above us, and then as I moved toward her, something large and heavy fell behind me, brushing the composite compressed air cylinder on my back and pushing me forward. The floor shuddered, and I stumbled into the room. More crap fell. A slow avalanche. Several lighter pieces hit my helmet and shoulders.

"Kitty! Get the hell out of here. Are you nuts?"

"Yeah, I guess I am. What was that?"

"I don't know. It sounded like an engine block."

In the corner of the room flames were growing rapidly, but that wasn't our concern now. The hose line was buried under a ton of junk. It was as if we were at the bottom of a garbage chute, stuff hitting my shoulders, bombarding Kitty, raining on us. We would be lucky to get out of here without one of us sustaining a broken neck.

As Kitty reached me and we turned to exit the room, I could feel the heat coming down on us. We got low, almost in a crawl, and headed for the door, but before we reached the doorway, another volley of debris dropped out of the ceiling, large chunks landing in front of us. The building shuddered, and it all stopped.

"You okay?" I asked Kitty.

"I don't know. I think my shoulder's hurt."

"Can you move?"

"As soon as I get all this crap off myself. Geez, it's getting hot."

"Don't worry. We'll be out in a minute."

62. I DON'T THINK SO

BARRY RENFROW

"How are we going to know he's dead?"

"I'm listening to the goddamned fire radios right now. Don't be worrying your butt off. This is going just fine. Every day a firefighter dies somewhere in the country. Today is Seattle's turn."

"How will we know things are going right? They won't announce it over the air, will they? They won't want the media to get it before the family."

"You want a blow-by-blow? The asshole's inside with his partner. I've got my charges set so when I push this button here, the first section of the ceiling caves in on him. Then the fire gets hotter. Then when the rescuers try to go inside, more of the roof caves in. That's when the exterior crews decide he can rescue his own ass. Trust me on this. I know how firefighters die. They'll make a valiant effort, but in the end no department wants to lose two or three crews at once."

"Are they going to know this was murder?"

"Firefighters die in arsons all the time. Nobody's ever going to guess someone would target an individual firefighter."

"When was the last time you had any trouble doing this?"

"*Never* had any trouble. Every one of them's gone off without a hitch. Trust me. I know what I'm doing."

"This guy's got nine lives."

"Maybe so, but there's only going to be *one* funeral."

The two of us are across the hood of my Ford Excursion, leaning on our elbows, binoculars to our eyes. I'd gotten the second pair of Bushnell's for Marci back when we were still together and had been bird-watching every weekend, driving to the swamps out in the lower Snoqualmie Valley to see the ospreys, to the rain forest in the Olympics for the warblers.

Back then I looked forward to the weekends. Hard to believe I haven't seen Marci in twelve years. Now this drugged-up clown from the Philadelphia Fire Department—retired—is scraping the zipper on his jacket across my paint job, and no matter how many times I remind him, I still hear the zitzing sound as the metal zipper makes tiny signatures in my Pueblo Gold finish. We are parked three blocks from the fire building, up the hill above a small strip mall. Oblivious to our presence, a rufous-sided towhee scratches furiously in the leaves in front of us.

Hackett has taken a saw out of his toolbox and cut down a couple of small branches so we can see the fire building. Just as predicted, Engine 28 is the first unit to reach the fire. Just as predicted, Brown and his partner march right through the front door. What a job. I've done some wild things in my life, but walking into a house fire was not ever one of them. I don't know why they're not scared shitless every time they do it.

"So what happens next?"

"Just like I told you."

"Tell me again."

"I knew I shouldn't have let you come. Usually I'm on my own. Gives me better mobility."

"Yeah, well, I was knocking out government ministers in South America when you were still sending applesauce through to your didies. What's next?"

"Next we wait until they're inside. I'll watch how much line goes in. That's my indicator. Then I dump the attic on them in stages. At the same time, the heat will build, and in five minutes they'll be with the angels."

"Are you sure they can't get out some other way?"

"Not after I bring the ceiling down. I spent two nights loading junk up there."

"Did you say 'them'? Are there two of them?"

"That's how Seattle operates. Everybody has a partner."

"We don't want two victims."

"You want me to run down and stop it?"

"Fuck you."

"You nail 'em both or you nail neither. You got a two-for-one deal here. I should charge extra."

"At the Z Club he was by himself."

"I read that. That was a special circumstance." He pushes a button on the box in front of him. "Look at that. See all that smoke billowing out like there was an explosion?"

"What does that mean?"

"It means your boy is dead. Or as good as."

I'm thinking this guy is a jackass, that I don't trust him any farther than I can carry him, and that after this is over I'm going to take him somewhere and make sure he never talks about this. He's got his suitcases in the back of my Excursion, so it won't be as if there will be any traces lying around. A guy takes a flight to Seattle and doesn't come home. Nobody'll know how he disappeared. Afterward I'll take the body down to the plating plant and slide him into the acid vats. Take care of everything, including that damned zipper.

I've been getting more and more depressed about everything. Depressed about being alone all the time. Depressed about being the mechanism that secures Trey Brown's end. Depressed over the fact that I don't want to kill him. I like Brown. He's plucky. In fact, I like him a lot more than I like his brother.

The only part that cheers me up is that we'll soon be driving toward the airport, that I'll take a couple of detours, get lost, and stick a .357 in this jackass's side and tell him goodbye. I know I'm not going to be thrilled about it later, but right now, standing beside this smug bastard, it cheers me up to know Brown and his partner aren't the only ones headed for the angels.

63. EIGHTY/TWENTY ON A BAD DEATH

TREY

When the building stops cascading onto our heads, I find myself in a sitting position with my back against the wall. I have a real bad feeling about this fire. In front of me I hear Kitty moving, and above us the crackling of the flames. The heat is becoming unbearable. It feels as if we've just put our heads into an oven.

Somehow I've gotten myself pinned under a massive pile of debris. I am thankful my face mask is intact and I am still breathing bottled air, otherwise it would be a lot worse. Something large and heavy is lying across my lap, from the feel of it, a beam. When I push against it, nothing happens.

"Kitty, are you all right?"

"Yeah. I'm out from under all this crap now. Let's go. Geez, it's hot. Let's go. Let's get out of here."

"I'd like to, but I have a little problem."

Kitty is making her way through the rubble toward where she believes the doorway is. I can feel her weight as it is added to the tonnage on my lap. "Jesus. Get off."

"What?"

"Get off. I'm under you." She steps back, and the load lightens. "There's something on my legs. I can't move it."

Slowly she makes her way to my position, and I feel her gloved hands as she palms my face to ascertain where I am. She begins removing articles from the heap, tossing each item over her shoulder as she disentangles it. It is dark enough that we are both nearly blind, although I've got my helmet flashlight on and I'm reasonably sure hers is on, too. After she's cleared some of the debris, I feel her on the pile again. She's not that large a woman, but like all of us, she wears fifty pounds of gear. "What is this? A girder?"

"Hell if I know. Maybe if we both try to lift at the same time." We grunt in unison, each working in our own way, but the beam refuses to budge.

"This is going to take at least four people," I say.

"How the hell did you end up here?" Kitty asks, annoyed at my carelessness.

I want to yell, "Because I had to come back for you, you freaking nutcase," but instead I say, "Listen. Get to the doorway before it's compromised. We're going to need another hand line. The heat's building."

"Sure. I can do that."

As she climbs over the beam and moves along the wall searching for the doorway, I take off my left glove and fumble my portable radio out of my bunking coat's chest pocket—I can feel the top part of it scorching my fingers when I push the tiny nipple on top, the emergency button. After what seems like an eternity, a female dispatcher says, "Engine Twenty-eight. We show your officer has activated his emergency button."

"That's affirmative. I'm trapped under rubble inside the building. My partner is trying to find the exit. We need a RIT in here now. It's getting hot."

"Okay, Engine Twenty-eight. We'll relay that to the IC. Get you some people. Can you give us your location?"

"Just inside the front doorway in the first big room to the left. We're maybe thirty feet inside the building."

"Okay, Engine Twenty-eight. Thirty feet inside the main doorway in a room on the left."

"Affirmative."

It all sounds calm and organized over the airwaves, but that's not how I'm feeling. I've never been in this kind of a pickle before. The Z Club was horrendous, but I had mobility and knew where the exit was until the very last. This is different. I'm pinned. I can't move an inch. I'm at the mercy of other firefighters. I'm in the position Vernon Sweeting found himself in. All I can do is wait.

Kitty remains in the room with me, looking for the door while I begin removing bits of debris from around the beam that pins my legs, clearing the space as best I am able. The beam is buffered by a thick layer of debris on my legs, which is probably why I can't feel the beam, just the weight. Outside I can hear Engine 28's motor but not much else. In fact, nothing else. No fans. No chain saws. No men yelling. Nothing but Kitty's footsteps in the dark. "You haven't found the door?" I ask.

"It's jammed."

"Can you bust it down?"

I hear her thumping for a few moments. "It's steel, for cripe's sake. Why would anybody put a steel door *inside* a building?"

"Don't worry. They'll be here soon." Kitty continues to search for an exit, and when that proves futile, tries to unearth our hose line so we'll at least have the protection of a water stream, but that exploration is just as futile. God, how I hate this. It is like being nailed to the floor, my back and bottle jammed hard against the wall. In fact, that's the only part of me that hurts, where the backpack is biting into my back. "Try to breach a wall," I say.

"Jesus, you think I'm Supergirl? I'd need an axe."

If he isn't already, the IC will be organizing a rescue effort. We have a lot of friends out there, and they won't let us down.

"Engine Twenty-eight?" the dispatcher says.

"Engine Twenty-eight, over."

"Update on your situation?"

"We're trapped in this room. I'm pinned. My partner can move but cannot get out of the room. The door's jammed. It's getting hotter, and we don't have a hose line."

"How much air do you have left, Engine Twenty-eight?"

"A thousand pounds."

"Okay, Engine Twenty-eight."

Then we begin to hear movement on the other side of the wall. Movement, hose streams, men yelling. The voices have the agitated character that marks a rapidly souring event. Taking a brick from the debris around me, I begin slowly banging on the wall at my back. At least they'll know where I am. I can give them that.

These are rapidly becoming the longest minutes of my life. How long have I been trapped now? Three minutes? Five? Half a lifetime? All I can do is sit and conserve air. "Hey, Kitty," I call out.

"Yo, boss."

"Sit down. Make your air last."

"Good idea. You think they're going to find us in time?"

"Of course they are," I lie.

Before she told me the door was jammed, I'd estimated our odds at eighty-twenty in favor of survival, but now I reversed the numbers. We are pretty much finished.

64. CANDY ASSES

JAMES RUMBLE

We are standing in front of the building when Trey shows up in the front door looking his normal confident self, even though it looks like somebody dumped a garbage can over his head. I am on my way over to say something funny to him when he turns and walks back into the smoke. No particular reason that I can see.

There is a high overcast today, not warm enough for shorts—typical goddamn Seattle weather—but I am sweating just from walking around in this heavy gear. It don't let you breathe, man. It's like when they were making *Goldfinger* and the prop guys painted that naked lady with gold paint and she died because her skin couldn't breathe. I *think* she died. Or maybe that was an urban legend. Anyway, we're in these turnouts sweating like we're going to die.

Allen, Bill, Patrick, and me are waiting for a definitive order. It would probably help if Trey and his partner would get out of there. The roof is roaring now, and we're going to fight this from outside. As soon as they get out. We start pulling lines along the ground. Another crew is carrying a monitor to the opposite side of the building to set up in the parking area. Citizens are scrambling to move their cars, no doubt recalling the ruined vehicles outside the Z Club. Allen and I are hauling a hundred feet of two-and-a-half-inch line to the end of the building. The eaves are smoking pretty good the first time we look, but now there's actual flame licking out. I'm thinking this thing is out of control.

As we move, there's another loud crash inside the building, and I think to myself, shit, if Trey's anywhere near that, he's in trouble, but then I don't think about it again for a few minutes. We're getting water on the line when I hear on the radio that Engine 28 is trapped inside.

I find it hard to believe, because I just saw Trey a few minutes ago. On the other hand, there was that loud crash inside. From where we're positioned I can see along the front of the building, where they've got crews masking up to go in and get him, and it's taking forever, dammit. Then they're crawling in through the front door, crawling under the heat, dragging a hose line, another crew on top of them with a second hose line. They're moving so damned slow.

They are inside less than a minute when they come tumbling back out, rolling along the ground like monkeys, a fireball chasing them. Somebody picks up a hose line in the yard and douses them, cools each one off. Their turnout coats let off steam when the water hits, so you know it was hot in there. They go over to the IC, a chief from the Seventh I've met but don't know real well.

I can feel the bile in my throat. Trey Brown is my best friend, and if he's trapped inside, we can't stand around with our dicks in our hands. I head on over to the IC in time to hear the crews telling him it's too damn hot inside. "Besides, the room is barricaded. We'd have to cut through the wall with chain saws."

The chief gives them a long, slow look, and I can see everybody digesting the fact that they are about to declare a couple of comrades dead and gone. I'm seeing this, but I'm not believing it.

"You fuckers!" I scream. "Get your candy asses in there! What the hell is wrong with you chickenshit motherfuckers! Do it!"

They turn around sequentially, some of them looking at me, others looking back at the doorway, which has enough flame now that the crew with the hose line is backing away—still squirting but backing away. I can see the fire is using the doorway as a chimney, and that fifteen feet inside the entrance it's not as bad. We all wait a few beats, the four masked firefighters, me, the IC, and my crew on Engine 30. I know you're not supposed to go berserk at fires, but when your buddy is inside and people are writing him off like it's a table exercise . . . that's when I feel like I'm in the loony bin.

"You motherfuckers better cover me," I say. "You damn well better cover me!"

Even though I'm moving now, my curses bounce off them like pebbles. They all just stand and gape.

I'm pulling my face piece tight, hooking up the air, engaging the regulator, pulling my gloves on, walking toward a chain saw on the ground, jerking on the starter cord, jerking again. It fires up on the third yank just as somebody tugs on my shoulder from behind. I'm standing near the doorway now, and I can feel the heat through the turnouts.

"They're dead!" somebody says. "Feel that heat. They're dead." Something deep in my gut tells me he's right, that it's too late, but that only makes me crazier.

As they try to pull me from the doorway, a radio transmission comes out of the building. It's a woman's voice. "King Command from Engine Twenty-eight. We're running low on air. King Command?"

"You fuckers!" I say, and head through the doorway, where the entire top half is flame. I squat low and walk right through it, and as soon as I get inside, the heat decreases. And then my backside and the entire doorway is showered in water as a hose stream hits my butt, and I feel the cooling effect, my back pounded by the hose stream, my front half baking.

I cannot see shit, and I don't know where I'm going, because I can barely remember the directions that were given over the air. That's when I hear the banging. Somebody's banging rhythmically on a wall. I follow the sound. Behind me, two crews creep along with hose lines flowing, water splattering the ceiling high above us, bouncing off the walls, splashing across my back. They're not putting out the fire, which is in the attic space above us, but they are cooling things a little.

I find the spot where the banging is coming from, next to a door, knock the safety brake off the chain saw with my wrist, and rev up the saw, a Stihl twenty-inch, with carbide tips on the chain for cutting through just about anything. With the nose of the chain saw, I touch the door and a shower of sparks shoots into my face. The door is metal. I move to the right and begin working. It takes ten seconds of pushing just to get the blade through the wall.

It's heavy sledding, but I'm not going to give up. Trey's on the other side of this wall. Trey and his partner. He's maybe two feet from me, and it's going to be something short of ridiculous if I can't get him out. The whirring motor shrieks, and I bury the blade and fight the contortions of the saw, the muscles in my arms and shoulders twitching with the effort. I feel sweat run down my spine.

From time to time sparks shoot off the chain. Three cuts, I figure. One across the top. One down the right side. One down the left side. Maybe another at the bottom. Then we kick it out. Damn, this is hard work. I know these guys want to spell me, but there's no way I'm letting these chickenshit motherfuckers take hold of this saw. They had their go.

And then the saw begins choking and shuts down. I pull it out of the wall, pull the cord and rev it up to get the rpms where they should be, but still, it keeps choking. Like us, any internal combustion engine requires oxygen to function, and like us, deprived of oxygen, it begins to misbehave.

65. TEXAS CHAIN SAW MASSACRE

TREY

Over Kitty's radio, we listen as the dispatcher informs King Command he has firefighters trapped inside the building.

I tell Kitty to check her gear and make certain no skin is exposed, and then I do as much myself. It is best to make these checks with gloves off, but when I touch my helmet, my bare fingers recoil from the hot plastic, so I put my gloves back on. Chatty Kathy is strangely silent. She thinks we're going to die. And she's wondering how the hell she ever got herself into a job where you can be cooked to death inside a layered Nomex suit—tall, slim Kitty Acton, who before joining the fire department wanted to be a veterinarian.

The airwaves are crackling. "Dispatch from King Command. Our RIT team is making entry." Moments later we actually hear firefighters through the thick wall behind us. I can feel movement through the bottle on my back, which is snug against the wall, can feel the vibrations of people moving. And then it is quiet for a long time, perhaps ninety seconds, maybe two minutes. Certainly long enough to cook to death.

"Dispatch from King Command. Our RIT team has been forced out of the building. Repeat. Our RIT team has been forced out of the building because of high heat. We're trying to cool the area now."

"Geez, they left," Kitty says.

"They'll be back."

"Dispatch from King Command. We're not going to be able to access this building from the front. We're going to look for another entrance."

"Jesus," said Kitty. "They're not coming back."

"Hold your horses. It's going to be all right."

But it isn't going to be all right, and we both know it.

Radio traffic has died down. It is rare to have zero fire traffic at a working fire, but that's what we are experiencing. Is it possible they are simply standing out there waiting for us to burn to death? If so, they won't have a long wait. I can hear Kitty burrowing into the debris looking for a cooler place, squirming down like a rat. It is getting hot enough that I pick up a piece of the ceiling board and prop it up to shield me from the radiant heat boring down on us from the fire above our heads. After a while the shield bursts into flame, and I toss it aside.

"Why can't they get us out?" Kitty asks despairingly. I do not reply. I am thinking this is the end. This is how it's going to end.

We all wonder at some point in our lives how we're going to finish. Unless we have a terminal illness or are sitting on death row, it is an enigma for most. Tonight I can verify how and when I am going to die. I'm going to heat up and lose consciousness and eventually burn to death in a smoked-up room beside a firefighter I've worked with for five years and can barely tolerate. It is remarkable to me that I am no more panicked than if I were sitting in the dentist's office waiting for an appointment. Maybe that's because there's nothing I can do about any of this.

There will be a whole lot of people at the funeral. Johnny will cry. My mother will handle it with the same stoicism with which she's handled all the bad luck in her life. Jesus will be her savior. There will be a massive department-orchestrated funeral, and our caskets will be lushly filmed for the news. They will remember that I was the hero at the Z Club and marvel that I could be dead a month later. People will give long, rambling speeches recalling trivia about my life that I don't even remember. The mayor will give a speech over my casket and tell the crowds he loved me like a brother.

There is a rattling, and something attacks the steel door, banging against it. After a moment, I decide it's a chain saw. The noise goes away. Then the wall directly behind me begins to vibrate. Moments later a chain saw blade pops through the wall.

"Goddamn," says Kitty. "You gotta love 'em."

The chain saw is high and to my left, working across the wall above me. Then the horizontal cut is ended and the saw is withdrawn. They begin another cut, this one vertically about four feet to my right, coming down the wall, the blade poking through on our side. Don't they know when you're cutting through a wall you don't bury the blade? You go by feel, and when the blade has barely breached the wall you hold it there. That is the procedure. Whoever is working that chain saw is working wild.

The vertical cut four feet to my right takes longer than did the horizontal one over my head. Perhaps the chain is becoming dulled. It isn't until the first downward vertical cut is almost complete that I try to recall exactly where the horizontal cut above my head began, because it is beginning to occur to me that the next downward vertical cut will be along my spine.

I'm jammed up against the wall and they're preparing to cut me in half lengthwise.

I push the send button on my portable radio and say, "Engine Twenty-eight to RIT team. Don't bury the saw so deep. I'm trapped against the wall opposite where you're cutting."

I wait a few moments, but there is no reply. The saw finishes its cut to my right, and a moment later it bulges through the wall directly over my head, showering sawdust over me. At the depth he's burying the blade, it will rip through my bunking coat. It will slice my helmet. It will open my back in a way that will probably kill me. I arch and look up, using the flashlight on my helmet, directing the beam so that I might know whether the blade is going to come down with surgical precision or gross imprecision. Someone's got it poised directly over my spine.

"Kitty!" I shout. "You gotta jam the saw! It's coming right at me."

As she begins to stir, the saw blade crawls down the wall toward me, three feet away, two and a half, two . . . with a grinding sound . . . "Engine Twenty-eight to command. The saw is too deep. You have to stop the saw."

No reply. I repeat my message as the saw blade moves toward me. To her credit, Kitty hits the wall hard. I don't know what the article is, but she holds it flat against the wall, and then the chain saw blade whips through it like a hot knife through butter. "God damn!" she says, scrabbling for another object to block the blade.

But it's too late. The blade nicks my helmet and specks fly off, then it passes my neck and I cringe. It spins and whirs on my composite air bottle and jams. The blade is stuck in the wall for a moment and then they pull it out. I whack the wall five times in succession, desperately trying to send a message.

When the dispatcher calls on my radio, I realize why I haven't contacted the fire crews. I've been on channel 16. Everybody else is on channel 1, the fire ground channel. The dispatcher says, "Engine Twenty-eight. Your message was garbled. Repeat."

"The saw they're using is going to cut me," I say as calmly as possible. Kitty is straddling me now, standing over me with a chunk of something else she's found in the rubble, her bunking trousers crotch in my face. "Tell the rescue crews they have to move the cut."

"Okay, Engine Twenty-eight. We'll relay the message."

When the saw starts up again and pokes through the wall, we can hear the dispatcher's warning on Kitty's radio, but it occurs to me that it will be impossible to pick up on the other side of the wall because of the roaring chain saw. The saw has been moved over a few inches, and I struggle to try to reposition myself so it will come down on the bottle again, but I cannot move. They're going to gut me from behind.

The saw moves faster this time, and I tell Kitty not to let the chain take a chunk out of her. Even as I'm speaking the blade cuts through whatever piece of junk she's jammed against the wall, and she falls backward in front of me, landing on the beam across my lap. It hurts, but it doesn't hurt as much as the chain saw blade when it zippers alongside my air bottle and shreds my bunking coat and goes deep enough so that I can actually feel the revolving steel in my back. I vow not to scream, but even before I complete the silent vow I begin screaming.

In the movies people pass out when they feel this much pain, but the blade rips into my flesh and continues down as if I'm just another layer of wallpaper, and no matter how badly I want to, I do not pass out. And then the blade is done, and they're hacking at the wall with axes, and moments later the heat lifts as I fall backward into the corridor with a large chunk of the wall. The idling chain saw on the floor is next to my head.

I watch Kitty being led to safety, and then they're lifting the beam off my legs and dragging me faceup, racing to the entranceway, and for a few seconds it's hotter than it was inside the room, and then we're in the parking lot and they've set me down. My legs are numb and my back is bleeding. My torn bunking coat is bright with blood.

I lay motionless in a tangle of gear and wait for them to realize I'm seriously injured. And then they're cutting my turnout clothing and mask backpack off with scissors and buck knives. There are five or six people working on me, and when my back is exposed to the evening air, one of the medics says, "Sweet Jesus. Get him on a backboard quick."

They roll me onto my side and lift me onto a backboard and into the back of the medic unit, the same basic procedure I've done with hundreds of patients myself.

Sitting beside me is my friend Rumble, blubbering and confessing that he was the man on the saw. A firefighter is taking my blood pressure while one medic puts an IV into my left arm. The other medic is behind me, and I can feel gentle pressure as he pushes 4x4s against my wounds. I do not ask how badly I am hurt. I can tell from the ministrations of the medic team that they are in a panic. If nothing else, I've lost an enormous quantity of blood. I can barely stay awake. Before I know it, we are headed to Harborview Hospital, a firefighter driving, the two medics remaining in back trying to keep me alive. Rumble to one side, his teary eyes huge with guilt and grief. I'm not sure I've ever felt this much pain.

"Don't worry about it. You saved my life."

"Geez, Trey. I can't believe I did that. I'm so goddamn sorry."

From what I can feel along my back, the wound is twelve or thirteen inches long and runs from my scapula to a spot near my hip. To say it hurts is an infinite irony. It is the worst pain I've felt in my life. Every breath is agony. I'm getting weaker by the minute. Can feel myself begin to nod off.

"Don't leave us, Trey," Rumble says. "Whatever you do, don't leave us."

I drift off.

66. THE MAYOR TALKS HIMSELF OUT OF A JOB

JAMIE ESTEVEZ

The waitstaff, male and female, was decked out in white tuxedo-style shirts and black tuxedo pants as they served between two and three hundred people gathered in the lower level of the Space Needle, 100 feet above the ground.

Stone Carmichael had chosen to build his public persona on events that in most families would remain private, sacrificing intimate moments for the greater glory of the family name. The room was full of the Carmichael family and friends. Kendra and her husband spoke to me briefly, and it was from Kendra that I gleaned that the anniversary celebration was a sham, that the Carmichael marriage was on the rocks, and that Carmichael had somehow coerced his estranged wife into participating. I couldn't help thinking Trey had something to do with their marriage going south, and the thought made my blood boil. We'd been getting along better lately, but he could still make me fume. I visited with Echo Armstrong, who was concerned that her husband was consuming liquor as quickly as he could locate it. The old man was there, too, Shelby Carmichael, who busied himself pestering a red-headed camerawoman working for the local ABC affiliate. I noticed Shelby's nurse following him at a discreet distance, as if he might keel over without warning. Every major city functionary I'd ever met was in the room. A half hour into it, Harlan Overby made an entrance. In his late sixties, he looked trim and fit, his silver hair slicked back, his suit tailored perfectly.

True to Carmichael's habits, the evening was preplanned, printed programs on rice paper available at the door. From seven until eight, there would be a cocktail hour with hors d'oeuvres. At eight: speeches, cake, music, and dancing. At eight forty-five, there would be an announcement. In a corner near the elevator, I'd glimpsed boxes of banners and buttons: "Carmichael for Governor."

Thankfully, eight o'clock came and the celebratory speeches about the Carmichael marriage were offered, toasts were proffered, cake was sliced and passed out. The lights were dimmed while Stone and India danced a spotlight dance in front of hundreds of admirers—you couldn't even tell they didn't like each other. Stone Carmichael was probably the most popular Seattle mayor in thirty years. You would have to say—if you didn't know he was a crook or that India had been having a fling with a captain in the fire department and was leaving him—that they were perfect together. She wore a black off-the-shoulder floor-length dress, her pale hair long and loose. Stone had doffed his spectacles and had the half-blind look habitual glasses wearers get without them. The only snag that came remotely close to spoiling the picture was that India was half a head taller; I noticed she didn't kick off her heels to lessen the discrepancy in height. After their solo dance, the lights brightened and the dance floor began filling up. Around the outskirts chitchat started up again.

I was headed for the restroom when I saw Trey Brown and another African-American male arguing angrily with the security guys. The man accompanying Trey was shouting, but the music was so loud I could barely hear. Finally he flipped some identification out and they were allowed into the party.

Trey wore fire department trousers with a shabby white cotton coat that I learned later had been lifted from the hospital. He had white cream on his ears, probably Silvadine, the common medication for burns. So did his partner. When Trey saw me, he stopped and introduced Rumble. The two of them looked as if they'd just gotten home from a long road trip, or just crawled out of a fire.

"You know about the tape, right?" Trey's friend said.

"The what?"

"This. This right here," he said, pulling a small tape cassette recorder from a pocket in his fire department coat. "His honor on the phone?"

"Rumble has a hard time keeping a secret," Trey said, wandering off through the crowd.

"What?" his friend shouted to Trey's backside. "I can keep a secret. It was your idea to do this. You're the one who's mad." My eyes followed Trey as he moved through the crowd. There was something wrong with the way he was moving.

"What's he mad about?" I asked.

"He thinks they tried to kill him."

I knew from conversations with Trey that Rumble was his best friend and had been ever since they came into the department together. "Aren't you guys supposed to be at work? Isn't Trey's shift working today?"

"We *were* at work," Rumble said. "Now we're here. Hey. You got any idea where the sound techies are hiding out?"

Not much later, while the police and fire chiefs and their wives were socializing near the windows on the west side of the room, somebody came in and handed a message to the fire chief, who in turn rushed the note to Stone Carmichael, who was about to mount the stage for the evening's centerpiece speech. The speaker of the state House of Representatives had halted the dancing and was giving a short talk, working up to the evening's announcement, I presumed, while Stone conferred with the fire chief.

Moments later, the speaker of the house ended his speech by announcing what we'd all guessed, that Stone Carmichael was in the running to be the next governor of the great State of Washington. Amid a chorus of whistling and party horns, thrown confetti, and a massive release of balloons, Carmichael leaped up the stairs to the podium and shook hands with the speaker, then with several other regional political figures. The band played a riff and ended with a staccato drum solo. Stone stepped up to the microphone, cleared his throat, and waited while the silence solidified.

"I'm going to talk politics in a moment, but first . . . Chief Smith has handed me a note that should give us all cause for concern. The fire department has suffered another tragic fire. A firefighter has been seriously injured. We don't know how seriously, but he's been rushed to Harborview. Ordinarily I wouldn't give out a name this early, but it's somebody we all know and respect. Most of you may remember Trey Brown as the man who made those valiant rescues at the Z Club a month ago. Right now our hopes and prayers are with this man."

A smattering of applause. A couple of amens. Only a few people in the room realized Trey Brown was thirty feet in front of me, but even so, I could see a portion of the crowd react around him like a ripple in a pool.

Trey stepped through the crowd to the front of the room and stood under the podium. Something had stained the back of his white jacket, and as I got closer, I realized it was blood. The realization that he was bleeding made me want to scream. Rumble hadn't volunteered any details about their evening, but at that moment the dark, brooding look I'd seen in Trey's eyes began to make sense.

"Well, here he is now," Stone said, noticing his brother for the first time. Again, applause halted the program. "Captain Brown, I'm glad to see you're here and apparently doing well. The report we received was alarming."

"Because I wasn't dead?"

"I don't understand."

"You've wanted me dead for years."

"Perhaps your doctor . . ." Stone addressed the crowd. "Did somebody come with this man?" By this time Carmichael had a simpering, half-embarrassed, angry look on his face. "I really think somebody should assist this man," Stone said, gesturing to persons in the crowd I couldn't see from my position. "He's apparently under the influence of medication. Get him out of here before he hurts himself!"

The two security guys I'd seen at the elevators grabbed Trey and began walking him through the throng. Trey didn't struggle, and because of this I got the feeling he was incapable of resistance. They hadn't gone far when there was a loud droning as somebody tinkered with the sound system, and then voices came over the room's speakers. I didn't recognize the first voice, but Trey had already told me who it was. *"Yeah. Thought I'd check in. I got that info. They're definitely going after the owners of the club."* Of course, the first voice was Barry Renfrow speaking to Stone Carmichael, but it wasn't until they'd had several exchanges that most people in the room realized they were listening to a taped phone call and that one of the parties was the mayor. *"Yesterday he called the King County assessor's office and then the city attorney's office. He's already got Silverstar Consolidated's name. It's only a matter of time before he finds out Overby owns Silverstar and has been funding your gubernatorial campaign and getting special favors in return. The direction he's taking isn't good. And we both know this isn't some kid you can intimidate. He's a captain in the fire department. He comes up with certain facts and people are bound to believe him. The whole city's watching these two investigate, and the worst part is, I don't know what the hell he's going to do next. We've got to figure out some way to control this report so it doesn't make us look bad."*

"Just keep an eye on Captain Brown and let me know what he's doing."

"It might be too late by the time we see what he's up to. I think something needs to be done now."

"Something harsh?"

"You can't treat a guy like this with kid gloves."

"Don't worry about it. I have an inside source. When things start to get too scary, she'll let me know and then I'll

let you know." The reference to me hurt, even though nobody else in the room except Trey knew what it meant.

"But, Stone—"

"Christ, Barry, I'm late for a ball game with my kids. Okay. Have it your way. Stop him. Maybe you can distract him or something. Get him a white woman. A fat one. All the black guys seem to go for that. Overby has raised a lot of money so I can be the next governor, and we don't need some hero messing it up by digging up the truth about Silverstar and our connection to the Z Club. But keep my name out of it. Keep my campaign out of it. Keep Harlan Overby out of it. Hell, Barry, you've been doing this for years. And I don't care if you have to hurt him. Listen, my boys are waiting with the bodyguard out at the car."

Stone Carmichael, who was beginning to shrivel in place, said, "This isn't what you might think." Everybody had recognized his voice, and it was common knowledge that Trey had been physically attacked on the street last week. Booing began to roll from the back of the room, then more from the front. I could see Stone's brain turning over the different ways he might spin this.

Harlan Overby made for the elevators. So did Shelby Carmichael and his nurse. India disappeared for a few moments but came up for air near one of the far windows, gazing out at the city lights with something that looked remarkably like contentment on her face. Almost as if on a signal, the local press in the room rushed the mayor en masse, three cameras and almost a dozen print reporters surrounding him before his entourage could mobilize and block the assault. One reporter was off to the side interviewing the head of the local chapter of the NAACP, who was saying, ". . . everything in my power to make sure he never holds elected office again. We're calling for a new investigation of the mayor and his participation in this cover-up."

A few feet away, Miriam Beckmann from Z Club Citizens for Truth was giving an interview. "This is racism bare naked." Several black people had angrily disengaged Trey from his two escorts and, free now, he made a beeline for India Carmichael at the windows. My heart broke to see him approach her, and it broke again when I saw the splotches of blood on the back of his jacket. Amid the uproar, nobody else in the room seemed to notice her. I remained far enough away not to impose, but close enough to come to Trey's aid should he falter. Rumble showed up about then, but I held him at bay with a hand gesture.

Trey and India looked at each other for a long moment, spoke a few words I couldn't hear, and then he turned and headed for the exit, draping an arm over my shoulders and taking me with him as casually as if he'd done it every day of his life. Rumble stared at India Carmichael for a few moments, then followed us. The ice queen, it seemed, had lost this round. It wasn't until much later that Trey told me she was the one who actually won it.

67. WHERE ARE THEY NOW?

TREY

"Hey, you're not going to eat the last piece of chocolate, are you?" Estevez asked as I dropped the entire chunk into my mouth. She let out a groan of mock agony. We were at my mother's house, Johnny wearing a fancy cummerbund over his church trousers and serving the food and beverages as if he were being paid to do it, Estevez and myself arguing over nothing, as usual. Rumble had brought his current girlfriend, and the women had been hovering in the kitchen preparing food while they talked about us. For months now Estevez and my mother had been getting on like sisters.

"I only had two chocolates," I said.

"You ate one whole row out of that box," Johnny said. "I saw you."

"Whose side are you on?"

"I'm on the side of the chocolate."

We all laughed. "I'm thirsty," I said.

"That's what happens when you take in too much sugar," said Rumble.

Estevez and I have been together for over a year now, one minor breakup in the middle of last summer, which involved Jamie being offered a job in Washington, D.C., that probably would have spelled the end of our relationship. In the end we got back together, and she decided she wanted to stay in the Northwest. She reads the news on the noon and late-night news hours, so her schedule is just as erratic as mine.

As far as the Z Club goes, the dust still hasn't settled. Maybe it never will. The lot has been bulldozed now, the land confiscated by the city, with plans for it to be turned into a small memorial park. There are half a dozen pending lawsuits, and rumor has it that Harlan Overby is doling out a small fortune to keep his business affairs out of the public eye.

Within minutes of the declaration that he was in the running for governor, Stone Carmichael announced he'd changed his mind. It would have been funny if it hadn't been so ugly. No matter how many times I hear that tape, it still makes me shake my head in disbelief. Two months after it first came to public attention, some reactionary antiracist clown punched Stone in the face when he spotted him outside a Starbucks. A white guy, even. Carmichael's candidacy made records for being the shortest in the history of the state. He was made fun of on *Letterman* and *The Daily Show* and has become a staple of comedians across the country.

In Washington State it is illegal to tape phone conversations unless both parties agree, but the tape became public the night we played it, and legal or not, it has been quoted liberally on all of the local television and radio stations. Grand jury investigations were opened with the intent of exploring the mayor's relationship to the Z Club and to the fire where I got chainsawed. It has become clear that Stone Carmichael has been linked to the Z Club fiasco from the beginning. Harlan Overby's policy was to cut corners to keep any moneymaking scheme in business for as long as possible, always trying to squeeze a few more nickels out of anything, and the operations of the Z Club were no exception. After the mayor told him he would make the violations okay with the fire department inspectors, everything became fair game. Whether or not the mayor actually interfered in the fire department inspections is still under investigation, but witnesses are beginning to come forward to testify against him. His promises were enough to let the club owners, Overby, et al. think they could get away with a series of fire regulation infractions. Using political influence to help out campaign contributors wasn't a particularly heinous crime, nor one we don't see every day, but using it to allow people to break the law had led to fourteen deaths in the worst fire on the West Coast in years.

Stone's lawyers dropped a protective umbrella of denial and obfuscation around him, and because of the smoke screen and the ponderous pathways of the judicial system, people are speculating that he may skate. Whatever else happens, his political aspirations are finished.

I've only been back to see my father once, and it did not go well. I denounced the old man for choosing the white son over the black one, for alienating me from my adoptive mother during her final years, and for taking advantage of my birth mother when she was sixteen; but instead of rolling over and playing dead, the old man accused me of playing the race card, saying he'd given me the best head start any black kid could ever dream of and decreeing that whatever success I had in life wouldn't have occurred without the substantial foundation I'd been given by him. He was, he claimed, personally responsible for my success.

I exploded. "You don't send two ex-professional boxers to beat the hell out of a kid and then tell him you gave him a head start in life."

"What boxers?"

"The two thugs who beat the crap out of me when I came back to the island to convince you I wasn't guilty."

"This is the first I've heard. It must have been Harlan. Harlan must have been behind it."

At that point the nurse asked me to leave. I was surprised she hadn't insisted earlier, since Shelby had been looking ill ever since I walked into the room. Weeks later I was told my father's health was in a steep decline; he's twice asked for me to visit and I've twice refused. When you think about it, it's kind of pathetic, a father who desperately wants forgiveness and a son who cannot give it. On the other hand, he still has not apologized or admitted any wrongdoing. It's not spiritually or emotionally good for me or for him, and I'll probably pay for it in the afterlife, but he sold me down the river and I will never forget it.

I see Kendra maybe twice a month, make the kids' birthday parties and all the rest of it. Kendra is the only member of the family who remains on good terms with me.

The night after the tape was played at the Space Needle, there was an organized street rally asking for the mayor's resignation, although for reasons nobody ever divined, Mayor Carmichael didn't resign until two days afterward. Maybe he couldn't get himself to give up the dream. Maybe he was up there alone in his mansion licking his wounds. Or maybe he was hoping the public would forget his current indiscretions the way his father had forgotten his indiscretions so many years earlier.

At the rally there were a few scuffles with the police—most initiated by knuckleheads—a couple of arrests, a couple of sprained ankles, and several people—Rumble included—who lost their voices from shouting. Johnny got his head busted again, this time by somebody in the crowd. We never got the whole story.

Our fire investigators said the fire where I got cut resembled the work of a well-known torch who worked out of Philadelphia, a former firefighter. Interestingly enough, two days after the fire, the suspected arsonist and another man were found shot to death on a side road near the Seattle-Tacoma Airport. The second man was Barry Renfrow, who the papers mentioned was an employee of Harlan Overby. For reasons nobody ever quite figured out, they'd driven out to a deserted part of the county and shot each other.

India Carmichael took her boys to Maryland to be near her mother. The divorce settlement is still pending and occasionally written about in the tabloids.

As far as Rumble goes, he and I still talk about everything except the fire where he saved Kitty and me. I know he still feels bad about chainsawing me, but I'm healed up now and have recovered most of my shoulder function. Rumble says if I'm ever fool enough to lose Estevez, he's going to jump in and give it his best shot, even though he has a new girlfriend he met in the condom aisle at Walgreen's, but that's another story.

Rumble and I had a long talk about the night I went from being a rich "white boy" to just another black kid in the hood. The Overbys had been duped and honestly believed I'd raped their daughter, so it was a miracle they hadn't prosecuted me or had me killed. Only their tight alliance and history with Shelby and Helen Carmichael had stopped it. After I heard the whole story and thought about it for a while, I had a hard time blaming a confused and shocked fifteen-year-old Echo for trying to shield the man she thought she loved. It was even hard to blame her for not having the gumption or impetus to change her story later.

I'm not holding my breath waiting for Stone to get what he deserves. The statute of limitations has run out for what he did to Echo, and the tangle over the Z Club may never be sorted out. Even though his political career is a train wreck, he's making money hand over fist in the private sector, but that doesn't surprise me; if you've been around a while, you know the rich don't always get what they deserve, at least not in this life.

I can't think of too much more to say. Everyone is in the other room gathered around the Christmas tree, and it's gotten quiet, so I have a feeling this would be a good time to waltz in, take Estevez by the hand and pop the question. I know from things she's said in the past she thinks it is unabashedly romantic when somebody proposes under a Christmas tree in front of family. The mistletoe my brother Johnny's tacked up won't hurt. Estevez is sentimental about mistletoe. I better get in there before I lose my nerve.

Read on for an exciting preview
of Earl Emerson's
next thriller

PRIMAL THREAT

Coming to bookstores everywhere
Published by Ballantine Books

Pedaling up into the first of the foothills, Zak felt a droplet of sweat trickling out of his helmet and down the side of his face, dangling for just a moment on the tip of his chin. The others had been sweating heavily all along, especially on this ferocious uphill. At some points on the gravel road they found themselves pedaling up grades so steep your average Joe would have a difficult time walking them, much less riding a bike—so steep that if they got off they would not be able to remount, each of them fighting hard to control his bike on the washboard fire road, each breathing in his own labored and painful rhythm.

The five riders were bonded by affection for this type of grueling exercise, intoxicated by the adventure of hard workouts, and addicted to the endorphins exercise produced. While other northwesterners spent the three-day weekend lounging around the house or semicomatose on a blanket at the beach, Zak, Muldaur, Stephens, Barrett, and Morse would be logging two hundred miles in the mountains, climbing fifteen to twenty thousand feet on fire trails, county roads, and overgrown logging roads.

For Zak and Muldaur it would be a calculated shock to their systems to help them prepare for a twenty-four-hour mountain bike race they planned to enter in three weeks. For

Stephens, who lived nearby, and for his friend Morse, the ride was an end in itself. Always game for an adventure, Barrett had tagged along almost as an afterthought.

Zak had been riding last in the string of five men, a position he took up from time to time in order to size up the opposition. *Opposition*. He liked that word. They weren't actually enemies—in fact they were friends—but he knew each climb on this trip would be a contest, and the best place from which to size up the other contestants was at the back. They were all competitive and more than a little vain about their prowess on a bicycle, and thus competition would be fierce.

The Northwest was suffering through the last days of August, and afternoon highs in western Washington had been languishing in the mid- to high nineties, briefly touching a hundred in some counties. In the mountains the evenings would be cooler, but the midday sun would also be harsher. Their plan was to traverse from the western side of the Cascade Mountains to the east, ending in Salmon La Sac, a journey Muldaur had promised Zak would be similar to running three or four marathons back-to-back.

Zak, Jim Muldaur, and Giancarlo Barrett were firefighters, while the other two were businessmen, friends of Muldaur's. Besides the five years they'd put in together working on Engine 6, Zak and Muldaur had raced mountain bikes and competed in road races together, traveling to and from many of the events in Muldaur's Subaru Outback with their bikes on a roof rack, so they knew each other's habits and predilections like brothers. At 160 and 165 pounds, respectively, Zak and Muldaur were the fittest in the group. In biking the most critical single factor in climbing performance was the combined weight of bike and rider. A pound or two might not make much of a difference in football or basketball, but people paid hundreds of dollars to shave a couple of ounces off bicycle components.

Muldaur's friend Steve Stephens was the chief financial officer for a successful local biotech company; his salary, bonuses, and stock options placed him in an income category none of the others could match, although his buddy Morse, a freelance labor negotiator, came close.

Thursday afternoon before Labor Day the five of them met at Stephens's house in North Bend, a burgeoning hamlet at the base of the Cascades and the last town before Snoqualmie Pass and the ski areas. Stephens lived under Mount Si, a rocky, four-thousand-foot monolith that jutted almost straight up from the valley floor. Originally eight men and one woman had signed up for this weekend, but the woman and one of the men bailed for family reasons. The last man jumped ship after hearing that the woods in western Washington had been declared off limits because of fire danger. The drier eastern half of the state had been in a condition of fire alert for the past month, but until recently spotty rainstorms had shielded the western half from sanctions. Now *all* the backwoods in the state were officially off limits to motor vehicles, hikers, bikers, and riders on horseback. Forest fires had consumed a record number of acres in eastern Washington, Idaho, and Oregon, and the governors of the three states had asked for federal help to finance fire-suppression efforts.

"It's bullshit," Muldaur said when they gathered in Stephens's driveway to discuss it. "We've waited too long. And now comes Labor Day weekend and the weather's going to be perfect and we can't go? We're not going to have a campfire, none of us smokes, and bicycles don't throw off sparks. The ban is to keep the morons out, and we're not morons."

"I agree," said Giancarlo.

"I also vote that we're not morons," said Zak, facetiously.

Stephens added, "You're absolutely right. That is . . . Well, after all, bicycles don't set off sparks. Everybody knows . . . I mean rules like this are, uh, to keep out the vast majority of the public, because they know if they let everybody up there on a dry weekend like this . . . I'm sure you'll all agree, uh, there'll be a certain percentage of the population who don't obey anybody's rules, and of course, as we've all discussed before, at least Morse and I have, all it takes is one."

Zak was beginning to remember Stephens from a ride

they'd been on together the previous year. In his late forties, he was two years younger than Muldaur, and he had a way of stammering out his thoughts as if English were a second language. In his own clumsy way he was fond of repeating important points others had stated, but at a torturously slower pace than the original speaker. It was almost as if he thought something hadn't been said until he said it himself. Muldaur once said, "I always wondered where the center of the universe was, and then I met Steve Stephens and realized he was it." Cruel, but there was a core of truth to the remark.

"It's a very dry forest," said Giancarlo Barrett. At 220 pounds, six feet three inches tall, Giancarlo had climbed Mount Rainier half a dozen times and had done STP, the Seattle to Portland bike ride, eleven years in a row. He and Zak had been friends since drill school six years earlier, and Zak was the best man at his wedding. "The weather guys said it was going to be dry and hotter into next week. More danger of fires. This'll be our best window."

"I'm going," Muldaur said.

Giancarlo turned on his impish grin. "I'm going too, then."

They would be riding north along the face of the mountain, circumnavigating it and other sheer peaks, pedaling up into a series of low, rolling hills that stretched into the northern part of western Washington. It was an area frequented by fishermen looking to be alone, loggers, mushroom gatherers, dope smugglers, and bear hunters.

A sign cautioned travelers that the road stretched twenty-six miles on gravel before ending, though Stephens assured everyone it was possible to ride mountain bikes all the way to the small town of Snohomish on Highway 2. But that wasn't where they were headed. They would trek five miles into the hills and then turn east into the real foothills. The first climb after they crossed the North Fork of the Snoqualmie River would gain four thousand feet of elevation.

The plan was to scout for a couple of hours on the rolling county roads and then climb halfway up the side of the Cascades to a camping spot at Panther Creek, where Stephens had paid to have a local man stash their gear. Framed by the summer twilight, they would have a splendid view of Seattle and Bellevue and the Olympic Mountains eighty miles away.

They would spend the first two nights on the western side of the Cascades and then thread their way along hiking trails and back roads until they traversed the Cascade Crest Trail and descended into Salmon La Sac, a small tourist town in central Washington.

They were carrying only rudimentary repair kits for their bicycles, CamelBak water bags, GU packets, Clif Bars, sunglasses, and other necessities: traveling as light as a body could travel in these mountains. At the finish they would savor a Mexican dinner in Salmon La Sac with a couple of the wives, who would caravan across Snoqualmie Pass to meet them on Sunday afternoon.

The part Zak liked best was that there would be no cell phones, no GPS finders, and except for their bikes no appurtenances of the modern age. For one weekend they would be largely independent of modern amenities, knights errant jousting with one another on the climbs, racing down the miles-long descents at breakneck speeds, roaming a section of the Northwest where they were unlikely to see another human being for at least three days.

They rode easily on the five miles of pavement that preceded the first climb into Weyerhaeuser property. Traffic in the upper Snoqualmie Valley was sparse, and the sunbaked tarmac roads gave off heat in waves they could see. In front of them to the east were the low, rolling green foothills of the Cascades they would soon be climbing.

The road pointed north with the sheer, rocky base of the foothills to their right and a series of low, forested hills to their left. Even though the Northwest had been suffering a drought for months, the stark green of the foothills never faded. They passed a Christmas tree farm and a few isolated houses. Then, while they were still on the paved road, four teenagers in a Honda sped past, honking and shouting. Muldaur, who was in the front next to Barrett, turned around with a smile and said, "None of that shit where we're going."

"No sirree," said Morse. "Nothing but bears, coyotes, and deershit."

Morse was a jolly man, repeatedly cracking impromptu jokes and launching into witty wordplay. The three firemen took to him and his self-deprecating sense of humor immediately, which was ironic because he didn't seem too concerned whether people liked him or not, in stark contrast with Stephens who worked overtime to make friends without accomplishing a whole lot. Zak tried to recall if he'd ever met anybody who wanted to be an integral part of the crowd as badly as Stephens did.

Muldaur, the second oldest and arguably the fittest, wasn't going to let anybody beat him to the top of a mountain if he could help it; Zak felt the same. Certainly Stephens, who had been a national champion runner in college, wasn't going to be outshone if he had any say in it. Giancarlo Barrett was tough but too heavy to be competitive on these long climbs. Morse would be at the back of the pack, and he made no bones about it. "Just wait for me, guys. I may be slow, but I'll make up for it by eating and drinking more than my share."

As they rode, Stephens dropped back and rode alongside Zak, attempting to be friendly, giving him encouraging words about how it wasn't going to be "that hard." Apparently he thought that because Zak was at the back, he was having a tough time keeping up. Stephens was six feet tall, almost the same as Zak, though built heavier, with pale skin he protected via gobs of sunscreen slapped on like paste. Zak learned as they talked that they'd been to many of the same biking events in years past: STP, Seattle to Portland; the Tour de Blast up Mount St. Helens to the observatory; and RAMROD, the one-day ride around Mount Rainier, 154 miles that included ten thousand feet of climbing. Like Muldaur, Stephens was in incredible shape, considering he was almost twenty years older than Zak and Giancarlo. Muldaur had the newest bike and, oddly enough, Stephens, who was the wealthiest, rode the oldest. Stephens also wore the tattiest clothing, most of it musty racing gear that was ten or fifteen years old. Zak wondered why a man would keep four luxury vehicles in his driveway, a speedboat, a new motor home, motorcycles, and Jet Skis—but then wear a cycling jersey that looked as if it had been in the doghouse.

At the point where the pavement ended, a sign was nailed to a tree. FIRE DANGER. UNTIL FURTHER NOTICE ALL WEYERHAEUSER PROPERTY NORTH OF THIS POINT WILL BE OFF LIMITS TO HIKERS, CAMPERS, HORSEMEN, AND MOTORIZED VEHICLES.

"Doesn't say anything about cyclists, does it?" Zak said.

"Typically," Stephens said, "they post a twenty-four-hour guard. But I don't see him." A steel gate had been swung across the road, and alongside the gate on a level piece of ground sat a black Ford Bronco coated in dust so thick, the windshield looked opaque.

"I don't see a guard," Muldaur whispered.

"I don't see a guard," Zak repeated as he dismounted and lifted his bike over the gate.

One by one the others followed. "I don't see a guard," said Morse, his voice softer than the others.

"Do you see a guard?" asked Giancarlo.

"Obviously . . . well, I mean, he's probably asleep in the Bronco, wouldn't you imagine?" Stephens asked, spoiling the joke for everyone.

As they rode up the steep hill and pedaled out of sight, they kept waiting for somebody to call them back, but all they heard was the soft crunch of tires in the dirt and the strong, hot wind blowing intermittent tornadoes of dust the height of theater curtains in front of them. The late-afternoon sun pounded their backs, and the heat flowing from the woods seemed almost too humid to inhale.

"It's going to be great," Muldaur said, speaking to no one in particular. "The whole area's closed off, so we won't have to worry about cars."

Less than ten minutes later, after they'd gotten off the steepest part of the road and onto a rolling section, Zak sprinted from the rear to the front of the group. "Car back," said Zak. "Car back."

"It's probably the guard," said Muldaur. "Maybe we should duck into the woods."

"I'm not hiding," said Giancarlo. "If he wants to throw us out, let him have at it."

They'd passed two gravel pits, a section of younger trees interspersed with hundreds of tall foxgloves gone to seed, and now were riding through a mature section of Douglas fir. If they were quick about it, they could conceal themselves in the woods alongside the road, and if they hiked far enough into the trees, they would avoid both the afternoon sun and the dust that coated everything within thirty yards of the road.

"The speed these guys are traveling," Zak said, "they're going to bury us in dust."

"There's more than one?" Morse asked, gasping for breath.

"At least two. Maybe three. Hear them?"

Traveling close to sixty and towing a gigantic plume of dust, the first vehicle, a white Land Rover, passed them on a section of small rolling hills. The fine-grained silt was light enough that even their bicycle tires were kicking it up, and when Zak looked down at his legs, his socks were tan with it. As the Land Rover overtook them, the air became saturated with a brown haze. Zak took a huge gulp of clean air and tried to hold his breath. In the miasma that was being created, the following vehicles had no way of knowing they were passing five bicyclists. It would be a miracle if one or more of them wasn't run down, crushed, or annihilated without the drivers even knowing they'd hit anything. One or more of them would be hit and dragged for a quarter mile. Any second. There was no escape. To Zak's mind, the actions of the first driver were criminal, the most reckless and infuriating driving he had encountered in a long time.

What saved their lives was Muldaur shouting "This way" as he bounced off the road, across a shallow ditch, over a log, and into the woods. All four riders followed in the nick of time as more vehicles roared past, four in all.